THE
RISING

THE
RISING

Olivia Coleman Suspense

_To Kim,
Enjoy Olivia's journey!_

Kerry Peresta

Kerry Peresta

This book is dedicated to my son, Andrew Jordan Lowery. Drew is a living testament to the rewards of perseverance in the worst of circumstances. He fought the good fight, and he is winning. Drew, this one's for you.

"You learn to rise above a lot of bad things that happen in your life. And you have to keep going."

~LAUREN BACALL

Praise for THE RISING

"With countless twists and turns, Kerry Peresta takes readers on a spell-binding journey in her new book, *The Rising*, the second book in the Olivia Callahan Suspense series. Strongly recommend!"—Dana Ridenour, award-winning author of the Lexie Montgomery FBI undercover series

"Kerry Peresta's *The Rising* is a page-turner that will keep you up at night, jumping at every unexpected sound! With twists and turns you won't see coming, Olivia Callahan, traumatic brain injury survivor, is determined to put the past behind her and regain her memories, both the good and the bad. Grab this one!"—Cathi Stoler, author of The Murder On The Rocks Mystery Series.

"In *The Rising*, Peresta's stunning writing and multi-layered depictions take readers into the heart of a woman struggling to reclaim her memories and her life. Hooked from the first page, I was right there with her, rooting for her every terrifying, twisty step of the way!"—Susan Crawford, Bestselling author of *The Pocket Wife* and *The Other Widow*

"Kerry Peresta's second thriller is as riveting and well-plotted as the first. Among the many pleasures in this taut and fast-paced novel is the protagonist herself. Because the reader gets to see Olivia Callahan from multiple perspectives, this intriguing and potentially unreliable character has a depth and complexity that transcends the genre. The multi-layered narrative spans several time periods in Olivia's fractured life, and all are rendered in clear and vivid prose. An evocative, moving, and satisfying read."—Lori Robbins, Author of the On Pointe Mystery Series, Silver

i

Falchion Winner for *Lesson Plan for Murder*

"Peresta's skill ensures that the central drama of the novel swells around the reader, leaving them to experience the protagonist as her investigator, witness, gossip, judge, friend and foe. An immersive experience. A carefully composed book, with a painter's eye for details that vivify."—Coy Hall, author of *Grimoire of the Four Imposters* and *The Hangman Feeds the Jackal*

"Olivia Callahan's search to find her lost memories, while sorting through a web of deceit and lies, grabbed me by my heart on page one and never let go."—Annette Dashofy, *USA Today* Bestselling Author of the Zoe Chambers Mysteries

"*The Rising* delivers a thrill ride with plenty of surprises and a twisty plot that keeps the reader on edge in the best possible way. Olivia Callahan's traumatic brain injury has left her with a new, more outspoken personality and a patchy memory. All she wants now is a job and a quiet life for herself and her two girls. But the quiet life will have to wait—her house is under surveillance by parties unknown, and then the trouble really starts. When Olivia finds her old friend dead, she has to wonder whether her ex is out for revenge and if she's next on his hit list. In this second book in her series, author Kerry Peresta has crafted another compulsively readable tale of suspense with relatable, complex characters."— Mally Becker, Author of the Revolutionary War mystery series

"With countless twists and turns, Kerry Peresta takes readers on a spellbinding journey in her new book, *The Rising*, the second book in the Olivia Callahan Suspense series. Strongly recommend!"—Dana Ridenour, award-winning author of the Lexie Montgomery FBI Undercover series

"Kerry Peresta's *The Rising* is a page-turner that will keep you up at night jumping at every unexpected sound. With twists and turns you won't see coming, Olivia Callahan, traumatic brain injury survivor, is determined to put the past behind her, and at the same time, remember her past, both the good and the bad."—Cathi Stoler, author of Murder on the Rocks mystery series

"Fascinating and masterfully plotted, *The Rising* grabs the reader on page one and doesn't let go until the book's twisty and surprising end! I couldn't put it down!"—Joan Long, author of *The Finalist*

"Fans of this suspenseful series will be thrilled to spend time once again with Olivia Callahan, as she continues on her unique and intriguing journey in the latest installment of *The Rising*."—Carol Pouliot, Author of the Blackwell and Watson Time-Travel mysteries

"Olivia Callahan just wants to live a plain, old, boring life. Fortunately for readers of *The Rising*, though, she can't seem to escape drama! As she strives to reclaim her memories after a life-changing assault and resulting brain injury, she must face the truth: her life is still in danger. This second volume in the Olivia Callahan Suspense series will keep readers on the edge of their seats as Olivia races to determine who can be trusted, and who is out for blood."—Susan Diamond Riley, award-winning author of *The Sea Island's Secret & The Sea Turtle's Curse*

"*The Rising* is a suspenseful game of cat-and-mouse. It's also a study in evolution as Olivia Callahan grapples with the next round of challenges and tries to recover her memory and her past. This time she's moving on, growing and evolving, making a new way for herself. You will root for Olivia as she shucks her victimhood for a new life of adventure and opportunity. She is learning to look for the silver lining and you will find yourself doing the same. The ending unravels with surprise twists as Olivia tackles another baffling case with Hunter. Cheer Olivia on as she turns a new leaf and gets the second chance most of us only dream about!"—Tina deBellegarde, Agatha Award nominated author of *Winter Witness* and *Dead Man's Leap*

"A propulsive and cleverly crafted thrill ride of a novel. Kerry Peresta brings the goods in this twisty tale where secrets, families, and missing memories come together in an explosive conclusion."—James L'Etoile, author of *At What Cost, Bury the Past,* and *Black Label*

Prologue

Earl shielded his eyes against the bright slash of morning sun as he cranked open his office window. The fresh scent of spring drifted into the room. A nasty, yakkity, crow touched down on the sill, cocked his head, and stared inside Earl's soul.

He shooed the bird away.

With an irritable puff of his cigar, Earl padded around his office in sock feet, wondering what the day would hold. His calendar was empty. Every so often, he'd sneak a glance at the small reception area adjoining his office, and then he'd remember that his receptionist had resigned three weeks ago. A satisfied grunt of pleasure escaped his lips at the thought. He'd never much liked her, anyway—the wiry-haired, old, bat—and he looked forward to interviewing her potential replacement, who was due to arrive in a couple of hours. He smiled. His former client, Olivia, would be a grand addition to his law practice.

He snuffed out his cigar in an ashtray. Olivia had no patience with his cigars, and he didn't want the smoke to linger, or...for that matter...set off the fire alarm. Earl waved his arms and batted the smoke out the window. He then sprayed air freshener, slipped on his shoes, and tugged his vest into place. Satisfied, he dropped into his leather chair and tapped his bratwurst-sized fingers on his desk. "It'll be good to have younger blood in here. Maybe she'll find us some new clients," he murmured to himself.

The door to reception opened, then closed. He heard a thump, as if a cat had batted a vase to the floor. Steps drifted through the outer room.

Earl scowled. Had Olivia gotten the time wrong? He waited for a knock on his office door. When none came, he called out, "Olivia?"

His door opened. A slender man dressed in khakis and a blue shirt leaned against the doorframe.

"Good morning," Earl said, rising from his chair to extend his hand across his desk. "I'm sorry, but, I don't believe we had an appointment, did we?"

The man's eyebrows rose as he shook Earl's hand. "Do you know who I am?"

Earl sat back in his chair. The voice *was* familiar. "Forgive me, but…well, my memory isn't what it used to be."

The man chuckled. "I've called many times since our initial conversations, Earl. Since you won't return my calls, my only option was to show up. I've tried very hard to be reasonable."

Earl's bushy, salt-and-pepper moustache drooped in disapproval. He remembered the man now, but only via phone calls. He'd been adamant about stirring up a case that had left the town in shambles a couple of years ago. No one would touch it, let alone himself. He'd laughed outright at the proposition, but the man had kept calling.

"You couldn't have been serious!" Earl exclaimed. "Why would I take on a case like that? I barely have any clientele left, and I'm close to retirement. What you want will take a huge effort, and…well, it just isn't possible at this stage of the game. Besides, you don't know the people around here…and I don't know you! I've got a reputation to think about. Now, listen here…I've told you to stop calling, and this…this…" His face warmed. His heart rate accelerated. Earl tugged at his collar and patted his chest. He held up one of his thick fingers and pointed at the door. "Look, you…whatever your name is…you need to leave. Please go. Or I'll…I'll file stalking charges."

The man's pale, blue eyes never left Earl's face. "All I wanted was a sit-down. So we could talk to each other like professional adults. And now… you treat me like I'm a piece of dog shit you scrape off your shoe?" He sighed. "There are other matters at stake, Earl. Just…give me fifteen minutes."

"I told you. No! Now…*leave.*"

Earl started feeling sweaty. Something about the look in the man's eyes was unsettling. Once more, he raised an imperious finger and pointed at the door. He lurched up from his chair with such force that it caused it to rocket away from the desk. "Go NOW!" he demanded.

Swift and silent, the younger man snatched up a large, elaborate, letter opener with a metal blade. He hefted it in his hand and stared at Earl. A flip of his wrist turned the tool blade-out, in his fist.

"Here now…what are you—" Earl's jowls went slack as the man approached. His eyebrows popped up. "No, no…let's talk. We can talk."

Tears of terror streaked down Earl's cheeks into his moustache. As he backed away, he held out his arms. "I'm sorry. Sorry! C'mon. Sit. Let's talk about this. Like you said."

The man jerked his arm up and let it fall, hard. The makeshift weapon tore through the cloth of the vest and shirt, but failed to find flesh. Earl stared at him with wide, heartbroken eyes. "What are you doing? Why?" he cried.

Breathing hard, the younger man changed his grip on the letter opener, ripped the tail of Earl's shirt out, and rammed the blade upward, underneath Earl's ribcage, into the soft flesh, the spleen and lungs. He pulled it out, then rammed it again. And again. Earl's eyes rolled back into his head, and a sigh puffed from his lips. His knees buckled and he fell backward with a ponderous thud.

Earl lay behind his desk in shock. He felt no pain, but a foggy numbness claimed his mind. Blood traced its way across his starched, white shirt, dress slacks, and onto the carpet. From his line of sight on the floor, he watched as his attacker pulled a document from his pocket, stared at it briefly, and tossed it into the trash container. Earl let out a rattling, shaky, breath. He felt sure the opener had pierced his lungs. He had moments, maybe seconds, to live. Earl's eyelids grew too weak to stay open. He heard the slight rustle of movement beside him, felt the warmth of fingers on his carotid artery. The smell of the man's morning coffee reached his nostrils, and breath warmed his right ear as he listened to the last words he'd ever hear.

"You should've returned my calls, you idiot. It didn't have to end like this."

Chapter One

"How low you fall points to how high you'll rise."
~Matshona Dhliwayo

Three weeks earlier

The stark buildings and barbed-wire-topped walls surrounding the correctional facility reminded me of a Hitchcock movie.

My fingers tightened on the steering wheel. I found a parking spot, and waited in the car a minute, taking in the starkness and finality of a prison compound. My heart did a little lurch when I thought about Monty—my ex-husband and the father of my two daughters—inside. *Incarcerated.* I guess since I hadn't seen him since his indictment, it didn't seem real.

However, I'd learned that having sympathy for Monty was like having sympathy for a snake just before it sank its fangs. "It's been eighteen months. You can keep it together with this psycho," I hissed to myself. I hiked my purse onto my shoulder and walked out into the buttery sunshine toward the visitors' entrance.

I presented my driver's license, endured a frisk, offered my hand for the fingerprint process, and walked through the metal detector, which of course, went off. With stoic resignation, I endured another frisk, a few hard glances from the guards, and eventually pulled the culprit from the pocket of my pants, an aluminum foil candy bar wrapper.

While I waited for Monty at one of the small, circular tables in the visitors'

1

room, I scanned the list of do's and don'ts. Hands must be visible at all times. Vulgar language not allowed. No passing anything to the prisoner. No jewelry other than a wedding band or religious necklace.

I stared at my hands, sticky with sweat. My heart beat in my throat.

I lifted my curls off my forehead and fanned my face with one hand. Three other visitors sat at tables. One woman with graying hair piled like a crown on her head stared at the floor. When she noticed that I was looking at her, she raised her head and threw me a sad smile. A younger woman at another table struggled to keep two young children under control, and an older couple with stress-lined faces whispered to each other as they waited. The room had tan, cinder block walls, a drop-in ceiling with grid tiles that probably hid video cameras, and a single door. No windows. A scrawny, fake plant in one corner made a half-hearted attempt at civility.

The metal door opened. My thoughts were mush, a blender on high. Could I do this? After two years of physical therapy, occupational therapy, and every other kind of therapy the docs could throw at me, shouldn't I react better than this?

Remember, they're only feelings.

I squared my shoulders. Wiped my palms on my pants.

As Monty offered his cuffed wrists to the corrections officer, he scanned the room under lowered eyelids. When he saw me, he gave me a scorched-earth glare. After the guard removed his handcuffs, he shook out his arms and rubbed his wrists. The raven-black hair was longer, and brushed his shoulders. He'd been working out. A lot. He wore a loose-fitting top and pants. Orange. As usual, he was larger than life, and in the bright white of the visiting space, surrounded by matching plastic tables and chairs, he was a raven-haired Schwarzenegger in a room full of Danny DeVito's. I'd once had hope for reconciliation. The thought gave me the shakes now.

He dropped into the chair across from me and plopped his hands on the table. "What do you want?"

I spent a few seconds examining his face—this man I'd spent twenty, long years trying to please, and the reason I'd been assaulted and left for dead by Niles Peterson, a wreck of a man whose life Monty had destroyed as well.

The man responsible for my convoluted recovery from a brain injury that stole my past. Even after two years, I still had huge gaps in my memory, and staring at him felt like staring at a stranger instead of an ex-husband. "My therapist says I need to look back to move forward. I wanted to ask you a few questions, that's all."

"Okay," he grumbled. "I'll give you a few minutes. Oh, and you'll love this. I have to attend counseling sessions about how to keep my 'darker dispositions' under control, and I have one of those in thirty minutes."

Resisting a smile, I quipped, "Are they helping?"

He rolled his eyes. "What are the questions?"

"I still have problems remembering stuff. There are things I need to… figure out about who I was before—"

"Before you hooked up with my ole' buddy Niles?" he interrupted, with a smirk. "Before you threw away everything we had? Before you got yourself in a situation that could've gotten you killed? Before you started treating me like a piece of shit?"

I was careful not to react. I'd had enough therapy to understand how to treat a control freak that tried to make *me* the reason he ended up in prison. That part of my life—the part where Monty had been in charge and his spouse had to obey or else—was over. "Are you done?" I asked.

He clamped his lips together.

I folded my hands on the table and leaned in. "I'll get right to the point. What drew you to me in the first place? What was I like before the accident, from your perspective?"

Monty tried to get comfortable in the plastic chair. Beneath his immense bulk, it seemed like a child's chair. "Is that how you're dealing with it?" His lips twisted in disgust. "It was an *assault,* Olivia. He tried to rape you, for God's sake."

I looked away. "It's over, and he's in the ground, thanks to you."

He crossed his arms and glared. A corrections officer lifted his hand. With a grunt, Monty slapped both hands on the small table where the officer could see them.

After a few beats, he sneered, "You mean besides the obvious attraction

3

of an older guy to a high school girl?"

"Give me a break, Monty."

He chuckled. "You were kind of...I don't know...*scared*. I was drawn to you in a protective way. You were shy."

I frowned. "What was I scared of?"

"Your crazy mom had married some jerk that kept you off balance all the time. Don't you remember him?"

I thought for a few seconds. Nothing came.

"That coma still messes with you, doesn't it? Well...might be good not to remember. Maybe he did things to you that he shouldn't have." Monty raised his eyebrows up and down.

I wanted to slap him, but I kept my expression neutral.

"A brain injury recovery is unpredictable. I still lose memories, even if someone has drilled them into me. I'm trying to use visualization. I have this feeling...that if I can see it, the rest will be like dominos."

"So you may not ever remember? Even the good things about our marriage?"

I laughed. "We must have very different perspectives about the word 'good', Monty."

Monty's jaw muscles flexed. "Next?"

"Was I a capable mother? Was I available and...loving to the kids?"

Maybe it was my imagination, but his lower lip quivered. Did the guy have a heart after all? I'd always believed he loved our daughters. I hoped this was true.

"Olivia, you were a good mother. We had our problems, but you made a good home, and took excellent care of the kids. You were at every freakin' event, every school fundraiser, *everything*." He scowled. "I took a big back seat to the kids."

"What problems did we have? When did they start?"

He leaned in. "You don't remember our sex life? How terrible it was? Nothing I could do would get you to...." He shook his head. "You couldn't even fix a decent meal. You should have been *grateful* you married someone like me so I could...teach you things."

"Keep your voice down!" I insisted, embarrassed.

He cocked his head and grinned. "You always had this...desperate need for my approval or whatever. And when you conveniently avoided telling me you weren't taking birth control it caused a lot of issues that could've been avoided." He snorted. "Like being in here."

I tried to rein in my disgust.

"So, let me get this straight. Your priority in our marriage was sex and good food and to pin all our issues on your child bride?" My tone hardened. "A young woman who came from a single-parent home? Who had no understanding what a good and normal guy was like?"

He gave me a look that could peel the skin off my face.

"How did you react when I didn't do things the way you wanted?" I continued.

"Like any man who'd been disrespected. I corrected the issue."

"How? By yelling? Physical force? Kicking your pregnant wife in the stomach?" This was a memory I *had* recovered.

A vein pulsed in his neck.

"How often, Monty? Were these reactions a...a lifestyle in our marriage?"

"Look," he snarled, "I don't know that this is productive."

"It is for me," I said, brightly.

I glanced at the closest officer. He had his hands full with an issue at one of the other tables.

"Mom told me that Serena and Lilly floated out to sea one time, on a rubber raft. Do you remember that?"

His eyes found a spot on the wall.

"So you do remember. What happened?"

"Look, they were, I don't know, four and six or so. I didn't think it would be a problem for me to run grab a drink from our bag, and come back. I was gone less than five minutes. How could I know they'd lose control of the raft?"

An earthquake of anger shot through me. "You turned your back on a four-year-old and a six-year-old and expected them to have *control* of a raft? They were *babies!*"

"Yeah. Well." He rose. "Looks like this question thing of yours isn't working for me." He pushed his chair in with a bang. The correctional officer gave him a look. Monty strode to the officer's station and held out his wrists. Adrenaline made me a little shaky after he'd gone, but it wasn't from fear of the man. My therapist would call this real progress.

I left the room and gathered my things from the visitors' processing center. As I walked out of the prison facility, all I could think about was…why? Why had I married this guy? And stayed for *twenty years*? I couldn't even remember myself as a person who could do that.

At least I'd dragged more information out of him. I was determined to piece together the puzzle of the past I'd lost.

Chapter Two

"Rising means we have opted for forgiveness, dropped the drama, the pity, and everything else in a lower vibe. It isn't complicated. Rise."
~Debbie Lynn, Author

"**A**re you sure?" Callie asked, her tone anxious.

"This is so wrong," Sherry said, shaking her head in disapproval as she walked along behind us on the quaint cobblestone streets of Fells Point in downtown Baltimore. Seagulls screamed overhead on their way to the Inner Harbor, and the sun was sinking fast. February in Maryland was a study in contradictions, and though the high had climbed to sixty degrees, snow was forecast tomorrow. I tugged my sweater tighter around me as we navigated the sidewalks. Tourists bunched in groups laughed and talked as they made their way to restaurants.

Hannah walked faster in an effort to keep up. "What's so wrong?"

I laughed. "Guys, I've come a long way since...the incident. I think it'll be good for me to see if I've moved on. Besides, didn't we say we wanted to expand our bar repertoire?"

Callie groaned. "Yeah, but all the way to the City? I haven't been down here in a long time." She stopped in front of a ponderous, carved-oak door, and pulled it open with a grunt. Callie was 5'2" worth of grit and energy but no match for the heavy door. I grabbed the handle and pulled with her. Once inside, I took time to assess the surroundings and think about the last night I'd been a content wife and mother. The night that had changed my life forever— Monty's abrupt departure from our marriage.

The hostess swept up four menus and motioned us in. We settled into our seats for our once-a-month wine event where we explored different kinds of wine, whined about our lives, and ended on a winning note. None of us had had a lot of winning notes lately, but we were trying.

I fidgeted with my menu. Should I tell them I'd seen Monty or keep that little nugget to myself? They were already worried enough that I'd lose it by being in this place. I cautioned myself not to overshare, but hey, wine and drunk blurting would cause it to come out anyway, so just roll with it.

I put the food menu down and picked up the wine list.

As usual, we took our time with the wine choices and tried to find one we'd never had before. I'd been told my ex had not let me drink in my former life. I wondered why. There were so many things I wanted to remember. *Needed* to remember.

After the charcuterie and wine arrived, we settled in to nibble and drink and talk.

Callie, in typical fashion, took the role of moderator. "So who wants to start?" she asked, holding up her wine glass. "This is very good, by the way. Rombauer. Napa Valley."

"I'll start," Hannah said, clearing her throat. She studied her wine. Her long, elegant fingers played with the base of the glass. "I'm having a hard time," she began.

Callie, Sherry, and I leaned in.

She sighed. "My marriage…it's…stagnating. No sparks, no excitement, nothing. I'm so *tired* of trying to wake him up!"

"David didn't take the marriage counseling to heart?" I asked.

Hannah grunted. "Of course not. It's life as usual." She lifted her wine glass and drank. "I know I should be more appreciative. David is a good husband, has never given me a reason not to trust him, and he'd do anything for me. But, our life is *so* boring."

"I *like* boring," I said.

Hannah laughed. "Well, yeah, after what you've been through." She shrugged. "So that's where I am. At least for tonight."

Sherry lifted her glass. "Here's to boring." We clinked. A thoughtful silence cloaked the table for a few seconds.

"How's it going with you, Sherry?" Callie asked.

Sherry smiled in Hannah's direction. "Honey, I'd take boring over what I'm going through any day of the week."

With a regretful look, Hannah said, "Oh gosh, I didn't mean to be insensitive."

She shrugged. "Just saying. I'd be thankful for boring. Especially...as money slips through my fingers for court costs, attorneys...and now... Clay wants *alimony*."

"What? How? He can't do that." I protested.

"In this state, he can," Sherry said, chuckling sadly. "My entire career I saved so I could retire early and enjoy financial stability." She snapped her fingers and said, "Presto! All gone. It is astounding the man thinks so much of himself. He lost jobs more times than I can count when we were together."

"How long, again?" Hannah asked, her voice kind.

"Seventeen long, stupid, wasted years." Sherry angrily drained her glass. The server scuttled over to pour her a refill. "It's been almost two years mucking through this divorce. Please, girls, pray that this is over. *Soon.*"

We all murmured that we would. Callie turned her attention on me.

Moisture gathered on my forehead. I reached for my napkin to blot at it. Like a lightning strike, my mind flashed to Monty. With me. At a table in this restaurant. Two and a half years ago. The way his nervous fingers had played with his white, cloth napkin. How he'd crumpled it into a wrinkled ball.

Glancing around the table, I blinked the memory away. *Tell them. You need accountability.* I finished my wine. Seemed like light-years ago that Monty had asked me to meet him here so he could begin—or maybe finish—the long and winding demise of our relationship.

"So what's happening with you? How's therapy?" Callie asked.

I cleared my throat. "I'm taking a break."

Callie's face melted into worry. "Do you think that's wise? It's helping, isn't it?"

"Sure, therapy has helped, but I have a roadblock to get past, and I'm trying to figure out how to do it."

Damn. I hadn't meant to even share that much. At least, not yet. I glared at my wine glass.

"Roadblock?" Hannah asked, her gentle, blue eyes widening. "What kind of roadblock?"

Sherry patted the air with her hands. "Let her talk, let her talk," she said, leaning forward on her elbows.

"Look," I began, "I can't seem to get on with life. Things are better, okay? I'm seeing improvement but—" I sighed. "I'm isolating more, not talking to Mom as much, and staying in bed later. All signs of textbook depression. But I hate those anti-anxiety meds. I can't take them anymore."

Callie nodded, her dusky blonde ponytail bouncing in a nod to the ex-cheerleader that she is. My neighbor and loyal friend has a heart as big as Texas, and I was forever grateful to her.

"But...everything I've been ingesting and regurgitating—"

"Eww," Sherry said.

"Sorry. The brain misfires continue. I'm getting better about that, though. What I meant to say, is that my therapy sessions point to knowing the past before I can move into the future." I shrugged. "The only one who knows my history, and everything that happened..."

Hannah sucked in a breath. "Is Monty."

Sherry's mouth dropped open.

A shadow flitted across Callie's features. "You're *not*."

Hannah's long, blonde hair whipped around as she jerked toward me. "Not what?"

"Nooo..." Sherry murmured. "You haven't ever been to see him in that... that horrible place, have you?"

"Actually..." I spread my arms for effect and looked around the room. "I don't feel that upset or morose or...anything by being here. Even though it's where he convinced me that I was meeting him for a date instead of a farewell dinner to run off into the sunset with..." I paused, thinking. Her name had become a curse word to me, so I was reluctant to speak it. Besides,

I couldn't remember it, anyway. "The bimbo."

Sherry scrutinized my face with her dark brown eyes. Sherry, with her upturned nose and light brown, curly, short hair, reminded me of Hallie Berry. "Coming here tonight…" I continued, "It's encouraging that I don't *feel* anything, one way or the other. Not sad. Not mad. Pretty much…fine."

"How far away is that prison?" Callie asked, as she poured herself more of the Rombauer and refilled Hannah's glass as well. Hannah and Callie usually split a bottle, and Sherry and I split the other. "An hour. Not far."

"I'll go with you if you want."

I smiled. *Vintage Callie.* Strong. Supportive. "Thanks," I said, with a sigh. "Look, I didn't want to get into it, but hiding anything from you guys is impossible. I went yesterday. I didn't tell anyone, not even Mom. Or my therapist, either; who would've thrown a fit."

After a blip of shocked silence, Sherry sighed. "Are you going to tell us how it went, or are you waiting for us to beg?"

I laughed. "I got through it. At least I didn't…you know…faint or anything. I think it was helpful. Hazel is always telling me I have to drop the chains of the past to move into the freedom of the future."

"Here, here!" Hannah murmured, lifting her glass. "We should make a meme."

Callie's stricken face told me she was so…*not* on board with the visit to see Monty.

"Callie, I know you're disappointed. I couldn't tell you, okay? You'd have worried yourself sick! Look, girls, life's not so fabulous right now and I'm …*stuck*." I put my book deal on hold, and my publisher is furious but trying to work out an extension; my sixteen-year-old, Lilly, is going through stuff that I don't understand and I need to spend more time with her; my mother is getting ready to marry my neurologist, for God's sake…" I frowned. "Crossing a chat with Monty off my list felt like a big forward step."

"Not at the risk of another seizure! My God, Olivia, you're still having memory issues and trouble keeping your balance!" Callie exclaimed.

Her feelings were valid. She'd been there for me when Monty had tried to wreck my life, and when he'd been locked up for manslaughter. But I *had* managed a conversation with the man without launching World War III.

An uncertain silence had snuffed out the fun. I was wearing these girls out with my ongoing drama.

I put my hand on top of Callie's. "There were guards."

"Yeah," she quipped. "And they're *so* vigilant."

"I was fine, promise. And just so you guys know, I'm making a trip to Richmond to see Mom and Serena in few days, and my neuro lives there, right? I'll have my own, personal doctor at my beck and call all weekend if there's any fallout from the visit to see my ex."

Callie grudgingly conceded, then changed the subject.

As Callie prattled on about the issues an uber-wealthy, happy-with-life-in-general woman encounters, like the perfect chandelier over the dining room table and the merits of an occasional tanning bed visit, I half-listened and stared off into the distance. It hadn't been so bad to share. These women were my friends and they hadn't judged me, they'd supported me.

Still. When Hannah glanced my way, it seemed like there was more she wanted to say.

Chapter Three

"Well, I like to think that my illness has prevented me from rising to any number of dizzy heights."
~Christopher Monckton

I needed a break from trying to dissect every decision I made.

Soon, I'd be on a plane to Richmond for a much-needed mental vacation. Visiting Mom and my daughter would provide a great diversion.

However, this would be the first time I'd been back since Detective Hunter Faraday and I had carried out his plan to interrogate my suspected attacker, and visit him unannounced. It had jump-started memories for me that helped Richmond PD get a warrant to search his place, sure; but on my end, it had been a nightmare I'd never forget. Hunter and I had been thrown together in such extreme circumstances that it had created a level of intimacy that I didn't know how to handle.

Probably still don't.

But…here I was, trying to figure out our relationship. Again.

I couldn't deny that the attraction was still there.

In an amazing twist of fate, my mom had moved from West Palm Beach to Richmond to be closer to her fiancée, the wonderful Dr. Grayson Sturgis, my neurologist. Now I had three reasons to visit. Mom, Serena, and my doctor. Four, if I counted Hunter Faraday.

I wanted to see him.

I raked my hands through my hair in frustration. There was nothing wrong with meeting him for coffee, right?

My cell buzzed with a text. My eldest daughter, Serena.

S - Are you coming?

Yep.

S - Driving?

Of course.

S - Has Grammy moved in?

She is moving into her apartment as we speak.

S - Wow!

I know.

S - I bet you're happy about that.

I'm ecstatic.

S - She'll be over here all the time.

That's why I'm ecstatic.

I paused mid-text to laugh. Mom would make sure my nineteen-year-old, strong-willed, bright sophomore in college was appropriately surveilled. She and Gray had a wedding date set now. Number three would be the charm, I could feel it.

My cell rang. I made a rude noise on behalf of my editor's number displayed there.

"Yep," I answered.

"Olivia."

"That's me," I muttered.

"I got an extension, but they aren't happy. The marketing team is throwing a fit."

"I'm sorry, Agatha. I'm still working things out."

"I know you are, sweetie, but the book is about the drama of what happened, not your bright future. Well, not completely. But it's the actual *experience* you suffered that's riveting...the life-threatening assault, admission to an ER barely breathing with no identity, the complete lack of memories when you emerged from a coma. Not to mention the final, bizarre conclusion...or lack of. It is kind of a mystery, isn't it? We need to get the editing process started, and honey, it's been months since we've talked. I don't have a single new page from you. You've completed so much therapy that it makes me want to find a book about the results of stuffing too much therapy into one person." Agatha paused to titter a few seconds to let me know she was kidding. I sighed.

"Yes, we were willing to wait for the full impact of the *emotional aftermath* of your experience, and how it's all worked out. We've talked about this… however—"

"I visited my ex in prison yesterday."

Long, quiet, seconds ticked by. I thought she'd muted herself when her squeal of delight nearly ruptured my eardrum. "You did? Olivia, that's *fantastic*! That is a perfect segue, absolutely perfect. We need to rethink the ending. This could be a sequel."

"See?" I purred. "If you guys will be patient, it'll be even better than you hoped."

"Did you journal it?"

I blinked. This editor-author relationship had become a little too close. "Yeah."

"Great! We'll process soon. Listen, we support you, Olivia. We do. But the contract states the book was due six months ago."

"I know, I know."

"Okay. How about two weeks? Let's at least set a meeting. Can you commit to a virtual meeting in a couple of weeks?"

Reluctantly, I agreed. We set a date and ended the call.

The front screen door banged shut. My head jerked up. Was it already time for Lilly to be home from school? "Lilly?"

"Yeah, hi Mom." She trotted into the kitchen, slid her backpack off, and opened the fridge. "Did you know there's a couple of guys walking around outside?"

I muttered dark things to myself as I walked down the hall and out onto the porch. What now? Sure enough, there was a white van parked to the left of my long, twisty, graveled driveway, and two men setting up equipment.

"Hey!" I yelled, stalking down the three stairs from my front porch, through the yard, and out into the driveway that wound a half-mile through mature, intertwined oaks to Highway 128 in lovely Glyndon, Maryland. "What are you guys doing?"

My house was close to the Glyndon Historic District, so certain repairs or adjustments were arranged without my knowledge, but only on the easement. These guys were on my property. Had I scheduled something and forgotten?

A fifty-ish, gray-haired man strode toward me, his steps crunching on the gravel. "Afternoon, ma'am, can we help you?"

"I think there's been a mistake. This is my property."

"I can give a number to call for verification. All we get is location and job description." He shrugged. "They don't give us details. We're done, anyway. We'll be leavin'.'"

I entered the number he recited into my phone. "Who should I ask for?"

"Wyatt Harp," he said.

"Ok, thanks," I said, and left. Glancing over my shoulder, I noticed him watching me as I left. He spoke to the other man, and both men got in the van and left.

A shudder ran through me. My mind leapfrogged back in time. I closed my eyes.

My hands death-gripping the steering wheel, I shot down Worthington Avenue to my house like a woman possessed. My breaths came in short gasps, my heartbeat battered my chest. I flew up my lane, spurting gravel under the tires in the bleak darkness. It had taken hours to wrap up Hunter Faraday's requested trip to Richmond, and now my daughters needed me. I skidded to a stop in front of the garage and exploded from the car. My steps whisper-soft, I ascended the white-plank stairs and listened at the door. Male voices growled at each other inside. My daughters stepped out from behind the bushes. "Mom! Those guys are back! They're arguing with Dad!" Serena hissed in the darkness. Lilly, her first two fingers stuffed in her mouth, tears streaming down her cheeks, ran to me and buried her face in my chest.

I blinked. The images, per usual, fluttered away like wispy clouds in a stiff breeze. I took one breath in, one breath out.

I punched in the number I'd been given. The person who answered had no idea what I was talking about and hung up on me. My steps heavy—because paranoia does that to a person—I went inside. Lilly called me into the kitchen.

"So what's up with the guys? I see they left." She took another bite of the sandwich she'd prepared.

"Did you see what it said on their van, honey, when you came home?"

"I don't think it had any writing on the side, Mom."

* * *

After Lilly raced off to volleyball practice, I searched out the location of the van. It had been raining off and on, and I saw the tire tracks were deep. Settled. That van had been parked a while. I tried to retrace the direction of their work, and plowed through the vines and overgrown shrubs, slapping limbs out of my way and avoiding thorny vines that gripped my clothes. Irritated at Monty for never clearing out this space, I wondered how many other things he'd promised to do but hadn't. I tripped over a root and landed on hands and knees. With a grunt, I pushed myself up and leaned back against the tree.

A breeze whistled through the leaves. Twilight seeped in, and the temperature dropped. I shivered. A cat meowed. My eyebrows shot up. "Riot? Is that you?" My cat had vanished out the front door to hunt, or whatever it is that tomcats do in the wild, and I'd feared he was lost forever. The meowing got louder. I squinted into the encroaching dark, trying to figure out where the sound had come from. "Riot!" I called happily when I spotted my lovable, ginger tomcat about ten feet off the ground, miserable and stuck in a tangle of vines.

I scrambled up, worked the vines loose, and held his thin, trembling body. As I tried my best to soothe him, a black, distinctly un-organic shape caught my eye in a nearby tree. Upon closer inspection, it had a lens, and it pointed both at the property beside the highway, and the entrance to my lane from the highway. A green electrical cord wound around the tree like a vine. I sucked in a breath, holding Riot close to my heart. "It's okay, boy," I murmured, as I slipped and slid to the lower branches, jumped to the ground, and inspected more closely. Those guys had been putting up a video system.

For what?

I bent down, careful to avoid being caught on video. The cord ended at the base of the tree, buried in the dirt. I had the barest expertise with electronics, but I knew there had to be a receiver somewhere. Riot started to squirm. I'd have to get him home before I figured out what to do. Who had the receiver to this thing? Were they watching right now? Were there other cameras? Holding Riot tight, I ran back to my house, locked every door, and gave Riot a warm bath.

While toweling off my bedraggled, hungry cat, I settled on questions: Was my ex still trying to control my every move? Even from prison? A tremor of fear slipped up my back.

Riot struggled out of the towel to a corner of the room to groom himself. Every few seconds he gave me a pouty look. As a peace offering, I gave him two cans of Fancy Feast. He finally passed out on his cat bed in the den.

I envied his simple, uncluttered sleep.

Chapter Four

Earl Sorenson, III; searched in desperation for the last, official cigar out of a box of Montecristo's a client had gifted him after a successful divorce settlement. "Damn!" he blurted, and stopped in the middle of the room, pinched his nose to think. After a few seconds, he smiled. "Don't have the dementia yet, old boy," he muttered.

His knees cracked as he squatted to reach the bottom drawer of his intimidating, mahogany desk. With a grunt, he extracted a final, somewhat withered, cigar; shoved the drawer closed, gripped the top edge of his desk, and hefted his bulk upright. He held the cigar between thumb and the first two fingers of his right hand and whispered, "You are a thing of beauty."

Earl walked to his desk, sat in his maroon leather chair, and cut and lit the cigar with great ceremony.

Quick steps on the hallway carpeting stopped outside the reception area. He willed the person to walk on by so he could finish his last cigar in peace. Raps hit the door.

Earl hurled an unflattering comment at the visitor.

He snuffed out the cigar and lay it reverently on the edge of an amber ashtray he'd preserved from the eighties. With a start, he remembered his assistant of fifteen years had quit last week, and he needed to open the door himself. He ran a hand through his wavy, gray mane, smoothed his wild eyebrows, and strode through reception to the door.

The slender woman standing in the hallway shot him a grin. "Hi, Earl. How have you been?"

A smile erupted underneath his moustache. "Olivia! You look stunning!

Come in, come in," he insisted, both his arms sweeping toward his office. "Have a seat."

She pointed at the empty desk. "Where's, uhhh…what's your assistant's name again?"

Earl walked back into his office and sat in one of the two comfortable chairs in front of his desk. Olivia followed him in and sat in the other one. "She quit. Last week."

"Well, I'm sure you've got a replacement lined up."

Earl laughed and shook his head. "You want the job?" he teased. "You have more than enough experience."

"Only with outrageous divorce demands," Olivia quipped.

Earl regarded Olivia with keen eyes. "Business has been slow anyway, so I'll figure it out. How are things with you? What brings you in today?"

Olivia looked pointedly at the cigar. "I see you're still sneaking cigars."

His gaze slid from the ashtray to her face. "Mind?"

She rolled her eyes. "Go ahead."

"The last one in the box," he explained. "Then I'm done."

"What is it with you smokers? My mom's the same way. She did quit, though."

He lit the cigar and puffed away. "Now. What can I do for you?"

Olivia's forehead furrowed. "I didn't know who to talk to."

"You know you have a friend in me, Olivia. Always."

She smiled her thanks. "A work van was out in my yard yesterday, on my property. I asked what they were doing, and they said they were there at the owner's request. I figured there was a mix-up. I went inside, called the guy's number they told me had ordered the job. But the person that answered had no idea what I was talking about. After the van left—it was two guys—I went out there to take a closer look."

Olivia leaned in, her eyebrows raised. "Earl, they put video equipment up in one of my trees!"

He squinted at her. "You order a security system? Maybe someone did it for you…that detective friend of yours?"

Olivia ran a hand through her hair and shook her head. "Nope."

"Your mom? She was always very protective—"

She thought for a moment. With her ongoing memory issues, her mom may have told her she was having it installed, but...wait. Didn't she call her mother about it? Yes.

"I called Mom last night. She didn't do it. So random. I'm thinking maybe Monty is staking out his territory." Olivia's shoulders hunched. "Doesn't feel right, Earl."

Earl scratched his head. "Isn't he in prison?"

"Oh, yeah. He'll be there a very long time. I've only been to see him once." Olivia smiled, looked away. "I don't know if it's better to keep him out of our lives or not with all that's happened. I went to try to dig up information about my past. Still having memory issues."

"I'm sorry," he murmured.

Olivia waved the words away. "It's fine. I remember most things, but as a young wife, a young mom...I can't get there. I thought he might be able to help, but he hates me more than ever. He was awful. I'd forgotten..."

"I can well imagine," Earl said, his voice somber. He snuffed out the cigar, then sat back and folded his hands across his paunch. "Did you take the system down, or disconnect it?"

"No." Olivia looked away. "I thought about it, but I didn't want whoever put it up to know that I knew. It was easy to avoid the lens trajectory. I've been racking my brain...only one person comes to mind that could be interested in who comes and goes at my house."

Earl nodded. "Monty, of course. You always were a smart one, Olivia."

Olivia smiled. "Well, *after* the accide—assault. I was a complete airhead before that."

"No. You were a teenager with a mom in crisis and a father that was out of the picture."

"Whatever," she said, with a frown. "What should I do, Earl?"

Hands tented, he stared at the floor a few seconds. "Try this," he said as he rummaged around in a drawer, then handed a business card to Olivia. "I haven't used him in a while, but Tom Stark is the best PI I've ever had the pleasure to work with. Known him for over forty years. If anyone can get to the bottom of this, he can."

"A private investigator..." Olivia murmured as she took the card and stared at it. "What a great idea. Thanks, Earl."

"Let's see what he turns up. If it becomes a civil issue—a violation of privacy—we can go from there, but the first thing he'll want to do is figure out who put that thing up."

Olivia nodded. "And why."

"Especially why," Earl added. "How are you doing otherwise?"

When Olivia smiled, her whole face lit up, Earl noticed. He remembered when, a couple of years ago, Olivia had been a pale, withered shell of a woman scared of her own shadow. The difference was remarkable. Her lovely, red curls reached to her shoulders. She wore ankle boots and leggings with an emerald-green sweater.

"I'm good. Recovery has gone well, and I think I'm done with physical therapy and all the other therapists my doctors threw at me."

Earl laughed at the sarcastic tone. "Therapy's a good thing, but it can be exhausting."

"Exhausting is the perfect word for it, and I've put it off for now. My girls are growing up, Serena's in college, in the middle of her sophomore year in Richmond, and Lilly is a junior in high school—very busy with drama team and sports. I'm closing in on an empty nest. I can't believe it."

"Wonderful to hear, Olivia. I'm so glad there's been a happy ending."

Like rain clouds in a windy sky, he watched her eyes drift as she thought about that. "We'll see. Not outta the woods, yet. But for the most part, yes." Her smile was uncertain. "My memory is not quite at a point where I can... trust myself. So I have to get confirmation from people I know." Her smile broke through again. "Like you." She rose, hiked her purse on her shoulder, and stuck out her hand. "Thanks. I'll call Tom the minute I get to the car."

Earl stood, shook her hand. "Are you staying busy? I heard about the book. How's that going?"

Olivia shrugged. "I'm stuck. Writers' block, maybe." She laughed. "I never knew that was really a thing, but, well...I guess it is. That's why I went to see Monty, and now this happened. I want to stay busy, but...the writing wasn't going well. I couldn't focus."

"Listen," he said, "I do have a need for a receptionist. A *paralegal-slash-receptionist*. Do you have any interest in working in the legal field?" He moved his eyebrows up and down. "It can get exciting."

Olivia laughed. "I'll think about it, okay?"

"Stay in touch, Olivia. Great to see you." He rose, and walked her to the door.

"You too." One more fleeting smile, and she left.

Earl heard her steps pad down the hallway, the slight ching of the elevator's arrival, and the shush of its closing doors. With a sigh, he went back to his office and stared at an empty calendar. Olivia had been a bright spot. Yes, indeed.

Chapter Five

Detective Hunter Faraday grabbed his cell and looked at the screen. The faint lines between his eyebrows deepened.

"Is it urgent?" his friend Shiloh asked, poking her fork into a salad.

Hunter let the text go unanswered. "Nope," he said easily, leaning forward on his elbows. "What's happening in your neck of the woods? All's calm for me right now, which is awesome." He took a few seconds to appreciate the way she looked. Shiloh had always been a gorgeous woman, he had to admit.

Shiloh made a cute, unhappy face, and sipped her lemonade through a straw. "They've got me on a desk. Something about inflammatory issues." She lifted one shoulder. "I live in Savannah. It's a small, sedate town. How many inflammatory issues can there be?"

Hunter laughed. "You're too hot to be on the street. Speaking of, you look great." His voice softened. "It's good to see you, Shi."

"You too," Shiloh murmured, munching a bite of salad, studying his face. Her cell rang. "One sec," she said, grabbed her phone, and walked away from the table.

The way her mouth was working, Hunter figured he had at least five minutes to respond to Olivia's text. His fingers lingered on her text. She'd be in Richmond this weekend, visiting her daughter, Serena, who was in college there and lived in an apartment. Could he meet for coffee? She hoped he was doing well. He tried to ignore the jab to his gut when he remembered the way she'd backed off their blossoming relationship. Should he see her? No. He should be busy.

Too busy to get sucked into that black hole again, anyway.

He folded his hands on the table with a heavy sigh.

Shiloh slid back into her chair. "Everything okay?"

"Yeah," he said, summoning a smile. "Why are you in Richmond, again? You take days off?"

She resumed forking the salad. "Now or never. Once school's back in session, there'll be all kinds of crap going on. Slow now, with spring break on the way and all. Kids and families run down to Florida from Savannah."

"I think I'd like Savannah. You ever regret the change?"

"It was a promotion. Had to take it." She grabbed a napkin, wiped her mouth, set her fork down, and leaned back in her chair.

"No, you didn't," Hunter said.

"I *did*," she insisted. "I had no future here. *We* had no future, either. I needed to go." She glanced around the patio of the restaurant, and into the Virginia Museum of Fine Arts. "Nice place. I'm enjoying this. I do miss things about Richmond, but I'm becoming a fan of Savannah. Did you know they are the number one haunted city in the US? Or at least that's what TripAdvisor says." She laughed.

"Bet you see a lot of weird stuff."

"Almost enough to make me believe in ghosts."

A silence settled over the table. Hunter glanced at his phone and frowned.

"You need to go?" she asked.

Hunter smiled, sheepish.

"Detective, remember?" With a smile, she rose. "Hey, I have people to see. Still have good friends here, and we're planning things for tonight. You free?"

"Shi...I—"

"Oh for God's sake, Faraday, it's an innocent question. I have no hidden agenda."

He smiled. "I'll think about it."

After a pause, she asked, "That text from your Maryland girlfriend?"

He was quiet.

Laughing, she grabbed her purse. "Remember, I told you not to get involved with the victim."

"I know," he muttered.

He watched her as she left, wondering if he'd made a mistake. They'd had a good thing six years ago, and now Shiloh was in the middle of a divorce. Though he could picture them together again, he'd learned from hard experience that dating a woman who'd not recovered from a divorce was a bad idea. And an even worse idea was becoming romantically involved with a woman recovering from a major brain injury, *and* a nasty divorce. Congratulating himself on his self-control and maturity, his phone buzzed with another text. Olivia again. She needed to talk to him about something when she came in. How about Saturday afternoon? Blowing out a breath, he made a decision.

Saturday's fine

He slipped the phone back into his pocket, paid the check, and left. "It's only coffee," he muttered to himself.

Chapter Six

"You're like a cake when you're young. You can't rush it, or it will fall or turn out wrong. Rising takes patience. And heat.
~Ann Quindlen

My cell rang as I was in the final stages of teeth-brushing. I rinsed, spit, and answered. "Hey, Callie. What's up?"

"Need to talk to you about something. Do you have a minute?"

I wondered at the somber tone. "Sure," I said, tentative. Maybe another argument with her daughter? I walked downstairs, and out to my front porch.

"Am I on speaker?"

"Yeah," I said, glancing at the birds and my gorgeous front yard that I adored. "Lilly's at school and no one's here, so..."

"Okay," she said, and paused. "Oh, hon, I'm sorry to be the one to tell you this. I thought maybe, I thought...well—"

Not again, Callie. I wanted to scream at her to come out with it. I loved this woman, but gosh, she took forever to get to the point. Through clenched teeth, I asked her to *puh-leeze* get to the bottom line.

"It's Hannah."

My mind flipped back to our latest girls' night. Hannah had been preoccupied, and it was a good bet Callie's call had something to do with that.

I waited.

Callie sighed. "She's been talking to Monty."

"What?" My thoughts slowed to a death march.

"Apparently for a while."

I didn't trust myself to speak.

"Olivia?"

I cleared my throat. "I'm here. I...I don't know what to say. Why? Why would she even *want* to talk to him?"

"I don't know. I guess she felt so bad about it that she had to tell someone and...well she talked to me."

"Everyone talks to you, Callie," I responded, my mind in the process of being completely blown. "They can't help themselves." I felt lightheaded. I told myself to breathe in. Breathe out. Repeat.

"I wasn't supposed to tell you, but—"

"Glad you did."

"I've known for a while, I thought it was simple curiosity, y'know? That it'd be like...an outreach to a prisoner. So he could cheer up, y'know? But she has feelings for him now."

"Oh good grief," I muttered.

"Yeah," she said, miserable. "I told her that he wasn't worth it."

"Well, that and the fact that she's *married*."

"She's bored," Callie stated, her voice flat.

A finger of anger played with my jaw muscles. "Oh, well, that explains *everything* now, doesn't it?" I jumped off the white wicker loveseat and stalked down the three stairs and into the grass that had yet to green up.

Hannah knew all my secrets and had supported and strengthened me during my recovery. Had taken my girls to school, and volunteered with me for sports events and homeroom activities. What was this? How should I feel? He wasn't my husband anymore, and would never be, yet...here he was, still having this ponderous, stifling effect on me. If I wanted *anything* in life post-Monty, I wanted him off my back and out of my life. I pictured him laughing his ass off in his cell when he thought about the effect this news would have on me. And make no mistake, this guy had wanted me to know. With nothing more to do than work out and macramé, or whatever it is that men do in prison, he was the type to amuse himself by staying in my head. Monty could not live with the fact that Hunter Faraday and I had tracked down the truth, and the jury had given him ten years, which was a crazy mistake, as far as I was concerned. Ten years for murder?

"Callie, do you think Hannah's…well, do you think they're more than friends?"

"It's more an emotional connection, I think." Her voice sounded doubtful. "At least she didn't *tell* me they're…a thing."

"Should I talk to her?"

"I don't know," Callie wailed. "Maybe I shouldn't have said anything."

"Yeah, and we'd continue our wine outings and I'd be clueless." I thought about our last meeting. "Callie, I could tell. She looked at me weird, do you remember? Like, a long time. I wondered what that was about, and now I know."

"Oh gosh. I don't know what to do."

I knew Callie inside and out. She was fragile. Sensitive. It had taken a lot of strength for her to admit this to me. "You don't have to do anything, Callie. I'll figure something out. See where she is with it."

"It's just…so bizarre."

"What else did she say?"

"Not anything specific, really…like…he's misunderstood, and you're being hard on him, that type of stuff."

My laughter had an edge. "Don't you see? He's a manipulator. He's working her."

"For what?" Callie asked.

"That's the question, isn't it?" I thought about the video setup in my yard and decided to keep that to myself. I still needed to call Tom Stark. This would be excellent insight for a PI. "Callie, don't worry about it, this isn't your fight. I'm sorry she shared that with you, because I know it's driving you crazy."

I heard her blow her nose. "She told me not to say anything, but I had to."

I knew I needed to get off the phone soon, before she got on my last nerve. Exploding all over her would not help. "Callie, I'll talk to you later, okay?

Let's keep this between us."

"Okay," she sniffled.

"Callie!" I pressed hard, hoping to interrupt her descent into an abyss of despair. "Stop! Look, I'm shelving this thing. I have a trip to Richmond coming up tomorrow, and I'm determined to be in a good mood for my mom and daughter. So let this go, okay? Let it go, Callie."

The sniffling stopped. I could picture her straightening, pushing her shoulders back. We were good for each other. Post-coma, my family and friends had told me that my personality had been rewired, and I believed it now. After being told how passive and unaware I'd been, I was proud of the way I dug in now. Callie's pathetic whining was getting on my nerves, and she needed to stop feeling so sad for a situation she had nothing to do with. It was Hannah that needed intervention. The poor woman had no clue what she was getting into.

"You're right," Callie responded, blowing out a breath. "Sorry. You know how I am."

I smiled. "You can choose *not* to be that way, you know," I said, my voice gentler. "Don't be sad, this is Hannah's thing, and I'll sort it out after my trip, okay? I'm good. You're good. *We're all good.* Okay?"

"Okay," she said, her voice stronger. "I'll let you go. Have a great trip. Don't worry about Lilly, I'll watch her like a hawk."

"Thanks, and I *will* have a great trip," I assured her. And I would. This bit of news was not going to derail my visit. Plus, I was going to see Hunter for the first time since the investigation into my case concluded. Not sure yet, if that had been a good decision or not, but I looked forward to it.

After we ended the call, I put the phone in another room. One of these days, I told myself, I'd fast from the phone and reset myself.

Later, I walked back inside after working in the yard. Nothing helped me like a few hours of pruning, fertilizing, planting, and raking. Sweating, but happy, I pulled off my garden gloves, and went inside for a shower before I started packing for my trip.

Lilly walked in as I slung the suitcase on the bed, unzipped it and opened it wide. Like clockwork, Riot appeared and curled himself into one side of the suitcase.

Lilly laughed. "Mom, why do cats love suitcases?"

I walked to my dresser, and grabbed socks, pajamas and tossed them into the un-catted side. "Are you sure you don't want to go? Grammy is dying to see you."

She shook her head. "Mom. I'm almost seventeen. I can take care of myself."

I resisted the obligatory sarcastic comment. "So you're staying at Callie's house, right? With Amy?"

She made a face. "Mom, I love Amy, but her mom? I know she's your best friend and all that, but she drives me nuts. Talk about hovering. OMGee! Is it okay if we hang out here during the day?"

I studied her. I had yet to understand why Lilly had such a problem with Callie. Amy was short and cute, like her mom. She'd convinced Lilly to try out for the school play, and now Lilly was all about the drama team, maybe looking at majoring in theatre.

"You know how I feel about leaving you alone, honey. I'd feel much better with you at Callie's house. At least for now, okay?"

I grabbed slacks, and threw them in. Since I never folded anything, packing was a breeze for me. I sniffed the underarms of a top to make sure it was clean. Satisfied, I tossed it in. Riot started giving himself a leisurely bath on his side of the suitcase. "Callie's got your room ready, she's looking forward to having you. Don't forget to feed Riot and clean out the litterbox at least once."

"You never pay attention to what *I* want, as usual," she spat, her face a thundercloud. She stalked from the room. "Play practice," she yelled across her shoulder as she clattered down the stairs. The front door slammed shut behind her.

I sank onto the bed for a few minutes, as the slam of the door echoed through the house.

I shooed Riot out of the suitcase, finished packing, and went to get a glass of wine.

Chapter Seven

Hazel Magelssen sat at her desk in Westminster, Maryland, staring at Olivia Callahan's file. She looked out her window at the hazy, blustery spring day, her fingers tapping. This was the normal time for Olivia's counseling session and Olivia had canceled the next two months' worth of sessions. Hazel's light blue eyes narrowed in disapproval, and the lines between her brows squeezed together. That would put their next session sometime in May.

Since she had no more appointments until two, she ran over to Birdie's Cafe and grabbed a sandwich, a coffee, and a muffin for mid-afternoon. Her cozy, small counseling practice nestled in between an Edward Jones office and a florist on the historically protected Main Street of Westminster. The buildings, zealously preserved and restored by the local historical society, were two- or three-story, white clapboard, narrow sentinels standing shoulder to shoulder in silent tribute to days gone by.

Hazel trotted up the narrow staircase to her second-floor office. Catching a glimpse of herself in the wall mirror, she tucked her wiry, short gray hair behind her ears and adjusted her round, translucent glasses on her tiny nose.

Her cell shattered the stillness with its ultra-loud, landline-imitation ringtone.

After a slight delay, a voice inquired. "Hazel? That you?"

Hazel's eyebrows drew together. *Sophie.* After a scant three family sessions, Olivia's mother assumed she had earned the right to inject herself into Hazel's counseling methodology.

"Yep."

Slight pause. "I wanted to let you know that I've moved to Richmond. I'll be much closer than the Palm Beach area now if you need me for, uh... future sessions. I can zip over anytime."

Hazel grimaced. "Thanks for the information, Sophie."

"I've heard that Olivia's...um... *interrupted* her therapy. Surely I misunderstood."

Hazel stared at a spot on the wall. "You didn't misunderstand her, Sophie."

"Oh."

Pause.

Hazel sighed. "You know I can't give you any information about this. Talk to your daughter." Hazel smiled at the gentle clank of the woman's bracelets as they talked, which she'd learned were Sophie's trademark—lots of jewelry. She glanced at the scarves hanging on her purse, her coat tree. Fiddled with her long, sparkly, necklace, and sighed.

"Yes, well, I...I did want to let you know I moved, and for a good reason. You're aware that Olivia's neuro and I—Gray—do you remember?"

"I do. You and he were romantically involved."

"We're engaged, now. That's why I moved."

"Congratulations," Hazel said, still wondering what, exactly this infernal busybody of a woman wanted.

"I wonder if you'd at least give me some indication that you think Olivia is doing well? For the life of me, I don't understand her interrupting her counseling sessions, and I think it ought to be—"

"Sophie." Hazel interrupted.

Pause.

"We've had this discussion. I do *not* have Olivia's permission to share her history with you, nor would I feel good about doing so. I repeat, talk. TO. OLIVIA."

Sophie sighed. "Okay. I guess I'm overstepping."

Hazel was quiet.

"I'll email you my new address."

Hazel put her hand over her face. "That'll be fine, Sophie."

"I just wanted to—"

"I know you did," Hazel jumped in, "and I appreciate it. I've got to go now."

Hazel finished her sandwich, licked her fingers, and leaned back in her chair, thinking that Olivia's mother was an entirely different behavioral issue in Olivia's early years that needed exploring. Her phone rang. She smiled. *What timing.*

She snatched up her cell. "Everything okay?"

Olivia laughed. "Why is it when I call that's your first question?"

"Sorry. I guess I've become a little like…"

"My mother," Olivia completed for her. "I can only handle one of her, Hazel."

"Funny. What's up?"

"I did it."

Hazel's forehead furrowed. "Did what?"

"Went to talk to Monty."

Pause.

"I don't want you to worry. It was fine."

"Describe for me, 'fine.'"

"No passing out. No fear paralysis. No weird anger. I'd describe it as… uncomfortable."

"How long were you with him?"

"Twenty minutes maybe."

"He ended it, didn't he?"

Pause. "How did you know that?"

"Classic narcissist. You are compelling and stronger now, and able to say what you want to say. Feel what you need to feel without apologizing. It's a good bet that direct questions put him on the defensive. Made him acknowledge his flaws, which he can't stand. He had to disconnect." *And it's a good bet his target on your back just got bigger,* she thought.

"Yeah. He did. I don't care. The information I pulled out of him was helpful. I promise I'll unpack it with you."

"In two months?"

"You know how I'm feeling right now. I want…no, I *need*…a break from working on myself. You told me you understood. Remember?"

"Sure." But, as always, Hazel knew the decision to resume counseling was much harder after an absence. "Remember, I'm only a phone call away."

"Thanks. I thought I'd give you a call today to keep you in the loop in case something happens to me."

"Not funny."

Oliva burst out laughing. "Couldn't resist."

"Your mom called."

Pause. "Wow."

"It's okay. I like your mom." She paused briefly to internalize the fact that she'd outright lied. "But she has to realize I can't talk about what you and I discuss."

"She knows," Olivia reassured her. "She hopes you'll have a vulnerable moment."

"I suppose a mother is justified when she's almost lost her daughter."

"Maybe," Olivia murmured. "Anyway, I feel like I climbed a huge mountain and planted a flag on top. I talked with Monty—*in prison*— without having a mental breakdown or a seizure or freaking out. Aren't you happy for me?"

"Of course I am, Olivia," she responded, noting the hopeful tone in her voice. A darker undercurrent played on a loop in her brain. Monty Callahan didn't mess around.

I hope you realize what you've started, Olivia.

Chapter Eight

"Life and death matter, yes. And the question of how to behave in this world, how to go in the face of everything. Time is short and the water is rising."
~Raymond Carver

Saturday dawned bright and sunshiny. I sprang from bed smiling, thinking about seeing Mom and Serena in Richmond. Also, if I were honest, catching up with Hunter in a few hours had a lot to do with my goodwill and bonhomie. I started making the bed, but I was too excited. "Forget it," I breathed, left it the way it was, and hopped into the shower.

Even now, after two years of recovery from the assault and subsequent short-term paralysis, taking a shower felt like a minor miracle.

I toweled off, threw on jeans, a cute T-shirt, and tennis shoes, grabbed my suitcase, and bumped it down the stairs to the foyer. "Lilly?" I called before I remembered she'd spent the night with Callie's daughter, Amy. I sent off a quick text to tell my daughter goodbye. She answered, even though it was seven a.m. and she couldn't be happy about a text this early. To my surprise, she answered.

have a good trip going back to sleep bye

On the heels of her text, one from Hunter flashed on my screen.

Have a good trip. Thinking of you, be safe. See you tomorrow at Millie's Café.

The little curls of excitement rolling around my stomach at Hunter's text did *not* make me happy. *Objectivity.* That's what would make me happy. I stuffed my cell into my back pocket, threw my suitcase in the back seat, and drove away. Halfway down my beautiful, tree-lined, lane, glaring my hatred at the videocam, I remembered I was supposed to call Tom Stark. I called him from the car and explained the reason for my call. His voice was deep and reassuring; with a drawl so pronounced, I wondered where he was from.

"Yeah, haven't seen Earl in a while. Surprised he's still on the job," he said.

"Really? He seemed fine to me."

"He's had health issues, maybe it's all fixed now."

"I'd think so. He has no plans of quitting, he even offered me a job," I said, hesitant.

"That right? He's a good man, Earl. Couldn't go wrong there. Now let's get to this video camera thing. And you said your ex-husband is in prison, right?"

"Yes. He should be in a while."

"But you think he arranged this…um, surveillance?" Tom asked.

"That's what I need you to find out. I can't think of anyone else that would do this. Because, why? All I'm doing is working on remembering my life."

Pause. "You're *that* Olivia Callahan?"

"Guess so."

"How's the book coming?"

I sighed. "Can we change the subject?"

"Sure," he said. "So you're leaving for a visit to…Richmond?"

"To see my daughter and mom. I'll be back late Sunday. It's fine with me for you to run by the house, check out the video camera, and around the area. I don't know, maybe you can track down serial numbers, find out who bought it, or where it came from. Figure out what it can do."

"So…you said you saw who put it up?"

"Yes," I said, pulling into the airport parking lot.

"You sure you didn't hire someone to do it and forget? After all, you did have a problem with memo—"

"Let's get one thing straight," I interrupted. I am not that person anymore. All my faculties are in order, and the only things I cannot remember have to do with childhood experiences, or years ago. Short-term memory is fine. And so is everything else. Don't treat me like an invalid." I jerked my suitcase out of the trunk.

A heartbeat of silence. "I'll get started, but we'll need to have a proper sit-down when you get back, that okay?"

I agreed, told him I'd text him all my contact info and anything I thought might help in his investigation, and we ended the call.

* * *

My suitcase sat on the conveyer belt in the Richmond airport like a beached whale. As usual, I'd over-packed and it was heavier than it should've been and I'd had to pay extra. I'd put a cute, red ribbon on it because I was told black bags 'all looked alike' and I had a good laugh at that because *my* bags always looked like they were about to burst open. The red ribbon only served to accentuate the fact that I abused my luggage.

Settling on a bench, I scanned the pick-up traffic for Serena's white, four-year-old Ford Escape. My phone buzzed.

MOM have you landed

I texted back. **Yes. Waiting. Got my bag.**

OMG I lost track of time be there in ten minutes

With a shake of my head, I texted back. **OK**

I spread my arms across the back of the bench and settled in to wait.

Have you landed? This is mom.

I laughed. It was nice to be loved. **Yep. Waiting on Serena.**

She's late, isn't she? I should've come. Are you okay?

I'm fine.

Do you want me to come? I can probably get there quicker than she does. (laughing tears emoji)

No it's fine. Are you moved in

Working on it. Gray is busy with a meeting at the hospital, but he's free this afternoon. Wanna meet for lunch?

Sure. I think Serena already planned on us having lunch together

Okay. Gray lives in an area called Three Chopt. Isn't that weird?

38

I'll have to learn everything about Richmond. My condo is about ten minutes from his house.

Tell us where to meet

After I put the address in my map, scrolled through messages, and checked the weather, Serena finally pulled up and jumped out of the car. "Mom! So sorry! How was your flight?" Her mouth dropped at the sight of my bulging bag, but gamely rolled it to the trunk. It took both of us to lift it.

The force of her foot on the accelerator pressed me into my seat before I even had a chance to buckle in. I smiled. Her driving mirrored her personality.

"So where to?" Serena asked. "How are you?"

One hand on the armrest and the other on the dashboard, I gave her a shaky smile as her car lunged in and out of traffic. "I'm good. We're going over close to Grammy's place. Have you been there?"

She groaned. "Are you kidding? She wants me over there all the time. I practically live there."

I laughed. "I'm sure that's not true."

"Just feels true." She sped through a yellow light a split second before it changed.

"How's school?"

She shrugged. I felt a warning bleep in my brain. "What's that mean?"

She threw me a sideways glance. I resisted telling her to keep her mind on the road and firmed up my hold on the dashboard.

"Do you think college is really necessary, Mom?"

Pause. "I think this is a conversation we should have when we are not in crazy traffic."

"This is nothing," she said, flapping her hand. "You should see it at rush hour."

In ten minutes, we alighted at a cute little café on a side street in an area Serena called 'Midtown'.

"Grammy bought a condo at Libbie Mill, it's adorable. Two bedrooms, but it's big and nice. End unit."

"Can't wait to see it," unbuckling and taking a breath. I whispered a little prayer of thanks that we'd survived Serena's driving. "After lunch, I guess I'm going to Mom's?"

"That's the plan," she said. "Look, how *cute* is this? Never been here."

We walked up a sidewalk and inside a café with green and white striped awnings and nice landscaping and flower boxes at the windows. Mom waved at us from a table across the room. She looked flushed and happy, but tired. It couldn't have been easy, moving from her beloved West Palm Beach to Richmond, and I hoped it had been the right decision for her to move to be closer to Gray. As for me, it would be a cold day in hell before I got married again. I hadn't even had a date in over a year.

We all ordered white wine too early in the day and enjoyed a lovely lunch and girl talk. To my great relief, we avoided any discussion of therapy, recovery, the assault, or Monty in prison. We focused on Mom's new life with Gray, their upcoming marriage, and Serena's college experiences. It was one of those delightful times to tuck away in my memory and pull out when life got hard and I found myself reaching out to my old friend, Oblivion, for peace. As Serena and Mom chatted about Richmond, my mind wandered. To the video camera in my yard. Up a tree. Recording every move of who knows what.

I told my mind to shut up and leave me alone.

* * *

Mom's condo was one floor with two bedrooms, a lovely view out back, brand new weathered-wood planking and huge windows. Huge closets. Light and bright and airy. "This is gorgeous, Mom!"

She glowed. "Thanks. I love it. My little place in West Palm was...I don't know, dated, don't you think? This is all brand new. I'm looking forward to decorating."

"With Gray?" I teased.

She fluttered her hands, which made her trademark bracelets jingle. Her dangling earrings almost brushed her shoulders. She'd let her hair grow out, and I realized there were almost no traces of red anymore, it was mostly gray. With a stab of sadness, I realized I wouldn't have her around forever. "It's my place, and it'll have my stamp on it. Not his," she said.

Serena laughed. "This place is already so…you, Grammy."

Mom and I looked at each other.

"I mean," Serena explained, "it's colorful, with a lot of personality."

Mom shot her a look. "Nice save." She turned toward me, sat in the matching chair beside mine. An end table with a pelican lamp sat between us. Mom might need to retire the West Palm décor. "What are your plans while you're here?"

"I'm pretty much open." I shrugged. "I'd like to see where Serena lives, and meet her roommate, maybe? I'd like to help you with placing furniture or unpacking…whatever you need."

Serena grunted. "*Mom.* No way you'd come here and not see your detective."

"He's not *my* detective," I insisted. "I do have plans to meet him for coffee tomorrow afternoon."

Mom winked at Serena. Serena laughed.

I rolled my eyes. "Stop."

A text vibrated on my phone. I glanced at it, then hurried into one of Mom's bedrooms and closed the door.

"Tom. What's up?"

"Olivia, I thought I'd better touch base."

My brows jerked together. "Why are you whispering?"

"You might say there are folks not too excited about me snooping around."

"What! No. *Tom.* Are you okay? Where are you?"

"I'm behind your garage. Two men are walking the property. One has a sidearm."

"Do you have—"

"Yeah. I do. It's in my hand right now. Are you sure you don't know what these guys want?"

"What do they look like?"

"One is older, gray hair, medium height. The other seems more like a kid, rangy, tall, brown hair and a beard."

"Tom," I hissed, glancing at the door and glad I'd closed it. "Those are the men I saw hooking everything up. You need to get out of there."

"Yep. After I get photos, I'm out…"

"Tom!"

The phone went dead in my hand.

* * *

I returned to the table a bit wobbly and dropped into my chair.

"What happened?" Mom asked. "You're pale as a sheet. Honey, are you okay?"

Should I say anything? I took in their beautiful faces, each so concerned that any second I'd faint, or have a seizure. Yes, I'd been assaulted, and yes, I'd survived a coma, but my loved ones had PTSD, too, and hovered over my every move. I couldn't burden them with this. Not until I knew more. I waved my hand in dismissal. "Oh, you know, I have these little episodes. A few minutes, and I'm back."

Mom let out a long breath of relief. "Oh, good. You sure it's not the wine?"

I shook my head. "Positive. What would I do without wine?"

We had a good laugh at that. I tried my best to stay engaged, but at the back of my mind, I wondered if I'd find a corpse on my property when I got home.

Chapter Nine

"Your fears grow smaller and smaller as you rise above them."
~Carol "CC" Miller

A constant buzzing dragged me from sleep. I stared at the ceiling and wondered for a second where I was. Ten-foot ceilings, soft, pale, sage-colored walls, and fresh pristine sheets and sunshine blaring through my window. Had I died? Was this heaven?

I rubbed my eyes. My cell buzzed again. Oh, yeah. I was in Richmond, at my mother's new place, and Tom Stark could be calling. I'd not slept well, anxious about what had happened with him yesterday, and worried sick about Lilly. I hadn't been able to contact her last night, but left a message with Callie. My cell went off again. I grabbed it.

I did not recognize the number. My hand shook as I answered. *"Mom? It's me. This is Callie's phone. Mine's dead."*

I breathed in the sweet whiff of relief. "Please tell me you slept at Amy's last night."

"I did. Amy's mom said I needed to stay here. What's the problem? I need to feed Riot."

My eyes felt like sandpaper. I stretched, sat up, walked to the bathroom. Road maps stared back at me. Must be pollen season in Richmond.

"I hired a private investigator, honey. His name is Tom, and he's a nice man. We're looking into a few issues with the property. Be careful."

Pause. "Issues? As in, Dad-related issues?"

I rubbed my forehead, thinking. I'd never get over the anguish I felt for my

43

daughters that they'd had to endure the newspaper headlines and rumors after Monty had been arrested for murder. Lilly still believed Monty was redeemable. Serena flat-out refused to see him. "There's a video camera on our property, now. I'm a little freaked about it, so I hired Tom to track down information. That's all."

"Wait. So…those guys in our yard? Was that what that was?"

"Yeah."

Pause. I could picture the steam rolling off her as her anger boiled over. I steeled myself for her reaction.

"WHY do you always do this, Mom? God! I'm almost seventeen. I can handle it! Stop treating like some ten-year-old you need to protect. If anything, it's you that needs protecting!" Her voice dwindled at the end of her tirade, but I could hear the frustration loud and clear. My daughters were tired. Exhausted. They'd gotten used to one crisis after another, and now, they were drained. The last three years had certainly done that to me, and I couldn't imagine what it had done to them.

"I didn't want you to think about it, Lilly. You've been through enough with—"

"Mom, I need to *know* this stuff," she blurted. "I'm a capable person. I can be helpful, you know. I want to help you, Mom."

"I know you do, honey. I'm sorry."

"I saw the guys. I think I might recognize them. So if I go over to the house, I'll take a bat." She snapped her fingers. "Amy has a German Shepherd! Best thing ever. I'll take him. He'd tear their throats out!"

I laughed. "That's perfect. Sending my daughter into the unknown before my PI even knows what's going on. Better tie the dog up on the deck though, because Riot would never, ever recover."

Lilly chuckled. "Riot wouldn't know what hit him."

"Let's not find out, okay? Anyway, ask Amy's dad to go check on things, please. See if he and Callie would mind if you kept Riot over there."

"I will." A breath of silence. "No more keeping things from me!"

I thought about how tough it was, watching my girls grow up. I sighed. "Okay."

What the heck had happened to Tom? I guess if I had a body on my property, Callie's dad would see it. I dropped my face into my hands. Would I *ever* have a nice, boring life? I thought about the conversation we'd had at our last Wine & Whine. Hannah had said her marriage was boring. Sherry had said she *liked* boring...and I had agreed.

I think.

Hannah's face loomed in my mind. Should I talk to her? I had no claim on him anymore, and well, thank God for that...but she could be in danger. Monty's superpower was pretending to be normal. Didn't I need to warn her? Seems like she could figure that out on her own. But at what cost?

I cursed. Loud.

I hated Monty Callahan with all my being. But more than hating him, I wanted to render him useless. Impotent. Unable to touch our daughters, friends, anything. But I had no control over Hannah, and didn't relish the thought of getting involved in this little side hustle thing she was doing with Monty.

"Stop thinking about this!" I exclaimed aloud, determined to stop the spiral. I picked out an uplifting playlist to re-route my thoughts and turned up the volume.

I would not give in to the darkness. Oblivion could just...back off.

* * *

After showering and getting dressed, I followed my nose to the tantalizing smells of coffee, bacon, eggs, and Mom's trademark hash browns. She mouthed 'good morning' and held up one finger to indicate she'd be off her phone shortly. I took one of the plates she'd set out and loaded it up.

Unpacked boxes lined the walls. It was clear what I'd be doing most of the day.

Mom ended her call and smiled at me, her cheeks bright pink.

"How'd you sleep?" she asked.

"Good. It took a second to realize where I was," I mumbled through a mouthful of scrambled eggs. "How's lover-boy today?"

She laughed. "Good. Every time I talk to him, I'm waiting for a shoe to drop. I try not to think that way, but I guess..."

"I guess you had too many experiences with masculine trauma. Kind of like me, huh, Mom?"

She gave me a regretful look and picked up a piece of bacon to munch on.

"I went to see Monty," I blurted. I knew I had to tell her, and I wanted to get it over with. "I needed to. Nothing happened, Mom."

After an initial stiffening of her shoulders, it looked like she would be fine with the news. My mistake.

Mom folded her arms across her chest. "What the heck is going on, Olivia? Be straight with me. You've canceled therapy, and now this. I'm...well, I'm *beyond* concerned. You're not all the way back yet, and you *know* you have to be—"

"Careful," I finished for her, heaving out an exasperated sigh. "Mom, I can't be careful forever! I need answers. I've gone as far as I can go without more information. I've been poked, prodded, tested, so many times I've lost track. Except for Hazel, I can't even remember how many therapists I've seen. I've done everything I'm supposed to. Don't have a fit every time I want to take myself for a test drive!" In a gentled voice, I continued. "I'm okay, Mom. Really."

Mom was tired of worrying about my progress, I knew. We all were. Probably Hazel, too, though she'd never let on. And maybe Gray, who'd been nothing but positive and supportive. But now, he'd have a recovering coma patient as part of his family. I felt a little guilty about that. God knows I didn't want my deficits to come between Mom and Gray.

Mom swiped angrily at tears. "I'll get better at this. I know you have a life to live and I can't always be there. You are stronger, now. I have to trust that you're getting there and that my prayers are heard. God is better at parenting than I am." She blew out a breath. "Are you still journaling?"

Relieved that our little skirmish had passed, I told her yes, I was journaling.

She nodded. "That will serve you well. When you do have little 'spells' as you call them, the information you write down will help you."

"Like yours helps you," I teased. Mom had been keeping prayer journals for decades.

She smiled. "One day, after I'm gone, I want you to read them."

My eyes widened. "I'm not sure I want to know your innermost thoughts, Mom."

She laughed. "But you'll want to know what my prayers were and how God answered them. Those journals were a lifeline during my stuff, too, you know."

I thought about that. Mom had had more than her share of hard situations and raised me mostly as a single parent. "Do you want to hear how it went with Monty?"

I went over the conversation as I remembered it, chewing mouthfuls of breakfast in between. "Monty mentioned a man that scared me? Made me nervous? Would you know who that would be?"

A smile played with her mouth. "The Dud, probably. Do you remember him?"

"The Dud?" I laughed. "I assume it did *not* work out."

She took a plate off the table and rinsed it in the sink. "It certainly did not. He was a horrible person."

"Tell me what he looked like."

Mom inserted the plate into the dishwasher. "Gorgeous man. Blond, thick hair. Classy. Tanning bed tan year 'round. The kind of guy women with my history fall for— a perfect jackass."

I cocked my head. "In what way? Were you married to him? I can't remember that at all."

"I was married to him for two minutes."

"Monty said he...messed me up when I was in grade school or something?"

Mom, tight-lipped, looked away. Dropped her head. "I hoped you wouldn't remember," she whispered.

"Well," I murmured, "I didn't. But Monty brought it up, and he said the guy bothered me or whatever."

"He was...inappropriate, honey. With you. It didn't get far, because you told me...and at least I had a chance to intervene. I didn't press charges, but I should have."

"What? Did he—"

"No." Her voice was firm. "I was listening, one time, and overheard him talking to you, and went ballistic on him. Thank God, you didn't even understand what he was talking about. Back then, we weren't sure what constituted sexual improprieties. It was a different world. But I kicked him out, had the marriage annulled, and I cannot believe Monty even brought him up." She walked to the fridge, opened it, put ketchup back, and slammed the door.

"So he didn't have a chance to…well, do what those kind of men do."

"Not that I'm aware of," she said, her eyes searching mine. "You were ten, I think. And we were only together a few months. I can't imagine how he could have, he was at work, and I was home most days."

I could not dredge up a memory of the guy. How had Monty even known? I couldn't imagine, at seventeen, when Monty and I had started dating, that I would mention it. Like a lightning bolt, a thought struck. "Mom!"

She jerked out of her reverie.

"Whatever happened to him?"

"Last I heard, he was in prison. I don't know what for."

I let that sink in. A dawning awareness crossed Mom's face. "It can't be…" she whispered, her voice trailing off.

"Let's hope not," I said, bitterly.

Chapter Ten

"The key to generating loyalty and rising above the general noise seems to be all about creating an authentic voice."
~Richard Branson

At mid-afternoon, the crowds in downtown Richmond had thinned out, and a pleasant mix of seniors playing checkers outside restaurants and young moms pushing baby strollers or walking dogs made for an idyllic scene.

I pulled into the parking lot of the restaurant, fluffed my hair, and told myself there was nothing to be nervous about. However, a fluttery feeling in my stomach said otherwise.

"What's up," I said, as I approached his table.

"Wow," he said, his eyes lighting up. "I can't even believe you're the same woman." He shook his head and smiled. "You look great, Olivia."

I sat in the chair across from him. "Thanks."

"What can I get you? Mocha latte?"

I laughed. "You remembered!"

He scraped back his chair. "Want anything to eat?"

I shook my head. "Had lunch at Mom's."

He shot to the barista and returned with two coffees. "It's been a while. How have you been?"

I fidgeted in my chair. What should I tell him? That I'd been journaling and visiting therapists and doing physical rehabilitation until I wanted to puke? That I hadn't been able to recover all my memories, even after almost eighteen months, and I was worried that I may never be able to? That I'd visited Monty for the first time and was now concerned that he was cooking up a bizarre plan to get back at me? That I still had nightmares about the attack, and Niles' remorse, and the crime scene?

I wrapped both hands around the warm mug. "It's really good to see you," I managed.

"You, too," he said.

"I don't know how to start." I gave him a look. "You should interview me."

He laughed. "I can do that."

"If I remember correctly, you do it really well."

He cocked his head and folded his arms. "Let's see. Ms. Callahan? It is still Callahan, right?"

Chuckling, I nodded, thinking back to our early interviews and my nervous, stuttering, answers.

"Since you are now famous, especially here in Richmond…" he spread his arms. "How is it coming with the book? Richmond awaits the true "Mercy's Miracle" story. Especially me. I'm the hero," he joked.

My heart swelled with gratitude. "To me, you will always be a hero. And the book is on hold."

The caramel-chocolate eyes that grew warm or cold depending on the topic, softened. "Why?"

I looked away. Folded my arms across my chest. "I got stuck. Needed a break."

"I can understand."

We were quiet. One thing I remembered about the man, he was okay with quiet. I liked that.

"Tell me about you," I suggested.

He shrugged. "Business as usual. Homicides are down this year, so that's good. My caseload is light right now. Richmond PD has been working on building relationships with communities."

I pushed the mug aside. Propped myself on my elbows. "Speaking of jobs, do you remember Earl?"

"The attorney?"

I nodded. "He's offered me a job in his office as a receptionist. With the caveat that I should take paralegal courses. Have any words of wisdom for me? I've never had a real job." I laughed. "Not that paid, anyway."

Hunter leaned forward, thinking. At this point, our noses were like…a foot apart over the small table. I leaned back in my chair.

"Really want my opinion?"

I frowned. "Why do people always ask me that? Like words will break me or something."

He chuckled. "Most people need it all sugar-coated with…I don't know, diplomacy? I'm more comfortable with direct."

"I'm good with direct."

He looked at me for a few seconds. "There was a time…"

"Stop that!" I protested. "That time is come and gone, okay? I'm so sick of people tip-toeing around me. Say what you want to say!"

"Okay. Sorry."

I sighed. "My reactions are too extreme, lately. Residual effects, I'm told." I lowered my eyelids and grinned. "But I *have* learned that a properly-timed temper tantrum can work wonders."

He laughed. "*Yes,* you should pursue a career. You remember when we went to visit Niles? To figure out if he was the guy?"

I gave him a look. The event was forever burned into my brain with a branding iron. "As if I could forget, Hunter."

"Right. Well, I noticed certain personality characteristics. So soon after an assault, many women would have refused to participate in that type of investigation. But you…even though nerves played a part…you wanted to. *Had* to. And you saw it through like a pro. I never shared my thoughts about it, but I've thought you'd be good in forensics, investigation…the legal world, sure, but you can go in many directions. Police force, even, um law school." He made a face.

I laughed. "Poor lawyers. They must fight that attitude all the time."

He scooped up our empty cups. "I'll get us a couple more. Have time?"

I nodded. Yeah, I had time, but my nerves would be raw and bleeding from all the caffeine. He took his place in a long line of afternoon caffeine-seekers. Yes, there was a time…when I'd never have looked into the legal field, or any field, for that matter except taking care of my family. I'd been so insecure and passive that now, with a brand new set of re-routed brain connections, I had a hard time believing what people told me about…me. What had been the catalyst for all that passivity? Not Mom, the woman that managed to alienate almost everybody in her wake. It had to have been from my father's side. And I hadn't had the pleasure of knowing him.

My cell vibrated with Mom's text asking 'would I like to bring the cute detective to dinner'? Um, no. Next. Lilly had texted to tell me everything was okay, Riot had been hijacked to Callie's house and her husband, Graham, had fallen in love with him. This revelation was accompanied by several eye roll emojis and one barf emoji. How could a daughter of mine not love cats? I laughed, put my phone away, and watched Hunter at the counter. The easy way he talked to people. The facile, precise motions he made with his hands. The way his hair kept falling into his forehead and he had to brush it away. How his profile sharpened when he smiled. How his face had looked that tragic day at the crime scene …

"You don't want to see this, Olivia. Stay in the car!"

Hunter's face was a mask of fury and sorrow, his stride measured as he walked across the cracked parking lot asphalt toward the motel on the main thoroughfare through Westminster, Maryland. He lifted the yellow crime scene tape and stalked to the gurney. As he huddled with the coroner, the patrolmen around the perimeter, and the forensics team, I overheard a couple of men talking. I crept out of the car to get closer, desperate to know what happened.

"…brains all over the floor, man. His eyeball was hangin' out of the socket, for God's sake. How does anyone ever get used to this?"

The other man put an understanding hand on his colleague's shoulder. "You'll get used to it. Everyone goes through this."

I raced back to the car, shaking and crying, and…then I was gone.

Hunter walked back, balancing our coffees, and set them on the table. He crossed his legs, picked up his cup, and gave me a look.

"I recognize that expression. What's happening?"

Still tangled in the past, I stuttered, "I-I-I…didn't…"

Hunter's expression radiated concern. "What? What is it, Olivia?"

I clapped my hands across my face. Counted my breaths.

"Do I need to call that neurosurgeon? Um…Sturgis?"

I shook my head behind my hands. "I'm okay," I said and whooshed out a final breath. With a light slap on the table, I picked up my coffee with a flourish.

Hunter looked confused. "What was that?"

"Kind of a declaration of victory every time I beat it."

"Ah. You've overcome the fainting thing."

"I'm pretty much free of those. Unless I get in a situation that causes intense, deep, emotional pain, I'm almost there." I smiled. "I plan to stay away from those situations."

"Almost?"

"My short-term memory is intact—well, most of the time—but my high school years and twenties, I can't get to those." I shrugged. "Not the end of the world, but my therapist says to move forward I have to look backward." I laughed. "Hazel may not get her wish."

"I'm proud of you, Olivia." Hunter looked at me over the rim of his mug. "Who's Hazel?"

His words "I'm proud of you," made me blush—the signature embarrassment of every redhead ever born. "Thanks. Hazel's my favorite therapist. My mom's worst nightmare."

Hunter laughed. "How's your mom?"

I scrunched my hair with both hands, an old habit; pondering the question. "I told you she moved here, right?"

"We haven't exactly been in touch," he said, drily. "She's here for Gray, I assume?"

I nodded. "They…the relationship worked out."

"That's great news. Give them my congratulations."

"I will."

We went silent. The awkwardness stretched. Maybe it was gone, I thought. Whatever we had, it felt different, now. Confused, I gathered my purse and pushed my chair back. This had been a mistake. "It's been *so* good seeing you, and now I guess I better—"

"Sit down, Olivia."

I sat. Like a reluctant puppy in training, but I sat.

"Why haven't you returned my calls? If you want me to back off, say so. Don't leave me hanging. I *would* like to know…if there's any point in pursuing more than a friendship." He cleared his throat, stared at the table. "I've been seeing someone. And to tell you the truth, she's probably a good fit for me. I've been…hesitant, to move forward." After a pause, he continued. "Because of us."

I felt warmth creep up my neck and onto my cheeks. "Hunter, I haven't meant to hold you back from relationships. I've still not sorted things out, you must *know* that, and I had to relearn how to…understand who I was… who I am *now*. I'm comfortable with my life, finally; but the past is a mystery. It's…unsettling. I shouldn't commit to you or anyone." I jammed my arms across my chest and looked away.

My gaze slid to his strong, beautiful hands; fingers tracing patterns on the table. My mind flew back to his office, a year and a half ago. Watching him trace those same patterns on his desk as I sat across from him, scared out of my mind about his plan to 'drop in' on my alleged attacker to get credible evidence for a search warrant.

I jerked my attention back to Hunter, whose mouth was moving but since I'd been self-basting in past trauma, I'd lost the train of thought. I needed to work on that. Too often I'd get lost in the past, and my present wouldn't get the attention it deserved.

"I get it, Olivia. But I need to hear the words." His hands stilled. "Are we done?"

Irritated, I tried to say those words, but the words would not come. My lips seemed…glued together.

Hunter laughed. "Well, there ya go. See? You can't even *say* it! Let's give it a chance, Olivia. How long are you in town?"

It was too much. I exploded. "Just because I *still* can't grab my words sometimes doesn't mean I'm hanging onto a romanticized version of our relationship, Hunter!"

"Yeah?" He grinned. "Seems to me you're pretty emotional about something that shouldn't mean much." He shrugged.

"Brain injury victims can experience extreme highs and lows in the aftermath," I informed him.

"Even two years after the fact?" He grinned.

He had me there. I sighed. He looked even better than I remembered, and I didn't want to address what I felt right now.

"You and all those psychological forensic or...whatever they're called... classes. Can't even fight fair with you!"

"Does that mean you'll go out with me again while you're here? Dinner? My place?"

The invitation hovered in the air.

Why was I so intent on running from Hunter?

His brown, wavy hair fell over one eye as he waited for me to say something. My first instinct was to say no, but why? To prove I could resist every man that showed interest, because the one I'd married had been so despicable? What was it about getting back in the saddle after you'd been thrown off...no. Bad metaphor.

"Okay," I said.

Chapter Eleven

Sophie held the cell between her shoulder and cheek, listening to her granddaughter. "I've tried to call her about ten times, Grammy. I'm getting worried."

"Honey, her phone must be dead. She went out to meet that detective. Remember Hunter?"

"What the heck, Grammy! How could I forget? So...are they dating again?"

Sophie paused. "They never really did date, honey."

"Yeah, well, you can tell yourself that, but I saw it."

Sophie's eyebrows drew together. When had her granddaughter become so...what was this? Rudeness? Too adult? She didn't know, but it made her uncomfortable. Maybe it was the sarcastic tone.

"We see what we want to see, Lilly. Your mom was confused back then, and going through a lot of trauma."

Lilly groaned. "I'm so over *trauma! Freaking over it!*"

Sophie blinked. Where was the sweet, younger sister of Serena she remembered? The innocent, precious, redheaded grandchild she'd known? "Lillian Elyse Callahan. Watch your language."

"You know what I mean, Grammy. Mom's been so...into herself. I know, I know...she's been through a lot. As I keep hearing over and over and—"

"Lilly! Stop! How can you minimize what your mom's gone through? She is doing her best, and it will keep getting better. What is going on with you? Is everything okay at the house?"

"I think so, Grammy," Lilly's voice held a shimmer of uncertainty, "But

Mom told me about these two guys that put up a video camera, and that if I went to the house I had to take a gun or a bat and—"

"Hold on—gun or a bat? What on earth! She hasn't mentioned that to me."

"Grammy," Lilly's voice sank to a whisper, "those two guys? They're here right now. And I don't know what to do."

Pause. "I'm conferencing in your mom."

"She won't answer, I've tried and tried."

Sophie shot up a quick prayer. "She better." Her fingers trembled as you pushed the conference function.

"Hey Mom," her daughter's voice answered. "What's up?"

"MOMMM!"

"Lilly! What's the matter?"

"Why does she need a bat or a gun?" Sophie demanded.

"Mom, those guys are here," Lilly hissed.

"Where are you?"

"In the trees. They can't see me."

"*Lilly.* I told you to stay at Callie's. Didn't you send her dad?"

"Yeah, but..." she mumbled. "...I can't stand Amy's mom! I had to get away for a while."

"Lilly! Get back to Amy's house right now! Hear me? Now!"

Lilly sighed. "But, Mom, why are we all upset because two guys put up a video camera? Isn't that a good thing, like, um...security?"

"I don't know yet, honey. That's why I hired a professional to look into it." Olivia hissed.

"Right after I got here, they drove up the driveway. In that same white van."

"Are they out of the van?" Olivia asked.

Sophie put her hand over her eyes. A sense of dread radiated through her body. Was her granddaughter in danger?

"Yeah. Walking toward that tree where the video thing is."

"Where is Graham?"

"Amy's dad? He's at work. Most people *work*, mom."

Olivia frowned. The moment she returned home, she'd schedule an appointment with Hazel for the both of them, and drag her there...whether she wanted to go or not.

Sophie thought she was going to have a heart attack. "Lilly!" she hissed. "Run back to Amy's house right now. We don't *know anything* about these men." She paused a minute. "Do we, Olivia?"

"It's a precaution."

Sophie chewed on her fingernail.

"Okay, Mom..." Lilly whispered. "I'm hiding behind the trees, almost up to the house. I think the azaleas all around the porch will hide me if I'm careful, and I can run to Amy's house the back way."

"Keep me on the phone," Olivia said.

Sophie held her breath.

Lilly's phone made shushing noises as she walked through the undergrowth. The steps quieted when she reached the lawn. "Okay, I'm good," she told them.

"The van pulled away, Mom. And I'm five minutes from Amy's."

"Stay there," Olivia said, her voice stern. "Riot's already with you at Amy's, right?"

"I *told* you that he was, Mom. When are you coming home?" Lilly's voice cracked a little.

Sophie smiled. Her heart slowed. Lilly was safe.

"Sunday night. Stay put, okay? Promise me."

She groaned. "I will. But get home soon."

"Olivia, can you stay on? Bye, Lilly. Love you," Sophie interjected.

"Love you too, Grammy." She exited the call.

"*What*, Mom?" Olivia asked, her voice cranky.

Sophie frowned. "What's going on? What is all this about a video camera?"

"I hired a PI, but he hasn't done much. I haven't heard from him since he checked with me yesterday."

"Have you called the police? Or talked to Hunter? Aren't you with him right now? Shouldn't you tell him?"

"Mom. I'll ask for your help when I need it, okay? Haven't we had this conversation about…a thousand times?"

"Forgive me if I want to help! Last I checked, parents do that all the time."

Olivia waited a few beats, then responded. "Sorry, Mom. I'm…on edge. This has made me…tense. It's probably nothing."

"You have this amazing detective at your beck and call and—"

"MOM." I interrupted. "You realize he and I haven't talked in a long time, right?"

"I assumed."

Pause. "Why would you assume that?"

Sophie sighed. "You had things to figure out."

"Yeah, but you, the queen of divorce, wanted me to jump right back in."

"I did not!" Sophie cried, pushing away hurt feelings from the remark. "What is wrong with you today? After so many bad choices in men, a woman learns to spot a good one. And I think he's a good man, that's all."

Silence.

"How did the coffee date go?"

"Fine."

Silence.

Olivia grimaced. "Okay, I'm going out with him again tomorrow. Dinner at his place."

Sophie laughed.

Chapter Twelve

I slapped my journal closed and slid my pen into the metal ring spine. My cell beeped with another text. I frowned, thinking, 'what now'? I'd already had lots of reassuring updates—Lilly had sent a photo of herself snuggled up with a comforter in front of a cozy fire at Amy's house, Callie had assured me all was well, and that Graham had walked my property after he got off work and found nothing amiss. He'd told her the videocam was still there, and also to tell me he loved my cat, and if I ever wanted to get rid of him, he'd be willing.

I gingerly picked up my phone and looked at it. A text from Tom. "About time," I muttered as I called him.

"Where have you been? What's going on?"

"All good, all good. No worries, Olivia."

His slow way of speaking was comforting but also annoying when I needed the bottom line.

I heard the shuffling of pages. His notes, I guessed. Well, at least he'd been working. "Let's see here," he drawled.

I stared at the ceiling in frustration.

"Here it is!"

I waited for him to spit it out.

"The van's rented. From Enterprise. To a Mr. Wyatt Harp. An individual, not a company." He cleared his throat. "An individual that has an LLC, though."

More shuffling of pages. "I talked to Mr. Harp. He's an attorney in… Harrisburg, Pennsylvania."

I waited for more, but nothing happened. "Tom," I said as gently as my exasperation would allow. "What did he say his reason was for installing a camera on my property?"

More shuffling. "Your property is on, what, about five acres?"

"Give or take," I said.

"The city of Glyndon, the zoning board, rezoned some of the more generous lots left around town. I guess you weren't aware?"

Why would I be aware, I thought, my tension building. I hadn't watched the news much.

"But what is this man doing with the camera…I don't get it."

"The surveyors have already been out. When I walked the property, I thought the markers were old but turns out, they were brand new." He cleared his throat. "I hate to bring bad news, well maybe it's not bad news, actually…"

I sighed. The man loved his rabbit trails.

"Mr. Wyatt bought about half an acre or so, of the land that fronts the highway. He was real nice when we talked. His mother is getting on in years. She lives in Glyndon, and he's been away a long time, so he decided to move closer to her. He found the property listed online, and he's already been down to check it out. The camera is so he has eyes on it until he gets his place built."

I thought about the private, curving, beautiful half-mile of gravel drive overhung by hundred-year-old oak trees that led to the main highway. "But how could this happen?" I seethed. "No one even contacted me!" Even as the words flew from my mouth, I saw Callie's face, insisting I get involved in a protest that involved zoning. Since zoning had been the furthest thing from my mind, I'd swatted her away and gone about my business. As it turns out, I should've gone.

My irritation level was about to hit boiling. "Tom. Let's talk about the guy with the gun that scared me out of my mind! And I couldn't get you on your phone after you told me that! I thought something happened to you, for God's sake."

Pause. "Huh. Well, sorry 'bout that. Had to get a new phone. Guess I should've told you. Took a day or two to get it, then I had to go into the store to get them to show me how to set it up. Did you, I mean, do you expect daily check-ins?"

Did I? What was one supposed to expect of a PI? I'd imagine more communication than I'd gotten from this one, that's for sure. After a pause, I continued, "How serious did he sound about this property, because I'm going to have to do...*something*."

"Pretty serious. He paid cash. Plans to live in half of the building and the other part will be his legal office. He's starting the build real quick, he said, if he can get all the permits, landscaping, and parking lot approved."

My fragile composure slipped away. "What? They've zoned the frontage property for business?"

"It's uhh...zoned for multi-use, actually."

Hunter approached, and mouthed, "You okay?"

I talked to Tom a bit more, we set a meeting time after I returned, and ended the call.

Yeah, it was good news, but no... it wasn't.

I looked at Hunter. "Is this real life? Can you like, hit me or pinch me, so I'll know this isn't a nightmare I'm having right now?"

His forehead wrinkled. "What happened?"

Early diners had crowded the parking lot. A middle-aged, balding man with two young children in tow passed us, smiling a greeting. Hunter and I moved away from the throng to the car that Mom loaned me. I leaned my back against it, crossed my arms, and stared up into the brilliant blue of the sky.

Hunter stood beside me. I filled him in on the van and the two guys.

"That re-zoning stuff happens all the time, Olivia. You've been in that house a while, right?"

"Fifteen years," I muttered. "I sweat blood to get that house to look like it does now. The yard, the front porch. Everything. And the whole point was *privacy*! This makes me sick."

"It's also the site of many bad memories. Don't forget that part."

I glared at him. "Oh, wow. Thanks. Just when I'm trying to forget ALL of that. So helpful."

Hunter looked at the pavement, then back at me. "It may be hard to hear, but…what if it's time to move on?"

My left shoulder throbbed in that way it had of telling me I was entering dangerous territory. When tension built, I could rocket from zero to sixty in about 1.5 seconds.

"That is not what I need to hear right now," I told him.

"Sorry." He tried to look repentant, but failed. "We'd love to have you in Richmond, though."

My smile was thin. "Who's 'we'?"

"Your mom. Serena. Me." He shrugged. "Dr. Sturgis. You have a ready-made family here, y'know."

He was cute, and it *did* drag my mind away from the looming fallout of someone building on my—what I'd thought was my—property. A lawyer, no less.

"You can talk to the zoning board, but if you weren't there at the front end, I'm not sure you'd do any good at the back end. Olivia, he'll be, what, over a quarter-mile away? Is it really that much of a thing?"

I rotated my neck to release some of the tension. "I don't know. I have to think about it."

"Okay." He patted my shoulder. "It's gonna be okay. And what if…" he paused, thinking. "You're thinking about becoming a licensed legal assistant. What if…"

I gave him a look. "Not in a million years. I thought about working for *Earl*, a man of integrity that I trust. Not some…some land-poacher from Harrisburg!"

He smiled. "Okay. What time tomorrow?"

I paused and made a quick decision. "Hunter, would you mind if I took a raincheck? I mean, I forgot that I told Lilly I'd be back Sunday night. With all that's going on, I probably don't need to…stay an extra night. I wouldn't be good company anyway."

He stared at me about two seconds, then gave me a half-grin. "Sure, Olivia. Okay. You take care of yourself." He walked away.

"Wait, I didn't mean, I don't want you to think—" I called after him.

But he gunned the engine and roared away without a look back.

Chapter Thirteen

Monty angrily shoved the pile of sheets off the bed onto the floor and sank onto the four-inch, stained, pad that passed for a mattress in his prison cell. Ever since Olivia had come to 'interrogate' him—not because she cared—but because she needed *information*—all he could think about was how to make her pay.

He'd already spent months fighting through the shocking, horrific reality of prison; then she shows up. His passive, shy little bride who'd changed into wifezilla after the damn coma that had made her a household name. A tribute to female assault survivors, and she was their figurehead. To top it all off, she got a book deal with an advance.

And here he sat, rotting in prison.

He stared at the stark white walls, the metal door which had a 24-inch tall, narrow window on the right-hand side. A pass-through like a mail slot opened in the door, and an envelope dropped to the floor. The pass-through was also used to slide in meals or allow Monty to back up to it so he could be safely cuffed. He picked up the letter. From Hannah. The damn woman had made it her mission to improve his 'prison experience,' as she put it. He threw the letter on top of the pile of sheets.

A CO peered through the window at Monty's laundry on the floor. "Pick that up, inmate. Now," he mouthed, the thick pane muffling his voice. He stood watching until Monty had scooped up the bundle and put it obediently on the bed.

"Permission to fold," Monty muttered, standing.

"Granted," the CO said and moved on.

An artery in Monty's neck throbbed, and his heart thrashed angrily in his chest at the humiliation. It could've been worse, though. As he folded, the words that had bought his ticket into minimum security instead of max trickled through his mind like cool, cool water. 'Grief over his ex-wife's health struggles relating to her brain injury caused a response parallel to the definition of insanity recognized by this Court. We ask the jury to consider that when a person is temporarily insane, they are helpless, and in no way responsible for their actions.' "Oh, yeah," Monty murmured the words that had won the day in the courtroom. "I was so *overwrought with grief*…that I couldn't control myself." And in a stunning turn of events, he'd been saved from a life sentence. In his current situation, the men went about their business like college students in a locked-down dormitory. Max security was a hellhole.

He made his bed with the clean sheets and deposited his underwear and socks in the metal, built-in drawer underneath. He'd served twelve months. He had nine years to go, but he was determined to be on his best behavior so the parole board would use him as an example of shining rehabilitation and grant an early release request. Every time an all-call was announced over the prison facility's loudspeakers, Monty made sure he was one of the first to volunteer. He'd heard through the grapevine that the warden had called him a 'model prisoner' once.

It was so easy to fool these idiots.

When he finished organizing his eight by six space, he walked to his narrow window and looked up and down the corridor. All clear. Then he walked three paces across the shiny, white, linoleum floor, skirted the stainless steel toilet bolted to the wall, squatted down, and reached behind it for the prepaid phone he kept there. A man in another cell block answered.

"Hey, is this a good time?"

"Good as any," the other man told him. "Got no plans."

Monty chuckled. "We're gonna change that," he whispered. "Hannah's my secret weapon."

"What did you do?"

Concern creased Monty's brow. "You're the one that came up with the idea."

"Yeah, but…hey man, I've only got two years left. I can't screw it up. I was only talkin'."

"You won't," Monty assured his new friend, Duds. He smiled at the memory of meeting Duds, comparing notes, and their shock at how they'd lived in parallel universes, if only for a few months. It was fate that they'd met, Monty was convinced of it.

"Think about how good this is going to feel. We'll be doing all the men in their lives a huge favor."

The sound of CO boots strode down the corridor.

"I'll call later. I'm working on it."

With a practiced squat and flick of his fingers, the phone was back in its hiding place. So far, the officers hadn't checked the small space between the back of the toilet and the wall when they tossed the rooms. Lucky for him, the floor had cracked enough to allow him to lift a small square of linoleum and slide the phone underneath. The sound of boots drew closer. Every few seconds, the footsteps stopped. Monty could tell it was Buddy by the weight of his footsteps, the guy must weigh 300 pounds. Monty had a good friend in Buddy, as long as Hannah kept bringing him pre-paid gift cards.

He'd always had a thing for Olivia's friend, Hannah, anyway, and he could tell she liked the attention. He'd written a letter suggesting disturbing, and mostly untrue; issues with Olivia. It had created a rift between them, and now, Hannah was jumping through hoops to bring him the money that he needed. He'd overheard her talking to the officers as he waited to be taken back to his cell, once. She had these COs wrapped around her little finger. This 'angel of mercy on a mission' act had worked out in his favor, and now Buddy would go to great lengths to do what he wanted.

His smile grew wider as his mind wandered to the incredible, wondrous fact that Duds had been married to Olivia's mom once upon a time. What were the odds? It had to be fate.

The strike of heavy boot soles was almost upon him now, in front of his door.

The boots scraped to a halt. "Callahan?"

Monty rushed to the window. "Here, sir."

Buddy smiled conspiratorially and dropped his voice to a whisper. "Can you hear me?"

Monty nodded through the narrow window. Buddy looked one way, then the other.

"Okay. The chick you put on your ex texted photos." Buddy slid his cell through the tray slot.

"Don't say I never did nothin' for ya," Buddy quipped.

Monty smiled. "Thanks, man. I owe you."

He took the cell while Buddy made up some ruse out in the hall to make sure they weren't caught on one of the many cameras bolted to the ceilings. "Two minutes," he muttered, under his breath.

Monty studied the photos. Olivia on her precious, goddam porch. The others, though, interested him. Four women, including Hannah and his wife, sat at a table in a restaurant. The place looked familiar. Eventually, he remembered. This was the same restaurant where he and Olivia had shared dinner and he'd made the big announcement that he'd met someone and wanted a divorce.

He stroked her face with his index finger before he slid the phone back through the slot. Buddy whipped the phone into his pocket. "And make sure you don't call me by my name in public, asshole. It's 'Officer Bromage', got it?" He left.

Monty flopped on his bed and put his hands behind his head. Olivia looked happy.

Too happy.

Chapter Fourteen

Shiloh's phone rang three times. She answered on the fourth. "Hey."

Hunter smiled. "Hey. How's it going?"

"Working a homicide, actually. Such fun on a freakin' Sunday."

Hunter grunted. "Wish I had productive activity going on. Domestics, here. Kinda quiet, really."

"Listen, Hunter, I'm busy, can we talk another time?"

"Sure. Only wanted to tell you how it went."

"What went?" she asked, distracted.

"With Olivia this weekend."

Pause. "Okay. Still only got a couple minutes, though."

"It's over, whatever we had. I wanted to let you know. That's it."

"Right," she said. "Still gotta go. Talk later."

The phone went dead. He smiled. He really did like this woman.

For the first time, he wondered if he could get a job in Savannah. Shiloh had a couple of kids, though, and that was another issue. She'd told him she and her ex got along well and worked hard at making it easy to parent as exes, but stepkids were way out of his wheelhouse. He had to admit to himself, he thought, as he stepped into the steamy shower and adjusted the rain shower head; that the idea of a relationship with Olivia Callahan had been put to rest. At least that part was decided. He wasn't getting any younger, and women in their late 30s and 40s usually had kids, so...why not figure it out with Shiloh? They had so much more in common than he and Olivia, and he'd have to move, but that was okay. Wasn't it? Hunter frowned and grabbed shampoo, squirted some on his head, put the shampoo back on its shelf, and scrubbed viciously. When he stepped out and started toweling off, he saw that he'd raked his scalp so hard that he'd drawn blood.

He stepped to the sink to wash under his nails. "Women," he muttered.

* * *

Hunter threw on workout pants and a T-shirt, grabbed his gym bag, and hopped into his 4-door Jeep Wrangler. Instinctively, he scanned the area under the dash, in the doors. Under the wheel wells. Car bombs were easy to conceal. Before he started his vehicle, though, a disturbance brushed his soul.

He sat there, thinking about the homemade bomb that had killed his partner eight years prior.

The only reason Hunter had survived was due to a delay getting to the vehicle. The force of the explosion blew out the windows, dinging him with glass and pieces of metal. His partner had incinerated instantaneously. Since the passenger side door had been closed, the explosion had been somewhat contained, and the paramedics hadn't had to slide him into a body bag alongside his buddy. He'd suffered deep cuts from the shards of glass flying through the air, and bits and pieces of screws or nails that had torn into his body through his clothes. The paramedics picked a few larger pieces from his face and forearms as the ambulance screamed toward the hospital. He'd had hearing loss for two weeks. The bomb had been meant for both of them.

The grief he carried didn't show up much, anymore—but when he'd had too much to drink, he'd pick it back up and pull it on like a backpack full of rocks.

Since that experience, he'd made a habit of searching the wheel wells, interior doors, under dash, and seats before settling in to drive his personal vehicle. Today, though, his gut felt off. Hunter would never forget the smell that hung in the air after a car bomb. Metallic. Acrid. Melted plastic. And if a body was present, the burning flesh smell stayed with a person for years. Gingerly, he tested the brakes. Moved the steering wheel.

The hard scrape from the undercarriage sent clanging alarms through his mind like shrapnel. He leapt from the car and ran to a safe distance.

"911. What's your emergency?"

"Detective Hunter Faraday. I'm off-duty. Suspected car bomb in my personal vehicle. Send Hazardous Device Unit and back-up ASAP." He rattled off his street address.

Patrol cars screamed down the street from two directions within minutes. The uniforms poured from their vehicles, parked a cautious half-block away.

One of the unis called Hunter's cell. "Bomb squad's on the way. Should be here in five, Detective."

Hunter nodded and gave them a thumbs-up.

The patrol cops glanced uneasily at each other. If it was a sound-detonated device, quiet was critical. No one knew what type of trigger might be connected to the device, or even if a device was present, but they backed off anyway, and kept their mouths shut. Most likely it was a remote-controlled, homemade situation, but you never knew. They began to set up a perimeter, and secure the area.

The HDU arrived, a white, Hummer-style vehicle. A white robot edged its way down the ramp placed at the back of the vehicle. Hunter breathed slow and easy, waiting, aware that he might've been a heartbeat away from being blown to bits. The last bomb crime scene he'd worked, the vic had only had to lift off the vehicle's seat a mere inch to trigger the tilt device that closed the electrical circuit that sparked the detonator. Car, driver, and passenger had been completely decimated, the bodies reduced to black, smoldering husks with claw-like hands.

He pushed away the shriveled, blackened images that still haunted his dreams.

He listened to the hum of the robot and watched its metal crab-claw appendage explore potential sites and common hiding spots. After an excruciating twenty minutes, the operator shot a thumbs-up at Hunter. The robotic claw hung in the air from the upraised arm like a Spielberg alien in miniature. Suddenly, it perked itself, and a slim, high-powered jet of water sluiced underneath the driver's side of the vehicle.

Hunter ran to join the patrol cops, who watched the operator finesse the drone-like robot with rapt attention. The drone had army-tank treads and an ability to climb stairs, if necessary. "No worries," the operator told Hunter, smiling at him. "Must've been an amateur, lucky for you, huh? We're using the spray on the wires as a precaution, but we don't even think the perp connected it as he should—"

At that moment, an explosion rocked his Jeep. Shards of metal and upholstery and glass flew through the air like a hailstorm from hell. The uniforms dove for cover. The operator's jaw dropped in shock as he scuttled backward. The robot, now dinged and dented, reversed its course. Its treads rolled through a haze of smoke to its docking base in the white Hummer.

"Shit!" the operator cried. "I'm sorry, man! Don't know what happened. Must've been on a timer." He scrambled for his remote and got the bot back on course.

"Good thing I got outta there, then."

"Wow." The operator stared at his shoes, then at Hunter. "Let me check the bot." He started toward the desecrated Jeep, now half-black, half-red, and certainly not drivable.

Hunter's arm shot out. "Wait. Could there be more?"

On cue, a dozen little explosions, like firecrackers, cascaded through the air, creating a billowy smoke storm that filled up the block. Hunter coughed and batted at the smoke. Paramedics arrived, their sirens shrieking on a loop. Two EMTs jumped from the back end of the vehicle and pulled Hunter into the ambo. "What the hell happened?" a young man asked. His starched, blue uniform shirt had "Tommy" written on the pocket.

Smoke layered the area in a dark fog. Broken pieces of glass, chrome, and metal lay in the street and on lawns. Pockets of neighbors gathered outside their homes. The damaged bot still clawed its way home, but couldn't find the docking station. The uniforms did their best to keep onlookers from contaminating the scene.

"We're gonna have to figure that out, Tommy," Hunter said.

Chapter Fifteen

"Since my house burned down, I now have a better view of the rising moon."
~Mizuta Masahide

Sunday night.

I didn't stay the extra night to have dinner with Hunter because Lilly was nervous and I needed to be here for her. The mystery of the videocam is solved. Re-zoning apparent. So...Hunter. Trying to process. He is as sexy as ever and still does that thing to me. It's scary. But I've made enough mistakes with men, and I've got to learn how NOT to do that. I won't be my mother, version two. That is all.

* * *

I put my journal away, yawned, and stretched my arms high. I was tired, but before bed, I wanted a cup of tea on my porch. Humming, I checked on Lilly before I went downstairs. Lilly's rose-gold curls fanned out on her pillow. Her chest rose and fell in sleep. I couldn't believe she was almost seventeen, and how I wished I could remember her as a young girl. I wanted these memories back. Even if it meant another trip to see Monty. The stairs creaked from my weight as I walked downstairs to the landing, and made a quick right into the kitchen. Hard knocks rattled my front door. I jumped.

Who would be visiting at 1:30 in the morning? I tip-toed down the hallway, into the foyer, and put my ear to the door. Men's voices. Cops. My hand shook as I fumbled with the lock.

Two Maryland State Troopers in their tan uniforms stood on my porch.

"W-what's happened?" I stammered, after the initial shock.

"Maryland State Police Criminal Investigation Unit, ma'am. I'm Detective Sergeant Caldone, and this is Detective Sergeant Henderson. May we come inside for a minute?"

My throat tight, I nodded, and unlocked the screen to let them in. They stood at semi-attention in the darkness at the base of the stairs. I switched on the lamp on my foyer table, crossed my arms, and stared at them, my heart pounding out a reggae downbeat.

One of them cleared his throat. "Olivia Callahan, correct?"

I nodded, one hand drifting to my throat.

"You're acquainted with Detective Hunter Faraday," the older of the two stated. It wasn't a question.

"Yes," I said.

"Ma'am, Richmond PD has asked that we coordinate with them in an investigation that may concern you. We would like to notify you we will be surveilling the surrounding area for a few days, maybe weeks. We have reason to believe that your vehicle might be compromised. May we have your permission to check? Right now?"

Concentrating fiercely, I felt a headache start to build. Stress caused my still-unpredictable brain to sidestep facts and create imaginary events. Like early-onset dementia that only appeared when I freaked out. Was this a *crisis*? Was Hunter okay?

"Why? What is this about?"

The two officers flashed a look at each other. I knew that look. It happened when on-duty cops didn't know how to diplomatically disclose something horrible. "What is it?" I demanded, my fists clenched.

"Mom?"

I looked up. My daughter rubbed her eyes and frowned at us. Her white and pink flowered pajamas made her look twelve years old. "Lilly. It's okay. Go on back to bed now." I attempted a smile.

She walked downstairs, brushing her hair out of her face. "No way, Mom. I told you. I'm almost seventeen. Quit keeping stuff from me." She stood beside me.

"Detective Faraday's personal vehicle experienced an explosion, ma'am. Car bomb."

I blinked. Had I heard them right? "A...c-ca—"

Lilly put her arm around me and whispered, "Car bomb, Mom." She turned to the cops. "Is he okay?"

They nodded. "Richmond PD is thinking that it might be related to... your troubles, Ms. Callahan."

"Mom?" Lilly took me by the shoulders, shook me gently. "Mom!"

My consciousness started fading around the edges, and the tunnel vision that preceded one of my damned fainting spells began. *No. No! This cannot happen right now!* "Lilly. Coffee."

She ran into the kitchen. Caffeine jerked me from the edge. Like a migraine, if I let it go on too long, I'd end up on the floor. I looked at the men's stricken faces. "I can catch this. Don't worry."

They shifted their weight back and forth, waiting. Lilly returned with the coffee. I finished it in ten seconds and re-focused. "Specifics, please."

The older cop, the one with kind eyes and graying hair, smiled. "Detective Faraday is fine, but pretty rattled. He...has history with this situation. Car bomb killed his partner."

My mind stuck there, on repeat. *Car. Bomb. Killed. His. Partner.* He'd never said a word. What must that do to a person?

"Whoever did this might be...a threat. If it has anything to do with the 'Mercy's Miracle' case..."

I flinched. Lilly's eyes flashed concern.

"Good thing he had this...intuition thing goin' on. He notified 911, and the bomb squad came out and, well...there was an issue, but the detective was already out of harm's way." The kind eyes brightened. "Some cops have better instincts than others, y'know? That's amazing to me, how he did that."

"Me too," the younger officer piped up.

"Thank God he's okay," I said. The caffeine sizzled through my veins. I put my hands on my hips and eyeballed both of them. Lilly stood beside me like an Amazonian princess, intense and protective. "Now for the good part," I quipped. "I know how you guys work. You don't make a personal visit at 1:30 in the morning for a...a *feeling*."

The older man reached into his pocket, pulled out his cell, and scrolled through his texts. Pointed the phone at me in silence. I took the phone from his hand.

There, in the small screen, was an enlargement of a dirty, dinged-up, black ballpoint pen with the name of Monty's correctional facility emblazoned down one side in white, bold letters. The drumming of my heart went into overdrive.

The kind cop murmured, "This was found on the ground underneath the car. You can see why we'd be concerned." He cleared his throat. "Detective Faraday's car was in Richmond, ma'am, and this...the facility where your ex-husband is incarcerated—"

"Is in Maryland," I announced, resigned. Would I ever be done with this nightmare? Would Hunter?

I showed it to Lilly. Her face fell. "Oh, Dad," she whispered. "He just couldn't, Mom."

With a sigh, I handed the phone back. He waited, his head tilted, considering me. "You okay?"

"Yep," I assured him. "I'll get a flashlight."

"Ma'am, you don't have to accompany us, we've got—"

"I want to be involved in every detail of this investigation," I interrupted. "So get used to it."

The men looked at each other, shrugged. "Let's do this," the older man said, smiling.

* * *

My jacket flapped in the pre-dawn breeze. The detectives chattered into their shoulder mics, as we walked single file across my lawn, through the gate, and across the gravel driveway to my detached garage. I pressed in the opener code. The old, wooden door creaked and complained as it opened. My shiny, black Discovery—my one splurge after the book advance— sparkled in the moonlight. I'd run it through the carwash as I'd driven home from the airport after my trip to Richmond. A lump formed in my throat. Cars were replaceable. The important thing was not to be *in* the car if it blew up.

I turned on the overhead garage light.

"Stand back, ma'am," the older officer said. He nodded at his colleague, who began inspecting the floor around the vehicle. "We're doing is a 'hands-off' perimeter and interior search," the detective explained. We are the initial discovery team, and in the morning, we'd like to let the trained technicians do a comprehensive search of the interior. Okay?"

I felt my head nod, but my mind was on autopilot. I tugged my jacket nervously. "So you're not even going to open the car doors?"

Detective Caldone shook his head. "These things can be triggered by pressure, motion, electrical impulse, or thermal and barometric systems. We're relieved to find you in one piece, ma'am." At my shocked expression, he winced. "Sorry. That was unnecessary."

"I can't believe this," I muttered.

"Understood," he said, watching his colleague scrutinize every square inch of the concrete floor around and underneath my car. "What do you see inside, Detective?"

The younger man peered inside the windows with a smile. He glanced at me. "Sure makes things easier when you don't tint your windows, ma'am."

"I wasn't thinking about bombs when I decided not to," I quipped.

"Sir, I see a backpack, a gym bag, or duffel and a bit of trash tucked into the side pockets."

"Would you step closer to the car, and confirm those are your items, and that you have placed them there, and that they have not been tampered with?"

I walked toward the car as close as they would allow.

Craning my deck, I confirmed yes, they were mine, and no, they didn't look tampered with.

"Call it in, Henderson." He turned to me as Detective Henderson reported the exterior scan had been completed. "First thing in the morning okay with you?"

My jaw twitched. I needed to get to bed. Maybe I'd sleep through their inspection, and if I was real lucky—or blessed, as my mom is fond of saying—the car would be clear of bombs and this whole situation would go away. "How long does it take to do this?"

"Three to five hours, depending. And you cannot, repeat...*cannot* go anywhere near while this team is working. They'll have specialized monitoring equipment, sensors, and will need total focus. It is in our favor that your garage is a good distance from the house."

"Ah. That makes me feel so much better."

"I should add that we will be containing the perimeter. You can expect a good bit of activity until noon, I'd imagine."

My mind was shot. My eyes wouldn't stay open. "Okay. I'm going to bed now."

The detective dug into his pocket and handed me a card. "I want you to think about where this car has been and how long it has been left alone in places that could give someone time to plant a device."

He gave me a look. "A device like this can easily be put on a timer. Go to bed. Don't think about it. Have a good evening, we'll wrap up and leave in a few minutes. It goes without saying that you cannot drive this vehicle until we're done with it."

Whatever composure I'd tapped into cracked wide open.

I stumbled through my yard back to the house. Don't think about it? I couldn't think about anything else.

My mind ripped wide open with a memory.

Monty scrambled into the bedroom, his voice cracking. "Olivia, my God, I couldn't get you on the phone. Where were you?"

I squinted at him. "Asleep." I glanced at the clock beside our dresser. "I unplugged the landline."

"Keep that damn Motorola handheld with you! How many times have I told

you?"

A shiver climbed up my spine. "Monty, what's wrong?"

He let out a breath. "There's been a wreck."

"Serena?" I glanced around the room. Shoved the comforter off me and ran into the hallway. "Serena!"

My eyes widened in horror. "Where is she?"

"Get dressed," he growled and pushed me toward the closet. I threw on clothes. He tugged me out the door into the car. "She's in the hospital," he said. "And before you say anything, it wasn't my fault!"

I rolled down the window of our car with the need for good, clean air in my lungs. Tears streamed down my cheeks. "Is she okay?"

He clenched his jaw and remained silent the rest of the drive.

I blinked. Both hands were clamped over my mouth, and my cheeks were wet. Clearly, I'd remembered Serena at three years old. Monty had picked her up from a play date, and I couldn't remember whose family, but Monty had stayed to have a drink. They'd ended up playing cards and time had gotten away from them, he'd said. Serena's car seat hadn't been properly fastened, and she'd been thrown out of the seat. She had a cast on her leg for weeks, and Monty had been charged with a DWI.

Tilting my head back, I forced myself to gulp in a lungful of air, hold it, and blow it out. The last thing I needed to do was to hyperventilate and faint right here on my front porch and scare Lilly to death. The memory was tragic.

However...my memory was returning!

Chapter Sixteen

"The dogmas of the quiet past are inadequate to the stormy present. The occasion is piled high with difficulty, and we must rise. As our case is new, so we must think anew and act anew."
~Abraham Lincoln

My nose quivered in appreciation.

The morning sun streamed through the room window and smells of bacon and homemade cinnamon rolls drifted into my bedroom. It became apparent that I'd slept half the day away, and Callie had come to rescue me. I clung to the banister and wobbled downstairs.

"Here ya go, hon," she said. I stared at the overloaded plate. Callie would always be a firm believer in the power of food to wave a magic wand over troubles and make them disappear. Today, I almost believed it. I scarfed down the feast, with intermittent sips of the orange juice she'd provided.

"Thanks so much, Callie," I said. "You've outdone yourself this time."

She waved a hand. "It's nothing, hon. I'm glad you left a message last night. I love to cook, and I love you, so I'm in my zone right now." Placing her hands on her generous hips, she cocked her head. "Lilly said you had quite a night. She was pretty upset, but I got her off to school with Amy, and she seemed okay when I dropped them off." With brisk steps, she crossed my kitchen and pushed the button on my Keurig. With a sympathetic pout of her lips, she pushed a fresh mug into my hands.

"What's going on out there?" I sipped the coffee. "I can't look."

She grunted. "Yellow tape and everything. It took a few calls for me to get in here this morning."

"Have you talked to them?"

She grinned. "Of course, I talked to them. How could I resist? No car bomb at last report." She lifted one index finger. "Wait. In cop-speak that's 'hazardous device.'"

I let out the breath I'd been holding.

Callie reached over and stroked my hair. "It's okay, Olivia. You're okay," she murmured. "They told me this is a precaution. They don't know if anyone is going to do anything to *you*. It's Hunter that may have an enemy out there."

"I hope no one's told Mom."

"Not that I know of," she said, chuckling. "But you know her, she's telepathic. She'll appear, poof! Like magic."

I thought about where she lived now. She'd probably already heard about Hunter through the grapevine. However, she hadn't lived there long enough to *have* a grapevine but..."

My front door banged shut. "Hell-ooooooo? Anybody home?"

Callie gave me a look and ran to the door. I heard a woman's voice, then two sets of steps walked down the hall. I groaned.

"Look who's here!" Callie beamed.

Hazel walked over, gave me a brief hug. "Guess who the little birdie was?"

I shot her a sideways glance. "My mother."

Hazel laughed and sat at my kitchen table across from me. "I'm checking in, per her request. You weren't answering, Lilly wasn't answering, and... Callie wasn't answering." Consider this a house call, free of charge. Are you okay?"

I smiled. When I'd first met Hazel, I'd been an emotional wreck. I'd already made the rounds of physical therapy, occupational therapy, and I'd been dumped on her doorstep as the media had made a circus of my case, and no one would touch me. By the time I reached her, I was angry, confused, and still grieving. In short, my brain had somewhat recovered but my emotional state had not. This was complicated by my inability to retrieve memories other than ones in the very recent past. Hazel had been a last-ditch effort to make me whole.

I told her it would never happen.

She'd said, "well, depends on how you define whole. How do *you* define whole, Olivia?"

Hazel helped me get as close to 'whole' as a person in my situation could, I thought…but is anybody ever whole? It was a trick question from the first day, and I'm still trying to figure it out.

My eggs had gotten cold. I pushed the bacon and eggs into a little pile and shoved them into my mouth with a fork. Hazel and I looked at each other for a few seconds, silent. "You're good?"

I nodded. "I am."

"Okay," she murmured. "That's all I needed, and your mother is waiting for my 'all clear' to call. So. No threats, then?"

"I don't think so," Callie replied, with a glance at me. "It should be over soon. Want me to check?" she asked, her eyebrows raised in anticipation. A forever fan of crime thrillers, a bomb scare was like crack cocaine to an addict with Callie. She shot out of the kitchen yelling, "Back in a flash!"

Hazel leaned forward. "Have you talked to Hunter?"

I looked away.

"Why not, Olivia?"

I took a minute to think. Finally, I responded. "I think…it's strange that we're still bound together by criminal situations."

"I believe that's a healthy and well-balanced observation, Olivia."

I grimaced. "Can we please ditch the analysis, Hazel?"

"I'm not sure I can," she replied, her brows pulling together.

I laughed. "Can you ever just be…fun?"

She frowned. "I can do 'fun.'"

After a pause, I continued. "I have no desire to cultivate a relationship with Hunter, and haven't wanted to find out why." I shrugged. "Too much work."

She reached out and patted one of my hands. "Sit with it awhile. You'll know what to do." She picked up her mug and sipped. "Besides, your mom is *praying* for you, she told me." Her exaggerated sarcasm made me laugh.

"Mom has always prayed for me," I said, my voice soft. "You don't believe in prayer?"

"Of course, I believe in prayer. But I believe in *hard work* more." She sighed, folded her hands—the only part of her that showed her age—on the table, and looked at me. "Maybe you should call Hunter. He'll be worried."

I pursed my lips. "Shouldn't he call me?"

"Does it matter?"

"I don't know."

Silence.

My cell buzzed. A text from Hunter.

Of course it was.

With a sigh, I showed her my screen.

Her gray, wavy hair bobbed along with her laughter. "Olivia, the common thread is Monty, of course. It isn't about whether you guys belong together, or need to start dating again—"

"It isn't?"

She squinted at me and crossed her arms over her chest. "Do *you* think it is?"

"STOP."

She flapped her hands at me with a smile. "Okay, okay. I'm leaving."

"Wait. Hang on a minute. I had a *memory*."

She blinked. "Tell me!"

I related the incident, grateful that it was still fresh in my mind. I needed to put it in my journal before it, like the others, floated away. "I'm hoping this one will stay—?"

Hazel cocked her head, considering. "Cannot predict an outcome, really. It is a good sign, though. But Olivia, even normal people forget things about their kids when they were young."

"Not traumatic things like a broken leg!"

She nodded, thoughtful. "I'd bet you buried it in your subconscious because it was so painful. Did he ever own up to his part in the incident?"

I shook my head. "I don't think so."

"Did you ever confront him about it? The drinking, I mean...and not

83

letting you know they were running late?"

"I don't know," I whispered. But in my heart, I did know. I'd been the classic victim, and said nothing. Why? I was so different now. I sighed. Maybe I shouldn't know why.

"Okay," Hazel said. "It's huge that you remembered. Even if you don't see Monty in prison again—which I strongly suggest—you can role play. It will feel good to say the things you should've said. Express your anger, then let it go. Maybe in front of a mirror tonight."

The room closed in on me a little. Maybe I shouldn't have told her. This felt...a little too emotional. Damaging. Heart-bruising.

With a shake of my head, I smiled at her. "Thanks for coming. I'll let Mom know I appreciated you coming."

Hazel looked at me with that insightful wisdom she radiated. "I'm glad I could help."

She gave me a hug and left.

I looked at Hunter's text.

All good?

My front screen door banged shut, and Callie walked into the kitchen. "They haven't found anything. They're packing up."

I closed my eyes. "Thank God." Maybe this would pass. I could get back to trying to make sense of my life. First thing tomorrow, I would tell Earl I wanted that job. I *did* feel an affinity for the legal field, the investigations, the work I'd watched Hunter do. Being a part of it might get me out of the black hole of trying to remember details about my life. Maybe it would give me purpose. Had I ever dreamed of fulfilling a purpose? Or careers I wanted to explore? Maybe this could be the start of a new direction.

I texted back.

Yes, all good. They've been here and didn't find anything. You okay?

Yeah. Looks like your ex found buddies in prison to do his dirty work.

You really think so?

I do. I'm sure you saw the photo of the pen. But it's early. I'll let you know what we find out. I'm going to send you a video of how we do a

quick search for vehicle IEDs (improvised explosive devices) okay?

No, my mind screamed. *That is not okay! I don't want to go back to a place of horror and fear! I don't want to be a part of another nightmare that won't end! Please, God please...*

I texted back.

Sure, that'll be fine.

Chapter Seventeen

"Those who keep learning, will keep rising in life."
~Charlie Munger

I n the best interests of everyone, my vehicle was checked, tested, dusted, probed, and scrutinized for five, long, days. It felt like an invasion of my personal space on many levels, and in the end, they concluded the only person that had put their hands on, in, or up my vehicle was me.

Yay for me.

Still.

Driving my once-adorable—and now suspect—Land Rover Discovery after I'd surrendered it to the human equivalent of a CT Scan coupled with a colorectal exam—was jarring. As I eased cautiously onto the driver's seat, I wondered if I'd ever feel safe again. Trust the science, they'd told me. I'd wanted to yell, *You trust the science! You drive the damn car!*

And they did. The team took my car out for a spin and returned intact and whole. This made me feel better, but...the fear remained.

Today, though, I had something to look forward to—my wine and whine girls had called a meeting. Steeling myself in preparation to actually start and drive my car for the first time after the cops had released it, I recited my mother's favorite scripture: "For God has not given us a spirit of fear." I repeated it aloud ten times, which hopefully would convince my mind to let go of the fear that was stuck there like gum in a toddler's hair. Before I could retreat, I pressed the ignition.

"Okay, okay, okay..." I whispered and took off down my lane. What *used* to be my lane. I raised the middle finger of my left hand at the video cam as I drove by, and hoped the new owner got the message.

* * *

Westminster's cute and bustling main street throbbed with activity. A quick twenty-minute drive from my house in Glyndon, Eddie's Bistro had become one of our mainstays. I hopped out of the car feeling a niggling relief.

Hannah, Sherry, and Callie waved at me. They'd managed to get our favorite table, the one by a window that overlooked the sidewalk. As I entered the restaurant, I noticed that the hostess stared at me with sorrowful eyes. I had to laugh...Callie had already spread the word about my IED event.

"Hey, girls, sorry I'm a little late," I said as I hooked my purse over the back of my chair.

"Hi, hon," Callie said, her voice syrupy with compassion, which I hated. *I'm fine,* I wanted to scream. Being the object of pity was getting old, and I'd thought all that was behind me, but...*Monty.* His damn tentacles even reached from a prison cell.

Callie raised a bottle. "I bought this. Want to split it? I know you love it." She proffered a bottle of red from Napa...Markham Merlot.

I smiled. "You kidding? This is the only place within fifty miles that carries it. You bet I'll split it with you."

She plunked the bottle down and filled the wine glass that had been brought for me. "If anybody deserves this, you do."

"How are you?" Sherry asked. "Callie filled us in, but wow, I...can't even imagine. Is your car okay?"

I let the wine nestle on my tongue before I swallowed. Then I picked up a piece of cheese on the charcuterie board in the middle of the table and studied it. "Interesting question. If my car is *not* okay does that mean you guys would be planning my funeral right now?"

"Olivia!" Hannah protested, folding her arms across her chest.

I looked at her a heartbeat longer than necessary, then popped the cheese into my mouth.

Callie, ever the harmony-builder, patted my arm. "Now, I know you've been through it. We understand." She looked around the table. "Don't we, girls?"

Hannah blinked. "How can we? I've never even gotten close to anything like a car bomb in my life."

"Opportunity never presented itself, huh, Hannah?" Sherry's reply was catty. Her eyes cut toward me.

"What does that mean?"

"Nothing," Sherry mumbled.

Hannah cleared her throat. "I want to say something."

The rest of us stopped chatting and waited. Hannah wanted to drop her own bomb, I figured. We all knew, by now, that she'd been communicating with Monty. However, did she *know* we knew?

"Olivia, Monty had nothing to do with the bomb scare."

Shocked to my core that she would toss out such a…a…*cataclysmic* opinion without talking to me first, I didn't trust myself to speak. My jaw clenched and unclenched in an effort to keep from going off on her.

Callie stepped in. "And you would know that…how?"

My heart started beating again. No way was I going to lose it in front of this…this *traitor!*

"I…I," she faltered. "I've been visiting Monty."

Sherry, Callie, and I looked at each other in collective understanding. Okay, so she *didn't* know we knew.

"You don't understand," she protested.

"Explain, Hannah. We are dying to know," Sherry said.

"Dying, being the operative word," I added for no reason other than a dig at her. I didn't even know what I meant. My brain was in a warp room all by itself right now.

She gave me an uncertain look. "Olivia, he—your—marriage is over! My gosh, it's been almost two years since the divorce was final, right? Doesn't he deserve a little mercy?" Her voice trailed away. Even she knew how ridiculous that sounded to all of us.

Callie broke the stunned silence, her voice gentle. "Do you think, honey, that you were the right one to do that? What we want to know is why you'd feel the need to do that because...um, Olivia?"

Hannah frowned at me. "I'm so sick and tired of everything being about poor, weak, abused, broken *Olivia*! Have we even considered Monty's side of things? Did he even have a chance? He went nuts because *she* decided, before the divorce was even final, to step out on him. It's all that horrible person's fault? Whatshisname...Niles? Monty was protecting his wife's reputation!"

Astonished that Monty had brainwashed her so thoroughly, a yelp of disbelief exploded from my mouth. Then I laughed... which sounded a bit hysterical, I guess, because Hannah, Sherry, and Callie looked prepared to cart me off to the ER. "Don't worry," I assured them. "I'm fine...but amazed at what I'm hearing." I took quick stock of my physical signals at this moment. Heartbeat, calm. Check. Headache, nope, Check. Racing, confused thoughts, nope. Check. Unreasonable rage reaction, nope. Check.

I pronounced myself lucid.

I folded my hands on the table. "Hannah. Look at me."

She lifted her head. I saw a dedicated anger in her face. *My God,* I thought, *she's still defending the guy.*

"Monty Callahan is a dirtbag. A textbook manipulator. Multiple therapists agree, and this is a fact. The way he minimizes and uses people is deplorable. His specialty is depressed or insecure women. Of which, in my over-analyzed and professionally dissected opinion, you are both."

Hannah rose from her chair, an inch at a time, never taking her eyes off me. "And you, Olivia...are dead wrong. You have a problem dealing with people who have different opinions from yours."

"Hannah, he's using you. I'm trying to spare you unnecessary carnage."

She jerked her purse over her shoulder. "That is none of your business. As to unnecessary carnage, as you put it, aren't you the queen of all that? You're famous for it. And Monty? He's a casualty."

I looked at my hands, folded on the table, deciding whether I should ask the question. But in my heart, I already knew the answer. "Are you giving him money?"

With a final glare at the three of us, she flounced out of the room.

I held up my wine as if toasting. "That would be a yes," I declared to Callie and Sherry who stared at our departing Hannah, horrified.

* * *

Trying to regain our bearings, we fumbled around more mundane topics, but eventually circled back to my car bomb search, the local headline of the year, probably. I didn't even want to look at Facebook or Instagram, or any social media, for that matter, let alone the local paper.

"Olivia, so what started all this? Why…is your detective involved? I heard that he was responsible for the…what was it?" Sherry asked.

"He sniffed out an explosive device. Literally." I smiled. "He has this intuition or whatever. It happened to his partner years ago, and I guess it really affected him. Anyway, he called a team in. His car was destroyed, but he wasn't." I shrugged. "They contacted me because they found…" I cleared my throat. "…a ballpoint pen from Monty's correctional facility underneath his Jeep. So they thought the events might be related to me."

Callie leaned forward on her elbows. "Have you been in communication with him?"

"My therapist says no matter what I think, for my protection, I should keep lines of communication open with Hunter, but it's hard. We keep getting thrown together for criminal reasons. Is that healthy?" I shook my head. "But yeah, we've texted. I'm not following up every day or anything, because it's weird. Have I told you guys he still wants a relationship?"

Sharp intakes of breath all around.

"Yep. That's 'my' detective. Hunter Faraday. Protector and pursuer of broken women."

I raised my glass at that one.

"You're really on point today, aren't you?" Sherry said, finishing the last of her wine.

"Sorry. I know I'm whining, right? None of this is a win. At least for me.

Do you guys see a win?"

Callie leaned in. Her dark blonde hair had already started lightening up. She worked in her yard if the temps were above 50, so she had a perennial tan. For once, she'd worn her hair down instead of the bouncy ponytail. It suited her. Her nails had been painted a blue so neon it made my eyes water.

"It's been long enough, don't you think, hon'? Long enough to trust your decisions? Maybe even long enough to trust your heart?"

I fidgeted with my wine glass. Callie grabbed the bottle of Markham and poured. I gave her a little 'that's enough' signal with my hand.

"You know me," she said, laughing, "I'm always the one that sees a win. I'm telling you, girl, Hunter Faraday is a win. I wouldn't ghost him or he'll be gone. I bet he's already seeing someone, it's been so long. Am I right?"

I squinted at her. "How'd you know that?"

"Guy's amazing. Plus he's a pretty boy. That isn't gonna stay single long." She shrugged.

"Whatever," I grumbled.

"I say take your time," Sherry added. "You're discovering what you're about without, as you put it, the worst manipulator on the planet jerking your chain."

We settled up with the server and prepared to leave. My mom's words flew through my mind. One thing that Mom had shared with me when we discussed things in light of her faith, was this: "Mercy doesn't mean *stupid*, honey." Right now, though Hannah's heart may be in a place of mercy, Monty didn't care. He'd chew her up and spit her out.

Sherry, Callie, and I trooped out the door, a little too cheerful on our collective wine highs, trying to mask the harsh realities that had invaded our wine and whine group this time.

I waved goodbye to the girls and started the car with nary a thought about explosions until after I was quite a bit down the road. Thank you, Markham Merlot.

When I drove down my lane, I saw that not only had Wyatt Harp installed a videocam, but also a spotlight. I slammed on the brakes, got out of the car, looked straight into his surveillance system, and told him what I thought about that. I smiled the rest of the way up my drive. *Our* drive.

Dammit.

Chapter Eighteen

"Wait, I can't...no that won't work...here now, wait a minute—" Earl M. Sorenson, III, shook his jowls in dismay as he stared at the handset. The caller had hung up on him. He slammed the handset in its cradle and stared at the calendar on his huge desk. It had been ten days since he'd posed the question to Olivia to work for him. Was she still thinking about it? The cigar habit he'd given up pulled at him now, and he made puppy-dog eyes at the drawer that he used to keep them in. He opened it, hoping for one he'd overlooked, but came up empty.

"Dammit, Sylvia," he muttered. "Life was much more enjoyable with you, dear." Earl smiled at the framed picture of them he kept on his desk; one of their most precious memories—when their first and only grandchild had been born. His arm circled his wife as she held little Earl, IV. How long had it been since he'd visited his son's family? Oregon was a long way from Westminster, and he was too old to survive cross-country flights very often. Maybe once a year. He rose from his squeaky-wheeled desk chair, found his hat and sunglasses, and prepared for his weekly trek to visit Sylvia at the cemetery.

* * *

Traffic was light in Westminster, and Earl made it to the charming, downtown cemetery in record time. He parked by the library, got out of his car, and jerked on the hat his dermatologist insisted that he wear. "It's hell getting old," he fumed, walking across the street and onto the soft grass.

Pausing at the black, wrought-iron gate at the entry, he bowed his head and made a little cross sign on his chest. He strode to a graceful tribute stone topped by an angel. He placed his hand on the angel's shoulder. "Hi, Sylvie," he whispered. "Me again. I love you. I miss you. Today is our fiftieth, honey. We almost made it, didn't we? And next month makes four years since I found you, resting…so peaceful in your recliner that you looked asleep." He squatted, holding onto the headstone for balance. "I haven't been to see Bobby. Our relationship has become so…strained. You were always better with him, Sylvie. I'm getting on in years, and I don't know if I can stand another five hours in planes to get there. Can't he bring little Earl and come see me?" He pulled out a handkerchief he kept in his back pocket, wiped his face, and blew his nose. "I'm so tired. It'll be better when I'm…when I'm up there where you are." He dropped his head. "I'm going back to church. I haven't been in a long time, and I know you'd be sad about that. I'm going back, sweetheart. I promise."

Earl tried to shut out the traffic noise on Main Street, the calls of passersby to one another on a bright, sunny, Friday afternoon. Gently, he brushed debris off Sylvia's headstone and stood upright. "I sure wish you were here to talk to. This man wants me to take a case and I said no. He won't quit calling, and he's not taking no for an answer." Earl sighed. "So if you have any strings up there…see what you can do, okay?" With a fond pat or two on his wife's angel, he started back toward his car. In his pocket, his cell vibrated with a text. He pulled it out of his pocket. Olivia would like to talk about the position he had open. A smile lit up his face. With a lighter step, and a playful right jab into the air, he returned to his car and drove back to his office.

Chapter Nineteen

"Acts of injustice done
Between the setting and rising of the sun
In history lie like bones, each one."
~W.H. Auden

Lilly made slurping sounds as she downed the rest of her orange juice. I looked at the half-eaten eggs on her plate and made a tut-tut face.

"Mom, I gotta go! I don't know why you do this! I don't even LIKE breakfast!" With a fast peck on the cheek, she added, "What are you doing today?"

I grabbed her plate and ate the rest of her eggs. "I'm getting a job."

Lilly laughed. "Good one."

"I am. Seriously."

"Right," she said, still laughing, and raced out the door. Seconds later, I heard her car speed down the drive to the high school, throwing gravel.

I leaned against the sink and looked out my window at the backyard. A small patio with two Adirondack chairs led to the space Monty and I had tended for the twelve years we'd shared life together in this classic Maryland farmhouse on five acres. My bramble roses covered my fencing now, and soon red, yellow, and pink roses would adorn the perimeter. With a smile, I thought about how I could use them in vases for Earl's reception area…if he gave me the job.

My appointment with Earl was at three p.m. I flipped through a multitude of cute tops and capris and jeans with a sigh. Did I even have anything suitable for an interview? To my surprise, in the depths of the closet, I found a narrow, black skirt and a white blouse, which I topped with the new, short, leather jacket I'd picked up at Belk. Three-inch heels, too. Earl would flip out. He'd known me as a 'soccer mom', and had never seen me in professional attire. I looked forward to surprising him.

* * *

After an hour of stuffing myself into the tight skirt, selecting the right bra for the silky shirt, and wedging my feet into the heels, I decided 'professional' attire was a curse from hell.

I had to admit though, I looked pretty good. Now if I could coax my wild and free auburn curls into submission, all would be well.

After deploying all the tricks that Hunter had taught me to check for an IED on my car, I still tried to make myself light and airy as I sat in the driver's seat. I wished I hadn't learned about pressure tilt triggers and barometric or sensory electrical connections that would cause a homemade explosive device to blow up. I waited with eyes closed and shoulders hunched for a few seconds, then took off. I stuck out my tongue at Wyatt's videocam when I passed.

It was Hump Day. The perfect day, I thought, to insert myself into the world of working women. I'd always wanted to work after the kids were old enough to be in school, but Monty had derided that idea, said he needed me at home to best serve the family's interests. Now I realized it had been *his* interests he wanted served.

* * *

The gold-plated typeface on the rippled glass had faded and cracked. I traced the letters with my fingertips, "Earl M. Sorenson, III, Attorney at Law."

The late-1800s redbrick building and its ancient hallways still smelled the same—the linoleum flooring reeked of ammonia. I put my hand on the doorknob and pushed open the door, my mind flooded with memories.

His receptionist wasn't at her desk. I started to sit in a chair to wait for her out of habit, but remembered that she'd resigned weeks ago, and I was interviewing for her position.

"Earl?" I called out. Are you back there?" The door to Earl's office was slightly open. The reception area was neat as a pin, although the magazines were two years old and the flowers were fake. The reception decor pegged somewhere between Elvis and Madonna. I pictured my own flowers in cute vases on every flat surface, and hoped he had enough budget to get new furniture. We'd take those fake plants from the 80's straight to the dump.

I walked over to a lamp that had fallen to the floor and put it back on the end table, which was tough in a tight, black skirt and heels. With a grunt, I smoothed the skirt back into place as I stood. I thought about the contentious divorce Earl and I had seen through together. Our attorney-client relationship had been difficult at first, but in the end, we'd shared a glass of Champagne over successful, hard-fought negotiations. We'd begun badly, but parted friends. When Earl had offered me the job I'd laughed, but the more I thought about it, the more I liked the idea. *Something* needed to get me out of the house and on with my life.

I folded my arms and paced around the space. It was ten minutes after three, now. I knocked on his door. "Earl?"

Nothing.

I opened the door and poked my head in. Then I walked inside.

The empty office felt like a refrigerator. I rubbed my arms. Where was he? I grabbed my cell. No text. The man was as dependable as a clock. He wouldn't forget the interview.

I frowned.

Earl's chair had been pushed back from the large, ornate wooden desk as if he'd left in a hurry. A file lay on the floor, the contents scattered. Maybe he'd had an emergency. I squatted down in front of the desk in the wretched, tight, skirt, scooped the pages back into the folder, and slid them onto his desk. A twinge of dark premonition nagged at me.

I sat in one of his two guest chairs to wait.

Fifteen minutes past three.

I crossed my legs and tried to ignore the stench in the office from his cigars. His office felt so familiar. The outdated, sad, avocado-green shag rug underneath the desk. A large, dark spot visible from the far side of his desk made me shake my head. Had the guy never heard of rug shampoo services? I sighed.

Twenty minutes past three.

Wait. Was the dark spot *growing?*

My mind stalled. Paranoia curdled in my gut. My fingers clenched the ends of the armrests. I eased myself from the chair.

My still-unpredictable brain flipped me back to my hospital room eighteen months prior, where for five weeks I'd counted each step my legs could manage. Mechanically, I started counting. One step. Two steps. Three. *Don't look down! Keep going!* Four steps. *Almost there! Then you can look down!* Five. Five. Five...I looked down.

A scream exploded from my lips and vibrated all the way down to my bones.

Automatically, I pulled out my cell to call 911, but...slowly put it back in my purse. I took a deep breath. Just hang on a minute. What would Hunter do? What should I do?

I made a strangled sound in the back of my throat.

One thing you won't do, Olivia Callahan, is nothing!

Earl lay behind his desk, staring at the ceiling. The tears came when I realized that he'd dressed up for me...like I'd dressed up for him. He'd even worn a vest, but his shirt was pulled out and the dark red of his blood had saturated his shirt, the vest, the floor. "Ohmigod, Earl," I whispered.

The floor rocked beneath my feet. I grew dizzy. Since the assault, stressful situations threw me into a seizure or made me faint. I heard my therapist's voice in my head: *Note your vitals!* Pulse, check. Sweaty forehead, nope, check. Fainting sensation? Nope. Check. I blew out a relieved breath. My eyelids fluttered open.

I balanced myself in a squat beside Earl. I could barely feel my hands.

His mouth underneath the bush of a moustache was slack. Earl's face was the color of dirty chalk. My gaze traveled the length of his body. Above the groin and below the ribcage, his trousers were wet with blood. I bit my fingernail. Hadn't Tom mentioned that Earl was in bad health? Could this have been...a health issue? I frowned. *All that blood.* An injury? A wound? The look on Earl's face told the story. *This is a homicide.* The bloodstain on the rug grew, and with a start, I realized this must've been very recent, or his heart wouldn't continue to pump blood. Would it? I thought about trying to help, but Hunter had taught me not to compromise a crime scene.

It doesn't matter. He's gone, Olivia.

Earl would never kill himself. Never. I ruled out suicide.

I pressed my fingers against his neck. Nothing. The body was still warmish, though. I examined the space around him. The desk, bookcases; the dented, metal file cabinets. The trash can beside the desk held a few crumpled bits of paper. I grabbed a tissue from the box on his desk and took them out. A paid invoice. A menu from a takeout restaurant. A folded visitor's form to the Maryland Correctional Facility. Moisture dotted my forehead. I rubbed my eyes in disbelief. I recognized this form. I'd had to fill them out for my daughter when she visited her father in prison. The form was identical, except for one horrific detail. The underscored blank for the visitor contained *my name.*

With shaking hands, I called 911.

After long moments of staring at the form, I put it in my purse. I'd taken Lilly to visit her dad, but as for me...I'd visited the Maryland Correctional Facility only once in the past eighteen months, because I didn't have *any* desire to visit my scumbag ex. Why...and how...would this form end up in my attorney's office?

With a backward glance at poor Earl, I walked out of his office and into reception to wait for the authorities. Cursing softly, I jerked the form from my purse to look at it again. My jaw dropped. The signature was mine, but the handwriting *wasn't.* Ice water poured through my veins.

The mystery of the form settled around my neck like a hangman's noose.

Chapter Twenty

Monty tried to chat up the correctional officer as he walked back to his cell. The man attending him was as silent as a stone. "You new here, sir?" Monty asked.

The young, thin, CO looked no more than eighteen. "Yeah." The officer waited until Monty had walked back inside his cell, backed up to the door, and offered his cuffed hands through the slot. The officer removed the cuffs. Monty rubbed his wrists.

"What's your name?" Monty shouted through the vertical window, his face planted against the glass like a lunatic. The kid needed help lightening up, he thought, as he pulled a "The Shining" moment. But the officer simply stood there, watching, his lips a straight line. Monty backed off the glass. "Seriously, sir, if you are going to be around, I'd like to know your name."

The young man studied Monty through the pane. "Officer, inmate."

Monty nodded. "I like you, Officer," he announced.

The next two cells promptly started making kissing and hooting sounds.

"Hey, where's Officer Bromage? Doesn't he usually do this shift?" Monty yelled.

The young corrections officer stared at him through the window a few seconds before he walked away.

Monty cursed.

He needed all the COs—even the young, new ones—to like him.

With a sigh, he lay on his bed, put his hands behind his head, and thought about Hannah's visit. She'd been all dressed up today, and upset. Even mad. He wasn't sure what that had been about. He jumped off the bed, approached his door and put his ear to it. After assuring himself all was quiet, he squatted down by his metal toilet and sink and plucked the burner phone from its hiding place to text Duds.

Is this a good time?

D - Yep

Hannah was here

D - How'd that go

Amazing. She is mad as hell at those women in that stupid group I told you about.

D - Wow. That's good, right?

Gotta get her mad so she'll have the balls to do what we want.

D - You want to scare her, right? Keep her like...messed up? Look, I need to be out of the loop on this.

Monty's face grew warm. What did he mean by that?

D - I can't do anything to compromise my last two years, dude

Monty sighed. **Olivia had a bomb scare.**

D - What?

Yeah. They think it was me

...

...

D - Was it?

How would I do that, man?

...

...

D - I guess you wouldn't.

Damn straight. I'm dumb but not THAT dumb. Loverboy almost got blown up

D - That detective?

Yeah. So they figured it might be related to me. Funny, though. They found a pen. With this facility's name on it. Under the car.

...

...

D - From here?

Yeah.

...

...

D - I don't want any part of that, dude

It wasn't me!

D - Gotta go, CO

Later

Monty lay back and put his hands underneath his head, thinking. Hannah had also told him about the new guy in town…the re-zoning issue and how Olivia had been upset. Monty's dimples deepened. Oh, life couldn't get more interesting. But the pen?

His brow furrowed. How had it gotten there? Could it implicate him?

He knew how things worked, now. The truth didn't matter. What mattered was building a relationship with the types of people that could be convinced to lie. And lie good enough to *sound* like the truth.

That's what mattered.

Chapter Twenty-One

"The sole art that suits me is that which, rising from unrest, tends toward serenity."
~Tom Seaver

I sat in the reception area answering an investigator's barked, blunt questions until I couldn't stand anymore. I raised my hand for him to stop.

"There's a breakroom downstairs. I'm getting coffee, and I'll be back if you need me."

He gave me a look, then told a patrol cop out in the hall to accompany me. With a toss of my head, I stalked down the hallway, hopped into the elevator, and pressed the doors closed before the cop was able to jump in. I wiggled my fingers at him through the narrowing crack in the doors.

Since law enforcement had cleared the building, the breakroom was empty. No one even manning the register. I walked to the self-service coffee kiosk and prepared coffee. Behind me, I heard the racing steps and muttered curses as the—probably a rookie— cop berated himself for 'losing' me.

He glared at me. "What was that about?" I rolled my eyes. "I've been sliced and diced and peeled like an onion. This is ridiculous. The real bad guy is out there." I made a circling motion at the hall with my hand. "I'm going to sit in one of these chairs at one of these tables and enjoy my coffee."

He nodded and stood guard at the only door to the room.

Seriously? Would I have called 911 if I'd killed the guy?

If these cops were any indication of crime scene organization, poor Earl's legacy would be compromised. He'd been (eventually) a good lawyer and a good friend and I wanted his reputation protected. What if they ruled it a suicide? I sipped my coffee. It was disgusting. I got up, poured it out, and pulled out a water bottle from the mini-fridge behind the counter instead. The young cop moved sideways to eyeball me, and I felt ever-so-surveilled by Westminster's finest. I grunted. None of them held a candle to Detective Hunter Faraday.

I glanced at the time. Five o'clock. I checked in with Lilly.

"Hey."

"Where are you?"

"At my attorney's office."

"*Mom.*"

I sighed. "You've heard."

"Everybody at school heard. The sirens, everything. Are you okay? It was your old attorney, right?"

"And here I was all set to go to work for him. My luck," I muttered.

"Mom!"

"Stop. I do this dark humor thing when I'm upset, you get that, right? Anyway, yeah, I walked in on him, and now they're interviewing me to death and I'm tired and sad, so...how was *your* day?"

"I'm coming, okay? I'll be right there."

"NO. Do not do that, please, honey? I don't want you involved in this mess. They may ask to talk to you to verify my story—"

"WHAT? They think you did it?"

I sighed. "It's their job to rule out who didn't, honey. And I'm the one who called. I'm all they've got right now."

Through the door, I watched the coroner roll through and stop at the elevator. My hands shook. I didn't know how much more of this I could take. All I could think about was the day I saw the same thing happen with Niles, but Hunter had been with me then. Now, I was alone. With a lift of my chin, I told myself not to lose myself in trauma again...a habit I needed to break.

"Lilly, you home for the night?"

"Yeah," she murmured.

"Don't worry about me, I'll be home soon, okay? They know it wasn't me, they want details that I remember while it's fresh, that's all. You want to start dinner?"

"Sure you don't want me to come out there?"

"Positive."

We ended the call. I heard the elevator open and the collapsible gurney roll inside.

The young cop hadn't moved an inch from his post at the breakroom door.

I drank coffee and checked my e-mail.

The elevator dinged, then opened. I watched the solemn-faced coroner exit the building with his deceased cargo from the windows in the breakroom that looked out into the parking lot. As they rolled past, one of Earl's arms slid out from underneath the covering. I saw that he still wore his wedding ring, though his wife had been dead several years.

"Bye, Earl," I whispered.

The cop sentinel walked to my table. "You can go, ma'am. Sorry for the inconvenience. Detective Caldone said for you to stay close, though."

"He was a good friend, and you guys better find who did this!" My voice blasted through the room, through my tears, through my heartache. "If you don't, I will." With that, I strode to my car and roared from the lot. On the drive home, I promised Earl I'd nag them to death until we had answers. I tried to push away the guilt that had begun to claw at my mind.

Since he'd been my attorney, and by proxy, involved with the "Mercy's Miracle" case, could this have been my fault?

* * *

Once I pulled into my winding, beautiful drive, I stared at the beauty of fresh growth, trying to let it go. Let *everything* go, even if only for a couple of hours. I lectured myself that I had no control over any of it, anyway, so why let it eat away at me? For all I knew, his health had deteriorated and the bleeding was the result. Maybe it wasn't a crime at all.

Stop thinking about it.

I choked out a final sob.

My locust and oak trees had budded and now blazed with the light green promise of a Maryland spring, and their branches reached across the road toward each other, creating a leafy bower. A few daffodils had sprouted alongside the drive. I smiled. Had I planted those?

A man stood in the middle of my drive, waving his arms. Terror streaked up my chest. I slowed to a stop. *Olivia. Let go. Let go of the past. Not everything is a threat.*

The guy looked to be in his forties, with light brown, sun-streaked hair. He wore an olive green T-shirt that had the words 'Life is Sweeter in Hershey, PA' emblazoned across the front. The jeans he wore were torn in places and looked work-worn, but I suspected they'd been made that way. He walked toward my car with a smile, his arms outstretched like a long, lost friend. I rolled my window down two inches and made sure my doors were locked as my car idled. He wrapped his fingers over the top of my window and leaned in. Obviously, the guy knew nothing about personal space. As he bent down, I smelled a fresh, clean scent. Either cologne or soap, but whatever it was, it smelled nice.

Really nice.

Still.

I looked at him in a way meant to intimidate.

No such luck.

"Hey! Thanks for stopping." He pointed. "I recently bought that plot of ground right there, and…" he paused. Stared at me and laughed. "You're that woman! The one who flips me off in the videocam, right? Who gave me a good talking to?" He shook his head. "Which I couldn't hear a word of, by the way, but enjoyed watching. I'm Wyatt."

I folded my arms across my chest and stared at him.

His lips parted in dismay. "Aren't you her? Oh, gosh, if you're not her, I'm so sorry, I've overstepped—"

CHAPTER TWENTY-ONE

"Of course I'm her, you…you trespasser!" I rolled the window all the way down.

"What are you talking about?"

I sighed. "I missed the zoning commission meeting. They took my… *your*… land right out from under me."

He blinked. "Man. I had no idea…I…I'm sorry? I guess?"

I groaned. "Can you back up, please? I'll get out of the car and act like a human being." I smiled. He backed away, but not enough, in my opinion. I got out of my car and offered my hand. "I'm Olivia Callahan, and my house is at the end of this road."

"Nice to meet you, neighbor," he said, smiling broadly. We shook hands.

"Anyway, I recognized the car, I've seen it coming and going in the video. Wanted to say hello and introduce myself." After a pause, he added, "Even if you had the wrong idea about me." He chuckled.

Yeah. Haha. I stared at him. "Great. Okay." I started getting back in the car.

"Wait!" he said, his expression concerned. "I haven't offended you, have I?"

I sat behind the wheel with my door open. "It takes getting used to, this dividing my lot thing. Plus, isn't it zoned for commercial or multi-use or whatever, now?"

"Look, I had no idea this would be a problem. If there was anything I could do, I would, but it was all that was available close to my mom, that I could get zoned for business and personal. She's sick," he explained.

I had already gotten that information from Tom. "Oh, gosh, I'm sorry," I murmured, hating myself, but at the same time, realizing how empowering it was to know background information before I was supposed to.

"Will she be all right?"

His face clouded. "They don't know. Her doctors are in Westminster, and, well, it doesn't look good. Alzheimer's."

That I didn't know.

"I'm so sorry."

"Yeah."

Silence. I watched him dig the toe of his tennis shoe into the gravel of my...*our*...driveway. He stuck his hands into the pockets of his jeans. "Guess I better get going. I have an appointment with a contractor."

I glanced at him. "Look, can you...keep me in the loop on who to expect out here? I assume you're going back to...?" Letting the question hang, I made my eyes real wide like I had no clue where he came from.

He pointed to his shirt. "Isn't it obvious?"

"Hershey?"

"Harrisburg. It's close to Hershey. But yeah, I'm from PA and I do have to go back and forth for a while." He pulled a business card from his wallet. "Here. This is my cell."

I took it. "Now I can call instead of flipping off the videocam."

He smiled.

"I got the videocam as a watchdog, which you have made very clear that you hate; but I've been the victim of arson and theft. He shrugged. "Doesn't hurt to be careful. Bright light is a great crime repellant."

"So, what type of law do you practice?"

"Civil." He frowned. "How do you know I'm an attorney? I only just got my Maryland license."

I thought about Earl. I looked away. It was so fresh, I thought I might lose it.

"You don't like attorneys?" he asked, looking at me.

"I lost someone today," I whispered. "I am coming back from..." My vision began to deteriorate. I felt woozy. I needed to go. "Wyatt. I need to get home, so give me a heads-up if you need anything while you're here, okay?" I raced down the gravel lane in my car, Wyatt Harp a blip in my rearview.

I'd think about things in the morning. For now, caffeine, food, a bubble bath, and a book were needed. In that order.

Chapter Twenty-Two

"Lessons are learned through making mistakes, falling and rising."
~Adelaja

The buzz of a text tugged at the fringes of my consciousness.

I rolled over and snuggled into my cushy mattress.

It went off again. With one eye open, I glanced at the alarm on the bedside table. 5:30 a.m.

I grabbed my phone and read the text.

Hunter. **You still alive?**

I yawned and stretched my arms overhead.

It's 5:30 in the morning

Oh. Sorry.

When Hunter was in the zone, he had no concept of time. I did remember that about him.

After I pulled on a pair of workout pants and a T-shirt, I walked down the hall from my bedroom to Lilly's, pushed open the door, and saw that she—like most sane people at this hour—was still sleeping. Her face at rest, threw me back to her toddler days. My body tensed. A memory! I closed my eyes and let it wash over me.

Monty had raced downstairs and into the kitchen to grab a cup of coffee before heading to work downtown. A four-year-old Lilly, her first two fingers in her mouth as she watched, stood still and silent, watching. My heart ached. This little girl loved her daddy so much, and he had no time for her. She'd finally given up stretching out her arms for him to pick her up, throw her in the air like daddies do. But this morning, magic happened. Though running late, he skidded to a stop in the hallway, put his briefcase and travel mug on the floor, picked up his little girl and hugged her, hard, to his chest and told her he loved her. Then he put her down, patted her springy curls, blew a kiss at me and ran out the door.

I blinked. Like fog, the memory dissipated with my return to the present. This was revelatory. I drifted downstairs, thinking. Had I ever had a good and kind memory of Monty since the assault? During the long and difficult recovery? I think this was a first. Was it possible that my friends hadn't seen this side of him? Maybe he was redeemable. My mother says everyone is redeemable. I made face at the thought. Everyone but Monty, of course. Mom could barely speak his name.

No wonder Lilly clung to the hope her dad would find mercy, if he'd—even occasionally—acted this way. Displays of affection were not words I'd use to define Monty.

I walked outside to my front porch with its white, wicker furniture, floral cushions, porch swing, and ceiling fan and sat in my loveseat.

After drinking half my coffee, I called Hunter in response to his text. He answered on the first ring.

"Hey. How are you?"

"Good. So far, no further incidents. Maybe it was a one-off."

"You really think so?"

Slight pause. "There's no way to know, Olivia."

"No problems on my end. They come at different times and go over my car, which I appreciate."

"A precaution. It'd be a stretch to think that he'd do that to you."

"Monty?"

"Who else, Olivia?"

I was quiet.

"I had a memory of him being nice."

Hunter sighed.

"Y'know, I've been having trouble with memories of my kids when they were young. Dr. Sturgis says it's common with injuries like mine, but therapy helps memory return. This morning, standing outside Lilly's room,

110

I saw him with her at about age four or so. He was hugging her, taking time with her. It was…an emotional memory."

Hunter grunted. "Olivia, you do know that sociopaths compartmentalize, right? They have these…I don't know…different facets of personality. I'm glad your girls may have had a nice father figure periodically, but—"

"Yeah," I interrupted, my thoughts coming fast; "but what if the way we painted him had a huge effect on the jury? What if the things I told my attorney put a shadow over everything?"

Hunter murmured, "You okay?"

I frowned. Cleared my throat. "Do you remember my attorney? My divorce attorney?"

"Yep. Earl, right?"

"We had this talk about me going into the legal field. Remember? And I was going to accept his job offer to be his receptionist and work on my paralegal certificate, and—"

"Wait," Hunter blurted, "Was?"

I bit my fingernail. "I found him dead on the floor of his office yesterday."

"Freakin' unbelievable," Hunter whispered.

"What?"

"Think about it, Olivia. First, a hit on me. Now, your attorney, the one responsible for your juicy settlement and Monty's financial problems."

"How could he do that…from prison?"

Hunter shook his head. "It amazes me how much a person can accomplish from a prison cell."

"I'll put a call in to Westminster PD, but I'm sure they're already thinking about this," he said, his voice brisk. All business, now.

I was quiet. When he was like this, his mind hummed along in a thousand directions. No sense saying anything, he wouldn't hear it.

"I'll suggest they up the surveillance and continue the bomb inspections. In the meantime, that neighbor? The one that put up the videocam and spotlight? He's your best friend right now. I'd have him check the video every day for fluctuations in visitors or suspicious activity. Have you met that guy yet? Didn't you tell me he's an attorney? See? Even better."

My gut clenched. Hunter could see the big picture and would now put a huge net over my existence to catch the bad guys—if there were any—when all I wanted to do was feel safe in my own little world and live my life. Be a good mother. Start a career. I made a mental note to return to therapy before I lost my mind. "Okay," I mumbled.

"I'm sorry, Olivia. It's only a—"

"Precaution, I know!" I snapped.

Hunter was quiet.

"What, do you think I'd be okay with all this? My attorney was probably *murdered*, for Christ's sake, Hunter! I don't trust the Westminster PD to do much of anything…they're small-town cops."

"I worked with them on your case, Olivia. I assure you, they'll look into this. They're professionals."

I folded my arms across my chest and stared at my front yard, which minutes ago had been a place of solace and rest. Now, all I could think about was getting back into Hazel's office.

* * *

"Hazel found an opening on her calendar, Mom, so that's where I'm going today," I told her as I drove.

"But honey, don't you think it's too soon? After all, this man has only been…deceased…two days. Isn't a little early to try to, um…figure things out As far as…your emotions are concerned?"

I sighed. "Hazel's a good listener, and can be objective."

Slight pause. "I'm a good listener."

Ah. Maybe this is why she doesn't like Hazel. Does she think my therapist is a replacement mother? "You are," I agreed. "But Hazel has insights that she's learned that are helpful, and—"

"Are you saying I'm not helpful?"

My grip tightened on the steering wheel, and I almost ran a red light. I stomped on the brake. The driver in the next lane glared at me. "Of course not! You are amazing! Hazel is my therapist. You raised me. Your perceptions are important to me, plus, without your prayers, I'd be in a lot of trouble right now."

She was quiet.

"Let me re-phrase that," I quipped. *"More* trouble."

Mom laughed.

"It's okay, I understand," she said.

Nope, I thought. She did *not* understand, but I'd leave it alone for now. We ended the call chatting about Serena. I was becoming jealous of the relationship my older daughter and mother had cultivated since they now lived in the same town. Maybe both of us were a little rattled about the shift in relationships going on.

A parking space opened up right in front of me, and I pulled into it before anyone else could snatch it. I scaled the two floors of steep stairs, circa mid-1800s, and rapped on her door.

"Come on in," she called from the small space she used as her office. She glanced at me from her computer screen on her desk at the back of the room. "Let me finish entering these notes, and we'll get started. You want coffee?" she asked in her Jersey accent. She jerked her head toward the coffee bar. "Help yourself."

I fixed myself a cup and sat in my usual spot, a comfortable, upholstered armchair next to a matching couch with an end table in between.

I loved being here. I'd loved it from our first session. She'd done a great job creating a sanctuary for her clients. With a contented sigh, I sank deeper into the armchair, feeling a restful release from the chaos of the last few days. Well, the last few months. No. Almost two years. My body tensed.

STOP.

Hazel rose from her chair. Closed her laptop. Strode around her desk in that brisk way she had, folded her arms, and stood over me. "Are you okay?"

My smile was thin. "Kind of."

She patted my shoulder, took her seat across from me. "Shall we begin?" I nodded.

"I read about Earl. Tragic. How are you feeling about that?"

Not the beginning I'd hoped for. What had I hoped? Why did I do that?

Set up unrealistic expectations? I wasn't supposed to do that. Was I? No.

"Hard to describe, Hazel. That's why I'm here. I need help."

I stared at the floor. Dust motes floated and danced in the sunbeams stretching through the blinds. "He'd offered me a job. I hadn't seen him in a long time, and…and I was there for an interview."

She waited. Hazel was a patient woman who had no problem with silence. Like Hunter.

"I…my first thought was…I couldn't believe it. I screamed…I didn't know what to do. How to feel."

Hazel leaned forward.

"After that, this amazing calmness washed over me."

"Huh," Hazel murmured, writing in her notebook.

"I squatted down to check if he was…gone. He was, but it had happened hours…maybe minutes…before I got there. He was still warm."

"Oh…*Gosh*," Hazel whispered, one of her thin hands touching her throat.

"Then I went into this…time warp. Like, I was a cop. An investigator."

She nodded. "Hunter Faraday's influence. He's been a powerful presence in your life."

"I knew this was as fresh as a crime scene could get. I swear, Hazel, and… the way I crept around the body, looking for clues. I knew I needed to call 911. Which I did, only *after* I'd done some digging around. They got there fast. I spent the rest of the day answering questions. Talk about a bad day." I pulled in a breath and let it out. "Plus, my new job evaporated in a puff of smoke. Isn't it awful that I thought about that? I'm a terrible person."

Hazel shook her head. "No. This is wonderful progress, Olivia. For someone who's been through a traumatic brain injury and had to recover speech, movement, memory…it's remarkable. If this had happened even six months ago, you'd been fighting for consciousness—you'd have had one of those fainting episodes that terrifies everyone. Instead, you assessed the situation in an objective manner, and remained calm." She thought a minute.

"You're giving yourself space to grieve, though?"

"A little."

CHAPTER TWENTY-TWO

She nodded, thoughtful. "Hm."

I slumped in my chair. "I hate it when you do that."

She smiled. "Your case is unique since your brain is still forming new connections. I'm wondering where it will land, how it will react...how *you* will react." She scraped a few curly strands of silver hair off her face. "In tragic situations, I mean."

"First I have to remember who I was," I said.

Slight pause. "Maybe it's better to...slow down on that, Olivia. I've been thinking about it. When you went to see Monty, I was surprised. When I'd had time to separate my personal concern for you from a... therapeutic objectivity, I concluded that it took real emotional strength to take that step. Courage, too. A significant contrast to how you have been described to me by friends and family. I don't know, since yours is such an unusual case with the flipped personality, if it's best to pursue memories when one's past is quite painful; or if it's better to let 'sleeping dogs lie,' as it were." She paused, thoughtful. "We're forging new paths, Olivia."

I smiled. "Well, I wish one of them would jump up and bite me on the ass so I'd know which one to take."

Chapter Twenty-Three

Sophie lit another cigarette. Blew out a long plume of smoke. Her new husband, Gray, sat beside her on the tidy patio of Sophie's condo. He reached for her hand. She smiled at him. "This is the last one."

Dr. Grayson Sturgis picked up a tumbler of bourbon with his free hand and sipped. "Babe, you can smoke 'til kingdom come if you want to, and I'd still be right here. I haven't quite quit myself."

Her eyes widened. "No!"

Gray's laugh lines deepened as he grinned. "Kidding. I have. Honest."

She glared at him. "Nice. I let myself trust you, and bam."

He kissed the hand he was holding. "I have."

"It's hard."

"Try the e-cigarettes. At least you don't get the nicotine."

She puffed on the last of the cigarette and snuffed it out, jamming her arms across her chest and pouting. "It shouldn't be this hard. This is the third time I've tried."

"Yeah, but the last time was, what, six months?"

She nodded. "Such a loser."

Gray pulled her in and kissed her full on the lips. "So *not* a loser, Mrs. Sturgis."

She laughed. "Should we have waited to get married? You know, the kids are going to be mad. Maybe disappointed is a better word," she amended.

He shrugged. "We could have, I guess. But I couldn't wait anymore. Plus, I wanted to do life with you now."

"What's your realtor saying?"

"She says my house should sell in ten days. Tops. The market's nuts, she told me."

"Good. Well, we have plenty of time to look. Isn't it amazing that I signed a six-month lease and not a year? Such a blessing."

"Pretty amazing," he agreed. "It'll be fun to find the right place. And six months is not too long in this..."—he glanced around the space—"... situation."

Sophie gave him a look. "You're the one that was all hot to sell your house. I was fine, here on my own. I could've waited." His beeper went off like a siren. He checked it. "Well, I couldn't," he said with a smile. "One of my patients is awake. Gotta go. Welcome to the life of a doctor's wife."

Sophie placed her forehead on his. "A *neurologist's* wife," she whispered.

Gray slapped his knees, rose, and trotted through the condo to his car. Sophie walked him out. As she returned to her condo, her cell lit up with Olivia's name.

"Hey!"

"Hi, Mom. You busy?"

"Nope."

"Went fine with Hazel today."

"It did? So...what wonderful nuggets of wisdom did she dispense this time?"

Two blips of silence.

"You really don't like her, do you, Mom?"

Sophie reached for a new pack of cigarettes and lit one. "We have very little in common."

Olivia hooted. "I think you two are clones of each other and that's why you butt heads."

"Not funny."

"How's your place shaping up? Have you got everything put together?"

She blew out a smoke ring. "Almost. We still need to move Gray's..." Sophie grimaced. Oops.

"Move Gray's what? Is he moving, too?"

"Uhhhh…"

"Mom! What are you not telling me?"

"We couldn't wait, honey," she murmured.

"What do you mean? Are you guys living together now?"

Sophie winced. She hadn't meant to tell her yet. She cleared her throat. "We did it."

Silence.

"Did what?"

"Got married. Don't be mad at me."

"But we had plans…what about the wedding dress, the shower, all the stuff we were going to do together?"

"I know," she murmured. "We were impulsive."

"Well…congratulations," Olivia muttered.

"We can still have a party! How about that?"

"So you eloped," Olivia stated, her voice flat.

"I guess you could call it that. We went to the courthouse here, dressed up a little, it was nice. I didn't mean you to find out this way."

"Yeah."

Silence.

Olivia sighed. "Things sure are different now."

"Who could've predicted I'd fall in love with your neurosurgeon?"

"Me. You guys were disgusting. The king and queen of PDA, just saying."

Sophie laughed. "We were not."

"It's all good, Mom. However…we'll have to adjust to the news. How's Serena? Does she know?"

"Nope." Sophie sighed. "I was going to do a group Zoom, but…oh, well! She's good, I think. She and her young man came over for dinner last week."

"Her young man? Don't you think you should've told me about that? She hasn't even told me about him."

"Seems I'm offending you with everything I say, today," Sophie shot back.

"I'm sorry, it's just…I'm having a hard time, Mom. Trying to figure out what to do with my life now that I'm 'recovered', whatever that means. Hazel says I should move forward and maybe not be so concerned with the past."

CHAPTER TWENTY-THREE

Sophie stiffened. "And what Hazel says is the gospel, I take it."

Silence.

"I better go, Mom."

The phone went dead.

"When are you going to learn to shut up?" Sophie berated herself. "Don't say everything that pops into your head!" She stalked to her car to drive to Walgreen's to buy an e-cig, or a vape, or whatever the heck they were.

Chapter Twenty-Four

"You like Bosch? Guys always watched it in college, but me? Not much." Monty lay on his bed, shirtless and sweaty from his workout—one foot on the floor, the other on the bed. Hoots and catcalls emanated through the corridors—sounds of the weekly TV binge of the crime series devoted to an unscrupulous and somewhat tilted protagonist.

"Naah, man, I was always high. I made it through high school, but college?" He laughed.

"How'd you make money, then?"

"The drugs, dude. It was a good gig until I got too messed up. You get sloppy. Don't recognize the feds when they come, in all their undercover shit."

Monty's thick, black eyebrows drew together. With his long, black, wavy hair and cool beard vibe, he doubted anyone would recognize him after he got out. He noted his arms, ropy as any punk-ass bodybuilder's guns, with satisfaction.

He scowled. *IF* he got out. "You ever think about getting out?"

"Don't we all?" Duds made a guttural noise. "Shit, man, I ain't getting out. I'm seventy-two years old. What am I gonna do on the outside? I've been here almost thirty years."

"Did you do it?"

"Cut that woman? Yeah." Monty heard him sniff. He'd bet a hundred dollar bill that Duds was still using, and he'd managed to get drugs. The guy was depressed one day, manic the next. Pure cokehead, Monty thought. Or meth, maybe.

"It was self-defense. She was comin' at me with a butcher knife. I grabbed it and turned it around." He chuckled. "My good luck that I nicked the right artery. Lot of blood, man." He closed his eyes. "Still can't get that outta my head. Gnarly, dude."

"The judge have it out for you? Self-defense? They didn't believe your story?"

"A small-time drug dealer like me, with a record? They threw everything but the damn refrigerator at me. I was lucky not to get the chair." He grunted. "The only reason I'm not in max security right now is that I'm getting short. Seventeen months and counting."

The men went quiet. The faint sounds of creative profanities played in the background. Reassured of another few minutes of respite from the barked orders of the COs, they continued their conversation.

"You got kids?"

Another long sniff. "Maybe."

Monty laughed. "Maybe?"

"I was high, man. I had sex with so many women, they all run together, y'know? I'm not proud, understand. Not at all. I woulda liked to have known if I had a kid."

After a few seconds, Monty asked, "You get my ex's mom pregnant, you think?"

Duds laughed. "That broad kept her legs together so tight she squeaked when she walked."

Monty eyeballed the ceiling. It looked good. They'd let him paint it, and he was glad. It made his cell look bigger. "Yeah, I figured."

"There was a couple times though…now, I ain't proud, understand…but I did slide a little crushed up 'lude into her wine. That woman loved white wine."

"Still does," Monty said, thinking. "Quaaludes? Was that the drug of choice back then?"

Duds laughed. "Everyone did 'em. It worked on Sophie. For sure."

"You think she ever got pregnant?"

"Only happened twice. We got married, so I didn't need to do that." He laughed.

"You sure?" Monty asked, thinking about Olivia. Wouldn't that be the most awful consequence Olivia could ever imagine…or Sophie, for that matter…if Duds was Olivia's father.

"I don't think so, dude. How old is her daughter, again?"

Monty thought a minute. "She's forty-one, now. No…forty-two."

"This is the issue. I wandered around most of the time in a fog. I can't remember dates very good."

"Approximately?"

Silence.

"Try," Monty urged.

"Thinkin'. Hang on a damn minute. How old's Sophie now?"

"She's twenty years give or take older than her daughter. So sixty. At least."

"No way I could be her kid's father. I was older than her by a decade. I remember now, she had a daughter in grade school. We weren't together long—six months, tops. She was crazy."

"The daughter you remember is my ex," Monty said. "She only had one kid."

"Sorry, my memory's got holes in it. I can't tell one day from the next these days."

"Ten years? Total lech, Duds."

"Tell me about it."

The men laughed.

"So," Monty said. "I'm still trying to figure out the best way to send a message she'll remember."

Duds sighed. "Why don't you drop that, dude? Forgive and forget and all that? I don't want no part of any of this."

"Duds," Monty's voice was silk, "you believe in fate, right? Why do you think fate brought us together?"

"Don't know, don't care."

Undeterred, Monty continued. "Okay, so Hannah told me that idiot attorney of Olivia's died, and she found him. We can use that."

"Yeah. This is why I want..."

"No part of it," Monty completed for him. "I get it. I'm bouncing ideas off you. Can I do that much?"

"Yeah," Duds muttered. "But I gotta get off soon."

"Why, you have a beauty appointment?" Monty laughed at his own joke. "I got married to Olivia because I knew I could...you know...train her. She was young, seventeen, and I don't think Olivia ever knew who her dad was. Olivia's mom told him to hit the road."

Monty took a deep breath, blew out a long, shuddering, sigh. "Our relationship worked okay for twenty years. I had no real feelings for her, to be honest. She was more like...a FWB. She gave me sex, ironed my clothes, cooked food, and had a couple of kids. I only did that because she wanted them, and... after they were born, I...I started to *feel* something. Made life worth it, as they say..." Monty sat up straighter on the narrow bed attached to the wall and let his legs dangle over the side. He grabbed the pillow the State had provided—a sad, thin, thing that barely pillowed—plumped it against the cinderblock wall, and reclined.

"Sounds deep, dude. Where you goin' with this?"

"I guess I'm...still rollin' around in it. It infuriates me...the trial, prison." His jaw clenched. "That stupid bitch. Niles fell for it. The lost, little girl act. No way it's not partially her fault that I had to end the guy."

"Your friend, um...Niles?"

"I *thought* he was my friend. Then he crawls all over my wife when I hire him to keep an eye on her."

"Why'd you hire him to do that?"

Monty stared at the old—but clean—linoleum floor in his cell. "I'd left Olivia for someone else and moved out. But Olivia was still my wife, so I wanted to make sure...I don't know, that she didn't get into trouble. Make sure my daughters were okay."

"Yeah, and you told me what happened. He invited her to his place, they had a fight or whatever...she got injured. Right?"

"No way to know for sure what happened, but who cares? The thing was, he was the worst kind of traitor, and after I'd done so much for him professionally and all…wow. You can't trust people. Any of 'em."

"Got that right."

"You're a great conversationalist, Duds, you know that?"

"What?"

Monty laughed at the sarcasm that, as usual, had sailed right over Duds' head.

"Dude. Where were you goin' with all that? What do you want from me?"

"I want to prove a point, I guess."

"Why? You could get years tacked on. Why risk it?"

Monty smiled. "I can't leave it that she *won*. She pissed all over me and…I walk away? I say okay, so I'm gonna lay down and rot in prison, now?"

"I don't know, dude. Sometimes you got no choice but to walk away."

"Quit calling me *dude*!" Monty screamed into the phone.

Chapter Twenty-Five

"Prayer is a rising up and drawing near to God in mind and heart and spirit."
~Alexander Whyte

"What the *heck*," Callie exclaimed, spitting out part of the wine in her mouth. She pointed at the door. "Look who's here."

I had to scoot my chair out and turn around to see. I blinked. *Hannah.* We'd written her off as a casualty of Monty's charms, yet she barreled toward our table with all the gusto of Rachel Ray selling her organic pet food on QVC.

Sherry raised her perfectly drawn eyebrows at me, and looked at me over the rim of her glass. I gave her a look. Like everything was A-okay with me. But it wasn't. Callie shot me a sympathetic look. I shook my head. *Do not paint me as a victim, dammit!*

Hannah's stride was confident, self-assured; as if she hadn't gutted and filleted me—well, all of us—with the news she'd been developing a relationship with Monty. In stark contrast to my actual feelings, I smiled at her. She smiled back. Hannah was a very pretty woman, I realized, especially when on a mission, which I sensed was happening right now. Her long, blonde hair fell in beachy waves around her thin face, and she'd worn lipstick, almost unheard-of for this girl. She put both hands on her hips before taking a chair. I noticed her wedding ring was missing from her left hand.

"Is it safe to sit?"

We looked at each other, uncertain. I needed to make the call. "Yes. Sit."

Hannah settled into the one remaining chair at our table, leaned in, and extended her arms on the table, her fingers threaded together in a knot. "Look, ladies, I know you think I'm the worst right now, but hear me out."

We all leaned in and mimicked her body language—plopping our arms down and clasping our hands together like hers, as if gearing up for a group high five and a team cheer.

I studied our collective arms and threaded fingers—Callie, with her perpetual tan and strong Spanish streak in her heritage; Hannah, of Irish descent and two shades removed from my pale, freckled, Anglo skin; and Sherry, the color of a Latte, compliments of a black dad and white mom. We were a Coke commercial, and we needed each other.

But I was hurt. And mad. And wounded.

Hannah looked at me. "I know I've hurt you, and I'm sorry. I've been an idiot. And I want to apologize." Her gaze took in all of us. I couldn't breathe.

"Especially to Olivia, but I do have a thought, and I wanted to share it with all of you."

"Wait," I sputtered. "That's it? I'm sorry? What the hell made you do it, Hannah? Give us a clue, okay? Let's not move on to your 'thought' just yet." I put air quotes around the word with my fingers.

Hannah smiled. "Let there be no doubt that Olivia is a changed woman, forever and ever, amen."

"Amen!" the others chorused, raising their glasses.

"Did anyone order wine for me?"

We shot blank looks at each other. "Hannah," I said in my most long-suffering tone, "we didn't think you were coming, duh."

Callie looked stressed. "Here," she blurted, shoving her bottle of wine toward her. "I'll get you a glass. You can have part of mine."

Hannah clapped her lips together while the server brought over another glass. After she'd poured, she downed half the glass, then set it down on the table with a firm hand. "You're right, Olivia. He is such a jerk. I went in, thinking the man needed ministry, right? Like…in church, they tell me to reach out to the forgotten, or whatever. The hurting ones. Well, I don't know, I thought about Monty at the cookouts, and our neighbor events and…I felt sorry for the guy." She glared at us. "Can't you understand that?"

After a few stunned seconds, we mumbled the words, but the thought was a collective NO. We did not, on any planet, for one second, understand.

After the rumbling stopped, I looked her square in the eye. "Hannah, could you see me doing that to your husband? If he'd been in prison? Wouldn't you still feel a connection, no matter how long, and for us to be such close friends, and through so much together, don't you think there would be a kind of…oh, I don't know…respect for each other? Lines that shouldn't be crossed?" I jammed my arms across my chest.

"I said I was sorry," she insisted, her voice soft. With a sigh, she swept her arm upward, so that the top of her hand, including a bare marital finger, was prominently displayed. "He had papers served on me two days ago."

I told her I was sorry. The words came out, at least. At my core, I was still mad.

Callie teared up, of course. She patted Hannah on the back. I rolled my eyes. Grabbed my wine glass and drank. It would be a two-glass night, for sure. Sherry remained neutral and impassive. Smart girl.

I stared at Hannah and Callie, wondering if I could trust either of them. My mother's voice came roaring back from my misspent youth. 'Perfection is not possible this side of earth, honey. We are all flawed, imperfect individuals with challenges and difficult situations. So be patient, and be kind.'

If my mother had taught me anything, it was that good can come out of the worst situations. Her favorite scripture to quote had been "With God, all things are possible." I looked at Hannah. I could do this. I can choose to be kind. *In my own way*, I added. With a glance around the table, and Callie still commiserating with Hannah, I decided this was my fight, not theirs.

"Callie," I whispered. "Are you done yet?"

She looked at me, bewildered. "Oh!" Her cheeks colored through her tan. "I went on and on, didn't I?"

"I want a turn," I told her.

She held up a hand in surrender as she returned to her chair.

After a deep breath, I addressed Hannah. "To be honest, I'm still upset that you thought that was okay. You could've at least given me a heads-up. It'll take a little while to get over it. So what happened that made you, uh..."

"That made me call him an asshole? I woke up. He was using me...to get to *you*. He said things, and I know they were *planted* bits of information, to make me...well, to divide us. I saw him as he really was, a pathetic, guilty guy not working on fixing his life, but trying to get back at the wife he abused!" Hannah started to cry. "I'm really sorry, Olivia."

After a slight hesitation, I walked around the table to her and did a little back-patting of my own. "I don't know many women that can see through his exterior, Hannah. Don't be too hard on yourself."

I glanced around the table. Callie gave me an approving look. Sherry drank more wine.

With a final sniff, Hannah lifted her chin. "You aren't going to believe what he told me to pass along to you."

I went back to my chair. Part of me wanted to trust her, and the other part wanted to slam a lemon meringue pie in her face. After a hefty swallow of wine, I leaned forward. "Try me, Hannah," I said, the tone of my voice daring her to betray me. Correction: betray me *again.*

Sherry fumbled for her purse. "Should I record this, Olivia?" she stage-whispered, her dark, brown eyes ultra-big and sincere.

I blinked. Looked around the table. We started with a titter or two, which developed into long, bellowing, laughter that broke through the tension like a child's finger through a soap bubble.

"Thanks, Sherry, but no, okay?" I swiped the laughter-tears from my cheeks. "Go ahead, Hannah. Tell us what my ex wanted you to pass along."

Hannah's California-surfer-girl face held conflict, but after a moment, she forged ahead. "He said you should *watch your back.* Then he laughed." She shook her head in dismay. "He's in a bad place."

I shrugged. "So? That makes two of us."

"His bad place is a thousand times worse than your bad place. Listen. He really is lost, Olivia. I don't even know...if he has a soul."

I started breathing again. I realized I'd been holding my breath through much of Hannah's revelatory speech. My peripheral vision started to go. I clutched the side of the table with both hands.

Callie jumped up. "COFFEE!" she yelled at the server, with frenzied gesticulations at Olivia. Alarmed, the server dashed back to the back and returned with a carafe, cream, sugar, and spoons.

"Anyone else?" he asked, worried.

Callie waved him off, poured the coffee, put the mug to my mouth, and made me drink as much as possible. She then offered water after every hot swallow of coffee. Hannah and Sherry gaped.

Callie wore her concern with practical efficiency—like a nurse's stethoscope. "She gets these stress things...you know, from the coma and everything. I think we got it in time."

"Wow," Sherry whispered. "This has been the...best meeting ever."

I glared at her. My vision cleared. Relieved, I sat up straight, rotated my head, and took deep breaths. "I'm good, girls. I'm good."

"Drink more coffee," Callie, ever competent and capable, insisted as she sat back in her chair.

"Okay," I said, after assuring myself the strange clouding of my eyesight had vanished. "Keep going, Hannah."

She waved her hands in dismissal. "We can talk about this another time, why don't you—"

"I really am okay. I've had these...a hundred times. We caught it. I'm fine."

Hannah let out a breath. "I acted like things were fine when I visited last time, Olivia. He has no idea I'd...I'd uncovered him, or whatever." She grimaced. "He was so ingratiating and complimentary it started making me uncomfortable." She looked at her hands, grown red and angry from the pressure of smashing them together as she spoke. "I thought about how he'd treated you and realized I was going down the same track as...oh gosh, I'm sorry."

I shook my head. "That was the old me. She doesn't exist anymore. Keep going."

"All he was doing was seducing me...to get me to do what he needed. I saw it plain as day, and it felt like I'd been violated." She looked down, then at me. "But two can play that game." She smiled under half-closed eyelids.

And just like that, the sun came out.

Whatever her idea was, I was all in.

Hannah gave me a long, hard, look. "Olivia, he's out for blood. He hates you. He thinks you're responsible…the reason he's in prison." She raised her arms. "It's not like…he said the words. It's the way he says your name, the way his face looks when he speaks about your marriage, or Niles."

I flinched. Brain bits and the picture of Niles' son were forever stamped on my forehead, and the mention of his name triggered it. I tried to think about the flowers in my front yard instead. Hazel had told me the brain could not hold two trains of thought at once. It worked.

"He told me to tell you it's too bad that your *attorney was murdered*. And he sends his condolences." She turned big, round eyes on me. "How could he know that your attorney was murdered? Have they even finished the investigation?"

* * *

A heavy fog obscured a tiny sliver of moon as I drove home.

Squinting, I tried to see through the dank, murky, dark, struggling to keep my vehicle in the right lane. Two glasses of wine plus one coffee equals alert with a side of loopy, so I thanked God all the way home that I lived close.

Was Hannah telling the truth? There didn't seem to be an upside if she wasn't. I found it hard to believe that Monty would risk losing his hard-fought, lighter, prison term by carrying out some nefarious plan, but I'd learned through experience that his rage trumped common sense. Every time.

My phone buzzed. My editor's name appeared on the display. I pressed 'decline', and powered my windows down for fresh air.

The graveled lane to my house appeared, and I turned wide, almost missing. The damn spotlight that Wyatt had installed was a blinding intrusion, and in its glare, I watched Wyatt walk his property. Against my better judgment, I decided to pull over onto the dirt road that had been cleared in preparation for—I shuddered—*paving*. The last thing I wanted was a paved drive and a commercial enterprise less than a half-mile from my house, but nothing I could do but accept it.

"Wyatt!"

He jerked around. Smiled. "Hey! What are you doing out this time of night?"

I got out of my car, swerving a bit, closed my door, and leaned against the car. Wyatt walked toward me, the night breeze whipping his light, cotton shirt tight against his chest. Wyatt looked better at night, I decided. Or maybe he looked better because I'd been drinking. I squinted at him.

"Finishing up a night of wine and song. You?"

He laughed. "You look nice."

I looked down at my leggings and boots. My hastily thrown on yellow and white tunic top, the bright color a nod to spring. I'd worn more makeup than usual, and it felt good to get a compliment. "Thanks. I may look okay, but inside, I'm wobbly with drink."

His eyebrows raised. "Sounds perfect. Wish I was wobbly with drink."

I waved my hand at the spotlight. "Can I ask you a question?"

"Sure."

"I won't go into gory details, but I've had a few things happen that may be related to my ex...and you've got a videocam up...and a spotlight..."

Wyatt cocked his head and smiled. "My answer is yes."

I laughed. "You don't even know the question."

"You want me to check the footage, see who's coming and going, right?"

I stared at him.

He shrugged. "You're welcome to check the footage whenever." He gave me a searching look. "I wondered why the cops were patrolling this road. Guess now I know. Want me to make you a co-administrator on the system?"

I pulled my chin into my neck in surprise. "You'd do that?"

He spread his hands. "I'm an attorney. What have I got to lose? My reputation? I don't have an issue with you having access. It goes both ways. You can also keep a watch out for any weirdos trespassing on my...um... *our*...property until I move down permanently."

131

"Wow. Sure. Did I give you my number? Here," I grabbed his cell and punched in my number. "Now you have it."

"Okay," he said. "I assume you have an attorney? I'd be remiss if I didn't ask."

A sad sigh popped out. "I did until a few days ago."

"What happened?"

"Earl Sorenson. He died. He handled my divorce, which was a long and hideous ordeal. I was even going to work for him, as a receptionist, and eventually paralegal." I stared at the grass and ground my palms together. "I found him on the floor when I went for the interview." I looked up, blew out a breath. "It's a suspicious death situation. Westminster PD is investigating."

"Whoa," he whispered. "I'm so sorry." After a beat, he continued. "Have you been interrogated?"

I nodded.

"Without an attorney?"

I shrugged.

"You know that's dangerous, right?"

I crossed my arms and looked up. The fog had lessened, and the crescent moon inched through the murk.

Wyatt ran a hand through his hair. "Look, I'm offering my services. And…you're in luck. I'm staffing up here, and I have an opening for both. Reception and paralegal. Sounds like fate, to me."

I couldn't believe what he was offering. He barely knew me.

"As an employee, you'd get a discount, or hell, maybe I can do a pro bono, we'll have to see how complicated things get. But it sounds like a very workable scenario, Olivia. So think about it. Shoot me your details…wait, you've got my card, right?" without missing a beat, he pulled out a card and handed it to me. "Shoot me an email with your experience, credentials, whatever. But this feels like a good idea."

"I…I don't know what to say." I studied his card. Now it would be my turn to Google him. Lilly already had. This was probably a *bad* idea.

"Think about it?"

"Sure," I said. The booze was wearing off, and I could feel the infernal

132

dark cloud I'd lived with for two years hovering; waiting for me to give it permission to infiltrate. I didn't have the strength to push it away. I pictured dark, vaporous, fingers reaching for—and entering—my brain.

I shot to my house, put the car in the garage, and locked everything down tight before I fell into a deep sleep.

Chapter Twenty-Six

"Hope is like yeast, you know—rising under warmth."
~Leif Enger

Coffee mug in hand, I walked from my kitchen to the front porch to watch the birds eat breakfast. My trees and bushes had started to flower, I noticed, with a rueful smile. Early spring in Maryland was a crapshoot...a sudden snow could kill everything, or...it could be the most glorious spring in years.

I sank onto the wicker loveseat. Cardinals fought each other for the fresh sunflower seeds I'd put in the feeders.

Lilly's light steps raced down the stairs inside. "Mom! Did you fix breakfast?" she yelled as she hit the ground floor.

"In the kitchen!" I yelled back through the screen, smiling.

Ten seconds later, the screen door banged shut, and Lilly sat on the chain-link swing at one end of the wide, white-planked porch. "Thanks," she said, as she inhaled mouthfuls of scrambled eggs.

"You're early this morning," I said.

She shrugged. "Can't believe you got in so late last night. Have fun?"

I cocked my head. "I wouldn't call it fun. But it was good."

Lilly didn't probe, for which I was grateful. "Did I tell you I checked out Mr. Harp? Not much there, just his attorney stuff." Lilly replied. "I didn't find anything bad, but he's not on Instagram or Facebook or anywhere."

I nodded, sipped my coffee. "He offered me a job."

She stopped chewing long enough to stare at me. "Seriously?"

I shrugged.

Her plump, pink lips pulled into a vicious frown. "Mom. You're *not* considering that."

"Why not?

"How can you…how can you…" her voice sputtered to a stop. She sighed. "Mom! You act all tough and fun and stuff now, but deep down you're scared. You're scared of everything! This guy, Wyatt…you made him out to be this dangerous intruder. Hired a private investigator and even made me get Callie's dad to feed Riot instead of me. And now you want to go to work for him?" She shook her head.

Her words stung.

But I knew she was right. There had been times over the past eighteen months that I'd get lost in fear and depression for days. I'd worked through the tougher issues with Hazel, but I still wondered if I'd ever feel safe again. I straightened my spine and pushed my shoulders back.

This had to change. It was affecting Lilly, now.

Lilly rocked the swing with her foot.

I tore my eyes away from the swing. A memory of my mother and me on the same swing threatened to catapult me back into the blasted crime scene. I wouldn't…*couldn't*…live there anymore. I had to move on. I'd limped along as the depressed and pitied victim for almost two years, *and it had to be over.* The PTSD I struggled with was not my problem alone, anymore. It was infecting my girls, too.

"Honey, you're right. This cloud of doom, or whatever it is that hangs over us since the assault, has got to go. Life is *not* made up of bad stuff all the time."

A tear straggled down Lilly's cheek. She looked away.

I got up and sat beside her on the swing. Put my arm around her. "We are going to *change this.*" Lilly buried her face in my shoulder for a few seconds.

"Pinky swear?" She smiled.

I held up my pinky, like I'd taught them when they were little. In my minds' eye, I saw Lilly wrap her chubby pinky around mine for the first time. I blinked. *A memory! A memory of her when she was two years old!*

She gripped my pinky with her own.

"I mean it, Mom. I'm totally serious."

"Me, too, honey."

* * *

Lilly headed to school, trailing clouds of gravel dust.

My morning passed in a flurry of cleaning bathrooms, mopping floors, and shaking out rugs. Riot looked at me like I was crazy and hid under a bed. I turned the music way up on my new Smart TV. Serena had insisted I get rid of our ten-year-old monstrosity, and patiently explained every app that came with the new one. Monty had done all the technology stuff when we'd been married, and in the aftermath of trauma, divorce, and trying to figure out who I was, I hadn't cared about the simpler joys of life, but now I was going to care about every freakin' joy of life out there, and furthermore, I was going to buy new stuff. A lot of it. Stuff that didn't have memories attached that put me over the edge.

I heard my cell from the laundry room and dove for it on the couch in the den. Mom. "Hey!"

"Hi, honey. You sound out of breath. Is everything okay?"

"I'm okay."

"Are you sure? Do you have a headache, or have you had any—"

"I'm *okay*," I insisted, cutting her off. I thought about my stake-in-the-sand decision earlier. My mother had also been traumatized, and not only by what had happened to me—but by the revolving door of men in her life when she was younger. "Mom, I want you to know I am cleaning my whole house. With the music up so loud I can hardly hear myself think."

Slight pause. "You must be in a good mood."

"Answer this question, Mom." I headed to my kitchen, with its huge window over the sink that allowed the sun to baste the walls in light. "Have I been in a gloom-and-doom funk for two years?"

"Oh honey, you've been through so much. The trauma has made you react in certain ways which…well, you haven't been yourself. We all know you're doing your best."

"But am I? Really? I think my mind has been…kidnapped. It's hard to… *enjoy*, y'know?"

Mom was quiet. I heard the soft snap of a lighter, an intake of breath. The clank of bracelets on her wrist.

"Thought you quit?"

"It's an e-cigarette."

"Oh. Good! Better, I mean. That's not quitting, though, right?"

"Let's get back to you." She blew out a breath. "I know what you mean. I went through a lot of years not understanding what joy was. I was so used to crisis or struggling to pay the bills, that enjoying life was not an option. My whole existence was *survival*. I think that mentality sucks the life out of you."

"Or surviving a brain injury and losing your memory. That sucked the life out of *me*. I think I turned a corner this morning. I made a decision not to be a victim anymore. "

"Do you think it's as easy as that?"

"I think the mind is a powerful thing."

"I have been waiting for you to…I don't know, let go? Relax a little? There is…was…an *atmosphere* around you. It's like, hunky-dory on the outside, but I could tell…"

"Tell what?"

"Stress. Anxiety. Fear."

I frowned. "First Lilly, Now you."

"You asked."

"I'm done. I *am*, Mom."

* * *

Later, I put chicken breasts in my crockpot to use for homemade taco soup and ran outside to check another item off my to-do list—mow the yard. When that was done, I was so tired and sweaty I needed a shower before I had my afternoon cup of tea and waited for Lilly to get home from school. I could not believe how much I'd gotten accomplished. Had I been wallowing in self-pity and fear so long that I'd let...everything go? How long? When had all that captured me?

STOP.

"You're learning, Olivia," I reassured myself. Like the bright flicker of a new flame, the spiral might start, but it didn't have to go anywhere. I had the power to stop it. A little prick of jubilation danced inside me. Maybe I'd seen the last of my old friend, Oblivion. Maybe I'd never need him again.

Then my phone ID told me Hannah was calling. My eyebrows drew together. Just because I felt jubilant didn't mean the hard stuff would evaporate.

"Hey."

"Hey."

An awkward silence lingered.

"Spit it out, Hannah," I said, my voice curt.

"I'm being careful."

"I know you are, Hannah. I appreciate it. I forgive you, okay? Don't worry. I won't hold it against you. He's a mess."

"Well, that's one way to put it."

We laughed.

Still awkward.

After a few beats, she picked up the thread. "He's devious, isn't he?"

I smiled. "I think you know the answer to that question."

"I want to get ahead of this, Olivia. Can you help? I have the tiny start of an idea. My concern is for you and the girls."

My composure cracked. A little moan bubbled up and out.

"What?"

"I'm so *tired* of this! The bastard thinks he can pin me up against a wall and pound me to death...*again*. Only this time, through you!"

"I looked up the information on sociopaths. He definitely hits all the signposts, don't you think?" Hannah asked, calmly.

"Hazel says so."

"And all of us know what Hazel says is the gospel," she quipped, quoting my mother.

I smiled. "Yes, it is," I joked. "She would be so against this idea—"

"She doesn't need to know. We have to do *something*, Olivia. He hasn't gotten better in prison—not that I knew him very well when he wasn't—but there's this darkness around him. Like...he's harder, maybe? I guess that environment can do that to a person."

"Monty looks like he's embraced the life."

She was quiet.

"*You* know," I said, testily. "You've seen him. He's all muscled up, he walks around like a prize bull, and the guards look the other way. I've only been to see him once, but even that small space of time told me a lot."

"How are the girls doing? Do they miss him?"

I took a few seconds to think how to answer. "Serena is living the good life in college in Richmond. Since Mom is there now, she has family and that has helped. But...she's angry. She's handling it the opposite of Lilly. Lilly gives him all the slack in the world and hopes he'll be rehabilitated. She prays for him every day. It breaks my heart because I don't think there's hope, but who knows? It only takes one person..." my voice trailed away. Did I really think there might be hope for Monty? Even after Hannah told me he had it out for me after all this time?

"I don't think he's worth it," Hannah said.

"I never knew *my* dad," I murmured. "So here I am, confronted by the same type of situation. Do I take them to visit him on a regular basis? Lilly seems to need to see him. Do I suggest Serena visit, even though she's un-daughtered herself?"

"That's a tough one, Olivia."

"How are you, anyway?" I asked. "Did you know this divorce thing you're going through...was happening?"

She sighed. "I was minding my own business, complaining about our marriage to the group with every breath, and he popped up with a divorce all on his own. Surprise! No wonder we were bored. He wasn't even trying, and I was settling for nothing. I guess one of us had to do it."

"So sorry, Hannah."

We were quiet.

Hannah broke the silence, her voice brisk. "That's enough of that. We both have new lives staring us in the face. What are we going to do about yours? I'm offering my help, and I'm willing to go undercover."

I laughed.

Chapter Twenty-Seven

"Nothing makes the enemy upset more than seeing a woman who was severely bruised, rising and shining bright, because no matter how much the enemy tries to prove a point, a powerful woman will always prove him wrong."
~Gift Gugu Mona

Finksburg, Maryland, was probably one of the last places in the United States that an undercover cop could go unnoticed, I thought as I looked at the somber-looking men in black suits that bookended the flower arrangements around the casket.

Hannah, dressed in a frilly, black dress that set off her blonde hair, sat with Callie and me in the middle of the right-hand section of the auditorium seating in the new funeral home tucked beside the Food Lion in Finksburg, Westminster's kissing cousin. The parking lot was jammed with trucks of every flavor, from duallies to extended-beds to quad cabs. People in funeral attire plodded toward the double doors at a snail's pace, pausing to discuss the deceased every few minutes.

Earl was the talk of the town.

My mind flipped to Wyatt. I knew for a fact that Earl had represented most of the farmers in Carroll County, and many of the families. All of that business was now Wyatt's for the taking. What timing.

I frowned. Paranoia was becoming a habit and I didn't like it.

Callie leaned across Hannah and asked me if I was okay. I pulled my lips back from my teeth to indicate that I was, indeed, okay. Sherry trotted down the aisle looking back and forth between the rows. Hannah lifted her hand and fluttered her fingers. Nobody even had to get up to let Sherry into the middle of the row because Sherry was about as big around as an average index finger, and slid past all the knees with no problem.

"What have I missed?" she stage-whispered.

The big organ droned a melancholy Bach dirge. Hannah leaned across Callie. "Nothing. Guests are still being seated."

We stared in solemn silence at the casket at the front of the room. Earl had been laid out in his Sunday best, a boutonniere stapled onto his lapel.

"He looks good, don't you think?" Callie cocked her head. Her lips curved in a sad smile.

I nodded. Not an empty seat in the place. Earl would be proud. When I saw the person entering through the back entrance, my breath caught in my throat.

"Look!" Sherry's voice soared through the space. Soon, every head turned toward the entrance at the back of the large room. "Isn't that your..."

I frowned. "He's not *my* detective!"

The tall, striking, man leaned into our row. "Room for one more?" His smile sparkled bright white all over us. Hannah nearly fainted. She'd never met Hunter before. But she'd heard so much about him that she'd become a virtual fan.

Why was he here? "Sure. We can move over," I said.

Callie and Hannah scooted, leaving a Hunter-sized space right beside me. I gave them a fierce look as he slid in beside me.

I glared at him. "You couldn't give me a little hint about this?"

He shrugged. "Well, you know...bomb and all...plus all signs point to a homicide. Called for a secret bolstering of the troops."

"Great," I muttered, wishing I hadn't asked.

One of the community pastors took the podium and began a scriptural exhortation about a life well-lived and the joys of eternity. All the while, video of Earl ran in the background on a life-sized screen. Tears slipped from my eyes, and I bent in half to pull a tissue from the box of Kleenex tucked under the seating at discreet intervals. Hunter, stoic, looked straight ahead, his gaze bouncing back and forth between the dark-suited men and the speaker. After an interminable amount of testimonies to Earl's character by family and community members, the service ended. Hannah, Callie, Sherry, and I, trailed by Hunter; gathered in a tight knot outside on the grass.

"Are we attending the burial?" Sherry asked, with a glance at the darkening sky.

I shook my head.

"Better if she doesn't," Hunter murmured.

"Right," Sherry responded, eyes wide. She gave Callie and Hannah a look, and the three of them drifted away, leaving me alone with him.

So...*not* necessary, ladies, I thought. Why on earth did it seem like everyone...wanted to throw us together? As if we hadn't been through enough.

"How you doin'?" he asked.

"There's no chance this is related to me," I muttered.

He stared at his shoes. Shifted his weight side to side with his hands in his pockets. Looked around the area at the lush foliage, rolling hills. "Nice scenery. Any idea where the burial will be? It wasn't listed in the obit."

"Why?" I snapped.

"Research. Olivia, this doesn't feel like a coincidence. You don't have to go. But I do."

"I'm not."

"Okay. I'll drop by the house later."

I thought about that. Would that be a good idea? I frowned at him. He smiled back, as if he could hear my thoughts. His look told me I had no choice.

* * *

Thoughts of Earl plagued me on the drive home. Would I forever see him as a bleeding-out corpse lying in green shag? I shook my head, but it was no use. The graphic images would take a while to dissipate.

I tried to ignore the nagging thoughts about the form with my name on it in Earl's trash. I knew it was significant, but I wasn't going to offer it up to anyone just yet. Besides, removing evidence is a crime. And, as a dismal sidebar...once again, I was in the news.

My editor must be going crazy with joy. This turn of events would increase my notoriety, and if I ever got the darn book written, sales would rocket.

I pounded a fist on the steering wheel as I turned into my lane. *Our* lane. Whatever.

I forced myself to answer the questions Hazel had encouraged me to ask myself during traumatic times. What is my takeaway from this experience? Where is the silver lining? Focus on that, not the darkness, and remember, trouble is temporary. It comes to pass, not to last.

Maybe so, I silently told Hazel, but I seemed to be the exception.

The silver lining was that I had been prevented from taking the job with Earl, which might have resulted in my own trip to the castle in the sky. Plus, now I was free to consider Wyatt's offer. "The takeaway experience," I whispered to myself as I drove, "has shown me that I insert myself because I want to know. Yes, I try to avoid knowing, but...I *have* to know. I feel guilty not giving Earl's death more hand-wringing time, but...wasn't it a good thing to be objective in situations like this?

I didn't know.

And besides, someone was waving at me. Who was that?

Wyatt?

What was he doing in my yard?

I stepped out of my car and approached.

"You're home," he said with a smile.

"And you're here," I responded, curt; walking through the gate. "Did you need something?"

His face crumpled in on itself. "You said you wanted me to show you how to work the video system. I knocked on your door, and you weren't home... so I was leaving, and...there you were."

Mollified, I invited him to sit on the porch. He chose the swing, and I, as usual, sat on my loveseat. The plump cushions whooshed as I sat. "Sorry for being…irritated. A funeral brings out the worst in me, I guess."

Wyatt took in my outfit. My sedate, navy suit and two-inch heels. The somber expression. "Yeah, I didn't know that was today. Stressful."

"The whole community showed up. He'd been around a long time." I crossed my arms and pretended to be nonchalant about his response. But I wasn't.

"The attorney-client relationship can become close. They'll miss him, I'm sure. Sorry I didn't get to meet him."

I looked at him under hooded eyes. Wyatt had responded without a hint of an underlying agenda, at least in my opinion. Maybe my suspicions weren't warranted.

"He was a great guy. Crusty, hard to take at first, but a wonderful man when you got to know him."

The only sound for the next few minutes was the creaking of the bolts that attached the chain to the ceiling, and the chirping of birds—the equivalent of a few moments of silence for the dearly departed. I looked at my watch. "I need to…I don't know, process. Can we do the video thing another time?"

"Sure," he said, rising. "But I thought you might want to know I noticed your daughter—Lilly, right?—on camera around three a.m. last night."

My eyebrows shot into my hairline. "Are you sure?"

He described her car.

"Can I see the footage?"

"Your laptop handy?"

He followed me into my kitchen and sat at the breakfast bar. I shoved my laptop under his nose and watched over his shoulder as he logged in and connected me to the security system as co-admin, in under eight minutes.

"You're good at this stuff, I see."

He shrugged. Pulled up the video from early morning. I watched as a family of deer gracefully walked through the space, twin fawns dancing and spinning in the dark; raccoons bustled by, too. The lane and trees lay dormant under the camera's lens for long seconds, until Lilly's white Mazda zoomed by.

"Pause it!" I cried, my hand on my throat.

Wyatt paused and zoomed in. Lilly's face was in clear view. Her face looked blotchy. Even I could tell she was stoned or high. I stared at the image for long seconds.

"I can see you had no idea," he murmured, mercifully un-zooming the image.

"I...I..." my hands shook. The words died on my tongue. Was there no end to the stupefying drama that was my life?

* * *

After Wyatt left, I stared at the four squares of footage open on my laptop screen; different perspectives of the same event, and now I had the power to surveil our lane. I was beginning to feel fear climb up my back. Again.

I shook off goosebumps, then fixed myself a cup of tea. After settling on the porch, I focused on how to handle the way-past-curfew situation with Lilly. Maybe she had a good explanation, like a friend in trouble, or...or... stop the *excuses*. I had to be clear-headed enough to listen for the truth, and accept that she might be acting out in ways I don't recognize. After all, it's not like I remembered our history. Not yet, anyway.

The tea was hot and sweet and creamy. I'd treated myself to my best teapot and teacup and saucer, and spent a few seconds admiring them. My mind went back to Earl's funeral. The stress of the investigators watching, and Hunter beside me, tense and alert. I wondered how the burial went and supposed I'd hear from Hunter later. So much for holding him at arm's length... were we destined to be thrown together...if not for love, for... what, to catch the bad guys?

I hadn't had a chance to tell him that Wyatt had offered me a job and that his suggestion in Richmond had been prophetic. He'd get a kick out of that. I picked up a cherry scone and munched, contemplating the twists and turns of my life.

Bad idea.

I jammed the rest of the scone in my mouth and drowned it with tea.

Lilly's car roared up the drive. She parked, pulled her backpack over one shoulder, and stared at her phone all the way through the gate, down the sidewalk.

As she walked up the steps, she seemed to wake up.

"Oh! Hi, Mom!" Her smile gleamed.

I was about to wipe that smile right off her face.

In deceptive calm, I set my teacup in its saucer. "Can we chat a minute, honey?"

Lilly grunted. "Here we go."

"Have a good day?"

She'd worn a paisley headband today, swiping her curls back so that her beautiful, youthful, freckled face was on full display. Her burnt-umber eyes, though, revealed a sleepless night.

"Took a history test. Think I did okay. Drama rehearsal tonight, so I'm gonna grab a quick bite then head back out."

In a flash of inspiration, I realized all these drama rehearsals could be a cover. Pondering how to frame my remarks, my mother's voice floated through my mind...*be compassionate, anger rarely has a positive outcome.*

With a sigh, I switched gears. "Turns out Wyatt Harp is quite the good neighbor."

Her forehead crinkled. "Yeah?"

"He offered to put me on his security system, so we'll both know what's going on."

Lilly put her index finger to her lips.

I could see the wheels turning. "When? Do you think that's necessary?"

I cocked my head at her. "Do you?"

She laughed, a little uncertain how to answer. "How should I know?"

Riot approached at the sound of our voices, meowed, circled once, twice, and dropped—a golden furball inside the front screen door.

"I think you know."

She stared at me, but said nothing.

"I saw your car at three in the morning. Mind telling me about that?"

She was quiet.

I was quiet, too. Seething, but quiet. I waited her out.

Her eyes darted right and left. "Look, you won't increase my allowance, so I came up with my own...um, plan."

My heart skipped a beat. "What does that mean?"

"It's okay. Dad told me it was fine."

Every antenna I possessed sprang to attention. "If it means you have to sneak out of the house at night, I doubt it's fine."

She stared at the floor, crossed her arms. Let out a frustrated sigh. "Amy's on Adderall, right? For ADD and that stuff? Well, she hates it, but her mom makes her take it, and she...she can't, anymore, so she gave it to me, and...what I get is pure profit, right?" She cleared her throat. "It's not like it's, umm...heroin or meth or something." Lilly's face hardened at my shocked expression. "All the kids do it, Mom. It's not a big deal."

"*What?!* Do you have any idea how illegal that is? Lilly! My God!"

"Last night was a...an emergency."

"What kind of emergency?" I squeaked, a hand over my eyes.

Lilly's expression darkened. "I can't tell you."

"You can and you will."

She lifted her chin. Rose from her chair, kicked Riot out of the way and went inside.

I ran inside, caught her by the elbow at the foot of the stairs. "*You,* young lady, are mistaken if you think this is over." I stuck out my palm. "Hand over everything you have, or my next call is to the police. Got it?"

"Mom! It's only Adderall! Besides, I don't have any more."

I sniffed. "And I'd believe you...why?"

She shrugged. "Search my room."

I glared at her and tightened my grip on her elbow. "That'll be a priority from now on. And by the way, the car is to school and back only. I'll check mileage, so don't try anything stupid. You need to go out for rehearsals or meetings at night, I'll give you a ride. Amy's mom and I will figure this out. This is going to stop, and you and I are going to counseling as soon as I can arrange it. Now get upstairs and do your homework. I want to see it when it's done, too." My nerves shattering, I screeched, "I don't need this right now, Lilly!"

148

Lilly jerked her arm from my grasp. "Of course not, Mom," she said, her voice like steel. "You don't *need me*, either...you don't need to come to my performances, you won't raise my allowance, you don't like my boyfriend—"

My mouth dropped open. "Is he a part of this?"

"No! For your information, he'd never approve." She dropped her eyes. "I haven't told him."

"Don't you think that should've *told you something*?" I jabbed my index finger at the staircase. "Upstairs. I want homework done before I take you to rehearsal. Do you really have rehearsal tonight? You know I can hop on the website and check."

She started to speak, but instead, put her arms across her chest and looked away. "I don't really have rehearsal," she mumbled.

"Okay. I appreciate the honesty. From now on, unless I see something on paper or online that proves you have a rehearsal or event, you're not leaving the house." I held out my hand for her keys. She fished them out of her backpack with a frown and dropped them into my hand. After making sure I noted the withering look she shot at me, she stormed to her bedroom and slammed the door, hard.

Chapter Twenty-Eight

The sky over Westminster's Main Street was the color of ash after a doused fire. As Earl's casket was lowered into the ground, a light drizzle sputtered and settled into an earnest spring rain.

Funeral procession vehicles lined Westminster's Main Street, and several onlookers gawked at the burial proceedings wrapping up behind the public library in the historic cemetery that held the remains of many prominent Carroll County families. Now, the slot beside Earl's beloved wife would be filled, and his date of birth and death added to the Sorenson family headstone.

After the conclusion of the ceremony, Hunter turned up the collar of his sport coat and hunched his shoulders against the rain as he walked toward his vehicle. Two investigators in black suits flanked him, the three of them making a nice show of force with their erect posture and watchful expressions.

A man holding an umbrella approached. The investigators threw wary glances at one another.

Hunter rocked on his feet, his hands in the pockets of his slacks, waiting.

A smile split the man's anxious face as he approached. "Hi. Sorry to bother you at this…uh, unfortunate time, but I was wondering if you'd…well, if you'd discovered what happened."

Hunter smiled a thin smile. "And your interest would be because…?"

"I am in the process of moving to Glyndon. I've moved my business here, and I—"

"What's your business, sir?"

"I'm sorry, name's Wyatt. Wyatt Harp."

Hunter grimaced. "The attorney?"

Wyatt gave him a look. "Yeah. How'd you know that?"

"You happen to be a neighbor of Olivia Callahan?"

Awareness dawned on Wyatt's face. "You're him, aren't you? The famous Detective Faraday? The one who took down the husband in the Mercy's Miracle case?"

"Not famous. Not anything. Doing my job."

The two other men relaxed, smiles teasing their lips.

Wyatt cleared his throat. "You can understand why I'm interested, Detective. She told me strange things had been happening, and that she found," he pointed toward the cemetery, "the deceased when she went to interview for a job. I've given her the ability to use my outdoor videocam as a protective measure, and I'm concerned, of course, that this man's death might not only affect her, but me and my business in the process. So I'm wondering what my, I don't know…my mindset should be."

Hunter scrutinized Wyatt. Took in the curly, brown hair, not unlike his own, the intense, blue eyes, and the intelligence behind them. Annoyed, he realized that he was thinking about how well Olivia knew this guy instead of the homicide case.

"Why don't I give you a call tomorrow?" Hunter said. "Understand though, investigation is ongoing. I can't tell you much. But maybe I can give you a feel for how it's going."

Wyatt reached into his pocket. "Here's my contact information. Talk then, Detective." He left.

One of the investigators punched Hunter in the arm, smiling. "Looks like you got a lot goin' on, Detective."

"Shut up," Hunter grumbled, sticking Wyatt's card in his sport coat pocket.

Chapter Twenty-Nine

"We rise by lifting others."
~Robert Ingersoll

After the traditional clink of wine glasses across the table, I waited for the collective shoes to drop. Callie, Hannah, and Sherry had called me after I had my meltdown with Lilly, and insisted on meeting at Eddie's Bistro. I felt ambushed, for some reason.

Callie leaned in toward me and threaded her fingers together. "How you doin', hon?"

"Fine." My fingers tapped random rhythms on the table.

They all started talking at once.

Hannah's voice rose above the others. "I've told them about what I want to do. You know. The plan."

My eyebrows pulled together. "Why?"

"Because we want to collaborate." Sherry declared.

"If there's any collaborating to be done..." I stage-whispered, "...keep your voices down!" I threw out my arm. "Look around! These are normal families having nice dinners. Let's not poison them with all the crap that I'm going through, okay?"

"Sorry," Callie whispered. "We're all...well, we're excited, I think."

"I wouldn't call it excited..." Hannah said, stroking her chin, and staring at the ceiling. Hannah always insisted on the correct word. "I'd call it... anticipatory."

"Okay," Sherry muttered. "I want to help. I don't care what you call it...

Olivia, Hannah and...well all of us—"

"Except *me*," I blurted.

Sherry nodded. "Except you...yeah. We're working on a plan to get Monty to back off."

I sighed.

"Now wait," Callie said. "This is good." Her ponytail whipped around as she searched our faces. "Isn't it? Don't you guys think it's good?"

"I'm trying to psych myself." Hannah cleared her throat. "Listen, I've repented, okay?" She tossed back a long drink of wine. "Call this making amends. Still...I'm nervous."

I closed my eyes, exasperated. "Tell me what this is, Hannah."

"What if...well, you know he still trusts me, right? So what if I, under the guise of still caring," she made a little gagging motion with her finger pointed into her mouth, "I brought him another Visa pre-paid..."

My eyebrows rose. "You've been taking him—"

She rolled her eyes. "Yeah, we're past that now, okay? But what if in a generous fit of 'mercy' I take him several of the damn cards, but they're expired, or...even better, if I buy them and remove the cash from the card. So when he tries to use them...well, he told me the guards sell phones in there, did you know that? Anyway—"

"Still trying to get past that you took him money like that."

She shrugged. "A woman in a bad marriage who is being ignored will jump through a lot of hoops for a guy who makes her feel like a woman again. Not proud of it, okay? You know darn well the Monty is hard to resist. It started out as a good deed, Olivia. We've talked about this. But he *is* a scumbag, and I have no problem giving it right back to him." Hannah plopped her arms across her chest and looked away.

"The scumbag part?" I asked with a smile.

"Whatever. I can be a scumbag, too."

"We noticed," Sherry said, her voice droll.

Callie tried to cover up her hoot of laughter with her hand.

Hannah's brows knit together. "Can we move past this, please?"

I gave Hannah a look. "We're trying. But you're going to have to put up with the jokes."

Callie giggled.

"Done?" Hannah asked, with an 'I know I deserve this, but stop' stare.

I grinned at Callie and Sherry. "Are we done, girls?"

"Yep," Callie said, raising her empty wine glass. I poured her more from the two bottles we'd ordered. The others followed suit. We were already down to the last half of the second bottle. The waiter trotted over, a big smile on his face for the ladies at his table that were sure to give him a huge, wine-besotted tip. We chose another bottle, this time a Chardonnay instead of a Cab.

I hoped my stomach would survive.

"I got a call," Hannah muttered after the waiter opened the second bottle and poured. "Monty got caught with a hidden cell phone. I don't even know if I can get in there now."

I frowned. "How do you know that?"

"He has this guard that's a fan. He's the guy that makes people fall all over him, remember? Buddy—that's his name—calls me for him. Said he doesn't know yet if visiting privileges are reinstated." After a beat, she continued. "Monty told me he's in so tight with this Buddy guy that when I visit, I kind of…get a pass when I walk through the scanning thing."

"Don't you think we can use this guard?" Callie said absently, stroking the stem of her wine glass. "If Monty can do it, you better believe that we… or one of us…can, too." She raised her eyebrows up and down.

"What is this, a sitcom? This is real life, ladies," I muttered.

They went quiet a few beats. I drank more wine. The white was refreshing after all the heavier red. I reached for prosciutto, Gruyere cheese, and Brazil nuts from the charcuterie.

"He knows me," Hannah whispered. "The guards—by the way, they are called 'corrections officers' in real life—are used to seeing me. I should be the one. I've been thinking about the worst thing that could happen to a guy in prison."

"Which is?"

"The hole."

CHAPTER TWENTY-NINE

"That's a real thing?" Sherry squeaked.

Callie frowned. "That's just in the movies."

Hannah shook her head. "It's what they call it. They isolate them in the cell if they have a major or repeated infraction. Monty told me. No interaction with other inmates. Outside, alone, for an hour a day. Other than that, he's in a cell in the basement. Think about it. Cockroaches, rats..." She shuddered. "Monty has been trying so hard, all this time, to be a model prisoner. He's proud of it, too. Convinced it'll affect his term." She shrugged. "So this phone thing happened. Now we can kind of...assist? Coerce? In making sure other incidents happen, too. It'll be solitary, for sure."

She took a breath and fisted her napkin. "*Buddy* is key. We can do our own scam with these pre-paids, right? I've read about what happens. They convince people to put money on the card, and give them the serial number. That way, they can get the money and be gone before the person knows what happens. Anyway, that's what I can use as an excuse when Monty throws a fit. But in reality, I'll use the card to put the money back where it came from."

Sherry added, "Buddy will get tired of getting pre-paids that don't work. That's all the loyalty that's between them, right? So he'll get mad, and Monty won't have protection?" Her eyes lit up. "He'll have an *enemy.*"

"I don't know," I said, shaking my head.

Callie's voice was urgent. "What you *know* is that the guy tried to kill your detective!"

"He's not *my* detective," I murmured, out of habit.

"And he could be trying to put a bomb on your car too, Olivia. Forget about that?"

Callie's expression was serious. I sucked in a breath.

She leaned back in her chair. "We need to...immobilize him. Like... strategize. This is what it is, hon. Nobody knows for sure what he's got going on in there. He's a charmer. And a...what, a sociopath, right? No telling what he's capable of."

A dull roar settled inside my head. I reached for my glass. Sherry leaned over and put her hand on top of my glass. "You've had enough for tonight, don't you think?"

I picked up my water glass instead.

In a burst of clarity, I knew what to do.

I dug into my purse. My fingers touched the folded piece of paper I'd studied and prayed over since I'd stumbled across Earl's body. I placed it on the table, opened it, and flattened the folds until the page lay flat.

Hannah reached out, and with two fingertips, pulled it across the table. The three of them squeezed in to look at it. One by one, I watched their mouths drop.

"But I thought you said you never visited him until, um…you know…that visit to find out more about your younger days or whatever."

Hannah studied me with calm curiosity. "Must be important. It looks like you've worn it out."

Sherry reached for more wine.

"I found this in the wastebasket at the same time I…" my voice faltered. "…found Earl," I finished in a whisper.

Callie put her hands over her mouth, her ponytail swishing in agitation. Looked at the visitor's form again. "Olivia," she gasped. "That's not your signature, is it?"

I shook my head. "Nope."

"Someone wants to send you a message," Hannah said.

"I wonder who," I quipped.

Sherry's mouth dropped open again. "Monty?"

"All I could think about was that I would be implicated, so I took it. Tampering with evidence is a big no-no. Let's keep this between us, okay?"

Hannah slapped her hand in the middle of the table, palm-down, and left it there. Callie followed, placing her hand on top. Then Sherry. Next, mine crowned the pile, my eyes growing wetter by the second.

God, I loved these women.

Chapter Thirty

"Rise and rise again until lambs become lions."
~Robin Hood

An angry, brilliant, sun woke me the next morning.
I glared at the window and rolled over.
I couldn't remember how I got home.
My head felt like it was caught in a vice grip. Did I have a hangover? My mind flew to the meeting with the girls at Ed's. Yep. I most certainly had a hangover. With a sigh, I pushed off the comforter and pulled down the blinds, wondering why the sun was so damn hot in April. Or was it March? A knock sounded at my bedroom door. I heard a muffled, "Mom? Mom? Are you okay? I have to leave for school."

I hopped up and ran to the door, which I had, for some godforsaken reason, locked last night.

"Morning, honey. Sorry. Don't know why I locked the door." I swept my hair off my forehead and made a mental note to schedule a haircut. "You get breakfast?"

She nodded, hiked her backpack on her shoulder. "You were hilarious when you got home yesterday, Mom. Do you remember?"

I put my hand on my head and looked at her with one eye. "That won't be happening again anytime soon."

Lilly reached out and tousled my bed hair. "It's okay. See ya after school… wait! I have rehearsal."

I squinted at her. "And you're still grounded. Come straight home after school. I'll give you a ride to rehearsal, and pick you up. Your car is grounded, too. Got it?"

"How 'bout I ride with Amy?"

I tilted my head and gave her a look.

"Fine. Whatever," she muttered. Gave me a quick hug. "Have a good day, Mom."

"I will. You too. Love you."

I trudged into my ensuite bath and turned on the shower. From my bedroom window, I watched Lilly's Mazda as she raced down the drive to school. My head pounded. I groped the wall for the medicine cabinet, opened it, found the ibuprofen, and tossed back four.

After a long, hot shower, the headache had lessened and I felt somewhat more human. Now...my mission was to find my phone, which in the aftermath of the Wine & Whine meeting I'd managed to misplace, and hoped like heck it was in the house. Or the car. Or anywhere except lost or broken.

I threw on a T-shirt that said 'Be Kind' and a pair of jeans. Slipped on my favorite tennis shoes which should've gone in the trash months ago, but I was having trouble giving them up. I rummaged through the bedclothes, the bathroom, and downstairs in the den, the kitchen, the patio. No phone.

I fixed a hurried breakfast and gulped it down. On my way to the garage, I frowned. Why had I left the garage open? I strode to my car and looked inside. There! Bright and shiny in its pink, glittery case on the driver's seat of my car. I thrust out my arm in relief, but at the last minute, I drew back.

I'd almost forgotten to check for an IED. Had I even *locked* the car last night? I'd gotten in the habit of locking it since the bomb unit had scared the heck out of me, but...I'd left the garage door open, and had been so looped I probably hadn't even thought about locking the car. I stood on tiptoe to try to see the locks without opening the doors. Unlocked.

Huh.

Had I left the phone on my seat like that? I usually put it in a niche in the driver's side armrest. I tried to remember the last time I'd had my phone in my hand.

It was hopeless.

I carefully lowered myself to the garage floor and stared underneath my car for evidence of electrical wires or weird things that shouldn't be there, as the police had taught me. I could swear I saw a few mysterious tail-like things. Could be my imagination. However...

I bolted from the garage. My thoughts raced. No phone, no landline, and I needed to call 911. Lilly's phone was with Lilly. I could go over to Callie's but I knew she'd be gone to one of her endless volunteer meetings this morning. Wyatt! Was he still here? And the videocam! Holding my stomach, still queasy from too much wine, I ran inside the house. The red, screen door banged shut behind me. Riot lifted his head in irritation.

"Hurry, hurry," I told the laptop as it booted up and found the four security screens. I wonder if Wyatt had checked it yet. The computer said it was nine o'clock in the morning. I didn't know if he was an early or late riser. "C'mon!"

The screens settled into view, and I scrolled through, to the middle of the night, slowing the scroll in the early morning hours. "What if they parked somewhere else and walked? They could've avoided the camera." I muttered to myself. My hand moved the mouse cautiously and slow through the dark frames. Once into the morning frames, I let out my breath in relief. No car visible on the lane but Wyatt's, and it had been headed toward town. But I still needed my phone. Dare I take the chance to reach into the car?

No.

I bit a fingernail. Was Hunter still in town? How the heck would I get in touch? "It's so stupid to be helpless without a cell phone! Get a landline!" I told myself. I walked all the way to Wyatt's place and knocked on the unvarnished door that led to his unfinished-but-getting-there house and office space. After a bit, steps arrived, and the door cracked open. A sleepy-eyed Wyatt peered at me. "You could've called first," he said, as the door slowly inched itself open. With a glance down and a quick apology, he swept the door back.

"Long story," I said. "Can I use your phone?"

I now knew he slept in the nude. I *so* did not need to know that.

"Hold on." He closed the door. When the door opened again, a lone arm stuck out with the phone. Once I had it, he banged the door shut.

I didn't care if I'd interrupted his sleep, I cared about making sure a freaking bomb didn't blow up in my garage. I punched in Hunter's number.

"Yep," Hunter answered.

"Are you still here?"

Pause. "Morning to you, too."

"*Are you?*" I demanded.

"Yeah. Why?"

"Y'know that bomb thing? Well, I think I may have one. I'm using Wyatt's phone to call, because my phone's in my *unlocked* car, and I can't remember if I locked it and...I left my garage door open because I...after the funeral we had a thing...anyway, I think I saw...I'm not sure...the bomb cops? They taught me about this stuff, and I almost forgot to check my car before—maybe I need to call them? Hunter, I don't know what to—"

"OLIVIA. Hold up. I'll be there in fifteen, okay?"

He ended the call. I stared at Wyatt's phone. Started back to his front door to return it.

His door opened.

Dressed now, he held out a steaming mug. "Coffee?" He smiled.

* * *

We watched for Hunter on Wyatt's security system, sipping coffee and being awkward.

I looked around at how he'd been living the last few weeks. "So, they're getting it done, huh?"

"If I keep on top of them, they are," he said, his tone dry. "I paid extra for them to stay on the job ten hours instead of eight, and gave them a finish date." He shrugged. "It's going okay, I guess."

"Have you shut down your Harrisburg office?"

He shook his head. "Not yet. I may sub-let. Haven't decided yet. My lease is up in a couple of weeks, but I've got a good relationship with the building owner, and he's flexible."

"I could never own my own business."

He smiled. "You could. It's not that tough."

Seconds ticked by.

"You going to work for me?" he asked.

I gave him an appraising look. The question was unexpected, but in the back of my mind…I'd already accepted. "I am, actually."

His only reaction was a slight grin.

My eyes sliced down my lane, toward the garage, where an explosion could be imminent.

The fingernail I'd been chewing on was surrounded by angry, red, flesh, now. With a frown, I jammed my hands under my legs.

"I want to gear up right away, if that works for you. That's why I've had them working on the office part first." He pointed to a hallway. "I've chosen the carpeting, chairs, desk and desk chair. Electricians are almost done, too. Maybe you can help with décor?"

Surprising tears sprang to my eyes. "Sure," I managed, remembering when I'd walked into Earl's office and mentally redecorated the waiting room. "I can do that," I said, my voice soft.

Wyatt's office was spacious, and the walls were mostly sheet rocked and ready to paint. Rolls of carpet in a utilitarian color had been stacked along the edges of the floor. Further down a wide, long hallway, studs marked out different room spaces for the living area.

"You sleeping on that?" I pointed to the couch, blankets, and sheets that had been thrown on one of the chairs.

He rubbed the back of his neck. "The sacrificial life of the entrepreneur," he quipped.

We heard the sound of tires on gravel. *Hunter.* With an apologetic glance at Wyatt, I ran outside, waving my arms like an irate traffic cop. Wyatt followed me as far as the porch. "Thanks, Wyatt," I called, and got into Hunter's car. We zipped up the lane in is his Richmond PD-issued rental.

When I looked back, Wyatt still stood there, watching.

* * *

I stayed on my front porch as Hunter examined my car. Every time he disappeared from view, I shuddered. When I'd handed over my keys, I'd wondered...if he'd come out alive. I clenched my hands into fists and squeezed my eyes shut. *Stop, Olivia, stop the spiral! It's probably nothing!* Forcing myself to turn away, I stalked to the swing, which did not allow me to see the garage unless I turned around. With my foot, I rocked the swing so high the ceiling hinges might give way, but at least I wasn't watching the garage anymore.

After five minutes of no news, I couldn't stand waiting.

"Hunter!" I screeched. "Are you okay!" I jumped from the swing, started down the steps.

No response. But no explosions, either.

I ran toward the garage. "Hunter!"

"Stay back!" he yelled from inside the garage.

I spun on my heel and ran back to the porch, clutching the banister. My breathing sped up. "What are you doing?" I yelled.

The rear hatch popped up, which meant he was *inside* the Discovery. I dropped my face into my hands. Long minutes later, I peered between my fingers at the sound of door slams and the hatch closing.

"All clear!" he yelled. He trotted toward the porch. "Not a bomb mechanism in sight, I think you're good."

I held my breath, still watching the garage. He walked up the stairs, put his hands on my shoulders, and gently shook them. "Olivia. You're good."

Blowing out a breath, I muttered, "What took you so long?"

Chapter Thirty-One

"Olivia's going to check with her new boss," Sophie said, walking around her condo and talking to her fiancé with her phone pinned to her ear. "She's pretty paranoid about the bomb scares, and...I don't know how much more she can take. She's supposed to start this week, but I thought I'd try to scoop up Olivia and the girls and have a last-minute getaway, before she's working full-time. I'm waiting for her to give me the green light."

"Sounds good," Gray said.

Sophie watched the world unfold outside her large, living room window. "I found a resort on the other side of the Island, where she won't be fighting off nightmares about that last night when Monty was taken down by an army of cops. That was a rough night for her."

"I remember," Gray murmured. "He's still incarcerated, correct?"

"You bet he is," Sophie said, her voice defiant. "I hope he never sees the light of day."

Gray was quiet.

Sophie pursed her lips. "I hope he hasn't ruined Hilton Head for her. She loves it so. Or used to."

"Serena going, too?"

"I've invited her but...she seems a little...oh, I don't know. Reluctant. Closed off. I'm not sure she'll go. Did I tell you she's decided to take a semester off?"

Voices blurted in the background. An alarm rang. "Sweetie, I'm sorry, I have to go," Gray said. "Catch you later." The call ended.

"You always have to go," Sophie muttered.

Her phone vibrated and lit up. Olivia.

"What'd your new boss say?" she asked, without preamble.

"It's a go. Wyatt's fine with putting off my start date a week. Let's do it!"

"I'm thinking the Sonesta, mid-Island. It's in Shipyard."

"Wait. Don't you want to go back to—"

"Of course not! And neither do you. Why would you?"

Olivia was quiet a few beats. "You're right."

"Honey, I know you've come a long way, but...certain memories have a way of hanging on for years and making you miserable."

Olivia groaned in protest. "I said you were right, Mom! I don't need one of your—"

"The Bible says to throw off every weight that hinders our progress. Throwing off does involve smart decisions, honey."

"Got it," Olivia muttered.

"Have you and...well, when you were married to Monty, did you and the girls ever stay there?"

"It'll be fine, Mom," Olivia said, her voice flat.

A short silence stretched between them.

"I've done it again, haven't I?" Sophie asked.

"I'm not in the best mood, Mom. It'll be good to go to a new place. I... it's strange, but it's been so long now, it seems like another life. Maybe my mind turned off that pain? I don't know." She paused. "I won't go back to The Boat House, where I met Niles, that's for sure."

Sophie laughed. "No problem at all, since there are, what, 300 restaurants on the Island? We'll stay closer to the south end this time."

"When are you thinking, Mom? Lilly will be so excited."

"This Saturday? Stay a week?"

"We can do that. I'm *so* ready for a break from my life."

"Sure, but are you sure about Lilly? What about school?"

"What do you mean, what about Lilly? Of course, she'll go."

"She's growing up, honey. She may have her own thoughts about the trip."

Olivia didn't respond for a few seconds. "Maybe so. However, she's grounded right now, so I think she'll be excited to go anywhere."

"What happened this time?"

"You don't want to know, Mom."

"Probably not," Sophie agreed. "Is…well, did she learn from it?"

"We talked it out."

"Good."

A silence lingered.

Olivia sighed. "*Not* going to share details, Mom. Is Gray going?"

"No. Just us girls."

"That sounds perfect. Lilly can do her schoolwork remotely. Shouldn't be an issue."

Sophie smiled. "I'll book it."

* * *

Hilton Head Island – mid-April

Sophie ran her fingers through her hair and threw off the white comforter, smiling at Lilly's light snoring in the other bed. After a quick shower, she did her makeup, put on a floaty, tie-dyed skirt and a white, scoop-neck, cotton top.

Slipping her feet into sandals, she added turquoise earrings and matching bead bracelets. She tossed her hair into a loose bun, let tendrils trail, and pinned it in place.

"There," she told her reflection, her hands on her hips. "At least *that's* done."

"Grammy?" a plaintive voice floated through the room.

Sophie smiled. "In here, Lilly."

Forty-five minutes later, she'd managed to shepherd herself, Lilly, Olivia, and Serena into the dining room of the ground-floor restaurant for breakfast.

The girls tossed around Hilton Head vacation memories, laughing and teasing each other. Sophie watched her daughter wince, and look away. Sophie continued to take bites of her omelet, thinking that memories for

Olivia were much different than those of her daughters. She'd spent her whole marriage believing the family dynamic had been healthy and normal, and now she was discovering it had been broken from day one. It couldn't be easy for Olivia to listen to their rehash of the 'good times.'

"Let's vote. Beach or shopping today?"

Serena looked up from her omelet. "I vote shopping."

Olivia's gaze riveted on her oldest daughter. "So, you got a job on this little…college time-out thing of yours?"

"Uh, not yet."

Lilly's glance bounced around the table. "She's looking, Mom."

"Breakfast good?" Sophie interjected.

Sophie felt helpless. Had they even talked through the semester off yet? Back away, she cautioned herself. She was unsure how to parent a forty-something adult. How much loving concern was too much? How much was too little? Did Olivia even want her advice anymore?

"Mom! Things are fine! I have lots of options," Serena protested. "Seriously, Mom, chill."

Olivia leaned across the table. "Chill? When this break of yours is costing us your scholarship? That's not coming back, you know."

Serena pouted. "You've got lots of money now."

Olivia drew her chin into her neck as if she'd been punched.

"Well, you do! With that book thing, and Dad's money."

"*Dad's* money?" Olivia asked, her voice barely above a whisper.

Sophie flinched.

Lilly pushed her plate away and stared at her lap. Olivia glared at Serena.

"What? When did you ever have a job, Mom? Tell me. When?"

"Serena," Sophie warned.

"It's okay, Mom," Olivia said. "I got it."

Serena shot a steely-eyed look at her mom.

"What's the problem, Serena?" Olivia asked. "This semester break thing came out of nowhere, and now you think I…what, *owe* you a college education after you've thrown away a full scholarship? Are you kidding me? Where is this coming from?"

Serena pushed her long, blonde hair over her shoulders. She folded her arms across her chest, a gentle motion with an initial glance at her stomach instead of the slash-and-burn anger that typified one of Serena's pushbacks.

Olivia's lips parted. She put her hand on her chest.

Sophie closed her eyes and put her hands over her mouth. Lilly leaned back in her chair, confused.

"Serena...?" Olivia asked.

The stony stare melted. Tears spurted.

"I couldn't do it, Mom."

Olivia gasped. Sophie heard her own sharp intake of breath.

"Do what?" Olivia whispered.

Lilly put her fingers over her mouth.

"Get an abortion."

A stunned silence draped the table. The friendly waitress approached and asked how everything was, but noticed the somber mood and slipped away.

Olivia reached for Serena's hand and held tight.

Serena's face crumpled in despair. Tears streamed down her cheeks. "I couldn't. I couldn't do it. I tried, Mom. I went to a clinic and everything. But..."

"What happened, Serena? I've tried so hard—haven't I—? To help you make good decisions? I-I..."Olivia closed her eyes. Her chin dropped to her chest. "I'm so sorry you've gone through this alone," she whispered. "Why didn't you tell me? Don't you trust me? I would've supported whatever you wanted to do."

The anguish in Olivia's voice made Sophie's heart break. She supposed having children gave them permission to break a parent's heart...over and over again, but should finding peace be this hard for her only daughter?

"It's not your fault, Mom," Serena said to Olivia. "But like Grammy says, sometimes hard things happen and God uses it for good." She shrugged. "The only thing I knew, was that when I was in that clinic, I could not make myself do it. I tried, but the feeling was so strong not to go ahead with it." She put her hand on her stomach and smiled slightly. "I think I can feel the baby, now," she said. "I know it's not the right time for a pregnancy, and I don't think the father...well, I haven't told him, Mom."

Olivia slid a little lower in her seat.

"It...we didn't..." Serena sighed. "We didn't really have a relationship. And, Mom, I didn't want you to worry. You've been through so much, and I couldn't add to that."

Sophie tucked her arms around her chest. Cleared her throat. "Honey," she said gently to Olivia, "you need time to process. I'm here. I'll help any way I can. And Serena, I am so glad that you've told us, and grateful that Gray and I are here to support you. You've had a really difficult few months, haven't you, honey?"

Serena nodded and looked away.

"We are all here for you," Sophie reassured her.

"I know," she whispered. "And I almost didn't come, Grammy. I didn't want to ruin everything."

Sophie looked around the table at the three precious, confused, blindsided faces, and since she was going to be the matriarch of now, *four generations,* she figured she might as well be the one to set the tone.

She pointed at Serena's half-full plate of eggs and hash browns. "Serena, all I can say, is you'd better clean that plate! You're eating for two now."

They would treat this pregnancy as a celebration. Period. It would take effort, but this family had weathered a zillion storms, what was one more?

Her mind flew back forty years, when she'd been faced with a similar decision.

* * *

The strong hands circled her neck. "You're not going anywhere, Sophie, until we get this thing settled." His voice sounded thick and gravelly. Sinister. Sophie's mind raced through several stages of despair. The 1980 Corvette's tiny interior didn't allow her enough room to defend herself. She gauged the distance between the car and her condo—fifty feet of sidewalk. Her porch light shone like a beacon of safety in the night.

"It's okay, Tony. I'm...uh, calmer now. I had trouble getting used to the idea."

She forced her face into a contemplative stare at the floor mats. "Abortion is...well, I never thought of it before. Now that you put it like that, it might be for the best."

The hands, one grotesquely large from years of handball, the other smaller, but still strong, turned her loose. Sophie took in a lungful of air and tried not to look terrified. "You're right, baby. It isn't the best time to have a child." Concealing her disgust, she planted her soft lips on his tense, mean ones. As their lips touched, her right hand crept up the passenger side door until it found the door handle. Locked. Stifling the urge to vomit, she pulled him to herself with her left arm and intensified the kiss. She reached back with her free arm, felt for the door's button, and managed to unlock the car. Breathing hard, as if she were becoming excited, she interrupted the kiss and felt for his belt buckle with her left hand while her right inched across the leather, past the strip of silver detailing, until she could firmly, imperceptibly, grasp the handle.

He sighed. His body relaxed.

Like a lightning strike, Sophie jerked open the passenger door and bolted from the car. Her shoes pounded the sidewalk. Frantic seconds later, she reached her front door. Sophie fumbled with her keys. Tony bounded from the Corvette. "Come back here!" he yelled, in hot pursuit. The few seconds of surprise had been enough to give her the advantage. She unlocked the door with shaking fingers, jerked it open, then swung around and slammed the deadbolt home. One heartbeat later, his fist broke the glass in the top half of the door. His arm pushed through and groped for the doorknob, but the shards of glass, held in place by mullions, prevented him from reaching the lock. "I'm calling the cops!" Sophie screamed as she scrambled to the upper level.

She pulled the landline to the balcony and put the phone to her ear. Tony stood beside his car, glaring at her up on her second-floor balcony and cradling his lacerated hand. When Tony heard her begging the 911 operator to send the police, he jumped in the car and stomped the accelerator. Sophie disintegrated into a sobbing wreck and collapsed on the balcony, her hand on her expanding belly. Abortion had never been an option for her. Not once.

The memory evaporated. She wondered if Serena had had to stare down the same ultimatum.

She leaned forward on one elbow and put her chin in her palm. "Who wants seconds? It's an all-you-can-eat buffet, so load up! Let's make this a great day."

* * *

A few days of beach time, dolphin tours, kayaking, and tons of fresh seafood had refreshed everyone, Sophie thought, with a smile. They had two days left, before heading back. She'd put the finishing touches on her morning lipstick when the first drops of rain spattered the window. Her cell rang.

"Girl trip getting old yet?" Gray teased his wife. "Miss me?"

"Always," Sophie assured him. "Clouding up today, so it's—"

"A shopping day," Gray interjected. "I know all about women and vacations."

"Oh, yeah?"

"Listen, I called to talk, but also, I read an interesting article on brain trauma and recovery."

Sophie's pulse rate sped up. "Bottom-line it, honey. They're all about to get in the car, and I'm not even ready yet. I'm putting you on speaker..."

"Okay, we've talked about this—that Olivia has done so well thus far, is fantastic, but...we still have to be vigilant. Have you noticed any problems speaking coherent sentences? Any noticeable lack of coordination? Problems hearing? I know her memory is coming back, and that's a good sign."

"You're scaring me." Sophie planted dollops of foundation on her cheeks and picked up a blending brush.

He took a deep breath. "How do you feel about Olivia's decision-making abilities?"

She applied mascara. "Full disclosure... I *have* noticed risk-taking behaviors."

"In what way?"

"Did I tell you she went to visit Monty in prison? Without telling anyone?"

Gray was quiet.

"And now...she's told me those girlfriends of hers are cooking up a plan.

170

She thinks Monty is...planting bombs and...I don't know. I can't...even think about it." her voice trailed away.

"I know Olivia has been through hell and back and I'm glad she's...doing better. But issues like these are what I'm talking about. Another concern in a healing brain is the patient's ability to reason, and also, in certain cases, their sense of reality is compromised."

Sophie stopped applying blush and sucked in a breath. "You mean she could be making this up?"

"Maybe. If she is, though...it's very real to her."

"So what do I do? How would I know she's in trouble or...gosh, we're going *shopping*. Does it extend to...overspending, lack of control stuff? Should I be...oh, Gray...I don't want to be her watchdog! We're having such a great..." She paused.

"Great what?"

"Time," she finished, lamely. *Except for that part about Serena's surprise pregnancy. Still reeling from that.*

"The truth is, sweetie...we've all been getting a little too comfortable. I suggest you jot down things that are concerning. It's about time for her CT and exam again, so that would be helpful insight. I wanted you to be aware."

"Thanks a lot," she muttered. "Couldn't this have waited 'til we got home?"

"I *did* give you a few days." Gray sounded hurt.

Pause. "True. Okay, I take it back."

"I thought it was good timing, with you guys being together for a while."

"I get it."

They ended the call. Sophie checked her face one last time, then ran out to the parking lot to join the girls.

171

Chapter Thirty-Two

Panic seized Monty by the throat.

He couldn't shake it.

He wanted out of the tiny cell.

Now.

He walked to the sliver of window. "Hey! Heyyyyyy!!"

Catcalls reverberated down the corridor. "Shut up, asshole!" "We still tryin' to sleep, man!" The men's voices blended together in a mixture of hatred, despair, and hopelessness.

Monty felt like he would go mad.

He flopped onto the cursed four-inch topper that passed for a mattress and stared at the ceiling. Chills shook his body. Could he have a fever? He put the back of his hand to his forehead, like Olivia used to. Like a bombshell, regret hit hard.

"What in God's name have I done?" he whispered, pleading with God. But God was silent.

Tap-tap-tap.

Monty jerked up from the bed and squinted at the window. *Buddy.* He launched himself off the bed. "Officer Bromage! Please! Can I get a minute… out of this goddam cell? Don't I have a visitor scheduled today? What day is it? Isn't it Hannah's day?"

Dawn snuck through the small windows from the floor above, signaling the start of another ten hours of slave labor, dirty jokes, and suspicion. Male snoring provided a dismal backdrop to the unscheduled visit from Officer Bromage.

With a glance up and down the corridor, Buddy unlocked Monty's cell and entered.

"Against the wall, prisoner," Buddy roared, loud enough for all to hear.

Monty gave him a look and backed up to the wall.

Buddy dropped his voice. "You woulda gotten to see Hannah today, but, y'know, those 'items' she passes to me had no cash on them this time. I gotta know that our agreement goes both ways. Otherwise, no deal. I'm in here for a cell check, it's on the books, so we good?"

"More than good," Monty muttered.

"You want favors, get this straightened out. You got me?"

"I'm begging you. Just a few minutes outside this cell. I'm going nuts in here."

Buddy scrutinized the bags under Monty's eyes. The way his clothes hung loose, now, after being confined as punishment for the phone.

"I don't know, man." Buddy shook his head. "We'll see."

Monty felt a spark of hope.

In a blur of motion, Buddy ripped the Taser from his belt. Monty yelped in shock and made gurgling sounds as the probes hit him in the chest. Gaping at Buddy, he collapsed to the floor, his body quivering and out of control. Buddy pulled Monty out of sight, and grinning, jerked the barbed probes out of Monty's chest, rewound the wires, and replaced the Taser in his holster. "Monty Callahan, you were warned," he called out. He squatted beside Monty's shuddering form. "Screw with me again, and I'll see you go in the hole for a long time, Callahan. I need you to make good on those cash cards." With a stern, just-a-CO-doing-his-job look for the hallway videocam, he left.

Monty's thoughts rattled around in his head with unrelenting purpose. It didn't matter, anymore, what it took, he had to get out. He could die in here. When he rose from the cold, bleach-scented linoleum half an hour later, his legs were rubber. His chest where the Taser barbs had been viciously pulled out, was still bleeding. He inched his body onto the cot into as prone a position as possible and wondered if his 'model prisoner' status was gone forever.

And what the hell was up with Hannah? Why had she brought dummy cards?

Monty snickered in sudden relief. "Who needs you, Bromage?"

He had a backup plan. Casey, the new CO. had warmed up. It would be easy to get him to call Hannah and put things right.

Chapter Thirty-Three

"Go on and try to tear me down! I will be rising from the ground."
~Demi Lovato

I stared at what I'd written, and threw my journal to the floor. Then I launched my pen as well. "WHY is Monty still controlling my life?" I shouted into the air. A couple of chickadees exploded from the bird feeder, and Riot scampered away from his spot inside the door. "And why," I cried, shaking a fist at the heavens, "don't I have more of my memory back?"

The fresh growth of spring had thickened the undergrowth all along the lane, and I couldn't even see Wyatt's place, now, or his spotlight or the lights he'd installed on the building. The trailing Wisteria had budded out along one side of my porch, weaving itself through the white lattice panel. I walked over and touched the buds with my fingertips. I thought about how long it took them to bloom. Had I bloomed? Would I ever bloom?

I needed to look up 'bloom'.

I smiled at the thought of how much Hazel would love this exposition. I would tell her at our next appointment—the one I hadn't scheduled yet. The one I may never schedule because…well, *because*. How much therapy is too much? How much is too little? She'd taught me critical thinking… playing out the story…*that to remember the past is to find the solution to the present.* Okay. Fine. But Hazel, I told her silently, trying to remember the past is putting me over the edge.

I felt pretty good about my first week on the job. At least I'd survived. No panic attacks, only…normal stuff. Stuff I handled.

I walked out into my yard and stood in the middle with arms spread and stared up, through the boughs and branches into a brushed, scrubbed blue sky, and asked God to restore the memories that would help me go forward. Amen. He could probably do it faster than therapy.

Like a cattle prod, my cell rang with my new boss' ringtone. I'd assigned him a text tone called 'Apex' as a nod to my personal growth. My forehead screwed into a knot. Why would he be calling?

Oh, yeah. You have a *job* now.

My hands flew to my mouth. Didn't we have a meeting or something?

I raced back to the porch, up the stairs, and scooped up my cell. Checked my calendar.

"No, no, no, no…" I exhaled, as I punched his number to call him back. Ten o'clock Saturday morning. Org meeting.

"You coming in?" he asked, his voice on the testy side.

"I'm so sorry! I've had a lot on my mind…and, can you wait until, I mean, I have on shorts, for God's sake, let me get ready and get down there. Listen, I—"

"Olivia, I'm fine. Come in shorts, it's not formal. I need to know if how I've set things up is okay. The laptop and monitors have been delivered, and more office supplies. And a couple of chairs. I need to know where you want everything. Also, I'm trying to get out of here, if you don't mind kind of…babysitting in the meantime. The PA office needs me for a few days. I'll probably head up there tomorrow…so this is all the time I have to help you move stuff around."

"I'll be there in two shakes, honest."

I changed and raced to my new office. I still had trouble believing I had a job, but like it or not, this was happening. Wyatt opened the door with a smile. "That was fast."

"Promise, it was an honest oversight."

"I understand," he said. "I don't usually make people work Saturdays. This won't take long."

I followed him inside and frowned at the chaos. "Wow."

He sighed. "I'm a decent lawyer, but not the best organizer. Where do you want stuff?"

I put my hands on my hips and considered. It took me about fifteen minutes to have furniture placed, supplies in the cabinets. Wyatt was stunned.

"One thing about me...I'm a bit OCD about being organized."

"I can see that," Wyatt said in appreciation. "I like it."

Walking around the space, I mentally added accent pieces, side tables, and art. Faux plants. "How long are you gone? Are you going to be available if I have questions?"

Wyatt lifted his head from staring at his cell. "Yeah. Text me. And...the paralegal courses are paid for." He fiddled with his phone. "Sent you the sign-ons. Next week there shouldn't be much to do, so you can get started on that stuff. Otherwise, uhhh..." he pulled out his wallet. Extended a credit card. "This is the card for this office. Charge any more office furnishings okay?" He gave me a generous budget to work with. "Oh, and also..." he smiled, walked to one of the cabinets, and took out a small box. "Had these made."

I grinned when I opened the box.

I had to admit, it felt validating to see my name on a business card for the first time. Just *my* name. No 'Mrs.' attached. An important personal milestone.

"Thanks, Wyatt."

"No problem. I'll check in next week and see how you're doing. So that's it. You can have your weekend back."

I took my business cards with me to the car. Wyatt took his suitcase to his car, locked the office, and told me to enjoy the week.

Chapter Thirty-Four

"Yes, you will rise from the ashes, but the burning comes first. For this part, darling, you must be brave."
~Kalen Dion

"I've been on my own a couple of weeks," I told Hannah. I squinted at my laptop screen in frustration, trying to make sense of an online tort law class. "I have one more week of babysitting. He's mostly been out of town wrapping up things in his other office."

"So how's it going?"

"I have a lot of time to work on these online classes since he's been gone longer than expected," I said, with a whiff of distaste. "He's got his social media up, so we've had a few calls. I've set up appointments for him when he gets back."

"You don't sound thrilled about the paralegal courses."

"Well, he's paying for it, so…."

"You can change your mind. Anyway, I called to let you know I can't get in to see Monty. I guess it has to do with the phone infraction."

I was quiet a few seconds. "But…you've made friends with that guard, right? What's he say?"

"Buddy. What's great though…is our evil plan—"

"YOUR evil plan…"

"Right. Operation Monty is *working*. He has no guard buddies to protect him, or…or do errands for him. Buddy always calls with subtle hints about what I 'might' be able to bring in the next time, but now, I don't even hear from him. So... yesterday I poked around."

I could hear the smile in her voice. Her dramatic pauses drove me crazy. "Hannah! Keep going."

She giggled. Hannah was one of the very few women I knew that actually... giggled. "Buddy acted like he didn't know what I was talking about. Monty must've overstepped, and Buddy has to...oh, I don't know...cover his ass? I'm positive Buddy is not on board anymore."

I chewed my lower lip. "I need more than that. Can't you get him to...I don't know...pretend you're impressed with what he's done or something? So he'll admit to stuff? The pen they found at the explosion site, the bomb on Hunter's car... the insurance company totaled his car, y'know. That could've *been him* blown up! And if Monty had anything to do with Earl's death, I...I..." my voice trailed off.

"He swears he doesn't," Hannah said.

I thought about all the bomb searches I'd performed in my own garage. It didn't take an actual bomb...just the threat of one...to keep a person on edge for life. I wondered how Hunter dealt with it, because I sure as heck wasn't dealing well. "What do you know about a guy named Dudley?" I asked her.

"Duds? Why?"

I gasped. "So he's mentioned him."

"Mentioned who? How would you know a friend of his in prison?"

Trying to talk myself out of full-on panic, I considered what it meant to lay it out for Hannah. After all, she'd visited my ex, developed more than a passing friendship, and now...should I trust her?

"Dudley. I repeated. "You think Duds could be short for Dudley?"

"It is. He called him by his full name once. They're friends."

I lay a hand across my face. "I bet."

Slight pause. "What does that mean, Olivia?"

"Can you maybe get to this 'Duds' guy?"

"Why?"

"Dudley was married to my mom when I was a little girl."

Hannah went silent.

"Monty says I didn't like him. Why, I don't know."

"Wow," she breathed. "He's been inside for twenty years, I think."

I grunted. "So it's two of them now, plotting to get even or whatever."

"Olivia. They're in jail cells, for God's sake."

"You told me they can do all *kinds* of stuff from prison. Plus, it's minimum security."

"Umhmm," Hannah agreed, "...and Monty can talk the birds off the trees."

"Not this tree!" I declared.

* * *

The next day, a perfect, clear morning, I walked to Wyatt's office instead of driving. It was that kind of day. The sky was the color of the Caribbean. A light breeze swept across my skin.

Lilly's white Mazda shot past me. I waved. The end of the school semester was only a few weeks away. One more year, and she'd be graduating from high school and off to the university. I hadn't even had time to think about empty nesting yet, and here I was. Maybe that was why I was re-inventing myself.

Oh, wait. Nope.

The last two years had already taken care of that.

I chuckled.

I strode the final few steps to the pavement, then walked up the steps to the door. Put my keys into the lock. Wyatt was due back soon, and at least I'd have some company.

My cell vibrated. I pulled it from my back pocket. Before I could say anything, Mom cried out my name. A chill zipped up my back.

"Olivia," Mom said, her voice throbbing with emotion. "You need to come. It's Serena." She took a deep breath. "She's lost the baby."

Chapter Thirty-Five

Hunter Faraday stretched both arms out across the back of the bench, waiting for Shiloh to stride out of the Richmond Police Station. He grinned. He'd chosen the first bench she'd see when she opened the doors.

Shiloh had been working undercover the last few weeks. Richmond was the perp's next target, he'd heard. The Savannah investigative unit couldn't and wouldn't give him details about Shi's whereabouts, but he'd found a way to finagle information from admin about this meeting.

So here he sat, on a sunny Richmond morning, waiting for her to appear from behind the double-glass doors.

Like a blast of ocean breeze, Shiloh powered through the doors, burst from the building, jogged down the stairs, and strode toward the parking lot, her blonde hair flapping around her face like a windswept photo shoot. She didn't even see him until she almost tripped over the foot he stuck out. Brow furrowed in consternation, she hopped aside, then turned to accost the jerk attached to the foot.

When she realized it was Hunter, she laughed. "Hey! What are you doing here?" She plopped down beside him. Hunter pulled her in for a hug.

"Waitin' for you."

Shiloh eyed him. "How'd you know I'd be here?"

"Can't reveal my sources."

She patted his knee. "I always *could* count on you to bring the clichés. Got time for coffee?"

"What do you think?" he said, propelling her across the street to his

181

favorite greasy spoon. They sat in a booth with cracked red leather seating, a Formica tabletop, and an overworked waitress.

The waitress put two mugs of hot coffee on the table, and barked, "Black, right?"

Shiloh laughed. "How could you know that?"

"Honey, all cops look alike to me, and they all drink black coffee." With that, she ripped out her ticket book. "What else."

It was more threat than question. "Pie," Hunter said.

"I'll have what he's having," Shiloh added.

The waitress left.

"She must know your pie of choice," Shiloh whispered.

He leaned in. "Same as yours," he murmured.

"Is it?" She sipped her coffee and stared at him with a look he interpreted as flirting.

A silence stretched. Hunter's cell beeped with a text. He stared at it for long seconds.

"What is it?"

Hunter tucked the cell inside his sport coat jacket. "A friend of mine. Her daughter miscarried. She's at Mercy."

She made a little dipping motion with her hand. "Go on if you need to."

Conflict flitted across his features. "I'll go later."

They chatted for an hour, made promises to get together that both of them knew they wouldn't keep, and ended the coffee date with a friend-hug. Disappointed, Hunter went back to his bench outside the station, sat, and thought about what kinds of feelings would compel Olivia to let him know her daughter's situation. He also thought about why her text robbed him of the ability to focus on Shiloh—a serious marital option. With a grunt of frustration, he walked to his brand new Jeep Wrangler 4-Door Hardtop the insurance company had provided, courtesy of the jerk who'd tried to blow him up.

Minutes later Hunter floored it all the way to Mercy Hospital—where one fateful afternoon two years ago, he'd met a Jane Doe that would linger in his mind...well, forever.

* * *

When Hunter knocked on the hospital room door, it was Sophie who opened it. Gray smiled at him from one of the chairs beside Serena's bed.

"Hey, doc," he whispered to Gray, as he gave Sophie a quick hug. "So sorry," he told her.

She nodded, swiping at her cheeks. "It was pretty early," she murmured. "That's such a terrible thing to say, isn't it?"

Hunter shook his head. "Terrible, any way you look at it. What can I do? Is Olivia...well, I assume she's on her way."

Sophie smiled. "She went down the hall, she'll be back in a—"

A sliver of light slashed the floor as Olivia entered. Her gaze landed on Hunter. "Hey," she whispered.

Gray rose. "Here, take my chair. I'll check in later. She's going to be okay." He hugged his wife and left. Sophie waved her hands at Olivia and Hunter.

"You two go chat in the hall, okay? She needs her rest. I'll come get you if she wakes up."

They walked to a waiting room and sat in a couple of tan, fake-leather armchairs while a TV droned in the background. An older man was asleep in a chair across the room, and a young mom watched, listless and lost, as her toddlers played at the toy table.

"This can't be easy for you," Hunter whispered, watching Olivia thread and unthread her fingers.

Her smile was thin. "It's not. But Serena's okay."

"I didn't even know she was pregnant."

Olivia's shoulders drooped. "Nobody did. We made a quick run to Hilton Head and had a chance to...catch up." She glanced at him and smiled.

He'd forgotten how much he loved her smile.

"She told us while we were there, and it was like...shattering...but we were figuring it out. She was happy, moving in with Gray and Mom for a while, and..."

Hunter put a hand on her shoulder. Olivia took a shuddering breath.

"It happened on Mom's front porch. When Serena saw the blood pouring out of her, she slipped on the stairs and cracked her nose on the concrete. Mom called an ambulance. It was so unexpected. No symptoms, a little cramping, she said, but Hunter, how could she even know the signs? She's still a baby herself."

"I'm so sorry."

Olivia stared at him with mournful eyes. It took all Hunter's strength not to kiss her. Self-conscious, he took his hand off her shoulder. "She's young. It won't take long for her to be up and around."

Olivia nodded. "I know, I know." But these things affect a young woman. When you start to bond with that little life…it's hard, y'know? To let go."

Looking at her, he thought *big lives, too.* "Yeah, it is."

She sniffed, wiped her cheeks. Smiled. "Nice of you to come. I…I…" she looked away. "I thought you'd want to know," she finished, quietly.

Hunter was quiet a few beats, realizing that his concern for Olivia and her family was real and solid. Lasting. The kind of stuff they make movies about. "Olivia, I…"

She waited, her forehead furrowing.

"What?"

Hunter blew out a breath. *Get hold of yourself, dude.* "How long are you in town?"

She shrugged. "Wyatt gave me as long as I need."

He blinked. "Wyatt? So you did go to work for the guy?"

"I thought you knew."

"Well…" he stumbled around, searching for words. Why was he bothered by this? "I think I knew he made an offer but I didn't hear anything else."

"I'm rattling around in that big Maryland farmhouse by myself. Lilly's gone a lot, and I've about had enough of therapy. Plus, I can do a lot of his stuff remote, and I live right up the lane, so…no-brainer."

Hunter nodded. "Congrats."

Olivia ran a hand through her hair. "You mind if we check on her?"

He slapped his knees and stood. "Let's do it."

Chapter Thirty-Six

"My sun sets to rise again."
~Elizabeth Barrett Browning

L ater, after Hunter went back to work and the setting sun's rays stretched through the half-closed blinds across the floor of Serena's hospital room, I mused about my own stay in this hospital—the fifth-floor room that had been my sanctuary for five weeks as I recovered from the brain injury that almost stole my life. Gray—at that time I'd known him as Dr. Sturgis, my lifeline and neurosurgeon—told me I was a miracle, and it stuck. The Mercy's Miracle story spread like wildfire, the media picked it up, and now my so-called adoring public waited for the full story. At least that's what my editor kept telling me.

I held my hands out and stared at them. Turned them palms-up, then down.

"How are you doing, honey?" Mom whispered, from the other side of Serena's bed.

I pursed my lips and kept my eyes on my hands. "Wondering when these slow, stumbling fingers can get back to my manuscript."

Mom smiled. "You never were much of a fast keyboardist. Accurate, though."

"The book keeps getting longer."

Mom gave me a look. "How much of present-day stuff are you going to include?"

"My agent is hoping all of it, since my life seems to be developing into your basic soap opera." I frowned. "Mom, I don't *want* my own reality show."

She laughed.

Serena stirred. I hopped out of my chair and sat on the bed. "Hey, sweet girl! How are you?" I brushed her hair away from her face. "You've been out all day. I got here this morning."

"I can't believe it, Mom." Tears swelled in her eyes.

I put my arms around her. "I'm so sorry, honey."

"I know it would've been hard, but...I...was okay with that." Her sorrow broke my heart. She pushed herself into a sitting position and leaned back on the pillows. "I already loved him, Mom."

"Did you get to see the baby?"

"I was further along than we thought. Three months." I reached out and held her for a long time.

When the sobs subsided, I went into the hospital room's bathroom...a replica of the one in which I'd relearned how to take a shower—found a washcloth, and wet it. Returned to Serena and gently wiped her face. Then the oh-so-familiar squish of soft-soled nurse's shoes reached me. I smiled. The door to Serena's room squealed open. I yelped in delight.

Sarah!

"Well, here y'all are in here, without a word to me and I had to hear it through the grapevine." Sarah shook her head and made tut-tut sounds. "No way to treat a medical professional, honey. No way, a'tall." She stepped over to the bed. Serena squinted at her.

"Oh yeah! You were Mom's nurse." She murmured, then clutched her stomach and lay back. Sarah fluffed the pillows, took a quick look at her tummy, and checked her chart.

Serena shook her head, shifted on the bed. "Hurts."

Sarah stroked her hair. "I know, honey. We'll fix that. You need another day, that's all, and you should be feelin' better. I'll get you somethin.'"

I watched with a smile as Sarah took care of my baby...like she'd taken care of me as a comatose Jane Doe when I'd been brought in by the EMT team. No one even knew if I'd make it, yet I'd clung to her optimism from the beginning. Before I could move or speak, and before anyone realized I could hear, Sarah was the one who believed I'd pull through. She'd become like a surrogate mom to me when I couldn't remember my own.

With Serena settled, Sarah turned her bright, blue eyes on me, her hands on her hips. "You better get on in here for a hug, Olivia Callahan!"

I laughed. She'd straightened her hair and lost a few pounds, but she still smelled of oranges and sunshine, and her hug felt like home.

"It's so good to see you, Olivia. You look fine, girl!"

I tucked my curly hair behind my ears. "Serena and Mom live in Richmond now," I murmured.

"Oh! Well, that's real nice. I did hear that Dr. Sturgis married your mama. So your girl here, she live here too? College, maybe?"

I nodded. "She dropped out, well…" I cocked my head toward her.

"Understandable," Sarah said. "She'll be okay." She turned toward Serena, who stared out the window at the encroaching twilight.

Sarah marched over to Serena and took her hands. "Sophie, you wanna join in here?"

Mom jumped up. "Isn't this against hospital policies, or whatever?"

Sarah made a rude noise. "Let 'em fire me. I pray for my patients all the time." She cocked her head at me. "Worked for Olivia, didn't it?"

I grinned and joined the circle. "Sure did."

We joined hands across the bed. Sarah's prayer was like a sweet, sweet, symphony.

* * *

Mom and I walked, slow and thoughtful, to her car after visiting hours. The night felt warm. Velvety. A thousand stars dotted the sky, glowing brighter as we walked away from the building, through the landscaped grounds, toward the parking lot.

"Wait," I said, as we passed manicured hedges beside the winding sidewalk. The area outside the ER had been turned into a garden of sorts, with winding paths and greenery and benches at intermittent points. A stirring fluttered in my chest. I pointed at a spot of grass. "I think that's where I was dumped."

Mom wrapped her arms around herself and stared in horror. "I don't even...want to know," she whispered. "I can't stand the thought of it."

"You go on ahead, Mom. Do you mind if I...stay here a minute and see if I remember anything?"

"Olivia," Mom protested, her expression doubtful.

"Why don't you go sit over there?" I pointed to a bench fifty yards away. "Then if I flame out with a memory episode, you can rescue me."

"You can't be serious!" she exclaimed, stricken.

"Kidding, Mom. Kidding! I'll only be a few minutes. I feel like I need to do this, okay?"

She walked to the bench, muttering under her breath.

"Love you, Mom!" I called after her. She wiggled a hand above her head without turning.

I shouldn't be so cavalier, but hey—my assault, my brain injury. I thought how different I must seem to my family. I'd emerged from the coma a complete opposite of the person I'd once been, which in my opinion—after hundreds of hours of therapy—was a big, freaking, *positive.*

"Sit down and try to remember, I reprimanded myself. "And seriously, you *could* have one of those seizures, so be careful."

I folded my arms across my chest, looked around to make sure no one was going to walk by and chat me up, then scrutinized every bush, every sidewalk direction, every light source, every tree.

"So..." I whispered to myself, pointing at the parking lot nearby. "...that's where he parked. It was still dark when they found me." I scanned the area. Busy at nine p.m. They'd found me barely breathing, lying in the shrubs, around three a.m. That means I'd been carried...and, of course! If anyone had been around at that hour, it would have looked like a husband carrying a sick wife inside. They would've bought his story that he'd not had the time to wait for an ambulance, or whatever he'd have said. However, he'd laid me behind the bushes. If anyone had seen, there would've been questions about that, right? I watched people hurrying back and forth, lost in their own little worlds, thinking about disease and suffering and surgeries...yeah, it was plausible that no one would've seen. Especially at that hour of the morning.

Lights from the ER strobed the small patch of ground at regular intervals. I guess it was some consolation that he'd tried to make sure I'd be discovered. I'd never thought the man who had assaulted me was a hardened criminal, but I'd never know, because he was killed before he could be questioned. Who knows what Niles would've exposed? Monty may not have been able to talk his way into a minimum-security prison, that's for sure. I craned my neck to find Mom. She remained glued to her bench, erect and watchful.

I smiled. My mother was a gift.

My eyelids fluttered, and within seconds, images swirled into focus.

I...I'm moving? My neck is on something warm. Am I being carried? Yes. My head is laying on an arm. A man is carrying me. He...he's breathing hard! Why? Has he been carrying me a while? His breath stinks.

Dark. So dark! I can't see. My limbs won't work. Where is he going? Did I get sick? Pass out? I Nausea worked its way up my throat, and though I tried, I couldn't lift my head to vomit. It lay in my throat like a clog in a drain. And the movement kept on...and on. When the motion stopped, the pressure on my head lessened. Why? He removed something from my head. I smelled copper. The smell of pennies. Blood. Blood? What happened? I tried to speak, tried to open my eyes, but nothing worked. Then, a slow, slow, descent. The feel of a breeze on my face. The sensation of light, then...oh, it felt so good not to move. Prickly. My cheek. The smell...grass. Earth. A yard? Why? A hand stroked my cheek. Who was he? What happened? What was he saying? I strained to hear. I could...make...out... "So sorry, Olivia. ...find you, they will..." His hands pressed a hard object into mine and closed my hand around it. Then I was alone.

Like the final revolutions of a carousel ride, the images swirled...slower and slower...and faded away. I clutched the fixed reality of the slats of the bench underneath me, and waited out the hangover to follow, hoping I wouldn't end up in a dead faint on the ground. Mom would go ballistic and freak out the entire ER.

Control your breaths. In. Out. In. Out. Don't hyperventilate. Did you have enough water today? Yes. Yes, I did, I reminded myself. What was my checklist? Remember! Remember *now!*

Hazel's voice funneled itself into my ears. *Olivia. Breathe. Think strength. Think hope. Think life. That's it, picture yourself standing. Good. Now stand. You are not a victim. You are a strong woman with confidence and a purpose. Breathe. Good. You have nothing to fear. Fear is the enemy. It is a coward. You can defeat it with your thoughts. With your words. Good. Good girl.*

Slowly, I stood. Inch by inch. I would not let these memories crush me, I'd use them to defeat my enemy, fear.

Mom appeared beside me, her arms by her sides. She was a veteran with these things and knew better than to interfere. If I was going to have a life, I had to get a grip and defeat the seizures. Mine had lingered, but with therapy, we'd discovered they were more psychological than physiological. So we'd come up with a response plan to move through and past them. Like now.

I jabbed a celebratory fist in the air. "Yeah!" I yelled, then coughed, because...Richmond's spring pollen.

Mom's forehead beetled. "Remember anything?"

"One more piece of the puzzle fell into place."

She folded her arms across her chest, waiting.

"I want to poke around the dump site." I lifted a leg and hopped across a row of boxwoods that had been shaped into sharp-edged rectangles. The ER's bright lights threw cautious shadows. I felt around in the grass. Squatted down in the center, glanced at Mom. I was compelled to lay down, but my mother might have had a heart attack.

I had this intuition thing going on now. I could...*feel* things. Whatever had happened to my brain, it had all kinds of bells and whistles now. I still hadn't fully realized the extent of the aftermath of my injuries, and how the brain can rewire itself in limitless ways.

"Mom! Turn around. For five minutes, don't look, okay?"

With a sigh of exasperation, she turned her back to me.

I lay on my back with my arms spread out, staring into the sky.

Took a deep breath.

"Olivia? You ok?"

I frowned. "Mom! Trying to concentrate, here."

"Can I turn around?"

"NO."

Silence.

I folded my arms across my chest.

Nothing.

I flipped onto my side, into a fetal position.

Bingo.

Flashes of light fell across my face. People's voices rose and fell. A whisper in my ear. A man's voice. A kind voice. It sent warmth through me. The clatter of wheels on grass and several shouted instructions as I was secured, slid onto a flat surface, lifted and rushed away.

Chills raced down my arms. My breathing sped up.

"Olivia? I'm turning around."

I didn't argue with her. She ran over to me and squatted down. "What on earth are you doing?"

I pushed up onto one arm. "This had to be the spot."

She groaned. "Did you need to know that?"

I gave her a stern look. *"Almost two years,* Mom. And I'm still having trouble remembering things, or even believing what I remember is real." I stamped my feet on the ground. "This is real! I know it." Popping over to hands and knees, I scanned the area around me. "Mom, can you turn on your phone flashlight?"

Resigned, she flicked it on. "What are you doing?"

"I'm looking for it," I muttered, my palms hovering over the area like I was about to hold a séance.

"Looking for what?" Mom asked.

"Something I had in my hand."

I ran my fingers through the grass. Mom's flashlight followed them like a searchlight. I probed every blade of grass, until finally, I felt a solid edge. A rock? An old juice box? Holding my breath, I told Mom to highlight the spot. My fingers clawed the dirt. I saw a glint of gold. I dug harder. My fingers ached with the effort. A couple of people drifted by, looking at us in disapproval. Mom smiled at them, but held her flashlight steady. I sat back on my heels to take a breath.

"What is that?" Mom asked.

I shook my head. "Not sure, but it feels…" I pointed to my gut. "…right, y'know? In here."

My fingernails now a nasty mess, I continued my excavation. The earth had been packed with roots over the years, and the deeper I went, the more roots I encountered. My arms ached with the effort. I maneuvered around the roots and scooped dirt away with my hands. It was here, I knew it.

Two minutes and three ripped fingernails later, I held up a dirt-caked pendant at the end of a ball chain, like the kind that military dog tags are attached to.

"This is it!" I declared in triumph.

She frowned. "What do you think that is, honey?"

I rubbed away the caked dirt with the end of my shirt. My mouth dropped open.

Mom squinted at it. "Greek letters?"

With a disgusted shake of my head, I spit out the words. *"Monty's* college fraternity, Mom." I frowned. "I remembered something being *put into my hand.* This must've slipped out when they rushed me inside." I examined the piece. The chain was rusty, but the pendant was still in good shape. I threw an inquiring look at Mom. "Niles was trying to give me a hint, maybe, that Monty was involved? Or throw the blame on Monty for the assault?"

She clicked off her flashlight and slipped her phone back into her purse. "You better tell Hunter about this."

"I will," I said, thinking. "But why would Niles have Monty's fraternity—?"

"Didn't you tell me they went to college together?"

"That's right," I whispered. "They might've been in the same fraternity."

"Olivia…" Mom began, tentatively. "Are you positive it was Niles who left you here?"

Chapter Thirty-Seven

The final two steps of the staircase loomed like a taunt.

Hazel had to stop and take a breath before ascending to her office door. She glared at the steep staircase behind her as she clung to the banister, then up at the thunderclouds that belched lightning. Big, fat, drops of rain fell on her face. "You'd think I'd have better sense than to rent a second-story situation," she muttered and climbed the last two stairs. With a quick punch of code, she entered her office seconds before the sky opened and a hard rain hammered the bank of windows on the street-facing wall. Like a wallop from God's fist, thunder bashed the sky.

She removed the scarf she'd wound around her hair and hung it on the coat rack beside the bookcase to the left of the entrance, along with her purse, which bore the requisite matching scarf. She fixed her morning coffee and settled into the chair in the coffee nook, musing that her life, for a seventy-odd-year-old babe such as herself, was pretty darn good. Maybe she shouldn't retire yet.

Her cell rang. She sat her mug on the end table beside the armchair and walked to the coat tree to dig it from her purse. Sophie's head popped onto her screen.

The lines between her gray eyebrows rutted until they almost met in the middle. She grunted. "What."

Pause. "This is Sophie. Did you expect someone else?"

"Nope." Hazel decided she was in no mood to mince words or pretend.

Pause. "Look, I know we don't see eye-to-eye on things, but this is important, Hazel. Olivia's, well…she's had a lot on her mind and is remembering stuff, and I'm concerned. I wondered if you'd reach out."

Hazel's sigh was long. "How many times do we have to have this discussion? If Olivia wants to meet with me, she'll contact me, don't you think?"

"I don't know. She's having these…intuitions about things, and I think she needs an objective voice to balance her frame of mind. Sooner than later. I'm only calling as a heads-up. Call or don't. Your choice." Sophie ended the call.

Hazel stared at the dead phone in her hand. Perhaps she'd been too blunt. She walked to her desk and lay the cell beside her desk blotter. She tapped her fingers, thinking.

Then she called Olivia.

* * *

"Sure you don't want coffee?" Hazel asked, arranging her notebook, recorder and files before folding her hands and peering over her reading glasses at Olivia. She'd rearranged her schedule to get her in. Yes, Sophie was intrusive, but…what if Olivia had an episode, and she could've prevented it?

Olivia shook her head. "I'm good thanks." She shrugged. "I was thinking of coming in, so it was kind of confirmation for me that you called."

Yeah, with a little help with a call from your mama. Hazel busied herself with the notebook. "Where would you like to start?"

Olivia drew circles on the end table between them with her index finger. "Memories are coming fast, now." She fixed Hazel with a look. "I've read that reality is often…mixed up for brain injury patients?"

"Are you…having trouble distinguishing what is real?"

Olivia shrugged again. "I'm sick of it. Trying to figure things out. And now…" she took a breath. "You won't like this but… I re-created the scene outside Mercy Hospital."

Hazel put her pen down.

"Excuse me?"

Olivia sighed. "It's complicated. I had to go to Richmond because Serena had a miscarriage, and—"

Hazel gasped. Her hand drifted to her cheek. "Oh, no! Is she okay?"

"I was NOT there to see Hunter, just so you know. And Serena's shaken up, but physically, she is fine."

Hazel smiled. "Okay."

"Hunter came to the hospital."

"Of course he did."

Olivia put her hands in her lap and stared at them. "Isn't it odd that we're always being thrown together in crisis? What kind of foundation is that for a relationship?"

"What do you think?"

"Stop!"

Hazel laughed. "With Hunter, the obvious thing to me is that he sincerely cares. What you two would have to be sure of, however, is how you'd feel in your relationship *without* crisis. That would have to be worked out...it *is* concerning that crisis seems to be a bond. When life is devoid of crisis, what kind of people are you when you are together? That's what you'd need to find out."

Olivia rubbed her cheek and looked away.

"How has Serena's miscarriage affected *you*?"

"It's been hard," Olivia admitted. "It...well, I did think about what Monty did to me. When he told me I'd had a miscarriage, but...hadn't. I was younger than Serena when that happened."

Hazel nodded. "I wondered if it would throw you back there. How did... the father deal with the news?"

Oliva frowned. "I don't even know. She hasn't told him."

"I'm sorry," Hazel said. "Poor Serena."

"I...I'm having trouble dealing with it. I don't know what to do for her, Hazel. I'm so not good with being...I don't know, sympathetic? I never know what to say." Olivia slumped in her chair. "Mom and Gray will take good care of her, she'll get better and the sun will rise, and she'll go back to school."

"You don't think she'll want to come home?"

Olivia shook her head. "I'm not stable yet. Getting there, but I don't want her in a position where she has to take care of me or whatever. Mom and I talked about it."

Hazel had to think about that. "Okay, so you were in Richmond for Serena, and you were on the hospital grounds of the trauma. Tell me what happened."

Olivia related, in detail, how she identified the site outside the ER, lay on the ground, searched with her hands. Found the pendant. By the end of Olivia's tale, Hazel would've killed for a shot of Tequila.

Instead, she said, "That is very brave."

"You think?"

Hazel turned the question over in her mind. On one hand, she'd seen Olivia progress and grow and mature into a different version of herself over the past year, and given what she'd been through with coma and memory loss and restructuring her life around a different personality which her brain had arranged as a dark joke...she couldn't believe what Olivia was telling her. Amazing! She made plans to start a paper about it the next day. Her colleagues would find it fascinating. This...courage and emotional strength comprised ground-breaking behavior. Or perhaps...unnecessary risk-taking.

"Olivia, what I think is irrelevant. What YOU think is what's important. Anything else?"

Olivia seemed to struggle with what she'd say next. Hazel sat quiet, waiting.

"I'm having premonitions. Intuition." Olivia gave Hazel a somber look. "My brain has become kind of...." She sighed. "I can see things. When I saw the site of my accident, oh whoops, sorry...assault...you told me to use honest words, right? Anyway, I was *certain* it happened there. Hazel, I'd never *been* back there. My mom insisted that I not know the exact location since I was having such a hard time, and...it's been two years. And I...just knew."

"Wow," Hazel murmured.

"I don't think that's normal."

"What do you think is normal?"

"STOP."

"I'll rephrase. How are you feeling about it?"

Olivia smiled. "I *love* it."

Hazel burst out laughing. "Hilarious."

"It is, isn't it?"

Hazel patted her chest. Blew out a breath. "I need coffee. Do you?"

"Sure," Olivia said, rising to follow her into the cozy nook.

As Hazel made coffee, Olivia dragged over one of the chairs from the client space. "Let's sit here. We can watch the rain."

Hazel beamed. "My thought, exactly." She gave Olivia a steaming mug.

Olivia stared out the windows. Hazel reflected that the two of them—sitting and staring and comfortable in the rain-patter-silence—seemed more like friends than therapist and client. The coffee nook she'd designed had that effect on people, Hazel realized. She knew, regrettably, that if she and Olivia became confidants and friends, it would not only breach her sworn mandate as a professional counselor, it would have a disastrous effect on their counseling sessions. She could not let that happen. "How's the paralegal course going?"

"Not good," Olivia said, sipping. "All that research and writing? I can't imagine. I'll answer Wyatt's phone, I'll be his gofer, but I'm not cut out to be a paralegal. Paralegals do, like…thesis documents all the time." Olivia made a strangled sound with one hand around her throat.

Hazel set her notebook aside and chuckled. "Off the record…"

"I love it when you do that."

"Off the record," she continued, "have you ever considered the peripheral fields around law? You know…like Tom?"

Olivia blinked in surprise. "How do you know Tom Stark?"

"My husband used him years ago, and they became friends. This is a while back, before my husband's death. Tom's had some wild experiences, that's all. I've heard he's retiring soon. And once he's gone…well, it takes a singular talent."

Olivia blinked. "Tom's retiring?"

She nodded. "He's my age, you know."

"How old are you, anyway?"

"Google it," she quipped.

Olivia laughed.

"There aren't many PIs around here." She sipped daintily.

"Crazy," Olivia murmured.

"What?"

"I would never have thought of that. But now that you put it out there, the thought is illicit."

"Think Erin Brockovich." Hazel was quiet a beat. "Illicit?"

"Intriguing, I think I meant." She rolled her eyes at the brain blip. "I don't have her moxie."

Hazel considered her for long seconds, then shrugged. "Maybe."

Olivia bit her lower lip. "My daughter says I'm afraid of everything."

Hazel put her mug on the end table, folded her hands in her lap. "Talk to Tom."

Thunder rumbled in the distance. The dark clouds were a low-lying, veiled, threat on the horizon. The pattering on the windows subsided.

"Tell me about your premonitions."

"Are we back on the record?"

Hazel laughed. "Yes."

"I don't know...I feel things. *Know* things. Like...when I laid in that spot outside the ER at Mercy, I didn't see anything, but I did feel that whatever it was...was important. It's...like little, mental pushes."

Hazel quietly pulled her notebook back into her lap and began writing. Then she finished her coffee and looked at Olivia. "Will you document these events? And let's make an appointment—"

Olivia shook her head. "I'll document them for you, but I can't go back to once-a-week sessions. Hazel, I'm all analyzed out. I—I—" She stopped short of completing the thought.

"Verbal lapses still there?"

"Pressure does it."

Hazel scribbled a few more lines and closed her notebook. "I do not want to cause pressure, I want to *relieve* it! How about three weeks?"

Olivia let out a nervous breath. "Three weeks is good."

Chapter Thirty-Eight

"Today, if anything is trying to hold you back, give no attention to it. Get your hopes up, get your faith up, look up, and get ready to rise up."
~Germany Kent

"Mom, what does 'incoherent' mean?" Lilly asked, looking up from her laptop.

The TV droned in the background at a soft level, and I tore myself away from the scintillating text I was reading about TBI—traumatic brain injury—and the pathophysiological processes that result in psychosis after a delay, and within one to five years.

Not exactly life-affirming stuff.

"Incoherent means rambling, or confusion, honey. As in 'she became incoherent after breaking down in tears.' What are you looking at, anyway?"

"Email. Serena said I was becoming incoherent."

"What?" I rose and walked over to her side of the couch and plopped down beside her. "Let me see."

After I read what Serena had written, I saw that she was the one who had become incoherent. I made a mental note to give her a call and see how she was doing. "Since when did you guys use email to communicate?"

Lilly shrugged. "She started it. What am I supposed to do...not answer?"

"No," I snapped, irritated. "That's not what I meant."

"Mom," Lilly said with a grin, "are you becoming incoherent?"

I walked back over to my spot by the lamp at the other end of the couch and sank into it. "That's nothing to joke about, young lady!" I said, louder than necessary.

"Okay, Mom. Gosh."

"Sorry." I blew out an exasperated breath. "Truth is, I'm having trouble learning this stuff about TBI."

"Yeah? What's it say?"

I smiled at her, a little sad, wishing that my girls didn't know so much about traumatic brain injuries and seizures and personality disorders that they could converse on the topic at an educated level. Gray had seen to that. And Mom was an expert now.

"It says that psychological stuff...like my rewired personality...can manifest different ways of reacting from one to five years later." I hooted my derision. "As if I need to look forward to anything else crappy happening."

I told her what I'd been reading.

My den glowed with the candles I'd lit on the coffee table and the subtle lighting of the end table lamps. We shared a big bowl of popcorn that Lilly had made for us. It had been a nice surprise that she'd be home, and I was determined to connect. She'd been trying hard to change her attitude, and I was trying my best to be more in tune with her. It seemed to be working.

"Maybe it won't be a bad change, Mom. Like...you know, you're more confident and strong now."

My forehead furrowed. "You said I was afraid of everything."

"Well, yeah, when you needed to be. I didn't mean...in general, Mom."

A few beats of silence ensued.

My research wasn't revealing a pretty picture, and I knew, as a survivor of a major impact to my frontal and occipital lobe and subsequent unconsciousness for more than a hundred hours...that I had been the recipient of some kind of miracle. According to what I'd read, I should be a highly medicated, uncontrollable basket case, yet I wasn't. Was I? Maybe I didn't know. My ability to adjudicate my condition was supposed to be impaired.

"Lilly, tell me how different I am. Do I get angry more? Am I less...able to explain things? Do I obsess about stuff?"

Lilly's cheeks colored, and she stared at the floor. Riot took that as an immediate invitation to a lap, uncurled himself from his spot, stretched, and leapt onto her keyboard. In practiced cat-mom precision, she held him up with one hand, closed her laptop with the other, set it aside on the couch, and placed him on her lap. His purring increased in volume. Distracted, she scratched his head as she thought about my question.

"You used to worry about us, Mom. A lot. Like…we couldn't do anything without you around. Now…you're…well, you've got a job now, and you're writing a book…and have that club."

"The Wine and Whine?"

Lilly rolled her eyes. "Yeah."

"Do you feel ignored?"

She shook her head. "Not at all. It's been…hard getting used to the new you but I think you obsessed *before* the injury, not after."

"Okay," I said. This was hard to hear, but I needed objectivity. Lilly, at least, would be kind. Serena, not on your life. They were so different, my girls. "What is the new me like…now? According to what I'm reading, recovery from a brain injury takes many forms. It evolves."

"Huh," she said, stroking Riot, who had turned over on his back so she could pet his fluffy, almost-white, stomach. His body draped across her lap and he was so long, only his midsection fit. His head dangled upside-down in bliss. "You have a *lot* of energy, Mom. And you get upset over stuff that never bothered you before. I mean really upset."

My lips tightened. "Example?"

"The hysterics when you went to stay with Grammy? Like, men were stalking me?"

I waved my hand in dismissal. "I was watching out for you. That's what moms do."

"You were paranoid, Mom. Those guys…they were doing a job for Mr. Harp. They had nothing to do with anything."

"Yeah, but…well, it could have," I insisted, like a pouting child.

Riot melted from Lilly's lap to the floor and sauntered away. "And Serena? Don't you think she needs you right now?"

"Mom's right there with her, honey. And Gray. I think she's better off—"

"What do you think she was emailing me about, Mom? She wanted to talk about how sad she was, over the baby. She wanted to talk to *me*, Mom. Not you."

"That's not—"

"I'm being honest, Mom." Lilly grabbed her laptop and put it under her arm. "I'm going upstairs, but you should call Serena."

I watched her trot upstairs, my mouth open. With a glare at the revelatory site on my laptop, I shut it down and stalked into the kitchen. Got a cup from the cabinet, and slammed a tea kettle on the stove. Grabbed honey and cream, and stood there, seething. What was wrong with me? Why hadn't I seen this? How long had it been since I'd called Serena? When the tea kettle screamed with the boil, I jumped.

* * *

"Honey? How's it going?"

I heard a sigh, then a sniff from Serena. "Okay, I guess."

After a beat, I said, "I want to be here if you need to talk." More sniffing, which I recognized belatedly were tears. "Serena, are you crying?"

"Yep," she blasted. "Been doing a lot of that lately. How about you?"

"I...I..." my mouth snapped shut. How did I handle this? How did I act in these situations before my injury? Before I'd become someone else? I concentrated hard on what to say next.

"Mom says you're doing well," I began, uncertain.

"I have to act like that for her, Mom! For God's sake, give me a break. I lost my baby! How would *you* feel?"

My mind hurtled back. Yes, I'd lost a baby but under the most horrific circumstances. This wasn't the same. Was it?

"Terrible. Horrible. I remember what happened with your dad..." I started.

"Don't mention him! I don't want to talk about him again! Ever!"

My heartbeat pounded in my ears. Lilly had been so right. Serena was lost right now and needed me. But a crisis like this was exactly why I'd gone to see Monty. How had I reacted under stress? According to him, I'd been scared of everything, so an honest, open response had probably not been my go-to. I decided now, honesty was best. Even if I screwed up, it still counted as trying to make an emotional connection.

"Serena, I love you. We're going to see this through together. Tell me what you need."

After a couple beats of silence, she murmured, "I don't know."

My heart ached for my daughter. "Have you heard from, uhh...?"

"No!" she blurted before I could remember the baby's father's name. Had she told me his name? "I did call, and let him know...what happened..." her voice trailed off.

"That's good, honey. He would want to know."

Pause. "You want to know what he said?"

"Sure." I put my palm over my eyes. No telling what he'd said.

"He said it was for the best." She sniffed. I pictured her grabbing tissues. "For the *best*, Mom! How could he say that to me? This was his baby, too!"

My pulse pounded in my throat. Instinctively, I knew I didn't have the emotional savvy to know how to comfort her as a mother should. The words wouldn't come. I felt anything I said would be wrong, so I was quiet. Hadn't someone, somewhere said that grieving people only need to be heard?

The silence stretched. Her sniffling stopped. She blew out a long, sad, breath. "I wonder if I'll ever get over it, Mom. Did you?"

The question took me by surprise. Did I fully remember that time in my life? I don't think I remembered specifics, but I needed to dig deep for my daughter and say something hopeful. "I think there'll always be a special place in our hearts for these babies. But grief tapers off. We have the memory, but the grief isn't as painful, over time."

"Grammy says my baby is waiting for me in heaven."

I smiled. "She says that about the one I lost, too. Let's hold onto that hope. You and me, okay?"

"Okay."

I heard the hint of a smile in her voice.

* * *

Two cups of tea and an hour later, I sat on my porch listening to the night sounds, watching the stars, and thinking about the sheer beauty of a mother's relationship with her children. We'd cried together, then talked, then cried some more. I'd tried my best to make amends. It was tough, but we agreed it was better that she stay with Gray and Mom. She said she understood.

My brain still flopped around like a dying fish, and I didn't know where it was going to land. If my reactions to a strained, or worse, an *emergency* situation could not be relied upon, where would that leave my Serena? I wanted her to be with people she could depend on for her journey—emotional and physical—back from the miscarriage. She'd sounded upbeat and positive, and happy I'd called. In the end, anyway.

How long would my girls have to tell me they 'understood'?

Fists clenched, I announced, "I AM going to be a whole woman, a good woman, a dependable and competent woman, and I don't care what the psychological studies show. I'll channel it into a victory."

A shuffle in the grass prodded my eyes open. The trees had leafed out to the point that Wyatt's spotlight a quarter-mile down the winding lane was more a mild glow than a glaring intrusion. A full, silvery moon made for decent visibility. I squinted into the trees.

A slim shadow darted from tree to tree and took off down the road. A black fury filled me.

I stalked to my garage and powered open the door. When I turned on the lights, they blazed like the sun. I'd changed the fluorescents to the brightest I could find. No way an amateur bomb-maker would turn me into a sniveling coward. I'd had enough of that life, and it had almost gotten me killed. If it was my time, I was determined to go out like a torpedo. Meteor. Whatever.

I walked in, got on my knees, and dropped to the floor to look underneath my car. By this time, I'd memorized its undercarriage, and nothing looked amiss. How could anyone have gotten in, anyway? I'd changed all the locks, they were iron-clad. The interior check made me more nervous. I'd learned all about bombs, and they could be remote-controlled which was unlikely this time of night, the perpetrator had to be close, but if it was on a timer, and cleverly hidden…I could be toast if I opened the door.

Slow and steady, I backed away until I was against the worktable on the wall, and slid up, stretching my neck to see inside the car. In the end, I held my phone up high, took a photo. When I enlarged it, I saw nothing sinister. Also, I could see from the fuzzy enlargement that the door was still locked. My hands were shaky when I closed the garage door and reset the lock. I left the lights on.

My mouth a stern line, I strode into the middle of my beautiful front yard and stared up into the sky, awash with twinkling stars. The Milky Way provided a comforting focal point, and I screamed up to the heavens, "I will not live this way! I will find out who is doing this to me...to *us...* and I will NOT believe that my life is forever damaged. I will use ALL of my mental capacity and ability...to find out what's going on." I thought a minute. "AND FIX IT!" I screamed.

At that moment, an engine roared to life somewhere in the vicinity of Wyatt's building and screamed away.

Filled with a determination that had expanded to majestic proportions, I stalked to my front porch and dropped onto the loveseat cushion forever indented with the shape of my behind. I fixed my mind on the effects of 'perseverant and aggressive and uninhibited behavior' indicated in the aftermath of a TBI. What Hazel said resonated in my spirit: To be a private investigator takes a *singular talent.*

Chapter Thirty-Nine

"Everything negative – pressure, challenges – is all an opportunity for me to rise."

~Kobe Bryant

T he large, circular clock on the wall told me Wyatt should arrive any minute.

After three weeks, he'd closed his Harrisburg location. Now, he'd told me, his focus would be on Carroll County.

How ironic that I worked for Earl's successor. I could hear Mom's voice saying, 'God works in mysterious ways.'

"Bizarre ways is more like it," I muttered.

I walked across the taupe, color-of-dirt, carpet that had been installed, and surveyed my decorating efforts. In Wyatt's absence, I'd ordered a couch, end and coffee tables, lamps, art. I'd gone with a light, breezy palette to temper the ugly carpeting.

I couldn't wait for Wyatt's reaction.

A car pulled up.

After a few minutes, Wyatt entered, pulling his suitcase and smiling a greeting. He walked through the space, dropped off his suitcase and leather bag, and returned to my desk. "How's it going?" He stretched and looked around the office. "Long trip. Everything looks great, Olivia. Thank you."

I let out a breath in relief. I'd sent photos, but he hadn't given me much indication if he liked it or not.

"Have you started on my office?"

My brows arched. "Did you ask me to?"

"Thought I did."

"Let's look at it," I suggested, feeling the sting of disapproval. Had he asked me to do anything with his office? Had I overlooked his request? My newfound confidence took a nosedive.

"Later, maybe…" he said, distracted. He stared at his phone. "You've scheduled a couple of appointments, right? Aren't they coming today?"

I nodded. "Yes, I texted them to you." I pulled up his calendar. "You've got an hour."

"Could've given me a little space for lunch," he joked.

But I caught the irritation behind his tone.

"Do you want me to re-schedule?"

He flapped one of his hands. "Not at all. It's fine." He strode into his office, closed the door. After a bit, he opened the door and called out, "Don't mind me, I went to visit Mom before I drove here. I'm not in the best mood." He re-closed his door.

After his two appointments, he left.

* * *

"Maybe I'm not cut out for this," I told Lilly over the dinner table.

"Why, what happened?" She dug into the casserole I'd made.

"I don't know…but…not what I expected. He's never there, for one thing. I don't even know what I should be doing."

She laughed. "Well, I think when a boss isn't there to tell you what to do, you can do whatever you want. Sound great to me. Like…free money."

I frowned. "When you get paid for a job, you need to do what they hired you to do, Lillian."

With a shrug, she hopped up from the table, rinsed her plate, and put it in the dishwasher. "Gotta go to rehearsal, Mom." She gave me a knowing look. "And, yeah, you can find it on the school website calendar, so we good?"

I laughed. "Better than good, honey."

As I cleaned up from dinner, I thought about how different Lilly had been, lately. Happier.

My cell vibrated. Hunter. I rubbed the tension from the back of my neck. It was sad that I associated Hunter with all things negative. Crisis. Crime. Helplessness. And yet, that romantic dinner at Harriman House in Westminster? I fixed my mind on this happy experience when we'd first met before I answered.

"It's been officially ruled a homicide, Olivia. Three stab wounds to the groin. Definitely not a pro."

I silently cursed the man's habit of leaping right in without preamble. "So I take it the autopsy results came in."

A beat of silence. "Sorry."

I laughed. "I guess we're too comfortable with each other?"

"Are we?" I could almost see him smile.

"Now you sound like my therapist."

"I doubt that's a good thing." He laughed.

"So how's his case going? I didn't realize you were still involved."

"All the investigators on this case believe there's a connection. The timing can't be an accident. And that bomb incident...well, give me a break. Who wants me dead? Or injured? Monty's trial got a lot of exposure, and so did you. We're proceeding with that as a viable premise. Earl's family's not happy. They're...well, they're looking for someone to blame."

My eyebrows rose. "He never talked about his family. Well, his wife...she died a while ago, but...his kids? He didn't mention them."

Hunter grunted. "They're a strange bunch. I can't read them, and they didn't want to share much."

An odd, suffocating sensation squeezed my chest. "They *can't* think I had anything to do with this. Do they?"

"The media spun it like you were unhappy with his representation, so naturally, they've gravitated to you."

"At first, maybe..." I sputtered in disbelief, "but I was coming out of trauma. I wasn't myself." I thought about the words. Would I *ever* be myself?

"Understand. But you know how that goes."

I shook my head in defiance. "It *cannot* go that way."

"Olivia…"

"Don't 'Olivia' me! I'm done being coddled and cossetted like a pet poodle! Monty has some kind of vendetta going on, and now you're telling me Earl's family is accusing me of his murder? This is ridiculous."

"Coddled and cossetted?"

"I never know what kind of words are going to pop out, you know that," I said with a sigh.

Hunter laughed. "Makes you interesting."

"Makes me crazy," I muttered. "Look, Hunter…TBI recovery takes a long time. There are stages. But they *must* know that I'd not be capable of such a thing."

"What kind of 'stages' Olivia?"

I paused. The question sounded clinical, not personal. "Anger. Obsessive behavior. Struggles with self-control." My heartbeat raced. I put a hand on my chest.

"Olivia, you couldn't have done this."

"I *didn't* do this. But could they make a case? Based on these findings?"

"They could try."

I thought about the note. The damn, incriminating, infuriating form that I had not signed, but somebody had. For what purpose? And who? I couldn't tell Hunter about it. Should I?

Not yet, a little voice whispered in the back of my brain.

"So what are the next steps in Earl's homicide investigation?"

"We're looking into the family. The backgrounds of the kids, that kind of thing. Anyone he had contact with in the final weeks before his death. You know if he had close friends?"

My forehead furrowed in concentration. Had Earl ever talked about his personal history?

"I don't remember friends…but I do remember him talking about a difficult client. A younger man, I think, from the way he described him. He'd get calls, and I could tell he was irritated by them, and we talked a little about that, but not much. The calls distressed him, though, I could tell he was rattled."

"Name?"

Try as I might, I could not dredge up a name. "I'll give it more thought."

"Okay. Any detail would help at this point."

"He wouldn't have told me, anyway, Hunter," I said, thinking about the direction I was considering as a career. Puffing out my chest, I decided to tell him. "I'm not going to be Wyatt's paralegal anymore."

"Okay." He waited.

"I'm going to be his PI."

Seconds ticked by. I pictured those eyes—the color of mud when angry or intense—trying to process the statement. "What do you think?"

"Are you out of your *mind?* I know what I said about peripheral career choices, but private investigation is risky. Dangerous."

I frowned.

"Olivia," he began, his tone that of a parent to a child, "...paralegal is a safe, dependable career you can count on. Do you know what it takes to be a PI?"

"You lost me at 'safe' and 'dependable,'" I quipped, and ended the call.

Looks like my first assignment would be pro bono. A hike up the Sorenson family tree.

* * *

The next morning, I decided to face Wyatt with the truth about how I felt about becoming a paralegal. After he had his first cup of coffee, I knocked on his door.

"Come in," he said, distracted and opening and closing drawers.

"What are you looking for?" I asked.

"Pens. I can't find them," he muttered.

I walked to a tall, black, metal storage unit tucked into the corner of his office and opened it to expose several tidy containers labeled with various office supply categories. With a Vanna White flourish, I extended my arm toward its interior.

Wyatt laughed. "Can I marry you? Like, right now?"

I laughed, pulled out some pens, and put them on his desk. "Have you got a second?"

"Yep," he said, depositing all but one of the pens in a drawer. He leaned back in his chair. "What's up?"

"It's so generous of you to pay for the paralegal courses, Wyatt."

His eyebrows popped up at my tone. "But...?"

I shook my head. "I can't fancy myself at a screen all day, writing papers, researching precedent."

"Is this an exit interview?" He asked, a puzzled look on his face.

"Nothing of the sort. It's more...an observation. I...know I'm not cut out for it."

An awkward silence stretched.

"However..."

Wyatt put his elbows on the arms of his chair and tented his hands.

"You could use a PI, right?"

"Everyone can use a PI."

"Well..."

"Olivia, private investigators... *investigate*. Do you have any experience?"

"No, but..."

"Aren't you still recovering?"

I shook my head. "That doesn't count at all. In fact, I've been reading all the aftereffects of a healing brain, and I've become this...I don't know... mega-me or something. Persistent. Aggressive. Traits I'm told I never had before, and all characteristics a good PI needs to do the job. Plus, I have a mentor."

"Who?"

"Tom Stark." The teensiest lie. I didn't have him yet, but I would.

He laughed. "He's on my schedule to call today."

"And he's retiring soon," I blurted. "So see? Fate."

He was quiet a few seconds, then rolled his chair closer to his desk. "I guess I should tell you why I was such a jerk yesterday."

I pulled on my earlobe. "Your mom?"

He shrugged. "I'd also gotten a call from Earl Sorenson's family. They found out you work here." He couldn't seem to look at me. "They want representation, but with a caveat."

I waited.

"I have to fire you."

My jaw dropped.

"Your ex-husband is a suspect in Earl's homicide investigation, and if that case falls through they want to pursue a wrongful death civil suit."

I let out a breath. On one hand, it sounded like they'd made peace with the fact that I didn't have anything to do with it, and on the other, Monty *was* a convicted murderer. "Makes sense," I muttered.

Wyatt frowned. "It does?"

Oops.

Make up something. Do *not* tell him about the form you spirited away from the crime scene.

I waved a hand around. "A'course it does. He's a murderer. Not a stretch."

"He pleaded temporary insanity."

I was quiet.

"What aren't you telling me?"

"Nothing." Gosh, another lie. Where was my sense of integrity?

He grunted. "So…how are we going to resolve this? I need a paralegal. I need someone to answer the phone. It'll take months…years, maybe… for you to do the PI thing. You got any ideas?"

"I've been looking into what it takes to get a license. I'll shadow him or whatever. I've read that experience takes precedence over education, and some private investigators don't take classes, but I'd like to take some anyway, to figure out the law and how to stay… uhh…"

"Honest?"

I shrugged. Wyatt laughed. "They have PI online courses, y'know. I can switch them," he said, his face thoughtful. "You could do that at home, and we'd avoid the conflict of interest with the Sorensons. We'd need to keep our relationship quiet. However…I still need an assistant, and hopefully, one that will transition into a paralegal."

I stuck my index finger into the air like a commandant calling out the charge command to his troops. "I know the perfect person. Can I schedule a meeting?

"Do I have a choice?"

"We always have a choice, Wyatt," I said, my voice solemn. "Do I like... need to leave the premises?"

"Should I take the case?"

"Of course you should take the case," I declared. "It'll establish your lawyerhood... attorneyship...whatever you call it...forever! You'll be made. No-brainer."

"Agreed," he responded. Wyatt bounced his fingertips together, thinking. "Okay. Let's do this. I *would* like to interview your friend. We'll go from there."

We shook on it. "Can you switch to the PI course pretty quick? I'm sinking to get started."

He gave me a look. *"Dying* to get started, maybe?"

"Whatever," I sighed.

Chapter Forty

"Rejoice not against me, oh mine enemy. Though I fall, I shall rise."
~*The Bible, Micah 7:8*

Hannah chewed a piece of a homemade hard roll. "Why do these things taste so good but break my teeth?"

Callie lifted her wine. "I got a zinfandel this time! Here's to a new grape!"

We lifted our glasses. "Here, here," we chorused. I leaned back in my chair and waited for the inevitable moderation from Callie.

"Who wants to go first?" she asked.

Sherry jumped in. "My divorce is final!" She lifted her arms high and waved her hands around. "I'm glad I got the news today, so I could celebrate with you guys." Behind her smile, I sensed regret. We all did.

"I'm sorry it didn't work out, Sherry," I said, setting my wine glass aside. I'd ordered an Argentinian malbec, which tasted like crap. Why did people like malbecs?

Her eyes misted. "Nahh. Don't be."

Callie jumped up, gave her a hug, and returned to her chair. Stoic and sad, Hannah's empathy drifted across the table toward Sherry like a cool breeze.

"It'll be okay," I said, wondering why. How the heck did I know if she'd be okay? I hated it when people said that (which was *all the time*) and here I was falling back on the old chestnut like an idiot. I grimaced. "I mean, I don't *know* if you'll be okay, but I'm hoping things get better."

Sherry lifted her wine glass. "It's a new day, girls. It *will* be okay, Olivia."

215

She shrugged. "At some point."

"Next?" Callie blurted after a respectful moment of silence for the death of a marriage. "Anyone have fun plans for the weekend? Or news?"

Hannah shot a nervous glance at me and folded her hands in her lap. I frowned. Hannah had the worst 'tells' of anyone I knew.

I cleared my throat. "I'll go. I've been shadowing a private investigator for two weeks. With my neurosurgeon's approval and a background check, I'll be working on getting my PI license the next few months."

"Wow," Sherry breathed. "You definitely win."

"It's been a good week," I said. "Hannah, tell them."

"Monty is out of business, as far as I know," she began. "By that, I mean his relationship with the corrections officer who helped him has been, uh, cut off."

"And how that happened..." I added. "Is she stopped giving him money, and this CO is furious, and taking it out on Monty. We're assuming he's no longer a threat."

Callie stroked the stem of her glass, thoughtful. "Monty called and talked to my husband last night."

My forehead beetled. "What?"

"Graham saw right through him, Olivia."

"What did he want?"

Her face clouded. "I think he wants to know if you're...you know, sleeping with anyone."

I laughed. "I'm trying to figure out my life, for God's sake, not who to sleep with! What a jerk."

Hannah tapped her chin. "He'd have to know you'd find this out, Olivia. Why would he want you to know that?"

"To play up the 'jealous husband' bit that he got off on? That's how he got a lesser sentence, you know. Pleading temporary insanity because he was so jealous. Now, if he sets me up to be the perpetual wandering ex-wife, it'd play well with the parole board." I stared at a spot on the washed oak flooring. We'd chosen a new place to meet, Speckles, in Owings Mills. The restaurant smelled of fresh paint and new flooring. Fresh-faced, young servers zig-zagged across the space.

"Let's look at the opposite end of the spectrum," Hannah suggested. What if you're…and you are…a responsible and upright citizen and mother and he has nothing?"

"He still wants to get back at me," I muttered.

"He wants you to let your guard down," Callie blurted. "That's what Graham and I think. Throw you off track. It's ridiculous to think you're sleeping around. Besides, what business is that of anyone's? You're a free agent."

Sherry looked at me. "Do you know very much about Wyatt? Don't you think the timing is interesting? I mean, think about it. His building project, the way he swept in and scooped up that land before you had time to blink… maybe you ought to take a closer look."

"I agree," Callie said.

I sipped my wine. "I can ask Tom—the man that's training me— the best way to go about checking people's histories." I went on to share with them the dazzling array of aftereffects I'd discovered regarding traumatic brain injuries. They thought lack of empathy, impulsivity, my personality change, and a nasty temper comprised a terrific bunch of attributes and didn't understand why the medical field considered them negatives.

* * *

I raced home after our meeting, hoping to check in with Lilly. It was Saturday, and I didn't think she had plans, so maybe we could do a mom-daughter thing. I strode through the narrow, covered, walkway from the garage to my patio, up two stone stairs to the back door of my kitchen. Lilly's lilting laughter floated from the den to the kitchen. I smiled and tossed my keys on the breakfast bar. As I walked toward the den, I heard a masculine voice. My blood froze in my veins. My fists clenched. *Wyatt?* What was he doing here?

Lilly hopped up when I entered. "Mom! Hi." A shadow crossed her face. "Was it okay to let Mr. Harp in? I mean, you work for him now and everything, so—"

I smiled. "We'll talk about it later, honey." I dropped onto the couch across from where Wyatt sat. "So, what's up?" I asked him.

Lilly slunk from the room and up the stairs.

His forehead creased. "I'm sensing a disconnect."

"And I'm sensing a young girl alone with a man we barely know. So…"

"I had no idea you'd be concerned, since—"

"No harm done, but it would be better…if you want to come over, maybe text me first?"

He dipped his head. "Lilly said you were out with friends, and that I could wait. I apologize for overstepping."

Bells and clangs and alarms sounded in my mind like a firetruck screaming down the freeway. Had he been pumping my daughter for information? Was he another of Monty's undercover spies? Like Niles, the man that ended up drugging and assaulting me?

I frowned. I'd become so paranoid even *I* didn't like myself. I switched gears.

"I talked to my friend Sherry and she's willing to interview. She's a former court clerk, and she's been at home for a while, but she's ready to go back to work, so…hope it works out." The girls and I had decided Sherry was the most viable candidate to replace me in Wyatt's office, with the double advantage that, one; she needed a paycheck until her divorce settlement was finalized, and two; she'd be able to do a little investigating of her own. Into Wyatt.

He stood in preparation to leave. "Your recommendation is good enough for me. I'll get in touch."

"You *cannot* be a spy," I mumbled before I realized I'd said the words I'd been thinking out loud.

He cocked his head. "Where did that come from?"

I picked at a loose thread on the couch, then looked at him. "Are you representing Earl's kids in a civil suit?"

He nodded. "You gave me the go-ahead, remember? I can't think of any reason not to."

"You don't think our being neighbors...or previously working together... is a conflict?"

He smiled. "You don't work for me anymore."

"Under duress. That's what the opposing side would try to prove."

"That won't fly with a judge. You left of your own volition."

I stared darkly at the floor.

"How does this even affect you? I mean, you found him, but it was happenstance...explainable. And look at you, you're what, five-foot-three? Earl was a big guy. Who could think you'd catch him off guard and stab him three times with enough force to kill him?" Wyatt said. "Any involvement they'd try to pin on you is simple dereliction of duty, and even that's a stretch."

My eyes widened. "Dereliction of duty?"

Wyatt shifted his weight from one foot to the other. "I'm sorry, I mean... the story of your assault got *so* much press, and the media ran with it... it's, well, the public will think what they think." He shrugged. "There's a peripheral argument that could be made about your close relationship to Earl, and that you had a duty to be circumspect by understanding the danger your presence might cause him, but it'd be clutching at straws, Olivia."

I thought about the form I'd taken from the scene. How it was an obvious attempt to implicate me in Earl's death. The fear that still consumed me... that Monty had hired someone to put it there out of his hatred for me. Should I tell Wyatt about the form?

No.

Wyatt sighed. "Look, the only reason we parted company was so I could represent Earl's family, and you agreed. After the case is settled, I can use you for investigation, if that's something you're still going to pursue. It was never personal, you know that, right?"

He asked to use the restroom, and I waved him down the hall. After he left the den, I stared at Wyatt's leather bag beside the couch. I heard the sound of the bathroom door closing. I yanked open the leather briefcase and grabbed a file.

I scanned pages. Earl's family had filed a wrongful death civil suit, and my name stood out in big, capital, letters at the top of the Motion. With a gasp, I blinked and looked again. No mistake, there it was. My name, all nice and cozy with Monty's.

I stuffed the file back in the bag and replaced the flap. Sat on the couch, my brain pinging like a pinball machine on steroids. No wonder Wyatt had been amenable to my pursuit of a different career venue. He'd needed to get rid of me so he could launch a huge, lucrative case painting me as part of the reason Earl had been in a killer's crosshairs. I'd even supported him in taking the case! At the very least, I'd be implicated in putting him at risk due to the notoriety of my assault case; and Earl, the poor, tortured soul who'd handled my divorce from a sociopath bent on destroying anyone who'd been involved.

I felt like I was drowning.

The toilet flushed. The bathroom door opened. Wyatt's steps approached. I rose from the couch.

Wyatt picked up his bag and hung it on his shoulder. "Would you send me Sherry's contact info? And thanks for suggesting her. I'll work out a date we can meet. Listen, I really am sorry for overstepping. Won't happen again. See you later," he said with a smile. My screen door banged shut behind him.

Like hell you will, I thought.

Chapter Forty-One

Detective Hunter Faraday had had just about enough of citizen complaints and equitability and social justice seminars. A cop's life was too complicated these days. He strode down the gleaming hall and out the glass doors of the Richmond PD building.

A hard, slanting rain pelted his face like darts. He squinted at the sky and decided to buy a sandwich from the machines in the breakroom and wait out the storm. He went back inside, trotted down a wide staircase into a large room that held aluminum tables and chairs and a sea of vending machines. As he was swallowing the last bite and wadding up the sandwich wrapper, his phone rang.

"Olivia," he answered, his voice rising on the last syllable.

"Am I interrupting?"

Hunter put his feet up in the chair next to him. "Nope. Shoot."

"I have a situation."

"Of course you do," he joked. "That's the only time I ever hear from you."

Pause. "I'm serious."

He pulled his feet off the chair. "Okay."

"First, have you guys made any headway on Earl's case?"

"Not much. Can't find the knife, or whatever it was with a blade. Autopsy was unable to pin down the weapon. All we know is the doer was an amateur. Cuts were not clean. Also, prints are inconclusive. Yours and Earl's, and the cleaning staff, that's about it. The top motive we can find is connection to you, and that's only a guess. We're all over it, though."

"Is it possible it *could* be related to me?"

Pause. "Why?"

Olivia exhaled. "A couple things. Yesterday, Wyatt was in my house alone with Lilly when I got home. I told him not to do it again unless I was home."

Hunter frowned. "And the second thing?"

"I...had this weird feeling. So...when he was out of the room I fished around in his shoulder bag and found a file. Guess what? Earl's family is suing Monty...*and me*...for wrongful death."

Hunter sucked in a breath. "You *are* talking about the guy you went to work for, right?"

"Yeah, but we'd talked about it, but the family wouldn't use him as counsel if I worked for him. We agreed I do the PI course instead of the paralegal course and I'd do it remotely. See? So then he could take the case. It'll be huge. But he never told me I'd be one of the defendants! I'm like...*what?* Don't you think it's...implausible? I mean, can they do that?" Olivia groaned. "You're one of the few people I can talk to about this. I don't want to worry Mom or the girls.

"Why would he do that? Thought everything was all rainbows and unicorns with you two." Hunter's mind went back to Wyatt holding an umbrella. Playing nice. Trying to dig for information. He'd not trusted the guy then, and he didn't trust the guy now.

"I did, too. I'd even approached him with the idea of shadowing Tom Stark—"

"Think you have enough men in your life?" he quipped, an edge to his voice.

Olivia went quiet a few beats. "He's the PI I hired when that videocam was installed. When I found out Wyatt bought that land without me knowing, and I was so upset?"

"I wasn't around much, remember?"

He listened to Olivia breathe.

"Sorry," Hunter said, scratching the stubble on his chin. "I...well, I still feel like I should be around to keep an eye out."

"I guess that means that you think I'm still the poor, helpless, victim?"

He groaned. "Of course it doesn't, but...the media made a circus out of what happened to you, and now….." He chuckled and shook his head. "You can't tell about people. It's amazing what can happen with that kind of exposure."

"I can't walk around *afraid* all the time, Hunter."

"I know, I know," he murmured. "I sure didn't see this coming, though."

"It feels…I'm not quite…." Olivia cursed under her breath. "Monty isn't this smart. I don't think this has anything to do with him."

"What *do* you think?"

"I was up most of the night trying to figure it out. And I need to get back pretty quick, I'm on a lunch break."

"From what? Thought you didn't work for Wyatt anymore."

"I was *trying* to tell you before you went all…Neanderthal on me…that after I took the job with Wyatt, I realized I hated the paralegal classes, but I loved digging into the facts to get to the root of things. I keep reading about brain injury trauma and recovery…it's pretty fascinating, and…long story short, Hunter, I'm shadowing Tom now—"

"Oh yeah," Hunter interrupted, his tone droll, *"Private investigating* with this Tom guy. If I remember correctly, you ended that conversation before we had a chance to discuss."

"But don't you see how perfect? Wyatt needed me gone. Earl's family wouldn't want me working for him. Why was I even there? He'd have to have been planning this ever since he heard Carroll Country's favorite lawyer had died. Don't you think?"

Hunter sighed. "What's the connection? Why would Earl's family seek you out? Why would Wyatt?"

Pause. "There's something I haven't told you."

"Well, there's a surprise."

"I found a form from the Maryland Correctional Facility right after I found his body. I, um…took it. A visitor's form. My name was on it." Olivia took a breath. "Something's going on, Hunter."

Hunter frowned. "Perfect. Now you're admitting evidence tampering. I didn't hear any of this, okay? But…it's a form. Why would it be an issue?"

"It wasn't the same date that I went. And the signature was *not* my handwriting."

"It was a plant," Hunter murmured, thinking.

"Yep."

"Proof of forethought."

"That's what I think."

"Have you done a thorough background on Wyatt Harp?"

"Could you?" Olivia asked.

* * *

Hours later the storm had moved on, and the setting sun cast long shadows through the windows of the Richmond PD Investigative Unit on the second floor of the white, sleek building at the corner of Grace and Jefferson.

Hunter held his breath and concentrated on the woman's soft voice. It appeared that he'd finally hit pay dirt after three hours of digging.

As Hunter listened, a jolt of dread started at the base of his spine and worked its way up. He asked the helpful employee of the Richmond Department of Social Services to email any information pertaining to what she'd read to him as soon as possible and ended the call. His hand lay on the handset of the landline on his desk for long seconds as he thought through the implications of what he'd learned.

He needed to set things in motion, and he needed to do it quick.

His expression hardened. Though he hated to further freak her out, he decided Olivia should be his first call.

With a sigh, he punched in her number.

Chapter Forty-Two

"The good, rising fastball is the best pitch in baseball."
~Tom Seaver

I listened to Mom's lilting voice, grateful that I'd kept her distanced from the current drama in my life, and also happy about what she was sharing about Dr. Sturgis. Meeting Dr. Grayson Sturgis was turning out to be a beautiful sunrise in her life that kept getting brighter, and no one deserved it more than she did.

For all intents and purposes, it appeared that he was one of the good ones.

Her voice was clear as a bell through the audio in my car; one of the many reasons this vehicle had been worth every penny. I stroked the dash with affection and turned into my lane.

"Tell me about Serena. How's she been?" I asked.

"Never better," her voice dropped, which told me Serena was nearby. "Now she can move on with her life. She's enrolling next semester, for sure. And I think...she told me not to say anything yet, but...she may be going for pre-med!"

"Seriously?" I exclaimed, watching Wyatt wave from his front porch as I drove past. A couple of men were installing his sign. A pang of regret hit me as I realized I should have nothing more to do with him.

"Yes," she whispered, conspiratorially. "And guess what specialty?"

My brow furrowed. "She's already thinking about a specialty?"

"Obstetrics."

After a few seconds, I managed, with a wobble in my voice, "Silver linings."

I returned Wyatt's wave. For now, I had to act the part of a clueless ex-employee. "Tell her I love her and I'll call her later, okay?"

We ended the call. My jaw set, I punched the accelerator and sped all the way to my garage, and after making sure it was locked up tight, I trotted into the house with the groceries I'd purchased, my cell vibrating in in my purse. Hunter. I'd call him back in a few minutes. For now, I wanted to put up my groceries in peace, fix a snack, and settle on my front porch underneath the ceiling fan with a cup of hot tea.

Summer was about to arrive, and I hadn't even had time to enjoy spring.

* * *

I stooped to pet Riot, who had so missed me so much with all the stuff going on that he wove himself in and out of my legs wherever I went, almost tripping me in the process. I'd taken the time to feed him and clean the cat box, which had further delayed calling Hunter back. In my heart, I sensed an urgency, and therefore, I procrastinated as long as I could. I stared into Riot's golden eyes and stroked his tiger-striped, orange fur. "Buddy, you're the safest place I've got right now. Thanks for that." I picked him up, buried my face in his chest, and listened to his rumbly, loud purr. He tilted his head and licked my nose. I laughed. "You understand, don't you?" I returned him to the floor and walked outside.

Riot settled, as usual, inside the door on the floor where he could see me through the screen. I dropped into my loveseat, resigned. My cell lay on the coffee table all alert and ready for me to call him back.

With a frown, I touched his name on the screen at the top of my 'recent call' list. His phone rang. And rang.

It was not lost on me that for him to answer on the first ring was *not* a good sign.

"What's up?" I asked when he answered, my stomach tight with dread.

"What took you so long?"

"I had to change, feed the cat and do the litterbox. Oh, and fix tea." I gave him a virtual salute with my cup.

He let out a long breath. "You're not gonna like this."

"Somehow, I knew that."

The rustle of paper told me he was thumbing through the little notebook he kept.

My heart thrashed like a snake at the wrong end of a hoe.

"Wyatt Harp was adopted."

The tightness in my stomach clenched into a huge knot. "Okay."

"His original last name was Peterson."

My brain stuttered to a stall. "Can you repeat that?"

"Peterson, Olivia. Think about it."

Niles. Niles *Peterson*. Hunter had told me he'd been a foster kid. "Niles," I whispered.

"Olivia, your attacker had a brother," he murmured, his voice gentle. Hunter, more than anyone, knew that my brain could become very fragile and used to tip over with the slightest breeze.

I steeled myself with all the positive self-talk that Hazel had taught me, plus a few of my mom's scriptures thrown in for good measure. "Is Wyatt…?" The question dangled helplessly.

"Wyatt is Niles' younger brother. And it's possible he's been planning this for quite a while. Buying the land, building the property, developing a relationship with you…pretty complex."

"But…but…." I thought about the videocam. The spotlight. I flailed at my words. Hunter could be wrong. Peterson was a common name. The records could be WRONG.

Couldn't they?

Of course, they could. "He's here to watch over his mom. What if he's… he's not who you think? She's in assisted living at…"

"That's a lie. His adopted mom lives in Hershey, Pennsylvania and she hasn't heard from him since he moved. She was glad to hear that he's fine. I made up a reason to call. She doesn't know I'm a cop."

I was quiet.

"He took his new family's name when he was adopted. That's why you couldn't find him. I got to a dead end when I hit his younger years, and on a hunch, I called Social Services."

"I...I..."

"Olivia. Are you okay?"

I straightened my shoulders. "Yes," I stated, my voice firm but my insides about as sturdy as Greek yogurt. "I'm fine."

"You sure?"

"Stop that."

Pause. "You parted on good terms, right? You're in the perfect position to keep an eye out, with that PI friend of yours. Check court records. See what he's filing. That's all public, this Tom guy can guide you through that. See if Monty's involved. I know you don't want anything to do with him, but didn't you say a friend of yours visits him? Can she be discreet? We need to get more details before we close in. I'm going to talk to Earl's family. Find out how they decided to come up with a civil suit and include you. In short, I'm hopeful that my unit chief will approve re-opening the case. I'll keep you advised, okay?"

Like a mic drop, the phone fell from my hands.

Chapter Forty-Three

"Let every sunrise be a reminder of your ability to ascend from darkness by rising up and shining your light."
~LaShaun Middlebrooks Collier

The day started out well enough.

But the way it ended was a body slam on concrete.

I arose feeling okay in spite of Hunter's revelations. Truth was, I always had a little bit of hesitation about Wyatt, and I wasn't shocked. More like...what now? It did no good to live in anxiety. As my mom said, I'd 'do what I could and leave the rest up to God'. I would still live my life with clarity and purpose, and besides, every day I learned more great tactics from Tom, and it felt empowering.

I would not live in fear.

But...I should buy a handgun.

Staring at myself in the mirror, I took stock of my current physical state. Hazel had impressed upon me the value of taking care of myself.

My hair looked good. I'd let it grow out, and my stylist had talked me into a layered cut, and I didn't have to do much but fluff it in the mornings. I circled my wrist with my thumb and middle finger. I made a mental note to load up on calories. Pinching the softness around my 42-year-old waist, I added walking or working out.

"Mom!" Lilly yelled up the stairs a few minutes later, "Going to work! Pool opened today!"

I walked to the top of the stairs and took in her sweet face, eyes the same amber as my own; the backpack slung across one shoulder in preparation for her lifeguard job at the YMCA, the same job her sister held for three years before leaving for college. Looking at Lilly was like a flash from the past. She looked like me at the same age. Wait…did I have a memory from twenty-five years ago? Yes! I did!

"Okay, when are you coming home?"

"I'll text. Love you."

The next sound was her car pulling away.

I patted on foundation, applied eyeliner and blush. I'd been told I'd not worn much makeup before my accide—assault. Which was interesting, because it had taken about two seconds for me to figure out that makeup was a miracle. I pouted my lips in satisfaction at my new lipstick color.

The media had pounded the story of a Jane Doe dumped in the bushes outside Mercy Hospital and the miracle of her recovery into public consciousness for two long years, until everyone, myself included, believed the hype. They painted me as a victim, and this mentality had embedded itself in my psyche. Somewhere along the way, the victim in me had breathed her last, and the latent warrior in me had arisen. The tougher the day in front of me, the more makeup I slapped on. Like armor.

I laughed. Riot lifted his head, realized that food was not in the offing, and lay back down again. With a yawn, he rolled onto his back. "Riot," I whispered as I got ready to go wait for Tom for another day in the life of a PI, "I'm getting more memories back!"

Riot did not seem impressed.

* * *

As I sat on the porch and waited for Tom's car to drive up, a thought struck so hard, I dribbled coffee on my pants.

"Crap," I muttered, thankful that the stains wouldn't show on the dark jeans. If people didn't look too close, anyway. I stalked down the stairs to the sidewalk that made a hard right toward the gate. Craning my neck, I could make out the silhouette of the videocam Wyatt had installed, which

I'd been ignoring. Since he now loomed on my horizon like a simmering storm, the smart money was on staying vigilant.

I wondered where the heck Tom was. It was almost ten, and he was a guy that hated being late. Our usual pick-up time was 9:30. I pulled out my phone. No text from Tom. However…I'd use it to zoom in on the videocam. I'd always hated that thing, and now…I wondered if it had been a forewarning. Positioning the phone, I zoomed in as close as possible. The camera, once focused toward the main highway and on the area closest to Wyatt's building, now pointed straight at *my house.*

Maybe a curious raccoon or squirrel climbed on it and knocked it around?

On cue, Wyatt came trotting up the lane toward me. He stopped fifty yards from me, and called out, "Olivia, have you heard from Sherry? She hasn't called me back to set up a time."

I circled my mouth with my hands and called out, "I'll talk to her!"

He smiled and gave me a thumbs-up.

I showed him all my teeth, but it was a fake smile.

I texted Sherry, and she told me she'd call him.

Tom's car edged up behind Wyatt. Wyatt watched the car drive toward me, and I could tell that he was curious.

I ran back inside, snatched up my purse and sunglasses, and joined Tom. His slow drawl, and calm manner, once such an irritation, now held blessed relief. And savvy teaching techniques as well.

Wyatt stared as we drove past in Tom's aging Pontiac. Maybe he wanted to make sure I was serious about becoming an investigator. I thought about how Wyatt had made me co-admin on his security system. I'd ignored the screens for a while. Needed to check on that.

Tom told me the lesson today would be surveillance and the best use of security cameras and tools needed.

I told him that his timing was impeccable.

* * *

Later, I walked out onto my porch and sat there a good ten minutes, staring at nothing. Tom had been informative about security cameras and the different ways in which they can be utilized and one sizzling-hot fact lodged itself at the front of my brain.

"Yeah, you know," Tom had murmured in his soft way, "the interestin' thing about these security systems is that people don't think about them goin' the other way, too." I'd looked at him in confusion. "You can see the footage, but the footage can also see you. The primary admin can reverse the screen, like on a cell phone. With a wary glance toward Wyatt's office, I'd led Tom to the tree covered in electrical cord connected to God-knows-where. "I remember this," he'd said, scratching his head through the wispy, gray hair, "but seems he's changed the camera, and now it's one of those hyper-powered doo-dads that can see in every direction, with enhanced thermal." He'd squinted at me. "I remember he was a lawyer from Pennsylvania. Is he the nervous sort?"

I'd made a little rude sound with my mouth. "Maybe. But I'm the one that's nervous, Tom. About him. "Come on," I said as we tromped through the brush, back to his car, "let me show you what's inside my house. He made me a co-administrator on the system. At least I think that's what he did."

But my mind was stuck on what he'd told me. "Cameras can go backwards *and* forwards." The words made my pulse race.

How much had he watched? And the location of my computer? How often had it been in my bedroom, or my kitchen? How often had I been caught walking around in my underwear? I dropped my face in my hands. I was—once again—caught unprepared. And Lilly! How often had the creep watched her? Earl had pointed out two small, dome-shaped cameras affixed to the ceiling. The ones that looked like simple dome lights. Wyatt had told me they were necessary for connectivity, when in actuality, they had watched and recorded every move we made.

I ran inside and got my high-intensity flashlight. Made sure Lilly was in her room, sleeping; locked her in, and put the house keys in my pocket. Wearing the epitome of cliché, the black hoodie; I tore off—a good distance from the lane—through the trees on my property to circle around behind Wyatt's videocam. Now that I'd been educated about every type of surveillance system, I knew what *not* to do.

Since my property still measured around four acres in spite of Wyatt purchasing the frontage, I had plenty of room to give the videocam a wide berth. Tom had told me the wired ones like Wyatt's can capture a distance of 1200 feet in daylight, but at night, it's limited to 100-200 feet, so I felt secure. In the undergrowth, my flashlight turned off, I listened to frogs singing, owls hooting. The lightning bugs had closed shop for the night. A light breeze rustled the leaves and swept across my sweaty face. I slipped closer to the base, looking upward to make sure the camera wasn't scrolling. When had he changed it? Why hadn't I noticed?

You dropped your guard.

Callie's words rang in my ears.

And Monty had called her husband, Graham. What was that about?

I stepped forward, cautious. Paused to listen.

No change.

Another step. Another. A loud rustle in the undergrowth. I jerked my head toward the sound. The outline of the back end of a white-tail deer dashed away. I'd startled him. Quick as my thoughts, two fawns and a doe leapt out in front of me and bounded after the buck. I was lucky not to get sliced with a hoof.

Relieved, I continued on. Another careful step. Another.

Five minutes passed like two hours. I shielded my cell with my hand to hide the light and tried to find the bottom of the electrical cord. The deer were a godsend, I realized. Any thermal imaging would pick up the deer instead of me. There! The thick, green cord wound around the tree had been hidden in the root system. I dropped to my hands and knees and felt around in the weeds and sticks and pine cones. The same intuitive feeling I'd had outside Mercy Hospital hit me like an electric jolt.

I knew what to do.

The blunt knife I'd brought felt clumsy in my icy fingers. With one hand, I clutched the electrical wire, and with the other, I sawed the heck out of the ropy, plastic-covered wires until the connection was severed. Ragged and rough, as if an animal had chewed through it. After the cut, I wiped down the wire with a clean cloth.

I backed away on all fours; alert and quiet as a cat, until I felt safe enough to stand.

I tore through the undergrowth back to my house and stole around to the back door off the patio. Once inside, I drove the deadbolt home, and rested my back against the door, breathing hard, a big smile on my face.

Chapter Forty-Four

Monty checked himself in the small, cracked mirror on the wall above the sink in his cell. Combed his hair, brushed his teeth. Grinned at his image, and winked. "Casey, ole' boy, favorite CO of the moment, you've sure come through for me." He walked over to the narrow window, scanned the walkway outside the row of cells. All clear.

Still smiling, he snagged his new cell from a different hiding place. Casey, bless him, had been able to secure a brief reprieve from the discipline protocols, and had arranged for Hannah to visit. He pressed in Dudley's number. Duds answered on the first ring.

"Today, huh?"

"Yeah," Monty answered, and sat on the floor as far away from the door window as he could get. This time, he'd hidden his phone in a blind spot that the OCs could not see from his window. He wouldn't get caught again, and he'd played up his remorse over the burner phone they'd found to the hilt. No way was one little blot on his record going to keep him from his goal—early release. "Have you tried the kid? Man, he's been so helpful."

"Naah, dude. That CO won't have anything to do with me. You must be special."

Monty thought about that.

"I don't know, man, I'm just looking forward to a woman to talk to."

Duds laughed. "Right."

"I'm tired. I think I need to...y'know. Move on. Drop the hate."

"You have a life change or somethin'?"

Monty grunted. "You might say I had a 'come to Jesus' moment. Jesus showed me I would end up in the hole if I don't keep it on the straight and narrow in herc."

"I'm keepin' my head down, that's for sure. Sixteen more months, dude, and I'm out."

Monty heard steps coming down the hall. Voices call out. "Gotta go." Monty replaced the cell, hopped up, and sat on his bunk. Casey appeared at his window five seconds later.

"Female visitor!" Casey declared.

Monty backed up to the tray slot and extended his arms. The CO cuffed him, unlocked the door, and walked him down the hallway to a litany of hoots, catcalls, and slurping sounds.

Monty grimaced. He didn't know how much longer he could take being in here. With a sigh, he followed the young corrections officer.

* * *

The bright white of the reception room was more than he could handle after his limited exposure to light in the hole. He blinked and put his nose into his shoulder, which did not work at all. Casey removed the handcuffs and walked out.

Monty approached Hannah and sat across from her.

"How you doing?" he said, with a smile, devouring her with his eyes. Hannah looked even more terrific than usual. She had a tan, now, accentuated by her long, blonde hair. Her wide, blue eyes held...he wasn't sure, tension? She seemed distracted. She wore a light green sundress with a V-neck, He couldn't take his eyes off her low-cut sundress, which highlighted the necklace she wore.

Only one other table was occupied. Two busy, young kids were wearing out their haggard-looking mother, and the inmate they'd come to visit looked as if couldn't wait to return to his cell.

"I'm good," she said, following his gaze to the family across the room. "I bet you miss your kids."

Monty tilted his head, considering. "Of course I do. Serena's...well, Serena is Serena. She's a tough, little nut to crack. Lilly's been here quite a bit, though." He frowned. "You have to know that, right?"

She nodded. "I'm just making small talk. How are you?"

"Good as possible, I guess. I'm outta the hole soon, I think. Did you talk to someone and get that done?"

"I didn't. That new guy, Casey? He likes you."

Monty blew out a frustrated breath. "Yeah, Buddy Bromage did a real number on me. He's still not talking to me. Got his shifts switched or something. Speaking of…did you get the card situation fixed? I thought that might've been why they backed off my time in solitary."

"I don't know what happened." Hannah lowered her eyelids and fidgeted with her hands. Monty frowned. "But I didn't make good on the money, if that's what you mean. Why should I? The cards were fine when I bought them. Haven't you heard about the scams with these? Someone must've written down the card numbers and emptied them." After a pause, she continued. "Why'd you call Graham? That wasn't smart."

A shadow crossed his face. "How'd you know?"

"Good grief, Monty, we get together on a regular basis. You don't think we talk about that stuff? You're one of the major topics, for God's sake."

Monty smiled. "I like that."

Hannah rolled her eyes. "You shouldn't."

"What the hell is wrong with you today? I haven't seen you in weeks, and I've looked forward to this." Monty fumed. "I called Graham to make sure the kids are…well, Olivia's not thinking straight, at least with me…and I wanted to make sure the girls are okay." His eyes fixated on the medallion at the end of her necklace. He leaned across the table for a closer look. Hannah was quiet, watchful. "How did you get in with *that* on?"

She shrugged. "I told them it was a religious necklace, since they don't allow anything else. They believed me."

"Where'd you get it?"

After a blip of silence, she said, "Why don't you tell me, Monty?"

Monty pounded a fist on the table. The officer at the door frowned at him. Monty cursed softly, leaned back in his chair, and folded his arms across his chest. Another warning look from the officer.

"Callahan! Hands where I can see 'em!"

Monty grinned, all peachy and innocent, and put his arms on top of the table. "Sorry."

Hannah bent her long, lean frame toward him. "You know exactly what this is, Monty. It's your damn fraternity badge, and Olivia thought you needed to know that she found it," she hissed.

Monty felt the blood drain from his face. His lower lip trembled. "Where did she find it?"

"Outside Mercy Hospital's ER, Monty. Give me a break. You *know* that. And we dug out your old college yearbook, found your fraternity pictures, and your good buddy, Niles, and guess what? He wasn't even *in* a fraternity. It couldn't be his. It's yours!"

Monty frowned and snapped his mouth shut.

Hannah leaned in further, a smirk playing with her lips. "So you see, asshole, you've been made. *You* were with Niles that night...you helped him or whatever, or maybe you're the one who assaulted her, who knows? Maybe you wanted to *watch*," she hissed. "How stupid of you to wear this," she said, fingering the pendant that dangled between her breasts.

Monty looked away, then back at Hannah, his fingers on his chin in speculation. "Does she know about us?"

Hannah's chin jerked into her neck. "Monty that was like...*fifteen years ago.* Let dead dogs lie, and all that."

Monty's eyes slitted. When he spoke again, his tone was hushed. "She'll never speak to you again."

Hannah glared. "We're human, and it was a long time ago. And only once. She'll forgive me."

He shrugged. "Sure about that?"

"What I'm sure about is that you deserve to rot in here, Monty. I don't know why I ever thought—."

Monty scrutinized Hannah from top to bottom, taking his time. "You're still a good-looking woman, Hannah. Even from a jailbird like me, you crave attention. Your dipwad of a husband couldn't ever give you what you needed." He laughed and noticed her ringless left hand. He smiled with half his mouth…a 'gotcha' smile. "He divorced you, didn't he?"

Hannah looked away. The kids at the other table had been given coloring books and busily colored. The inmate and his wife were holding hands. Hannah smiled at that.

"Monty, I have a lot to learn about…relationships. And I thought I could come and…cheer you up…be a friend…but I guess all you have on your mind is how you can *use* people. She cleared her throat, turned her face to his. "By the third or fourth visit, I realized all you wanted was my help in paying off the guards, and information about Olivia. In short, I'm another one of the many people you've used to get what you want." She shook her head. "Pathetic. I'm pathetic, but you're *more* pathetic."

He laughed. Then he lurched forward and ripped the necklace from her neck before she could react. Her hand rose to her throat. The CO went all psycho and threatened Monty with his expandable baton. "Whatever you took off her, I want it, Monty. Now." He stuck out his palm.

Pale and shaken, Monty realized he'd crossed a big, freaking line and he'd be headed for solitary again. He threw the pendant at the CO. Hannah, smiling a secret smile, touched her lips, and glanced at the guard. "Good thing you gave us a heads-up, Hannah."

"It's all on video, right?"

"Yep," he said, and dropped to the floor, scooped up the pendant, and put it in her hand. "Guys we stationed out in the hall have instructions to take him where the sun don't shine. You take good care, now."

Monty's jaw dropped.

"Thanks. And this?" she asked, smiling at Monty as she pulled a taped wire from the depths of her top with a slight grimace. She handed the wire to the CO.

Monty scowled as he watched Hannah wave and waltz away, the scent of her cologne and glimpse of cleavage pasting desire across each tired and over-worked CO's face.

Muttering an expletive under his breath, he strode down the hall in cuffs between two very pissed-off COs.

Chapter Forty-Five

"The wise will rise, but the fool will duel."
~*Gena Showalter*

My visit to the Carroll County Clerk's Office had been revelatory.

First, Wyatt had filed the lawsuit before I'd even agreed to work for him. Second, he'd already deposed Monty, and neither Monty nor Wyatt had said a word about it. And third, Hannah chattered in my ear like the neighborhood gossip with all the gory details about the culmination of our 'evil plan,' as it would henceforth and forever be known.

Thirty minutes. No pauses, breaths, nothing.

The situation was *so* absurd.

I had to laugh.

Hannah stopped in mid-sentence. "What's funny? *Nothing* I said was funny."

"I was thinking that you and I should team up. Maybe start a business."

"A business?"

"Hannah, I'm amazed you pulled that off, and I'm proud of you, but...my ear is tired."

"Well, pardon me for being excited," she grumbled. "What kind of business? Like...stalking husbands in prison?"

We both laughed hysterically. It felt like a release valve for the tension that had been building for weeks.

"What if that's really a thing," Hannah asked. "There are tons of women that have husbands in prison, what if they could use...creative investigative work?"

"*Creative* investigating?"

"Callahan and Summers. Creative private investigation."

"I wonder how the licensing board would feel about that tagline. And the cops." I quipped. "Besides, I think that with the PI career path, 'creative' is a given." I smiled at my little joke. "So you think Monty is wrecked. For good?"

"When we started working this out, Casey told me that baiting him like that would make him go ballistic."

I smiled. The statement threw me back two years to the beach in Hilton Head Island, where Hunter and I had made a similar plan. Monty's bells were not hard to ring. I shook myself from the memory of sand dunes and the way it felt, my feet slipping and sliding in an attempt to outrun an outraged husband.

"The COs put Monty in the 'hair-trigger temper' category. So he got the other guards...I mean officers...set up outside the door." She paused. "Y'know, Casey wasn't there when it went down. I wondered at the time, but everything went so seamlessly..." her voice trailed off.

"My original question...?"

"Casey said it was like, a 'two times you're out,' and Monty would get isolation for six months and the parole board...well early release would be off the table. So I think he's out of the picture...your picture, anyway...for a while."

We listened to each other breathe in silence.

"You okay?" I asked.

"I still feel like an idiot...that I ever thought the guy was in any way—"

"Redeemable? Don't beat yourself up anymore, Hannah," I interrupted. "He makes a science out of manipulation. Look at it this way— *you* pushed him to admit he'd been with Niles when they dumped me. I always wondered how Niles did that. He was a bicycle guy, muscular and lean, but short. Almost...fragile. It was a stretch to believe he could carry me that distance. Now, Hunter has enough to re-open the case, and Monty can maybe sit on what he's done long enough to figure out he needs to change."

Hannah grunted. "Like he can."

"Never say never."

Hannah was quiet. "For his sake, I hope he changes, Olivia." After a beat, she continued, "For ours, too."

* * *

After we ended the call, I pressed in Hunter's number. It rang and rang and rang. With a frown, I tried again. He answered on the third ring.

"Busy?" I snapped.

Pause. "Yep," he said.

In the background, I heard voices, the sound of clinking and laughter, a woman's voice.

"Do you have a few minutes?"

"Hold on."

The cell went silent. He'd put it on mute. I fumed as I waited. What was so important he couldn't spare a few minutes to talk about the case?

"Okay," he said when he returned. "I'm good. Go ahead."

"What are you doing?"

Pause. "Having lunch with a friend, Olivia."

My forehead beetled. The woman he had talked about, he was with *her*. The woman he said was a better fit for him than I was. "So much for wanting to pursue a relationship, right?"

After a beat of silence, he responded. "Yeah, I'm having lunch with a *woman* friend, and it's really...none of your business, okay? You've made your lack of interest real clear. I got the message. Now, what's up?"

Struggling, I told myself to shut up about it before I lost whatever relationship we did have. I needed him. In clipped tones, I told him what Hannah had done and Monty's response.

"What? How did you..." he sputtered, exasperated. "You didn't tell me you found something at the site!"

"There's a lot of stuff I don't tell you," I said. "We have the video, and of course, the COs witnessed the whole thing."

"Wow."

"Yeah. Hannah did it. We planned it, but one of the guards collaborated because Hannah had developed a relationship with him through Monty."

"How'd she do that?"

I thought about how to answer. Should I tell Hunter everything? He was bound to uphold the law to extract justice and all that. But me? I was a private citizen, and what good would it do to tell him that my Wine & Whine girls had all supported me in getting Monty off my back and onto a road more suited to his disposition—extended jail time.

Yeah, Hunter didn't need to know that.

"I'm not sure," I lied, "but she's pretty good at persuading, um, men to do things for her."

"Okay," Hunter conceded. "But how do we explain the form in Earl's office? The one I've never seen or heard about?" he asked, his tone sarcastic.

Those dots didn't connect at all. I couldn't imagine who would've done that, but in the back of my mind, I knew there was a connection.

"I can't explain that."

"We need to."

"Isn't that *your* job?" I asked, with a voice all sugary-sweet.

"Very funny. The chief is looking at re-opening it. I quote, "Anything connected to helping "Mercy's Miracle" helps the Richmond PD's reputation.""

"Good to know," I said.

Hunter grunted. "Chief Satterfield has no idea what you're capable of."

"Let's keep it that way," I quipped.

* * *

Lilly's car zipped up the lane and jerked to a stop in front of the garage. She jumped out of the car, backpack slung on her shoulder. I watched her from my spot on the front porch, where I was enjoying tea and scones I'd purchased from Santoni's, a local fresh market a few miles from my house. I'd left my phone in the house so I wouldn't be tempted to think about

Monty, or Wyatt, or the plethora of unanswered questions.

"Why didn't you answer, Mom?" she asked, trotting from her car, through the white, wooden gate, and up the sidewalk to the porch. She dropped the backpack on the floor and hopped onto the porch swing. Every time I looked up at the hooks that held the swing, it made me sad. Monty and I had spent so much time painting it to match the furniture, hanging it. We'd made it fun, back in the day. That must've been about thirteen years ago, I thought. Right after we bought the house.

"Mom! What are you thinking about? Helloooo?"

I blinked. Stared at her. "Oh. Sorry. Thinking about when your dad and I put up the swing."

"I don't remember that. I remember that you guys were always remodeling, though."

I was quiet, smiling.

"You loved him once, right, Mom?"

"Of course, honey," I answered. "But I was a much different woman."

"He wasn't different?"

I cocked my head. Sipped my tea. "I don't know. I'd love to grab more of those memories, but I'm not sure I'll get them back." I brightened. "But I did have a memory of you, a couple days ago. I looked at you and flashed back to your toddler days, so there's hope!"

Lilly rose and planted a kiss on my forehead. "That's great, Mom. I'm going to get a snack." She grabbed the backpack and bounded into the house. Riot jumped a foot, circled, and re-settled on the floor, his wide, ginger face and golden eyes fixed on me.

My tea had gotten cold. So, feeling an inexplicable need to apologize for wasting the tea, I emptied the cup over the front porch railing into the grass. As I pulled back my cup, I noticed a bump underneath the railing. I squatted down for a better look. A white button had been attached. I took a photo of it and sent it to Tom. He got back to me fast. A bug. My flesh crawled. Wyatt. I'd forgotten about him in the midst of 'Operation Monty.' I texted Tom back.

Tom what the hell do I do?

T - It's wireless. Relocate it where it won't matter. Don't destroy it. You may need it. Move it with nitrile gloves. Did you buy them?

Yeah. Didn't think I'd need them so soon.

T - A good PI is never without them. Move it to a tree or anywhere you can't be heard having a conversation. He'll show up and see how you're doing, you watch. Any word on the videocam disconnection?

Not yet. Are you sure it's a bug?

T - Yep. Cheap one. He'll show up anytime now. I bet he's not getting feeds at all. Are you sure you don't want to get the cops involved yet?

I'm sure I want to trap this jerk and get hard evidence first.

T - You on for tomorrow?

I sent a thumbs-up icon and pocketed the phone. Now, I could focus on Wyatt, and figure out his end game. Was it money? Proving himself in the community? Whatever it was, I felt a fresh determination sizzle through my chest. One thing I'd learned on my brief tour as a brain injury survivor was that people might want to stay out of my way when I felt like this.

Chapter Forty-Six

Hunter stared at the flat, white ceiling and blinked. Carefully turning his head, he saw an IV in his arm and heard beeping sounds.

Damn.

He was in a hospital.

A nurse bustled in, lifted his wrist to take his pulse, nodded in satisfaction, and adjusted the IV. Hunter croaked, "What am I doing here?"

"Welcome back! Your car was, um, the victim of an explosion. You were in the vicinity and sustained a concussion and cuts from glass and metal pieces. You'll be fine though."

Dazed, he tried to remember. "When?"

"Yesterday afternoon, late," she said, typing notes into her electronic pad. She finished, put it underneath her arm, and cocked her head. "Second attempt, I understand."

Hunter slid up on the pillows, his head starting to pound. "Yeah. Wow."

She patted him on the shoulder. "You'll be fine. Doc'll be in soon."

He must've gotten knocked out, because he hardly remembered what happened. But one thing he knew…whoever was doing this knew his history. Watching his partner's flesh melt away, on fire and beyond help in their PD-issued sedan, Hunter had never felt so helpless and frustrated. His partner had died the worst death imaginable. Hunter bowed his head, closed his eyes, and prayed for him, a habit he'd developed right after the funeral. He didn't know why it made him feel better, but it did. He prayed for his deceased partner, hoping maybe he'd hear him upstairs; and the family left behind. Jaw clenched, he tried out his arms and legs. Everything worked. He needed coffee. He ripped the IV needle from his arm and slung his legs over the side of the bed. Sat still a moment, to let the wooziness settle. He could tell he'd not been hurt that bad. He'd be damned if he'd lay in bed doing nothing while some sociopath was getting a good laugh. For what purpose, though?

He frowned, thinking. He—or she—*would* be brought to justice.

The door opened, and Chief Satterfield walked in. "Hey." He smiled. "See you're feelin' better. I guess it's a safe bet they haven't discharged you yet?"

Hunter's smile was wobbly. "I'm good. Gettin' outta here."

"What are you thinking?"

"I'm thinking...message received, but not sure what the message is. Find anything at the scene?"

The Chief crossed his arms, stared at a spot on the wall, and attempted to patchwork the events together. "First the ballpoint pen, and now...a delivery form from...guess where?" He shook his head. "This has to be connected to Callahan."

Hunter rubbed the back of his neck. "The guy has the longest reach of any mental case I know."

"How so?"

"Look, I haven't had time to unpack everything I've learned from Olivia. She and her friend have sort of...neutered Callahan. He's in solitary right now. I was on my way to talk to you...when..."

The Chief walked to the door and closed it. Returned and sat in a chair beside the bed. Folded his hands and straightened his shoulders. "So talk."

Two hours later, the case had been re-opened, Hunter had secured his release from the hospital, and a rental had been delivered. As he was about to get in the rental, Dr. Grayson Sturgis tapped him on the shoulder. "Hunter!"

The familiar voice stirred Hunter with emotion. Dr. Sturgis had been invaluable in early interviews while Olivia was still re-learning how to speak, and had been a strong ally in the investigation. Hunter had seen him when he'd visited Serena, but only for a few minutes. The men stared at each other in mutual appreciation until, eventually, Dr. Sturgis pulled him in for a bear hug.

"Was on my way to check on you, but you were already gone." Dr. Sturgis clapped him on the back. "You okay?"

"I gotta get this person." Hunter looked away. "Enough's enough."

Dr. Sturgis nodded. "Any ideas?"

"It has to do with Callahan. It has to."

"He's behind bars. What can he do?"

Hunter blew out a breath. Turned and leaned against his rental. "Yeah, and in solitary from what I understand. We're re-opening the case. Effective now."

Dr. Sturgis's eyebrows shot up. "What's going on?"

Hunter shook his head. "Can't say."

Dr. Sturgis put his hand on Hunter's shoulder and looked him in the eye. "Sophie and I are available. If you need anything—*anything*, hear me?—call."

The men shook. Hunter stomped the accelerator and pulled out into the street, wondering how long it would take to replace his Jeep this time.

Chapter Forty-Seven

"You learn who you really are in a fight—what you're really made of. You have to face yourself and rise above your own fears and failings."
~Tami Hoag

I walked into Wyatt's office on the pretext of saying hello to Sherry, but in reality, to test the waters of Wyatt's suspicions.

It had been a couple of days since I'd sawed off the videocam connection, and I'd put the bug he'd planted on my deck on the garage, too far away to be intelligible but close enough to hear voices. Hopefully, he'd think the bug had malfunctioned and remain unaware that I had discovered he was spying on me.

Sherry lifted her hands from her laptop and smiled when I walked in. "Hey! What brings you out here?"

"How's it going?" I asked. "Thought I'd drop in and say hi," I said, with a meaningful glance at Wyatt's office door.

"He's such a good boss!" she exclaimed for his benefit. Then, lowering her voice, she continued. "I haven't seen your civil suit cross my desk. I don't know what's going on with that. But Wyatt's been a basket case the past couple days."

I nodded. "Okay," I said, louder than necessary, "I'll take off. Tell Wyatt I came by."

Like a shot, Wyatt's door flew open. "Olivia! I thought that was your voice. How are you? Come on in a sec. You got time?"

My resolve wobbling, I followed him inside. When he closed the door behind us, I felt like a mouse in a trap.

He flapped his hands toward the chairs facing his desk. "Tell me all about the PI course."

I murmured a few obligatory thank-you's and course descriptions and that I enjoyed it and how much I'd learned in the few weeks I'd been shadowing Tom. From his reaction, I couldn't tell if he had any doubt that I was acting as agreed—waiting until I got my license so he could use me on a case.

Without warning, however, he changed course.

"Are you still checking the videocam screens? Mine is…having issues. Is yours working?"

I stuttered, "I-I…do you think there's a reason I need to keep watching?" I mustered a smile. "You're here all the time now, right? For your mom? So I've kind of put that on the back burner."

He nodded, nice and slow, his eyes never leaving my face.

"How is she, anyway?" I asked, the picture of innocence. I knew damn well he'd never had anyone in that nursing home.

"As good as can be expected, I guess." He shrugged. "I don't think she's got long."

"Very sad."

Without quite looking at me, Wyatt asked, "Have you received anything?"

I blinked. "Say again?"

"I…Olivia, I hate to have to tell you this. The Sorensons insisted that I include you in the suit. I'm sorry. The Westminster Police got it yesterday. Thought you'd be served by now."

Of course, he'd have to tell me. It couldn't come out of the blue. I'd wondered why I hadn't been served yet. I decided to act like it was a big nothing-burger. "I'll look for it."

He squinted at me, perplexed. "You're not upset?"

"I've been through worse, trust me."

"That's for sure. I followed the Mercy's Miracle case. Our local media picked it up. Every detail."

"Huh," I blurted. "You never told me that."

Misgiving shot across his features. He hadn't meant to reveal that much,

I realized. "That's right," I murmured, thinking. "Niles Peterson was from that area, right? Before he moved to Richmond?"

He nodded. "The media painted a horrible picture of him."

My eyebrows rose. "You knew him?"

He waved a hand. "A little. Saw him around."

"But…you're from Hershey. He was from Harrisburg."

His gaze hardened. "Like I said. Saw him around. Hershey is a suburb of Harrisburg."

I went quiet. This was a huge revelation, and I tried not to show how shocked I was. "Well, it was tragic. I never thought he was a horrible person, just a down-on-his-luck guy that made a bad decision. The injury was, well, in my opinion…an accident. A sickening accident." I watched him closely. His reaction would tell me a lot. Tom had taught me how to play it naïve and ignorant in order to elicit information. And my favorite, plant seeds of solicitation; little bread crumbs to lead the unwilling to the edge and see if they jump. I gave myself a mental pat on the back.

In reality, it had been a good thing the truth had come out, or Niles might've continued down the road of drugging and assaulting women.

A kaleidoscope of emotions flew across Wyatt's face as I waited him out. Agitated, he paced the office. "He never had a chance," he muttered. "He was a foster, did you know that? Bounced from house to house. All his life."

"Thought you didn't know him well, Wyatt."

His complexion colored. He stopped pacing, put his hands in his pockets, and looked at me. "An attorney is a student of the human condition. I always thought his was a tragic case. A lot of foster homes take great care of the kids, but many don't."

I stared at him. He sank into the chair beside me with a deprecatory wave. "Sorry for the over-reaction. It's outrageous, the way things turned out. Your ex got ten years…for *murder!*" He shook his head angrily. "He deserved to die, too. Or at least, life in a cell."

"Wyatt." I took a deep breath and made a quick decision. Since he was diving over the edge, I might as well join. "I know that Niles was your brother." After a pause, I continued. "I'm so…*so* sorry for your loss."

His fingers dug into the armrests of the chair.

I tried to clear the lump in my throat. "And I know that you were a foster kid, too."

A vein throbbed in his temple.

"How long have you been planning the civil suit, Wyatt?" I asked, my voice hushed.

He paled. Kept his eyes glued to the floor. "All that matters is that piece of shit husband of yours gets his due."

I rose from my chair. "We're agreed on that, Wyatt. But he is my *ex*-husband. So why am I on the suit?"

"The clients insisted," he said, with a shake of his head. "I need the cash. It's a solid case, and I thought, after the deposition—"

My brow furrowed. "What deposition?"

"The one I scheduled in two weeks. You'll get the paperwork."

"Haven't seen a server. No note, nothing."

"You had nothing to do with Niles' murder, I know that now. In my deposition, I plan to show you as a product of your environment—an emotionally unstable woman with a brute for a husband that controlled your every move."

"Boy, talk about research," I muttered.

"Like I said, I'm a student of the human condition. You think a controlling husband is bad? You ought to represent clients from foster care. It's chilling. I got into this business to change the system. Weed out the evil idiots that only take in the kids for the money. My foster family was fantastic. And eventually, they adopted me. I was lucky." His forehead furrowed. "When I think about what my brother went through…"

"Detective Faraday told me about Niles' history," I said. "He can testify that I was *not* one of those who wanted to see Niles get life in prison or the death penalty. I would've voted for therapy and a lesser sentence if that had been on the table."

He gave me a skeptical look. "What about your husband?"

"It's complicated," I said, carefully. I wouldn't let Wyatt twist my words, or use them in court against me. But what *had* he heard in my house on his video system?

"Besides," I hissed, "the cameras you were so diligent about making me co-administrator on and installing...you must know my innermost thoughts on the subject already."

A dawning realization cleared his countenance. "It was *you!*"

"What was?" I tried to look bewildered, but I didn't think he was buying it.

"I thought an animal had chewed through the wiring. But you did it, didn't you?"

I laughed as if his words were preposterous. "I have no clue what you're talking about."

The lines between his eyebrows deepened.

We stared at each other.

A chess game.

"What about Detective Faraday's Jeep, Wyatt?" I blurted, breaking the silence.

He frowned. "The detective who investigated the case? What does his Jeep have to do with anything?"

Interesting, I thought. No anger, no hatred, or any emotion other than curiosity. Was the guy really this good at lying? "Right. As if you don't know about the *bomb,* Wyatt. Give me a break."

"What bomb?"

I stared at him. *Was he on the level?*

"Seriously. A bomb? I'm clueless here, Olivia."

"My God, you don't know," I whispered.

"I had nothing to do with a bomb, I swear! Did someone try to kill Faraday? Is that it? I would've heard about that. Wouldn't I?" Wyatt had gone pale, tugging at his collar. "Olivia! Tell me what happened. When? Where?"

Obviously, he was upset. To the extreme. Something else was going on.

I stared at him. "Wyatt. It's all right. Detective Faraday is okay."

He went quiet, thinking. His lips trembled. He stared at the ceiling. Finally, he squeezed his eyes shut and put both hands across his face. "Oh, *no.* No, no, no! My God, Casey," he whispered in despair.

A twisting, coiling, wildness slithered through my veins. "Did you say Casey? Casey, *who?*" I demanded, thinking about the infamous guard—Casey—at Maryland Correctional Center that Hannah had beguiled into helping with Operation Monty.

"Olivia," he said, his voice resigned. "Casey is Niles' son."

My mind flew back two years. To Hilton Head Island. The star-studded night had been so beautiful...and it had been the second time we'd run into each other.

A thin ghost of a cloud drifted across the moon. A smattering of stars glinted in the darkening sky.

"Well, yes, I think...I'm happy."

Niles, sitting beside me, shook his head. "Don't you know?"

I stared at the boats. Life was so simple for boats, I thought. "I don't know what to think."

Niles raised his eyebrows.

I stared at the moon.

He smiled and drained the last of his beer, then twisted around and looked at the restaurant entrance. "Sorry, but I gotta get goin'. I just came in for a quick drink and to listen to the band until Casey was ready to go." He turned and pointed at his leggy, tall, teen-aged son with a couple of other boys. Niles waved, and Casey began walking in our direction. "Enjoy your night," he said. Then he was gone.

I remembered Casey. He'd been a high school senior, Niles had told me, later, when our chance Island meeting had turned into more. Hunter had filled me in during his investigation into Niles' family after the assault. Casey had been angry and defensive, and his mother had declared there had never been hope for his dad anyway. I could completely see how Casey had been driven to avenge his dad's murder.

I closed my eyes and saw Niles' mouth pleading with me to go easy on the assault charges when he ambushed me outside my attorney's office.

My eyes widened. Of course! They'd have to think Earl was a direct conduit to me, and maybe complicit in his father's indictment, when the truth was, poor Earl had nothing to do with anything other than help me through a difficult divorce from Monty. Niles had begged me to talk to someone, do something…he was terrified of losing his visitation rights. Casey had meant more to him than his own life, and when the police had found him in a hotel room, shot to death; a wallet-sized photo of Casey was in his hand.

"You're…his *uncle*," I whispered, astonished.

My mind screamed across the past few weeks. I spun around to confront Wyatt. *Tell him. Make him understand.* "Casey's still torn up with grief. He's just a kid. Are you sure? Is he capable of installing a car bomb?"

Wyatt let out a long breath. "Think about it. His dad never even had a chance to contest the charges. The first time I even heard about it, Casey reached out to tell me that his father, *my brother,* had been shot. Casey was devastated. I guess Niles told him about me, I don't know, but it was the first time I even knew I had a nephew, or where Niles ended up. I don't even know how he found me. But Richmond is a long way from Hershey. I felt so…helpless. Here was a blood relative, in desperate need of legal help… and emotional support. But the words out of his mouth…" Wyatt looked away. "First, I didn't even know I *had* a nephew, and second, he suggested we collaborate. Make a blood oath or something. He was…almost incoherent with grief and rage. He…he was so…*insistent.* Determined."

I let out the breath I was holding. My mind raced with possibilities. Tom had taught me a lot already, about getting information out of people, and one of the best tools was empathy, he'd said. Wyatt stared at the wall, squeezing his hands together over and over, as if he were cold.

"Sounds like an impossible situation," I murmured. "I'm sure you did the best you could."

A smile touched his lips. "When we talked, neither of us knew Niles had left Virginia to confront you personally, much less what he was thinking. I hadn't seen Niles in decades. The adoptions were shuttered—the parents thought it better that we have no contact. Casey must've…gotten the contact information of the adoption agency and talked them into letting him know where I was." His expression hardened. "Then, when it all came pouring out of Casey…when I realized what my brother had gone through—the blackmail situation that Monty had him in, the fostering nightmare— it was like gasoline on a fire, I guess." He stared at his shoes. "My brother, *murdered!* What was I supposed to do? My first allegiance was to this brother I'd lost, and when Casey reached out…I felt I had to make up for…lost time." He chuckled, sadly. "Believe it or not, I was trying to help."

I reached out and put my hand on his arm. "I know you were, Wyatt."

"My God, Casey, what have you done?" Wyatt whispered to himself.

I didn't know where to go next with this discussion, but I knew I needed a record of it. Excusing myself, I left the door open and approached Sherry.

"Sherry, I need you to join and record this. Okay?" I whispered.

She bobbled her head up and down, grabbed a notebook and her phone. Wyatt didn't even notice our return. His thoughts were elsewhere, maybe on the only blood relative he was aware of. How old would Casey be now? Seventeen when I'd first seen him, which would make him at least twenty, now? Most kids this age were so technically advanced that I'd bet he could've figured out a simple, homemade bomb and a remote trigger. All these kids needed was a YouTube video.

"Wyatt." I patted his arm. He startled, and came out of his trance. He looked at Sherry sitting on the couch. "Oh. Hi, Sherry. Did you need me?"

With a glance at me, she shook her head.

"Okay, Wyatt, why don't you tell us more about how you helped Casey?"

He recited facts like a robot, his mind on autopilot. I wondered if he was in shock. "I helped Casey research people involved with Niles' murderer. Since Earl was the Mercy Miracle attorney, of course, anything that went on with him was of interest to us. It was my idea, really…to move my office to Maryland." He shrugged. "There was opportunity here, because when I realized how old Earl was, I guessed he was getting ready to retire. Then I saw an ad for the frontage of your property and… it was like…a sign. A sign from Niles, maybe? I don't know, but I jumped at it. The land was listed at a reasonable price, and I needed to be onsite to figure out how to best approach…well, Casey called it 'justice.' He raised his head. "That's when we came up with the idea of applying for the corrections officer position. He could keep an eye on Monty, and I was supposed to take care of the legal end. I'd already taken Maryland's exam for out-of-state attorneys. We'd planned it all out." Wyatt stared out a window. "It would've made it easier to partner with Earl, but he was so damn against it, we had to recalibrate."

I felt like I was watching this play out like a documentary. Like the *ending chapters of my book.*

The hairs on the back of my neck stood up. Sherry, quiet as a mouse, tried to make herself invisible.

I couldn't believe Wyatt had no objection to the recording. One could make a case that he wasn't made aware of being recorded, so I tapped the phone and looked at Wyatt. "Wyatt, do we have your permission to record?" His vacant eyes looked at me, then dropped to the phone on the desk. He nodded. My shoulders sagged with relief. No one would believe this without proof. And now it would be admissible in court.

Wyatt seemed intent on the information dump. I wasn't sure what was going on with him...whether I should call for backup or sit still and listen.

He made that decision for me when he picked up the thread of our conversation.

"What better time to approach Earl's family with the possibility of a civil suit? After all, Earl's death was the result of his involvement with you, Olivia." He raised his head and looked at me. "I'm convinced of it."

A tremor of fear shook me. "It was? How do you know?" Earls' homicide case was still open, as far as I knew.

His nostrils flared, his mouth slightly open, Wyatt's eyes darkened.

I felt fear seeping up through the floor. Sherry's face was pale and drawn. She felt it, too.

I told myself to keep it together.

Wyatt continued. "After Casey and I developed...oh, I don't know...an *understanding*... I called Earl Sorenson. At first, I asked if he'd like to join forces since he was about to retire, and he responded like I'd popped him one in the face." Wyatt scowled and crossed his arms. "My nephew and I needed justice. He needed clients. I thought it was a reasonable request."

My mind flew back to the difficult conversations Earl had been having with a male client. *It had been Wyatt.* My voice whisper-soft, I asked, "And then?"

Wyatt's scowl deepened. "You'd thought I'd broken some godforsaken code of honor. He ripped me up one side and down the other. I chalked that up to a bad day, and called several times after that, but only got voicemail. Can you believe that? The guy was ghosting me. I was trying to give him a way out."

"No. I can't believe it, Wyatt. That was rude. What do you mean by 'a way out'?"

"He demanded that I never call again. So unprofessional! I've hammered out a practice and developed a reputation. I have more than ten years' experience and my clients are…were loyal. This simply…doesn't happen. Professional courtesy is taken very seriously where I come from." He sniffed in disgust, remembering. "I relocated my practice to avenge my brother's death. Pure and simple. To see that he got justice in the wake of his murder. These are *honorable* goals, right?"

He looked at me. I guess in some world, somewhere, these are honorable goals; if they align with our legal system, I thought.

"And he was appalled. Not supportive in any way." Wyatt shook his head, smiling a little. "The old guy was bleeding clients. He should've retired years ago, and yet here he was, staring at a great opportunity to partner with a younger, more aggressive attorney, but I was an outsider, and wouldn't understand, he said. There were circumstances beyond his control that I couldn't *fathom.*"

I prodded. "It's shameful, Wyatt. What he did. How he acted. Um, what do you mean you wanted to give Earl 'a way out'?" I asked again.

His head jerked at my question. He frowned, glanced at Sherry. "What's she doing here?"

"I asked her to come in to record our conversation and you agreed. Now, can you explain why you were trying to give Earl a 'way out'?

He put his hand over his eyes. "Casey was out of his head. Every time he asked if I'd talked to Earl, he'd be furious that I hadn't. When he learned that Earl was ignoring me, Casey started talking crazy." Wyatt studied the floor. "The kid had lost his dad and to his mind, his self-respect; and he was determined to do something. I was afraid he'd go after Earl."

CHAPTER FORTY-SEVEN

My eyes widened. "But, why? Earl hadn't done anything to Niles."

Wyatt sighed. "I think...he wanted someone to pay, that's all. To his view, Earl was a link to you, and in his twisted way, he blamed you by proxy for his dad's death. Does that make sense? If Earl had taken even ten minutes to hear me out when I went to see him." He dropped his head.

I shook my head. "No. It doesn't make sense. *Monty* killed his dad."

Wyatt raised his head. "Because of you."

I started to say something, but paused at Wyatt's set jaw and narrowed eyes.

My mind stumbled, then snagged the words: *when I went to see him.*

"When did you go to see Earl, Wyatt?"

His eyes darted right and left. He licked his lips. "I, uh...can't remember."

My hand rose to my throat. "What did you do, Wyatt?"

He stared at one of the faux plants I'd bought to put in the office. "Casey told me he wanted to *kill* the guy. And he meant it." Wyatt whooshed out a breath. "I couldn't lose a nephew *and* a brother. I just couldn't. I made a trip to Sorenson's office." Wyatt shook his head. "The old man had no idea what was coming, and the clock was ticking."

Wyatt closed his eyes and sighed. "All I kept thinking was that Casey would be safe. Casey would be...safe," his voice dropped to a whisper.

I held my breath.

Like waking from a dream, Wyatt straightened in his chair and pushed his shoulders back. After a contemplative look at me, he folded his hands on his desk.

"I think I'll stop talking, now."

Sherry slipped over to the edge of Wyatt's desk, picked up her phone, and left the room. I heard her voice as she called 911 from reception.

Wyatt began to shake. He tried to hide it, but he couldn't control himself. The man was having a meltdown. Either that, or going into shock. I put a hand on his shoulder. He looked up, stricken. "Casey? Please find out about Casey? He's been through so much." He frowned, and looked away, rubbing his hands. His head jerked up at me again. "Listen, Casey wants to bring Monty Callahan to his knees. Justice for his dad. He's in that prison now, and I don't know what he's capable of."

Sherry walked back in, her mouth opening and closing in disbelief, like a fish gasping for air. I kept my hand on Wyatt's shuddering shoulder. I doubted he'd registered the full impact of what he'd told me. When he did, he was going to need medical attention.

"Olivia," she whispered, sidling up beside me, giving Wyatt a wide berth, as if he were a rabid dog. "Cops and paramedics are on the way. But when I told them you were here too, they asked that I tell you that Hunter is out of the hospital."

The ground beneath me shifted.

Wyatt wasn't paying the slightest bit of attention to anything but the shrunken orb of his own little world, so I grabbed Sherry's arm and propelled her across the room.

"Is he okay? What happened? Don't tell me it was another—"

"Bomb attack. It was. He wasn't in the car, though."

My knees went weak. Sherry gripped my shoulders and held me up. "He's okay, Olivia. Mild concussion."

"I need to talk to Richmond PD ASAP." I cocked my head toward Wyatt. "Casey is behind the IEDs, Sherry," I said, punching in 911. "Would you go ahead and call Hunter? He'd want to know, regardless."

She grabbed her cell as I recited the number. She held the phone to her ear.

"Casey came up with the bomb stuff all by himself. Wyatt didn't have any knowledge of that, and I believe him, but he admitted he'd been to see Earl. Wouldn't tell me when."

Sherry blinked. "You don't think—?"

I threw up my hands. "I kinda *do* think."

"Holy crap."

"Yeah."

I glanced at Wyatt. The shaking had intensified. "The way he dumped everything…I think the guy's eaten up with guilt. I don't think it'll be long before our favorite detective will have a confession. Just a hunch."

Richmond PD answered. I summarized what I'd discovered, and they said they'd alert the appropriate channels. I emphasized the importance of Casey's position as CO at the correctional facility.

After we ended the call, I felt numb.

Sherry told me she was still trying to get Hunter on the phone.

"Hunter was already re-opening Monty's case—with new evidence." I groaned. Sherry listened, fanning herself with a brochure. She'd been freaked out, too. We were both trying to come off the adrenalin rush that had kept us going. "If Casey had known that Monty was going to get justice after all…" The wall of self-control I'd erected came tumbling down. Sherry gave me a hug.

I cried hot, angry, tears into Sherry's shoulder. For Hunter, for Niles' family, for the futility of revenge. For poor Earl, too; caught in a storm he didn't see coming.

And for me too, a little.

Chapter Forty-Eight

Monty paced his cell like a neglected lion in a cage. His black hair, a mass of oily tangles, reached below his shoulders now. The COs let him have only one quick shower a week. A sliver of sunlight graced the small space for a few minutes each day, the result of a high, rectangular window. The COs didn't seem too interested in wasting electricity on the floor that held the solitary cells. The food, though, was good enough, he had to give them that. He counted his steps. Ten steps in one direction, eight in the other. Though it was dark and musty and bug-infested in the basement, the cell was bigger than his other one.

Monty had learned to find the good in things.

It was either that or go completely mad.

He completed his steps, then dropped to the floor for fifty push-ups. The concrete floor felt like ice underneath his hands. He hopped up and rubbed his arms. He wondered what month it was. May? June? With a sigh, he picked up one of several books they'd allowed him to have, flopped on the bed, and began reading, a curious peace comforting him. The white-hot anger at the sound of his ex-wife's name had withered away to mild disgruntlement. Whatever state of denial he'd been living in had been stripped away. When Hannah had confronted him with the fraternity badge, plans for revenge seemed ill-advised against the backdrop of the overwhelming proof that he'd been an accomplice to Niles' crime.

He sighed. What a ridiculous oversight to lose it, and now they would tack on years.

He thought back to the night that had kicked everything off...the night that changed everything.

Niles had called, his voice sticky and fragile and panicked.

"I...I..."

"Spit it out, Niles. What is it?"

He looked at the clock on his phone. Why was he calling at midnight?

"I know you told me to watch her. I know, man, but, things went way wrong. And I'm sorry. I'm sorry, okay?"

Monty felt his heart stop beating for a second. "What did you do?"

Niles began to cry, which developed into long, racking, sobs. Monty held the phone away from his ear, damning the day he'd even taken this idiot under his wing in college. With a sigh, he got up from his bed, stretched, and sat in the hotel room's armchair. "C'mon man, it can't be that bad."

"It is! It is, Monty. I can't do this by myself."

Monty was quiet. "What could go wrong? Dammit, can't you at least keep an eye on someone without turning it into roadkill?"

Niles' sobbing stalled.

"What have you done?" Monty roared, jumping to his feet, clenching his fist. "What did you do, you sniveling, little—"

"It just...happened, Monty. She's a beautiful woman, and I found myself, I, uh... found myself...well, I fixed her dinner at my place, and she was so beautiful..."

"Good God," Monty whispered, placing a palm across his eyes. "You didn't."

"We've had some good times, haven't we? With those women?" Niles whimpered. "I...remembered those times, I guess. It was wrong. It was a terrible choice."

"So...you used drugs on my WIFE?"

"I'm sorry! I know it was wrong, but...but...there was an accident. I need help."

He hadn't meant Niles to do anything but watch her and give him updates. There had never been a chance of the guy getting involved with her. He should've known, though. When had Niles ever been dependable?

"What happened?" Monty asked, resigned.

"She's injured, man. It's bad. She fell. She hit her head. She's bleeding out in my bedroom."

Monty groaned. Like hell she 'fell'! But he couldn't get emotional, he had to think.

"Okay. Stay with me, here. I'm in Alexandria on business, so I can be there in an hour or two if traffic's light. Wrap her head, okay? Get a towel, and wrap her head tight. As tight as you can, to stop the bleeding. Make her comfortable. Try to get water down her. I'll be there as soon as I can."

"Should I take her to the hospital? She's cold, man. She's not waking up. She's not...well, gone...but I don't know—"

"NO. Do you want to have an assault charge? Do I want to go down with you? NO. Look, I'll be there soon. Hang tight. Do not call anyone! Repeat that for me, Niles. Can you say the words?"

"I won't call anyone," Niles promised.

"I'll be there soon."

Monty stretched his bulked-up arms over his head on the narrow cot, interlaced his fingers, and put his hands behind his head. He'd arrived at Niles' place in seventy-five minutes, and they'd wrapped Olivia as best they could and deposited her in his vehicle at two a.m., still unconscious, but alive. Monty followed Niles to Mercy Hospital in his car, careful to avoid the hospital's security cameras. After they'd scouted the area, they both carried her to a patch of bushes outside the emergency room and lay her in a space between. They'd raced away, secure in the knowledge that both personnel and patients walked past at all hours. She'd be found. But without her ID. Monty knew his wife's fingerprints weren't in the federal database, and facial rec would take a while to implement. He'd insisted all Olivia's personal items—wedding ring, earrings, purse, car—be trashed. It had taken them the rest of the night and into the next day. They scattered everything in the trash bins of neighboring small towns and drove Olivia's car into a lake. Monty heaved out a breath, remembering. Watching it sink had been hard. The complete waste of a late-model vehicle. Had to be done, though. As the sun powered up and Niles looked like something the dog had thrown up, Monty drove the two of them to a Dollar Store and bought a strong bleach cleaner for Niles to use on his carpet.

Monty had demanded that Niles never contact him again. He agreed.

And he had been true to his word.

Until the little brat had come to Maryland to beg his ex-wife for forgiveness and a reduced sentence.

That had been a tipping point. How dense do you have to be to confront the victim right before her case became the story of the year? It had been bad enough that Olivia had become the media's favorite feel-good event after she survived, but Niles had to *compound* his stupidity by showing up in Maryland.

What a fool.

So he'd walked into Niles' scummy little hotel room and taken care of it.

People that stupid *deserved* what they got.

* * *

The clomp-clomp of heavy boots sounded in the hall. He heard the rattle of keys from a pocket. Monty's brow furrowed. The checkpoints did not happen at this time of day, and a random CO visit to his cell didn't make any sense in solitary.

Keys jangled in the lock mechanism.

The deadbolt slid away.

Chapter Forty-Nine

"I need to talk to Detective Hunter Faraday," Sherry insisted. "It's urgent." She heard scuffling sounds, and in minutes, Hunter was on the phone.

"Hunter, it's Casey! Casey's behind the bombs!"

"Slow down," Hunter said, scratching his head, wincing a bit as he did. His head still rocked from the blast. "Who is this, and I need you to lower your voice. Who's Casey?"

Sherry took a breath. "This is Sherry, Olivia's friend."

A deep groove appeared between his eyebrows. "You guys are gonna get yourselves arrested."

"Wait," she said, her voice clipped and serious. "Olivia had a talk with Wyatt Harp. He confessed *everything*. I've texted you the recording. I'm not sure how much you already know, but Wyatt is Niles Peterson's brother, and Casey, who's a CO there, is Niles' son. The son is responsible for the bombs, Hunter. Casey is unstable and pissed off."

Hunter barked out questions, all business now. They talked a few minutes more and ended the call.

Hunter ran toward his vehicle in the Richmond PD lot. On the way, he pulled in a uniform. "Thomasson!" He called out to a cop on the front steps of the building. "I need you! Come with me. We'll call for back-up on the way."

They flew toward Hagerstown. Hunter called the warden and asked to keep more eyes on Monty.

When they pulled up three hours later, the warden waited outside, nervous and shifting his weight from one foot to the other, wringing his hands. He ushered them in. The three men trudged downstairs to solitary.

"Can't locate the CO you mentioned," the warden whispered. "He's not responding." He shot a worried look at Hunter. "Hope we're not too late, son."

"I know where he is," Hunter said, his jaw clenched and hand poised over the holster on his belt before he remembered he'd had to lock up his weapon in processing. He cursed.

They raced down three flights of stairs to the basement, to the disciplinary segregation unit. A chill crept into Hunter's bones. Quiet, they made their way down a long, dim, depressing hallway that led to a series of cells, each with a tray slot and a peephole. "These accommodations aren't fit for a slop hog, warden, much less a human being," Hunter commented.

"I inherited it, son. You gotta get budget for upgrades." He shrugged. "We got none."

"You could keep it clean, at least," scowling as he avoided another puddle of greasy water and a crowd of cockroaches feasting there. The patrol cop he'd recruited followed the men, scrutinizing every square inch of space as he pulled up the rear.

"Yeah, well, we could do a lotta things." The warden pounded on the cell door. "Officer Peterson! You in there?"

"He's not in here, Warden," Monty replied.

"Move," Hunter hissed, and stepped forward to peer into the peephole. He could make out the business end of a weapon pointed at Monty, who sat on his cot and stared at the floor. The gun barrel waggled at Monty. "He's not in here, Warden," Monty repeated.

"Gun," Hunter whispered to the warden, who moved further down the hall, speaking softly into his cell phone. He gave Hunter a thumbs-up as he ended the call.

Hunter nodded, feeling more secure now that the prison's extraction team had been activated. In minutes, officers in riot gear, helmets, and shields would crowd the space, awaiting instructions.

"*Casey*. This is Detective Faraday. We know about the bombs. We know everything. You need to put down the weapon and come out. *Now.* Right now, Casey."

"I ain't got no choice!" Casey called out, his voice like that of a child. "He took it all. My dad. My mom. Mom killed herself, you know that? He took my whole life!" he yelled. "This bastard right here!"

"Casey! Wait! Monty's going away for a long time. It's a sure thing, Casey. Your dad will get his justice. Your family will get justice. If you kill him, he won't have to serve his sentence. You want him to get what he deserves, don't you?"

Hunter peeked inside. The boy had fallen to his knees, the gun clutched in his hand. Monty sat on the bed, detached and staring. He snapped his head around to the warden. "Get a medic down here. You have one onsite right?"

The warden glared at him. "A'course we do!" He pressed buttons on an intercom system affixed to the wall and spoke into it. "On her way."

"He deserves to go to hell where he belongs!" Casey cried.

Hunter had a flashback of his interview with Casey's mom, Niles' ex-wife. What a monstrous woman. She'd shouted the same words to her son about his father. He felt a rush of compassion for the lost young man inside Monty's cell. "I agree with you, Casey. But this isn't the way. You don't want to live your life in prison, like Monty's going to. Come out. Let's talk about this."

Fingering the full-face respirator mask he'd been given, he eyed the men that had assembled and jerked his head at the door. The warden nodded his approval.

One of the masked officers stepped forward, lifted the tray slot, and tossed in a tear gas grenade.

The warden stepped back and away. Hunter followed, motioning to Officer Thomasson. The three men huddled and pulled on their masks.

A shot exploded in the room, its sound muffled by the heavy, steel door. The thump of dead weight on concrete followed.

Hunter closed his eyes. The warden unlocked the door with shaky hands.

The door gave way, and five men in tactical gear rushed into the room, screaming instructions, shields lifted.

Casey's anguished cries echoed up and down the corridor, ending in a coughing fit. No sounds from Monty.

With a groan of exasperation, Hunter moved past the warden and ran into the cell. One of the men had Casey pinned against the wall with his shield, his chest heaving with effort. "My eyes!" Casey screamed, succumbing to fits of coughing.

Hunter watched Monty's blood carve a small stream on the floor. Cocking his head, he saw that the blood originated from his throat. He punched one of the tactical team on the shoulder. "This man needs a medic. Now!" Desperately searching the cell, batting away the tear gas fumes, he found Casey's firearm. He picked it up and passed it to Thomasson, at the door. The warden entered, took command of the situation, and instructed the team to get the injured inmate to the elevator, where the nurse waited with a gurney.

By now Casey was a handcuffed, screaming, coughing, mess. One of the COs gripped his arm and shoved him out into the hall. "Thirty minutes and he should be able to talk to you," the Warden told him.

Monty nodded. He and Thomasson accompanied the tactical team and warden to the elevator, where a short, efficient, woman with salt-and-pepper hair dropped her fingers to Monty's neck, examined him a few seconds, and indicated with a curt nod that he'd make it. "It looks like it didn't hit a main artery. They'll be in the infirmary."

After a tense thirty minutes in the correctional center's breakroom, Monty and Thomasson strode to the infirmary, where a young woman with long, blond hair buzzed them in. She led them to a large room with several cots and left. The uni found a chair and waited, unsure of his role, but available. Hunter smiled at him. "Hey. Thanks for the support. I know you got a job to get back to."

"No problem, sir," the cop said.

The warden walked in. "I need to be present at the interview."

Hunter frowned. "Ok."

Casey lay propped up on a cot, his coughing diminished. Eyes closed, he scratched his face with both hands and rocked back and forth.

Hunter grabbed a chair and dragged it over beside the cot.

The warden assumed a stance beside them and crossed his arms.

"Feel better?" Hunter asked, ignoring the warden.

Casey wiped his nose with the back of his hand. Shook his head.

"It'll take a while to wear off," Hunter said.

Casey trembled, all the bravado and faux determination gone. All Hunter could see was a confused young man with a chip on his shoulder for his dad—a man that may not have been worth what Casey had done, but his dad, nonetheless. Hunter turned toward the warden. "Can we take off the cuffs?"

The warden shook his head with a firm no.

Hunter sighed. "I need to ask you some questions, Casey, that okay?"

Casey nodded, coughing until his lungs rattled, then said, "Okay."

"What was up with the bombs, Casey?" Hunter asked.

Casey coughed. "Never meant to hurt anyone."

Hunter gave Casey a look. "Do you understand the power of those damn things? I could've gotten killed! Everybody in the vicinity could've gotten killed! There'll be serious charges, son. You know that, right?"

Casey scowled and rubbed his thighs, his cheeks, his eyes. "It would've been a life for a life, is how I see it." More coughing.

Hunter had been willing to give the kid a chance.

Chance just got real slim.

"All I wanted was to get someone to listen!" he shouted." He coughed and rubbed his eyes until they were blood-red when he stared at Hunter, and whimpered, "Will I ever get out?"

Hunter glanced at the warden, now across the room, talking on his cell in low tones. "I don't know."

Casey straightened his shoulders. "Dad would've wanted me to do the right thing."

"And you think shooting Monty was the right thing? Setting up a couple bombs?"

"Damn straight," he hissed, his red, watering eyes little slits of hate.

270

"And the attorney, son?"

Casey cursed. "That pig! Uncle Wyatt called him, all respectful and proper…" Casey tried to open his eyes, but couldn't quite keep them open yet. "He's a real lawyer. Knows his stuff."

Hunter nodded. Kid needed someone to be proud of. "Go on."

His chin quivered. "I…I couldn't get my head around it, y'know? He didn't want my Uncle Wyatt to team up with him? How could he be that dumb? I was gonna *make* him listen." He sneered. "But someone got there before me. Karma, man."

Hunter was quiet. So who killed Earl? He still had to gather enough evidence to figure that out.

"I'm tired of people tellin' me how horrible my dad was, and now I find my uncle and he's got a good job and a freakin' law degree, and he's not good enough either? Screw 'em!" Casey's cheeks reddened. A vein popped in his neck.

"Calm down," Hunter cautioned. "You're gonna give yourself a stroke."

Casey dropped his legs over the side of the bed, then swayed to his feet. "I'm not gonna calm down!" he screamed. Thomasson raised his eyebrows at Hunter. With a sigh, Hunter nodded and flapped his hand at the door. As the boy was led away, Hunter heard him yell with his raw, tear-gassed vocal chords, "Monty Callahan, fry in hell! Fry in hell for what you did to my dad! Fry in hell, you bastard!" His voice bounced off the infirmary walls and into the corridor. Hunter glanced over at the cot where Monty lay, oblivious and out of it. They'd probably stuffed him full of pain meds.

With a heavy heart, and even heavier steps, Hunter left the infirmary and started down the corridor.

Today, he hated his job.

Chapter Fifty

"There ain't no troubles that we can't rise above, with a handful of faith and a heart full of love."
~Tim McGraw

Three weeks later

Tom Stark dropped me off, gave me a thumbs-up and a warm smile, and left. I studied the four-door, dark blue sedan in my driveway that I didn't recognize, and wished I'd asked Tom to wait until I'd checked it out.

With a sigh, I walked closer and recognized the subtle indications of a government-issued vehicle.

Hunter.

I pushed open the white, plank gate, and ran up the sidewalk, my stuffed backpack bouncing on my spine. I jerked it off and dumped it on the porch. Hunter stood in the foyer behind the red screen door, smiling. He lifted the glass in his hand toward me. Opened the door and walked onto the porch. The loveseat cushions wheezed pleasantly when he sat and crossed his legs.

I laughed. "Lilly! Why didn't you tell me Hunter was here?"

Lilly walked down the hall. "We wanted to surprise you, Mom."

I sat on the other side of the loveseat, a scant four inches between me and the warmth of his leg. My daughter lurked behind the screen watching, her grin as wide and bright as a summer morning. "I'll have what he's having," I told Lilly.

"What, iced tea, like Hunter's? You don't want hot tea? Are you kidding, Mom?"

"I want to try it," I said, with a glance and a wink at Hunter, who often teased me about my disdain for iced tea. In Maryland, one's tea must be hot.

Lilly brought me a glass of the sugary tea with lemon.

Hunter and I sat content and quiet, admiring the sweet, cool, afternoon hush, which whispered the promise of autumn. The birds swooped in, complaining that the feeders needed filling.

"Hunter. It'd be easier to talk to you if I didn't have to crane my neck. I wiggled my hand at one of the chairs across from the loveseat. "Sit over there."

"Don't want to."

A blush crept up my neck, and onto my face. I sipped my tea, winced, and gamely took another sip. "Are you okay?" I asked him. "I never got a chance to ask you about that last hospital stay. I heard you had a concussion."

Hunter scooted closer until our legs touched. My heart rate sped up. "What's the matter?" he teased.

I glowered at him. "You're enjoying this."

Pause. "Aren't you?"

I stared into those killer chocolate eyes, warm with affection. Smelled the familiar cologne and breathed it in along with the clean, fresh scent of his aftershave. His hand found mine and held it. "How's the PI business?"

I opened my mouth, but found it hard to form words. I frowned. Why was I having a hard time getting words out?

In the next few seconds, Hunter swept away every thought by planting his warm, full, lips on mine. Like a homing pigeon, I leaned into the kiss. I didn't want it to stop, but it did, and we sat there like teenagers, awkward and happy and…well, anticipatory, I suppose.

Riot decided he needed attention, too, and started yowling. Like an old married couple, we rose and went inside. Hunter picked up Riot and walked into the den. He sat on the couch and put Riot on the floor, but Riot was having none of it. He jumped onto Hunter's lap, started kneading his legs, then formed himself into his typical doughnut position, and settled there. Hunter chuckled and raised his palms. "Guess I won't be helping with dinner."

I tried to make light of how magical and sweet it was that Riot trusted this man.

But I couldn't.

Lilly and I fixed dinner, chatting about mundane things, boring things, surface stuff, like the weather. I thought of our Wine & Whine girls, and when we'd decided that a boring existence definitely had its benefits.

I smiled. After a tense few weeks avoiding getting shot or arrested, dragged by my hair down a rat hole, or blown up by a bomb, I looked forward to boring.

As Lilly set the table for dinner, I slipped away. Entering my bedroom, I ran my hand across the smooth, marble top of the 1800s piece that Monty and I had reclaimed from some flea market somewhere in the Maryland hinterlands. I bent down, pulled out the bottom drawer, and located the Ziploc baggie I'd hidden there.

"Hey." He smiled at me as I entered the dining room. "We're ready to eat." He squinted at the baggie in my hand. "What's that?"

"First…." I smiled back, and sat at the table. "Let's pray."

After thanking the good Lord for everyone's safety, I said 'Amen' and handed him the baggie.

He held it gingerly between his thumb and forefinger, scrutinizing the document inside. "Is this the evidence that I'm not supposed to know about?"

* * *

After dinner, Lilly said she'd clean up and shooed us onto the porch. She even brought out a bottle of wine, a wine opener, and two glasses, and sat it between us. I opened the wine and offered Hunter a glass. Hunter took a quick sip, and settled into his chair. "Tell me about Wyatt Harp. I got the short version from Sherry, but what happened after he was arrested?"

"I spent an hour at Westminster PD with...can't remember who...and he got my story down, then I went home, took a sleeping pill, and slept like a baby. Now *that*...felt good. I hadn't been able to sleep for a long time."

"They keepin' him?"

"They assigned him an attorney. He seemed...relieved, Hunter. No problems whatsoever with the arrest. Y'know...I believed him when he said he didn't know about the bombs. He was horrified."

Hunter grunted. "Well, I can believe it, after dealing with Casey." He stared out into the night. "We still haven't nailed down the identity of the killer."

I lifted my glass. "To Earl." Our glasses clinked in a somber toast.

"What's happening with the lawsuit?" he asked.

"It'll have to be declared moot, right? Vacated? I don't know what they call it—"

"You are gonna have to learn that stuff, Ms. Olivia Rosemary Callahan, Private Investigator."

"Yeah, whatever. I will. Anyway, they have no case anymore. All I know is... it's off the table and I can sleep at night." A happy thought bounced through my brain. "I can catch up with Mom and Serena! Maybe I'll go see them next week."

"Works for me," he declared. "I want an exclusive on any time you don't need to be with them next week."

I laughed. "So...Casey? What happened?"

"Here I was, fresh from another bomb scare, walkin' around with a concussion, and this woman from Glyndon, Maryland screams into my ear, "It's Casey! It's Casey!""

"Got your attention, though, right? It blew my mind that the kid went to such lengths. And I remember...I *remember* him from when Niles and I were in Hilton Head. I met him, I think...or saw him. Not in a thousand years would I have thought he'd work himself into the prison system where Monty was—"

"So he could kill him," Hunter interjected. "Revenge is a nasty habit."

"Hunter...how did Casey get the gun in there? Corrections officers don't carry guns."

"Broke it down in pieces and snuck it in." Hunter stared at his hands. "He also wasn't even 21…he had a fake ID so he could meet the age requirements for a CO position." Hunter shook his head. "If things hadn't turned out the way they did, he'd be up for homicide."

"And you were getting ready to re-open the case, right?" I stared at him. "Did you?"

"Yeah."

I was quiet a few beats. "So everything Casey did…was pointless." I ran my hands through my hair. "I guess I shouldn't be surprised that Monty would help his best friend clean up the mess he made," I said. "But still…it hurt to know he could leave me there like that."

"It'll be a long haul with the new charges. The DA will make a case for accomplice to a crime. Withholding evidence, maybe." He shrugged and picked up his wine glass.

"Speaking of…" I grimaced.

"The form you took? Look, I think you did the right thing to remove it. After I tell them you accidentally lost it, or whatever I come up with, it'll go away. The point is, we have it now."

"Thanks. Seriously."

He waved one of his hands and grunted. "You'd just stumbled across a corpse. No way you knew what to do. Even if the investigative team wanted to make a big deal out of it, you were under duress. Scared." He shrugged. "It wasn't pre-meditated."

I chuckled. "Right."

"Don't push it," he stated. At my expression, he laughed. "They're tired of this case, and I know how it works. It won't be an issue at this point. It might not even give us any traction…but…" He lifted the bag and stared through the plastic. "Once forensics gets it, my bet is they can match the handwriting and that'll give us more to go on. It depends on whether we have samples."

"Of course you have samples," I blurted. "His office is right down the road. Samples are everywhere. I don't think anyone's been in there since he's been gone."

"You sound pretty sure you know who killed him." He cocked his head.

"I'm ninety percent sure."

He offered his hands over the small wicker coffee table between us. I put my hands in his. "I need to get on back, Olivia. I'm gonna rush the form tests, so we can be done with it. So...until next time. There *will* be a next time, right?"

I nodded, a twinge of electricity shooting through my chest. "I'm willing if you are," I said.

His jaw flexed, his chin lifted. An acknowledgment, sure...but also a movement with finality...like he'd settled something in his mind. "Okay, then," he said and rose. "I'll get back to you."

Lilly walked outside.

"Perfect timing, honey," I said, with a smile. "He's just about to leave."

Hunter walked over to Lilly and gave her a hug. "Thanks for the chat and for dinner. See you soon, okay?"

He trotted down the steps, to his car and drove away.

I watched his tail lights get swallowed up by the dark.

I already missed him.

Epilogue

I fluffed my hair, checked my makeup, and answered the Facetime call. It had been an anxious seven days of waiting. He better have news.

"Hey, gorgeous!" Hunter said.

"Don't do that to me. What did you find out?"

He laughed. "No chance you'd think this was a social call, huh?"

"None. It's a video call. When do we ever do that? Never. You must have something!"

"You got me. Okay. Yeah, it was a pain, but finally, we pinned it down," he said.

"Why? What was a pain?" I bit a fingernail.

He chuckled. "All that PI instruction and you haven't covered handwriting analysis yet?"

I groaned.

"Here's a quick summary, Olivia. Typically, if someone wants to sign someone's name they at least try to match the actual handwriting style. Even practice the signature. In this case, he—"

I pounced. "HE?"

"Hold on, hold on, let me finish!"

I rolled my eyes.

"In this case, he disguised, or tried to…his handwriting, but did *not* try to recreate your actual signature. Which means he probably made the decision at the last minute. We subpoenaed several samples and finally had a conclusive result. We almost had to bring him in, but the examiner found overwhelming similarities.

"Hunter...what the heck...who is *he?*"

"It was Wyatt, Olivia," he said quietly.

I'd known in my heart this was probably the case, but the truth hit me like a wrecking ball. Wyatt had seemed like such a great guy. My emotions surprised me.

"We brought him in. Showed him what we'd discovered. He confessed. Real quick, like he expected it."

"That's how he was with me, too. He...he wasn't comfortable with his actions, he got caught up in something so huge, I mean...think about it... he'd found a nephew and lost a brother all at the same time. That would mess anyone up. I don't think he's a murderer."

"But he is."

"Yeah."

We both went silent.

"I'm sorry, Olivia," he said.

"Me, too. This whole thing...Niles, his family, their history...it seemed they were marked for destruction or something. It's horrible."

"People can change their future, Olivia."

I made a little snorting sound. "Yeah. Like Monty. Prison's done wonders for his personality."

Hunter cleared his throat. "Wyatt's attorney's looking for involuntary manslaughter, I think. Says his client was under intense stress, not in control of his actions."

I nodded slowly, thinking. "I believe that. He was so desperate, even talking to me. He only wanted to protect Casey and re-establish a relationship. But Casey was...so eaten up with hate."

"I hear that's catching."

"Guess so."

Hunter sighed. "Anyway...he'll probably take a deal. Maybe get ten or fifteen. He used the letter opener, by the way."

My brow furrowed. "The letter opener? For what?"

Pause. "To kill Earl."

"How...completely hideous," I whispered, stunned.

"That's why we couldn't figure out the murder weapon. He used a damn letter opener. Must've been a heckuva letter opener to do that much damage."

My mind went back. I tried to remember Earl's desk. I'd sat in front of it a hundred times. An image popped into my mind. I had studied it as I sat in Earl's office as he pontificated from behind the enormous desk. Looking at it was how I'd tried to distance myself from his words, the divorce, my whole world crashing in on me. "It had a huge, carved ivory handle with this long, silver blade. I remember thinking…wow! That looks dangerous."

"Turns out…"

"…it was," I finished.

"It has its upside," he suggested. "You can include this as kind of a… postlude…right? In the book?"

"In fact, my editor is delighted that I've started working on the manuscript again and really sappy and suck-uppy about this turn of events."

"I bet," he said, chuckling.

"SO…not funny," I quipped.

"I know. Sorry."

Lilly crossed in front of me to the end of the porch and sat in the swing. I turned my camera around. Lilly waved at Hunter's image in the screen.

"Y'all are cute," Lilly trilled from the swing. Her curly, ripe strawberry-colored hair had developed highlights over a summer in the sun, and her skin was freckled and tan. Soon, she'd start her senior year. Slender and graceful, she'd have her pick of young men to date. Now, I thought, I'd have time to connect with her. I would make sure of it.

"So, Mom," she began, her head tilted. "Mr. Harp is going to prison for a long time, then?"

"Probably," I said.

"Definitely," Hunter echoed from my phone.

"I was thinking…Mr. Harp went to all that trouble to buy our land, build that building, and now…you need an office, right?"

"I do," I whispered in surprise. "Plus, a quiet place to finish the 'Mercy's Miracle' book."

"Bet he'd sell chee—eaap," Lilly sing-songed. "He has lawyers and stuff to pay, right?"

My cell buzzed. Callie's number. I switched over to her call. "Hey."

"Hi…" she managed before she broke down.

With a pained look, I told Lilly I'd be right back. I walked down the porch steps and out into the yard to talk to my friend. The sun had started its descent behind the trees. The birds, for once, were quiet.

"What's wrong, Callie?"

"It's Graham. I think he's having an affair."

"That can't be true! Graham? Not *Graham*. I can't believe it!"

"I've found things. Receipts. A new credit card. I haven't started checking mileage on his car yet, but I'm about to."

Seconds of silence ticked by.

"I don't know what to say."

She sniffed in disgust. "I'm sad, but I'm not blind. I want to know what's going on. I want to hire you, Olivia. I need evidence."

I blinked. "What?"

"You've been learning stuff for what, six weeks? Eight? Don't you know enough to follow people?"

"Well, yeah, but…"

"Girl, I want you to!"

"Let me talk to Tom—"

"Perfect. This can be on-the-job training or whatever. Text me your rate, or his rate…whatever." She ended the call.

Which caused me to also end Hunter's call by accident.

I walked back to the porch, slow and deliberate, ticking off a to-do list in my head.

First, I'd approach Wyatt's attorney about options for the property, and when and if I could buy it back.

Second, I had to figure out if I was on the right track. Does Tom support my belief that I could make a decent private investigator? My jaw clenched with purpose. I was so close to a full recovery, and Tom told me he planned to work a couple more years. Plenty of time to prove myself.

Third, I needed to finish the manuscript and get it to my agent.

And last, when Lilly and I drove to Richmond, I needed to check in with my favorite neuro, Dr. Sturgis, and make sure my brain hadn't performed somersaults or vault dismounts or any other assorted gymnastics that needed attention over this pithy crapshoot of events I'd endured.

I couldn't wait for the next Wine & Whine. I had bunches to share, all good things.

Resolved things, at least. Tilting my head back, I breathed a prayer of thanks up into the heavens. For life. Truth. Resolution. Restoration. My daughters. Mom. And…Hunter. I even added Hazel.

At that moment, the sun disappeared behind the trees and the small, white, promise of a full moon appeared, on the rise.

I jogged up the stairs to my porch and Facetimed Hunter back.

Hunter shot me a puzzled look as he answered. "What happened?"

"Sorry, but it was important. Wait a sec." I reached for my wine.

With a smile, I raised my glass at Lilly on the swing, and Hunter on my cell phone screen.

"Congratulate me! I just got my first client!"

A Note from the Author

This book is about overcoming. It's a given that all of us will experience hardship and trauma...some more than others. In my life, I have found that there is no circumstance, or terrible relationship, or consequence, or *any* obstacle too intimidating to overcome. We must simply make the choice to rise.

Acknowledgements

First, I want to thank my husband for his support and patience as I spend hours planning, researching, outlining, and writing. Though he doesn't exactly understand or delight in the writerly world I embrace, he staunchly defends my right to be involved. Plus, his favorite way to introduce me is, "This is my wife. She's an author." I so appreciate you, honey.

Next, I want to thank Brian Thiem, author of the Matt Sinclair crime thriller series, and retired homicide detective; for his help with the cop scenes, James L'Etoile for his input about prison systems, and my beta readers, Linda Lovely, Bonnie Miller, Dana Ridenour, and Mally Becker for their perspectives and suggestions. My appreciation grows with each manuscript I submit to Harriette Sackler and Shawn Simmons, principals of Level Best Books, as they are invaluable assets in the process of publishing an enjoyable, well-thought-out story that we are all proud of. Big, fat, kudos to you both.

And finally, I want to offer my thanks to the one that I consider the greatest and most creative being in the universe, my savior, Jesus Christ. Without this relationship, I would be gutted in a dark, back alley somewhere, wondering what went wrong. I am beyond grateful for second chances.

About the Author

Kerry's publishing credits include a popular newspaper column, "The Lighter Side," (2009—2011), and magazine articles in *Local Life Magazine*, *The Bluffton Breeze*, *Lady Lowcountry*, and *Island Events Magazine*. She is the author of three novels, *The Hunting*, women's fiction, *The Deadening*, Book One of the Olivia Callahan Suspense Series, and *The Rising*, Book Two. The third book in this series releases in 2023 by Level Best Books. Kerry enjoyed a thirty-year career in advertising as an account manager, creative director, and copywriter before she became an author. She is past chapter president of the Maryland Writers' Association and a current member and presenter of Hilton Head Island Writers' Network, South Carolina Writers Association, and the Sisters in Crime organization. Most recently, she worked as editor and contributor for Island Communications, a local publishing house. Kerry and her husband moved to Hilton Head Island, SC, in 2015. She is the mother of four adult children, and has a bunch of wonderful grandkids who keep life interesting and remind her what life is all about.

SOCIAL MEDIA HANDLES: https://www.kerryperesta.net
  https://www.twitter.com/kerryperesta

https://www.instagram.com/kerry.peresta
https://www.facebook.com/klperesta
https://www.facebook.com/kerryperesta
https://www.linktr.ee/klperesta

AUTHOR WEBSITE:
https://www.kerryperesta.net

Also by Kerry Peresta

The Deadening, Book One in the Olivia Callahan Suspense series, published February 2021.

The Hunting, women's fiction, published November 2013.

CPSIA information can be obtained
at www.ICGtesting.com
Printed in the USA
LVHW100324010522
717404LV00001B/2